Praise for *The Selected Prose of Fernando Pessoa:*

"Imagine if, some day back in the 1950s, an American poet named John Ashbery had not only written a few of his own highly original poems, but in an ecstasy of creative surfeit, had invented three other poets— Kenneth Koch, Frank O'Hara, and James Schyler—and then, over the years, proceeded to write poems *as* them, even entire books. It sounds fantastic, but that is what Pessoa actually did. Nor was it just a whimsical creative exercise. In *The Western Canon*, that ultimate literary proving ground, Harold Bloom named Caeiro and de Campos as 'great poets' in their own right. . . . Fascinating."
—Brendan Bernhard, *LA Weekly*

Praise for Fernando Pessoa:

"Portugal's greatest poet since Camoëns . . . [with a] wide range of talent, craft, intellect, and poetic achievement."
—Christopher Sawyer-Laucanno, *The Boston Book Review*

"The saddest of our century's great literary modernists and perhaps its most inventive . . . the finest poet Portugal has ever produced."
—*The Boston Phoenix Literary Section*

"Pessoa's writing, the whole of his extraordinary opus, [is] a major presence in what has come to be known as 'modernism' in the European languages. . . . Almost any commentary of any length on Pessoa's writings, sensibility, and imagination is bound to convey a glimpse, at least, of its intensity and elusiveness, its apparently endlessly unfolding hall of mirrors."
—*The New York Review of Books*

"If [Pessoa] never achieved such renown during his life, the years since he died have elevated him to a numinous status among European poets, and writers as idiomatically disparate as Jorge Luis Borges, Octavio Paz, and Antonio Tabucchi . . . have acknowledged his potent sway."
—*The Times Literary Supplement*

"Fernando Pessoa (1888–1935) is one of the great originals of modern European poetry and Portugal's premier modernist. He is also a strange and original writer. Other modernists—Yeats, Pound, Eliot—invented masks through which to speak occasionally, from Michael Robartes, to Hugh Selwyn Mauberly to J. Alfred Prufrock. Pessoa invented whole poets."   —Robert Hass, "Poet's Choice,"
The Washington Post and *San Francisco Examiner*

"Pessoa would be Shakespeare if all that we had of Shakespeare were the soliloquies of Hamlet, Falstaff, Othello and Lear and the sonnets. His legacy is a set of explorations, in poetic form, of what it means to inhabit a human consciousness. . . . What makes Pessoa's thought and poetry compelling is not that he picks up and develops the forms and themes of Whitman and Emerson and retransmits our patrimony back to us—though this would be marvelous—but because in the poems and prose he has passed a judgment upon the twentieth-century rejection of individualism."   —Richard Eder, *Los Angeles Times Book Review*

"The amazing Portuguese poet, Fernando Pessoa . . . as a fantastic invention surpasses any creation by Borges. . . . Pessoa was neither mad nor a mere ironist; he is Whitman reborn, but a Whitman who gives separate names to 'my self,' 'the real me' or 'me myself,' and 'my soul,' and writes wonderful books of poetry for all of them."
—Harold Bloom, *The Western Canon*

"[Pessoa's] work is never more profound than when it is most ludicrous, never more heartfelt than when it is most deeply ironic. . . . Like Beckett, Pessoa is extremely funny. . . . His work is loaded with delights."
—*The Guardian* (UK)

"There are in Pessoa echoes of Beckett's exquisite boredom; the dark imaginings of Baudelaire (whom he loved); Melville's evasive confidence man; the dreamscapes of Borges."
—*The Village Voice Literary Supplement*

The Selected Prose of
FERNANDO PESSOA

The Selected Prose of
FERNANDO PESSOA

Edited and translated by
RICHARD ZENITH

Grove Press / New York

Published simultaneously in Canada

Library of Congress Cataloging-in-Publication Data

Pessoa, Fernando, 1888-1935.
   [Prose works. English. Selections]
   The selected prose of Fernando Pessoa / edited and translated by
Richard Zenith.
      p.   cm.
   Includes bibliographical references.
   ISBN 978-0-8021-3914-6
   1. Pessoa, Fernando, 1888-1935-Translations into English. I.
Zenith, Richard. II. Title.

PQ9261.P417 A288 2001
869.8'4108-dc 21   2001018997

Design by Laura Hammond Hough

Grove Press
154 West 14th Street
New York, NY 10011

18 19 20 21   6 5 4 3

CONTENTS

GENERAL INTRODUCTION

Fernando Pessoa has the advantage of living more in ideas than in himself.

Álvaro de Campos

Fernando Pessoa the Man and Poet

When he died on November 30, 1935, the Lisbon newspapers paid tribute, without fanfare, to the "great Portuguese poet" Fernando Pessoa, who was born in Lisbon in 1888. He was remembered for *Mensagem* (Message), a book of forty-four poems published in 1934, and for some 160 additional poems published in magazines and journals, several of which he helped to found and run. The author, a single man survived by a half sister and two half brothers, had the peculiarity of publishing his poetry under three different names besides his own—Alberto Caeiro, Ricardo Reis, and Álvaro de Campos—which he claimed were not mere pseudonyms, since it wasn't just their names that were false. They were false personalities, with biographies, points of view, and literary styles that differed from Pessoa's. They were names that belonged to invented *others*, whom their inventor called "heteronyms." Pessoa also published over a hundred pieces of criticism, social commentary, and creative prose, including passages from *The Book of Disquiet*, whose authorship he credited to "Bernardo Soares, assistant bookkeeper in the city of Lisbon." Another peculiarity about this author—mentioned by the literary compeer who delivered the brief funeral address—was that he wrote poems in English, some of which he published in chapbooks, for the benefit (according to the compeer) of "the literary *cercles* of serene Albion." In fact, scarcely anyone in Portugal had read them. French was the second language of those who had one.

Still another peculiarity—this one a complete secret—was that Pessoa's death marked the birth of a far larger writer than anyone had imagined. It was a slow birth that began only in the 1940s, when Pessoa's posthumous editors opened up the now legendary trunk in which the author had deposited his legacy to the world: twenty-nine notebooks and thousands upon thousands of manuscript sheets containing unpublished poems, unfinished plays and short stories, translations, linguistic analyses, horoscopes, and nonfiction on a dizzying array of topics—from alchemy and the Kabbala to American millionaires, from "Five Dialogues on Tyranny" to "A Defense of Indiscipline," from Julian the Apostate to Mahatma Gandhi. The pages were written in English and French as well as in Portuguese, and very often in an almost illegible script. The most surprising discovery was that Pessoa wrote not under four or five names but under forty or fifty. The editors timidly stuck to poetry by the names they knew—Alberto Caeiro, Ricardo Reis, Álvaro de Campos, and Pessoa himself—and further limited their selection to manuscripts that were easy to transcribe. It wasn't until the 1980s that reliable, relatively complete editions of poetry by the main heteronyms began to appear, and no such edition has yet appeared for the poetry signed by Pessoa himself, much of which still needs to be "lifted" from the manuscripts. Pessoa's English heteronyms and his one French heteronym remained virtually unpublished until the 1990s, when many of the minor Portuguese heteronyms also began to make their way into print.

It's impossible to know how much psychological and emotional space the heteronyms occupied, or opened up, in their creator. In the real world Pessoa was a loner, by choice and by natural inclination. He was in love once, if at all, and his intimacy with friends was restricted to literary matters. As a young man he moved from one neighborhood to another, staying sometimes with relatives, sometimes in rented rooms, but from 1920 on he lived at the same address—with his mother until her death in 1925, and then with his half sister, her husband, and their two children. Family members have reported that the mature Pessoa was affectionate and good-humored but resolutely private.

Pessoa the child was the same way, according to people who knew him at school in Durban, South Africa, where he lived from age seven to seventeen. His father had died when he was five, and his mother remarried Portugal's newly appointed consul to Durban, a boom town in what was then the British colony of Natal. Shy foreigner though he was, Fernando Pessoa quickly stood out among his classmates, none of whom could surpass him in English composition. English writers — including Shakespeare, Milton, Byron, Shelley, Keats, and Carlyle — were the formative influence on his literary sensibility, and English was the language in which he began to write poetry. Pessoa returned to Lisbon to attend university but soon dropped out, and it was his knowledge of English that enabled him to make a living as a freelance, doing occasional translations and drafting letters in English (he also wrote some in French) for Portuguese firms that did business abroad.

In 1920 Pessoa's mother, once more a widow, also returned from South Africa to Lisbon, accompanied by three grown children from her second marriage. Pessoa's half brothers soon emigrated to England, and Pessoa thought to do the same toward the end of his life, though probably not very seriously. Since stepping off the *Herzog*, the ship that had brought him back to Lisbon in 1905, Pessoa had never strayed far from his native city, which became a more frequent reference in his writing as he got older, especially in *The Book of Disquiet*. In a passage dating from the 1930s (Text 130) Bernardo Soares, the book's fictional author, called Lisbon the "crucial address" of "the main literary influences on my intellectual development," which were none other than the common, everyday people whom the bookkeeper worked with. Had Pessoa written those words in his own name, they would have been an exaggeration, but the people who were part of the scenery in the Lisbon he inhabited — shopkeepers, restaurant waiters, streetcar operators, sellers of lottery tickets, fruit vendors, delivery boys, office workers, schoolchildren — are a striking presence in his literary work, partly because of the absence of more intimate kinds of social contact: romance, close friendships, family life. It seems, for the same reason, that a few of those almost anonymous people were a strong, if quiet, presence in Pessoa's sentimental life. It was the case, probably, of the tobacco shop owner who inspired poems signed by Campos and by Pessoa himself. And it was surely the case of the barber who made cameo appearances in *The Book of Disquiet* and elsewhere. Among the family members and the literary people at the funeral on December 2, he was spotted—the barber—paying, or repaying, a kind of respect.

Fernando Pessoa, Prose Writer

"I prefer prose to poetry as an art form for two reasons, the first of which is purely personal: I have no choice, because I'm incapable of writing in verse." To be able to make such a statement, Fernando Pessoa—the greatest Portuguese poet of the last four centuries—lent his typewriter to Bernardo Soares, a literary alter ego who wrote only prose. But what was the point of having Soares write, not just a simple statement of personal preference (or competence), but a five-paragraph eulogy for *The Book of Disquiet* (Text 227) that defended prose as the highest art form, greater than music or poetry? No point at all. It probably just reflected how Pessoa felt, in the persona of Bernardo Soares and even in his own person, on the 18th of October, 1931, the day he wrote it. Pessoa made his fame as a poet, but he embarked on literally hundreds of prose projects large and small: dozens of short stories, twenty or more plays, detective novels, philosophical treatises, sociological and psychological studies, books on Portuguese culture and history, a tour guide of Lisbon, pamphlets about sundry political and economic issues, astrological works, essays on religion, literary criticism, and more. Few of these ever arrived at or near completion, but as the years went by and Pessoa launched new projects, he did not abandon the old ones. *The Book of Disquiet*, which he worked on furiously from 1913 to 1919, yawed in the doldrums in the 1920s, to return in its fullest splendor in the thirties, though it proceeded, as it always had, without firm direction, never finding nor even seeking a port of arrival.

"What's necessary is to sail, it's not necessary to live!" shouted Pompey the Great to his frightened sailors after ordering them to weigh anchor in a heavy storm. Those words, reported by Plutarch, became Pessoa's motto, which he expressed—like his own self—in multiple versions, including "It's not necessary to live, only to feel" (*The Book of Disquiet*, Text 124) and "Living isn't necessary; what's necessary is to create" (in a random note). Pessoa's world was almost all ocean, dotted by occasional islands of truth and its corollary, beauty, though he realized that those might after all be illusions, the reward of much sailing. There was also, as if it were a motive for the voyage, a not too insistent hope, or belief, in unknown lands that were perhaps worth discovering. But it was essentially a voyage of self-discovery, or self-invention ("To pretend is to know oneself")—an existential circumnavigation that would not end until Pessoa did. In the last years of his life, that self-exploration became less "inventive" and more investigative, more urgently expository, as if Pessoa sensed that time was running out. He tried to get to the heart of the matter he called the soul, and prose—in his letters, in *The Education of the Stoic*, and especially in *The Book of Disquiet*— became a privileged vehicle. Which brings us to the second and real reason Bernardo Soares preferred prose to poetry:

> In prose we speak freely. We can incorporate musical rhythms, and still think. We can incorporate poetic rhythms, and yet remain outside them. An occasional poetic rhythm won't disturb prose, but an occasional prose rhythm makes poetry fall down.
>
> Prose encompasses all art, in part because words contain the whole world, and in part because the untrammeled word contains every possibility for saying and thinking.

In Pessoa the untrammeled word did not necessarily probe more deeply than poetry, but it drew a closer, more naked picture of its subject. This was particularly true in the 1930s when, with no more youthful striving after literary effects, that word became truly, completely free.

Pessoa's prose was even more fragmentary than his poetry, or more conspicuously so. His failure (except in *Message* and *35 Sonnets*) to organize his poetry into neat and orderly books hardly affects our appreciation of the individual poems that would have gone into them, and the same holds true for many of the finished and even unfinished passages from *The Book of Disquiet*. But the page of perfectly gauged dialogue, the exact explanation of a protagonist's motives, or the paragraph that lays down an astonishingly clear argument, necessarily suffers without the rest of the play, the short story, or the essay for which it was written. Suffers, that is, in its ability to make an impact on the reader. Pessoa wanted to make such an impact, even if the only reader would be him, but he couldn't stand to put the final period to a work that was less than perfect. Most writers put it there anyway, because life is short, but Pessoa's destiny—or so he wrote in a letter breaking off with Ophelia Queiroz, his only paramour—belonged to "another Law" and served "Masters who do not relent." He patiently endured under the weight of his written fragments, as if waiting for the Architect to reveal the plan.

In 1928 Pessoa invented what was probably his last variation on himself, the Baron of Teive, a proud perfectionist whose major frustration—the one that leads him to commit suicide—is precisely his inability to finish any of his literary works. In that same year, several countries north and east of Portugal, Walter Benjamin published *One-Way Street*, which contains a seeming homage to Pessoa qua Baron:

> To great writers, finished works weigh lighter than those fragments on which they work throughout their lives. For only the more feeble and distracted take an inimitable pleasure in conclusions, feeling themselves thereby given back to life. For the genius each caesura, and the heavy blows of fate, fall like gentle sleep itself into his workshop labor. About it he draws a charmed circle of fragments.

Pessoa's charmed circle was not, however, so gently static. More than a diligent genius surrounded by his unfinished creations, Pessoa was a creator god standing at the center of his orbiting creatures, who were themselves creators, or subcreators, with Pessoa's literary works circling them as satellites. It was a dynamic system, in which all the elements interacted, meaning that even the apparently finished works were in truth fragments, since they were only what they were (and still are) in relationship to the rest of the system. The only whole thing—Pessoa's one perfect work—was the system in its totality.

Fernando Pessoa, English Writer

Pessoa's original literary ambition was, naturally enough, to become a great English writer. All of his schooling as a child in South Africa was in English, his extracurricular readings were mostly in English, and his first poems, stories, and essays were all in English. In 1903, when he was just fifteen years old, Pessoa won the Queen Victoria Memorial Prize for the best English composition submitted by examinees (of which there were 899) seeking admission to the University of the Cape of Good Hope. It's no wonder that Pessoa, after returning to Portugal in 1905, continued to write almost exclusively in English for three or four years. By 1912 Portuguese had overtaken English as his main language of written expression, and it was clear, from several articles he published on contemporary Portuguese poetry, that he was setting the stage for his own arrival. But his English poetical ambitions did not totter. He self-published slim collections of his English poetry in 1918 and 1921 and organized yet another book of verses, *The Mad Fiddler*, which he submitted to an English publisher in 1917. It was turned down, and the self-published volumes—which Pessoa sent to various British journals and newspapers—received guardedly favorable reviews. At that point Pessoa's production of English poetry dropped off considerably (though he continued to write poems in English up until the week before he died), and he redirected his British publishing hopes to the realm of prose. In the 1930s he was writing various long essays directly in English, including *Erostratus*, and he felt confident that he would be able to publish "The Anarchist Banker" (1922) in an English version, for which he translated a few pages.

　　With few opportunities for him to speak the language, Pessoa's English inevitably strayed from standard usage as he got older, sometimes lapsing into Portuguese syntactical patterns, but even as a student at Durban High School his English was not quite like everyone else's. Pessoa had little social involvement with his classmates, and Portuguese was the language spoken at home, so that his excellent mastery of English derived mostly from the many books he read and studied. It comes as no surprise, therefore, that the language of his English poetry tended toward the archaic ("Mr. Pessoa's command of English is less remarkable than his knowledge of Elizabethan English," commented a review of his 35 *Sonnets* (1918) in the *Times Literary Supplement*), and if his English prose often delighted in being humorous and colloquial, the humor was literary and the colloquial expressions came from Dickens, not from what Pessoa heard on the streets of Durban.

Though he readily admitted that his French was deficient, Pessoa seems not to have realized that his English was different from what an Englishman speaks. This was probably because Pessoa, who is reported to have spoken his second language with no accent, also spoke and wrote it with absolute fluency, in the most literal sense of the word. His English was spontaneous, it flowed without impediment, but it was *his* English—a bit stiffer, wordier, and more bookish than the native variety. This difference proved fatal when he applied his English to poetry, where the words themselves are the artistic point. But the words of prose are less self-referential, and here Pessoa's English often served him quite well—occasionally crabbed sentences and infelicities rubbing shoulders with lapidary expressions that no native English writer could have cut with more grace and precision.

About This Edition

The universe of Pessoa's prose is so vast and varied that no single volume could ever hope to represent it adequately, but this edition attempts to give at least a sense of how far it reaches, and by what diverse paths. The selections are drawn from the whole length of Pessoa's writing life, beginning in his teens; from the three languages in which he wrote, namely Portuguese, English, and French; from the various genres that his prose entails—drama, fiction, essay, criticism, satire, manifesto, diary, epigram, letters, autobiography, and automatic writing; and from more than a dozen of his literary personas. Although I theoretically object to heavy editorial intervention, the nature of this edition, and of this author and his oeuvre, has led me down that road. Pessoa's work is so fragmentary, and at the same time so interconnected, that any partial presentation—anything less than the whole universe—is liable to create wrong impressions. My introductions, by supplying background information, are meant to minimize that danger.

Works published by Pessoa are (with one exception) presented here in their entirety, and his letters are presented virtually entire; the occasional excluded paragraph usually deals with a specific personal or literary matter that would interest few readers. Most of the works not published in Pessoa's lifetime are bunches of fragments, whose individual integrity—in the case of the Portuguese texts—I have endeavored to maintain. The pieces taken from *The Book of Disquiet*, for instance, are complete pieces; none has been abridged. A few fragments from other Portuguese works have been cut short, but not cut and spliced.

The writings in English, on the other hand, have been frequently pruned. Rather than "clean up" grammatically problematic passages through heavy editing, I have usually removed them. And Pessoa's critical writings in English, which often run on at some length, have been freely excerpted. Pessoa's English has been quietly edited in the following ways: the spelling has been Americanized, the punctuation has sometimes been altered, a few words have been transposed, erroneous pronouns have been replaced, and an occasional definite article has been added or dropped. All other changes to the English texts are recorded in the notes or else indicated by brackets (in the case of an added word or two). Bracketed words in my translations from Portuguese and French are editorial proposals for blank spaces left by the author in the original.

The selections have been placed in roughly chronological order, conditioned by thematic considerations. The major displacements are

Álvaro de Campos's *Notes for the Memory of My Master Caeiro*, which dates from around 1930; Professor Jones's "Essay on Poetry," whose initial drafts were written in South Africa, before 1905; and Jean Seul's "France in 1950," which was conceived in 1907 or 1908. Most of Pessoa's literary criticism is difficult to date, but parts of "Concerning Oscar Wilde" were surely written in the early 1910s. One of Pessoa's notes suggests that his writings on American millionaires date from around 1915.

The bibliography contains a complete list of the published Portuguese sources for the translated selections; in cases where there may be doubt, the notes specify which title from the bibliography contains the source text for a given selection. All selections written by Pessoa in English were transcribed directly from the original manuscripts; instances of previous publication are noted. The archival reference numbers for all previously unpublished manuscripts and for all newly transcribed ones are recorded in the notes, which also elucidate historical, biographical, and cultural references. The frequent alternate wordings that Pessoa jotted in the margins of his manuscripts have not been recorded except in one or two instances.

This edition would never have been possible without the pioneering work of Teresa Rita Lopes. Her various books have made available several hundred previously unpublished poems and prose pieces by Pessoa. Her *Pessoa por Conhecer*, in particular, mapped out vast areas of the Pessoa archives that had been all but unknown.

Symbols Used in the Text

...... place where the author broke off a sentence or left blank space for one or more words

[?] conjectural reading of the author's handwriting

[. . .] illegible word or phrase

[ ] word(s) added by editor

(. . .) omitted text within a paragraph

... one or more omitted paragraphs (the three dots, in this case, occupy a separate line)

* indicates an endnote

Thanks . . .

to Teresa Rita Lopes for all her distinguished work in the Pessoa archives and for her personal help and encouragement;
to Luísa Medeiros and especially Manuela Parreira da Silva for their help in deciphering;
to José Blanco for his help locating and supplying source materials;
to Manuela Correia Lopes, Manuela Neves, and Manuela Rocha for their help interpreting;
to Anna Klobucka, Carlo Vinti, Didier Povéda, and Oliver Marhall for their research assistance;
to Martin Earl and Amy Hundley for their help in making selections and reviewing the essay matter.

Lisbon   Richard Zenith
December 2000

The Selected Prose of
FERNANDO PESSOA

ASPECTS

Pessoa probably wrote this preface, which would have appeared in the first volume of his complete heteronymic works, in the early or mid 1920s. In fact, Pessoa, as was so often the case, left several pieces for the preface—two of them typed, one handwritten—without articulating them into a final version. The handwritten fragment (not published here) explains that the heteronyms embody different "aspects," or sides, of a reality whose existence is uncertain. For more details about the heteronyms and their origins, see "Preface to Fictions of the Interlude," *Thomas Crosse's* "Translator's Preface to the Poems of Alberto Caeiro," *Álvaro de Campos's* Notes for the Memory of My Master Caeiro, *and most especially Pessoa's letter of January 13, 1935, to Adolfo Casais Monteiro.*

The Complete Work is essentially dramatic, though it takes different forms—prose passages in this first volume, poems and philosophies in other volumes. It's the product of the temperament I've been blessed or cursed with—I'm not sure which. All I know is that the author of these lines (I'm not sure if also of these books) has never had just one personality, and has never thought or felt except dramatically—that is, through invented persons, or personalities, who are more capable than he of feeling what's to be felt.

There are authors who write plays and novels, and they often endow the characters of their plays and novels with feelings and ideas that they insist are not their own. Here the substance is the same, though the form is different.

Each of the more enduring personalities, lived by the author within himself, was given an expressive nature and made the author of one or more books whose ideas, emotions, and literary art have no relationship to the real author (or perhaps only apparent author, since we don't know what reality is) except insofar as he served, when he wrote them, as the medium of the characters he created.

Neither this work nor those to follow have anything to do with the man who writes them. He doesn't agree or disagree with what's in them. He writes as if he were being dictated to. And as if the person dictating were a friend (and for that reason could freely ask him to write down what he dictates), the writer finds the dictation interesting, perhaps just out of friendship.

The human author of these books has no personality of his own. Whenever he feels a personality well up inside, he quickly realizes that this new being, though similar, is distinct from him—an intellectual son, perhaps, with inherited characteristics, but also with differences that make him someone else.

That this quality in the writer is a manifestation of hysteria, or of the so-called split personality, is neither denied nor affirmed by the author of these books. As the helpless slave of his multiplied self, it would be useless for him to agree with one or the other theory about the written results of that multiplication.

It's not surprising that this way of making art seems strange; what's surprising is that there are things that don't seem strange.

Some of the author's current theories were inspired by one or another of these personalities that consubstantially passed—for a moment, for a day, or for a longer period—through his own personality, assuming he has one.

The author of these books cannot affirm that all these different and well-defined personalities who have incorporeally passed through his soul don't exist, for he does not know what it means to exist, nor whether Hamlet or Shakespeare is more real, or truly real.

So far the projected books include: this first volume, *The Book of Disquiet*, written by a man who called himself Vicente Guedes;* then

The Keeper of Sheep, along with other poems and fragments by Alberto Caeiro (deceased, like Guedes, and from the same cause),* who was born near Lisbon in 1889 and died where he was born in 1915. If you tell me it's absurd to speak that way about someone who never existed, I'll answer that I also have no proof that Lisbon ever existed, or I who am writing, or anything at all.

This Alberto Caeiro had two disciples and a philosophical follower. The two disciples, Ricardo Reis and Álvaro de Campos, took different paths: the former intensified the paganism discovered by Caeiro and made it artistically orthodox; the latter, basing himself on another part of Caeiro's work, developed an entirely different system, founded exclusively on sensations. The philosophical follower, António Mora (the names are as inevitable and as independent from me as the personalities), has one or two books to write in which he will conclusively prove the metaphysical and practical truth of paganism. A second philosopher of this pagan school, whose name has still not appeared to my inner sight or hearing, will write an apology for paganism based on entirely different arguments.

Perhaps other individuals with this same, genuine kind of reality will appear in the future, or perhaps not, but they will always be welcome to my inner life, where they live better with me than I'm able to live with outer reality. Needless to say, I agree with certain parts of their theories, and disagree with other parts. But that's quite beside the point. If they write beautiful things, those things are beautiful, regardless of any and all metaphysical speculations about who "really" wrote them. If in their philosophies they say true things—supposing there can be truth in a world where nothing exists—those things are true regardless of the intention or "reality" of whoever said them.

Having made myself into what I am—at worst a lunatic with grandiose dreams, at best not just a writer but an entire literature—I may be contributing not only to my own amusement (which would already be good enough for me) but to the enrichment of the universe, for when someone dies and leaves behind one beautiful verse, he leaves the earth and heavens that much richer, and the reason for stars and people that much more emotionally mysterious.

In view of the current dearth of literature, what can a man of genius do but convert himself into a literature? Given the dearth of people he can get along with, what can a man of sensibility do but invent his own friends, or at least his intellectual companions?

I thought at first of publishing these works anonymously, with no mention of myself, and to establish something like a Portuguese neopaganism in which various authors — all of them different — would collaborate and make the movement grow. But to keep up the pretense (even if no one divulged the secret) would be virtually impossible in Portugal's small intellectual milieu, and it wouldn't be worth the mental effort to try.

In the vision that I call inner merely because I call the "real world" outer, I clearly and distinctly see the familiar, well-defined facial features, personality traits, life stories, ancestries, and in some cases even the death, of these various characters. Some of them have met each other; others have not. None of them ever met me except Álvaro de Campos. But if tomorrow, traveling in America, I were to run into the physical person of Ricardo Reis, who in my opinion lives there, my soul wouldn't relay to my body the slightest flinch of surprise; all would be as it should be, exactly as it was before the encounter. What is life?

You should approach these books* as if you hadn't read this explanation but had simply read the books, buying them one by one at a bookstore, where you saw them on display. You shouldn't read them in any other spirit. When you read *Hamlet*, you don't begin by reminding yourself that the story never happened. By doing so you would spoil the very pleasure you hope to get from reading it. When we read, we stop living. Let that be your attitude. Stop living, and read. What's life?

But here, more intensely than in the case of a poet's dramatic work, you must deal with the active presence of the alleged author. That doesn't mean you have the right to believe in my explanation. As soon as you read it, you should suppose that I've lied—that you're going to read books by different poets, or different writers, and that through those books you'll receive emotions and learn lessons from those writers, with whom I have nothing to do except as their publisher. How do you know that this attitude is not, after all, the one most in keeping with the inscrutable reality of things?

. . .

THE ARTIST AS A YOUNG MAN
AND HETERONYM

Fernando Pessoa's adventures in heteronymy began in his early childhood, according to his own account, which he might well have fabricated, but we know that self-multiplication was the main generator of his writing life by the time he reached puberty. Pessoa's archives contain a number of make-believe newspapers that he began to create when he was thirteen. These are elaborate, three-column productions containing real and invented news, poems, short stories, historical features, riddles, and jokes, signed by a gallery of writers with distinct interests and literary styles. The papers were written in Portuguese, mostly in 1902, when the family had gone to Portugal for a year to visit relatives, but Pessoa penned at least one newspaper back in Durban, in 1903, and there's even one that dates from September of 1905, right after he had returned to Portugal for the second and last time. A biographical sketch for one of the pseudo-journalists, Eduardo Lança, reports that he was born in Brazil in 1875 and immigrated as a young man to Portugal, basing himself in Lisbon but traveling all over the country. And several of Lança's colleagues — Dr. Pancrácio, Gaudêncio Nabos — weren't limited to their newspaper collaborations but signed poems and prose pieces as well.

Far more prolific and psychologically complex, Charles Robert Anon and Alexander Search may be considered the first veritable heteronyms. Anon came first, when Pessoa was still in South Africa, and then Search, who may not have been conceived until Pessoa returned to Lisbon in 1905. Pessoa even had calling cards printed for Alexander Search, whose output includes over 150 English poems (some dating as late as 1910), essays, commentaries, and a short story titled "A Very Original Dinner," in which human flesh was served to the unsuspecting guests. Search, who was born in Lisbon on the same day as Pessoa, had an older brother, Charles James Search, who was a translator of Portuguese and Spanish literature into English. The two brothers had a French-language colleague, Jean Seul, who was a poet and a writer of moral satires, including "France in 1950," found further on in this volume. Curiously enough, Alexander Search, in the passage from this section dated October 30, 1908, refers to his "Jean Seul projects." This would suggest, though it seems rather unlikely, that Pessoa intended Jean Seul to be a French heteronym of his English heteronym. Pessoa did not leave us any biographical information about C. R. Anon, whose last name perhaps indicates that this anonymity was deliberate.

Search and Anon incarnated the anxieties and existential concerns of a young intellectual entering adulthood, but the two heteronyms were more stridently outspoken than Pessoa himself, and more virulently anti-Catholic. Their styles are not easy to distinguish, and Pessoa may have meant for Search to replace Anon. A number of poems originally signed by the latter were subsequently attributed to the former, and there's even a poem (revised and recopied) signed "C. R. Anon, id est Alexander Search."

The transition from his South African childhood to life as a young adult in Lisbon, separated from his mother for the first time, brought Pessoa new kinds of stress and insecurity that came to a head in the year 1907. The usual pressure felt by a nineteen year old to define or discover himself was magnified by his sense of geographical and linguistic displacement and by the lack of structure in his daily life, especially after he dropped out of the University of Lisbon. His paternal grandmother, who had been in and out of mental hospitals during the last twelve years of her life, died in a state of advanced dementia in the summer of 1907, and Pessoa seemed to be quite sincerely afraid of going mad himself. Living under the same roof with her (along with two great-aunts) and reading, during the same period, Max Nordau's Degeneration *(1892) set him to thinking and writing almost obsessively about the relationship between genius and madness (his archives contain over a hundred texts on the topic, nearly all of them unpublished). Perhaps his main problem was that very obsessiveness. At the end of the above-mentioned passage signed by*

Alexander Search in 1908, we read: "One of my mental complications— horrible beyond words—is a fear of insanity, which itself is insanity."

Pessoa remarked, in The Book of Disquiet *and elsewhere, that a madman is not liable to see the madness of his own ideas, which may explain his keen interest in learning how other people saw him. Knowing that he would probably never return to South Africa, he decided to go for broke, writing several of his former teachers under a false name, as a psychiatrist requesting information about his mentally deranged patient, namely Pessoa. In a letter of inquiry to Clifford Geerdts, a former classmate, the phony shrink was to announce that Pessoa had, apparently, committed suicide. Pessoa did not strictly follow his plan, but we know that in 1907 Mr. Belcher, who was Pessoa's English teacher in Durban, did receive a letter from a "Dr. Faustino Antunes" asking for information about his former student, and Geerdts was also sent a letter—not the rough draft published on pp. 12–13, but a letter like the one to Belcher, stating that Pessoa was suffering from a mental disorder. Both men duly replied, and Geerdts's letter—which was the more forthcoming—included the following observations about Pessoa:*

- *"He was pale and thin and appeared physically to be very imperfectly developed. He had a narrow and contracted chest and was inclined to stoop."*
- *". . . he was inclined to be morbid."*
- *"[He was] regarded as a brilliantly clever boy."*
- *". . . he had learned [English] so rapidly and so well that he had a splendid style in that language."*
- *"[He was] meek and inoffensive and inclined to avoid association with his schoolfellows."*
- *"He took no part in athletic sports of any kind and I think his spare time was spent in reading. We generally considered that he worked far too much and that he would ruin his health by so doing."*

In fact Pessoa, with incredible sangfroid, first wrote to Mr. Belcher in South Africa, waited for his reply, then wrote Geerdts at Oxford (where he had gone to study), relaying some of Belcher's comments and asking if Geerdts agreed. All of this in the name of Dr. Faustino Antunes, who turns out to be more than just a clinical psychiatrist, for he was also the signing author of an "Essay on Intuition."

From the schoolboy script in which it was written, we know that the opening passage in this section probably dates from when Pessoa was still in his teens, but he posed as an old man looking back: "I was a poet animated by philosophy," and, in the penultimate paragraph, "There is for me—there was—a wealth of meaning (. . .)". Whether writing under his own or an invented name, Pessoa already revealed what he called—in a passage signed by Alexander Search—"an inborn tendency to mystification, to artistic lying."

"I was a poet animated by philosophy"

I was a poet animated by philosophy, not a philosopher with poetic faculties. I loved to admire the beauty of things, to trace in the imperceptible and through the minute the poetic soul of the universe.

. . .

Poetry is in everything—in land and in sea, in lake and in riverside. It is in the city too—deny it not—it is evident to me here as I sit: there is poetry in this table, in this paper, in this inkstand; there is poetry in the rattling of the cars on the streets, in each minute, common, ridiculous motion of a workman who [on] the other side of the street is painting the signboard of a butcher's shop.

Mine inner sense predominates in such a way over my five senses that I see things in this life—I do believe it—in a way different from other men. There is for me—there was—a wealth of meaning in a thing so ridiculous as a door key, a nail on a wall, a cat's whiskers. There is to me a fullness of spiritual suggestion in a fowl with its chickens strutting across the road. There is to me a meaning deeper than human fears in the smell of sandalwood, in the old tins on a dirt heap, in a matchbox lying in the gutter, in two dirty papers which, on a windy day, will roll and chase each other down the street.

For poetry is astonishment, admiration, as of a being fallen from the skies taking full consciousness of his fall, astonished at things. As of one who knew things in their soul, striving to remember this knowledge, remembering that it was not thus he knew them, not under these forms and these conditions, but remembering nothing more.

"The artist must be born beautiful"

The artist must be born beautiful and elegant; for he that worships beauty must not himself be unfair. And it is assuredly a terrible pain for an artist to find not at all in himself that which he strives for. Who, looking at the portraits of Shelley, of Keats, of Byron, of Milton, and of Poe, can wonder that these were poets? All were beautiful, all were beloved and admired, all had in love warmth of life and heavenly joy, as far as any poet, or indeed any man, can have.

"I have always had in consideration"

I have always had in consideration a case which is extremely interesting and which brings up* a problem not the less interesting. I considered the case of a man becoming immortal under a pseudonym, his real name hidden and unknown. Such a man would, thinking upon it, not consider himself really immortal but an unknown, [destined] to be immortal in deed. "And yet what is the name?" he would consider. Nothing at all. "What then," I said to myself, "is immortality in art, in poesy, in anything whatsoever?"

Three Prose Fragments

Charles Robert Anon

1.

Ten thousand times my heart broke within me. I cannot count the sobs that shook me, the pains that ate into my heart.

Yet I have seen other things also which have brought tears into mine eyes and have shaken me like a stirred leaf. I have seen men and women giving life, hopes, all for others. I have seen such acts of high devotedness that I have wept tears of gladness. These things, I have thought, are beautiful, although they are powerless to redeem. They are the pure rays of the sun on the vast dung-heap of the world.

*   *   *

2.

I saw the little children . . .

A hatred of institutions, of conventions, kindled my soul with its fire. A hatred of priests and kings rose in me like a flooded stream. I had been a Christian, warm, fervent, sincere; my emotional, sensitive nature demanded food for its hunger, fuel for its fire. But when I looked upon these men and women, suffering and wicked, I saw how little they deserved the curse of a further hell. What greater hell than this life? What greater curse than living? "This free will," I cried to myself, "this also is a convention and a falsehood invented by men that they might punish and slay and torture with the word 'justice,' which is a nickname of crime. 'Judge not,' the Bible has it—the Bible; 'judge not, that ye may not be judged!'"

When I had been a Christian I had thought men responsible for the ill they did—I hated tyrants, I cursed kings and priests. When I had shaken off the immoral, the false influence of the philosophy of Christ, I hated tyranny, kinghood, priestdom—evil in itself. Kings and priests I pitied because they were men.

3.

I, Charles Robert Anon, *being*, animal, mammal, tetrapod, primate, placental, ape, catarrhina, ... man; eighteen years of age, not married (except at odd moments), megalomaniac, with touches of dipsomania, *dégénéré supérieur*, poet, with pretensions to written humor, citizen of the world, idealistic philosopher, etc. etc. (to spare the reader further pains) —

in the name of TRUTH, SCIENCE, and PHILOSOPHIA, not with bell, book, and candle but with pen, ink, and paper —

pass sentence of excommunication on all priests and all sectarians of all religions in the world.

Excommunicabo vos.
Be damned to you all.
Ainsi-soit-il.

Reason, Truth, Virtue per C. R. A.

"I am tired of confiding in myself"
July 25, 1907

I am tired of confiding in myself, of lamenting over myself, of pitying mine own self with tears. I have just had a kind of scene with Aunt Rita* over F. Coelho.* At the end of it I felt again one of those symptoms which grow clearer and ever more horrible in me: a moral vertigo. In physical vertigo there is a whirling of the external world about us; in moral vertigo, of the interior world. I seemed for a moment to lose the sense of the true relations of things, to lose comprehension, to fall into an abyss of mental abeyance. It is a horrible sensation, one that prompts* inordinate fear. These feelings are becoming common, they seem to pave my way to a new mental life, which shall of course be madness.

In my family there is no comprehension of my mental state — no, none. They laugh at me, sneer at me, disbelieve me; they say I wish to be extraordinary. They neglect to analyze the *wish to be* extraordinary. They cannot comprehend that between being and wishing to be extraordinary there is but the difference of consciousness being added to the second. It is the same case as that of myself playing with tin soldiers at seven and at fourteen years; in one [moment] they were things, in the other things and playthings at the same time; yet the impulse to play with them remained, and that was the real, fundamental psychical state.

I have no one in whom to confide. My family understands nothing. My friends I cannot trouble with these things; I have no really intimate friends, and even were there one intimate, in world's ways, yet he were not intimate in the way I understand intimacy. I am shy and unwilling to make known my woes. An intimate friend is one of my ideal things, one of my daydreams, yet an intimate friend is a thing I never shall have. No temperament fits me; there is no character in this world which shows a chance of approaching what I dream of* in an intimate friend. No more of this.

Mistress or sweetheart I have none; it is another of my ideals and one fraught, unto the soul of it, with a real nothingness. It cannot be as I dream. Alas! poor Alastor! Shelley, how I understand thee! Can I confide in Mother? Would that I had her here. I cannot confide in her either,* but her presence would abate much of my pain. I feel as lonely as a wreck at sea. And I am a wreck indeed. So I confide in myself. In myself? What confidence is there in these lines? There is none. As I read them over I ache in mind to perceive how pretentious, how literary-diary-like they are! In some I have even made style. Yet I suffer nonetheless. A man may suffer as much in a suit of silks as in a sack or in a torn blanket.

No more.

[An Unsent Letter to Clifford Geerdts]

Faustino Antunes

[I am writing you about the] late Fernando António Nogueira Pessoa, who is thought to have committed suicide; at least he blew up a country house in which he was, dying he and several other people—a crime (?) which caused [a] great sensation in Portugal at the time (several months ago). I have been requested to inquire, as far as is now possible, into his mental condition and, having heard that the deceased was with you in the Durban High School, must beg you to write me stating frankly how he was considered among the boys at the said institution. Write me as detailed an account as possible on this. What opinion was held of him? Intellectually? Socially? etc. Did he seem or did he not seem capable of such an act as I have described?

I must ask you to keep, as far as possible, silence in this matter; it is, you understand, very delicate and very sad. Besides, it may have been (how I wish it may have been!) an accident, and in that case our hasty condemnation would itself be a crime. It is just my task, by inquiring into his mental condition, to determine whether the catastrophe was a crime or a mere accident.

An early reply will [be] very much obliged.

Two Prose Fragments

Alexander Search

1.

Bond entered into by Alexander Search, of Hell, Nowhere, with Jacob
Satan, Master, though not King, of the same place:

1. Never to fall off or shrink from the purpose of doing good to mankind.
2. Never to write things, sensual or otherwise evil, which may be to
   the detriment and harm of those that read.
3. Never to forget, when attacking religion in the name of truth, that
   religion can ill be substituted and that poor man is weeping in the
   dark.
4. Never to forget men's suffering and men's ill.

October 2nd, 1907

† Satan   Alexander Search
(his mark)

2.

30 October 1908

No soul more loving or tender than mine has ever existed, no soul so
full of kindness, of pity, of all the things of tenderness and of love. Yet
no soul is so lonely as mine—not lonely, be it noted, from exterior but
from interior circumstances. I mean this: together with my great tenderness and kindness an element of an entirely opposite kind enters into
my character—an element of sadness, of self-centeredness, of selfishness, therefore, whose effect is two-fold: to warp and hinder the development and full *internal* play of those other qualities, and to hinder, by
affecting the will depressingly, their full *external* play, their manifestation. One day I shall analyze this, one day I shall examine better, dis-
criminate, the elements of my character, for my curiosity about all things,

linked to my curiosity about myself and my own character, will lead to an* attempt to understand my personality.

It was on account of these characteristics that I wrote, describing myself, in "A Winter Day":*

> One like Rousseau . . .
> A misanthropic lover of mankind.

I have, as a matter of fact, many, too many, affinities with Rousseau. In certain things our characters are identical. The warm, intense, inexpressible love of mankind, and the portion of selfishness balancing it—this is a fundamental characteristic of his character and, as well, of mine.

My intense patriotic suffering, my intense desire of bettering the condition of Portugal provokes in me—how to express with what warmth, with what intensity, with what sincerity!—a thousand plans which, even if one man could realize them, he would have to have one characteristic which in me is purely negative—the power of will. But I suffer—on the very brink of madness, I swear it—as if I *could* do all and was unable to do it, by deficiency of will.

          . . .

Besides my patriotic projects—writing of "Portuguese Regicide" to provoke a revolution here, writing of Portuguese pamphlets, editing of older national literary works, creation of a magazine, of a scientific review etc.; other plans consuming me with the necessity of being soon carried out—Jean Seul projects,* critique of Binet-Sanglé,* etc.—combine to produce an excess of impulse that paralyzes my will. The suffering that this produces I know not if it can be described as on this side of insanity.

Add to all this other reasons still for suffering, some physical, others mental, the susceptibility to every small thing that can cause pain (or even that to a normal man could not cause pain), add to this other things still, complications, money difficulties—join all this to my fundamentally unbalanced temperament, and you may be able to *suspect* what my suffering is.

One of my mental complications—horrible beyond words—is a fear of insanity, which itself is insanity. (. . .)

Rule of Life

1. Make as few confidences as possible. Better make none, but, if you make any, make false or indistinct ones.
2. Dream as little as possible, except where the direct purpose of the dream is a poem or a literary product. Study and work.
3. Try to be as sober as possible, anticipating sobriety of body by a sober attitude of mind.
4. Be agreeable only by agreeableness, not by opening your mind or by discussing freely those problems that are bound up with the inner life of the spirit.
5. Cultivate concentration, temper the will, make yourself a force by thinking, as innerly as possible, that you are indeed a force.
6. Consider how few real friends you have, because few people are apt to be anyone's friends.
7. Try to charm by what is in your silence.
8. Learn to be prompt to act in small things, in the trite things of street life, home life, work life, to brook no delay from yourself.
9. Organize your life like a literary work, putting as much unity into it as possible.
10. Kill the Killer.

THE MARINER

Pessoa wrote his only complete play, O Marinheiro (The Mariner), *in 1913, a year before Alberto Caeiro, Ricardo Reis, and Álvaro de Campos burst onto the scene, and the essential drama, or non-drama, of the mature author is all contained here, in seed form.* Perhaps not by accident there are three characters in the play who act, or who don't act—three women who impassively sit, watching through the night over the corpse of a fourth woman. A fifth character, intuited but not actually perceived by the women, seems to hold the perhaps nonexistent key to the mystery of their lives, which is really just the mystery of what makes them talk, for that is the only thing that sets them apart from the dead woman in the coffin. Everything else in this strange play is suspension. But, come to think of it, even the phrases spoken by the three women are suspended. Like Symbolist precursors of Beckett's Estragon and Vladimir, they spin words that lead to no conclusion, while waiting for they don't know whom, or what.*

Pessoa's "static drama," to use his self-contradictory epithet (drama deriving from a Greek verb meaning "to do, to act"), reads like a program or prophecy of the then young poet's life, for he spent the rest of his years leading a largely solitary existence but producing an astonishing quantity of words so as to make himself into fictitious others, whose reality threatened to overshadow his own. The heteronyms were like the watching women's verbalized dreams, speeches that seemed like people, a series of nonexistent mariners who noisily occupied the stage of Pessoa's outwardly quiet life.

The notion that our lives are but the stuff of dreams is a stock theme of classical European drama, as important to a playwright such as Calderón de la Barca as it was to Shakespeare. Pessoa's point of view was more complex, and in a certain way more optimistic. While endorsing the premise of Calderón's most famous play, Life Is Dreaming *(whose Spanish title is usually and less accurately rendered as* Life Is a Dream*), Pessoa was ultimately more intrigued by the reverse formulation: dreaming is life.* The Mariner *is negation, the unending night, a senseless vigil that humanity keeps over its own corpse, its future death, but against this bleak background or, if you will, this blank canvas, a certain kind of life—the dreamed life—thrives. The Second Watcher's observation that she and her companions could just be part of the mariner's dream is anathema to their egos but pays homage to the power and possibility of dreams.*

The mariner is of course Pessoa, who was notoriously silent about his true past and whose ship blew off course from the world of love and social engagement, depositing him on the isle of his literary imagination. Pessoa is also the Second Watcher, who dreamed up the mariner and the mariner's dream. And Pessoa is Pessoa, who dreamed the watcher who dreamed the mariner who dreamed a past life that was, perhaps, Pessoa's.

Renouncing all action, plot, and progress, The Mariner *is as much an antidrama as a static one, and Pessoa's dozens of unfinished plays, including a monumental but vastly disordered* Faust, *have few positively dramatic qualities to offer. Describing his life's work as "a drama divided into people instead of into acts," Pessoa specialized in inventing characters without true plays (or stories) for them to inhabit, and the larger characters—his heteronyms—ended up haunting him, not because they were convincing replicas of carnal realities but because Pessoa felt, or decided, that their other-world reality had every bit as much right to exist. No matter how ethereal a dreamed thing may be, it is in some sense an object of experience, as real to an unbiased sensibility as any other object, only more mysteriously so. Pessoa escaped from the world of material chaos into dreams, whose more obscure and endlessly proliferating reality proved to be even more disquieting. No wonder the Second Watcher, in the second half of the play, desperately pleads with her two companions: "Talk to me, shout at me, so that I'll wake up and know that I'm here with you and that certain things really are just dreams. . . ."*

She pleads in vain. No dream, for Pessoa, was just a dream; every dream, every fiction, every vision, every passing thought, was its own small but infinite universe, full of unknown wonders—and horrors—for the adventurer who dares to explore it. Pessoa would never have said that truth is stranger than fiction. What he did say was that truth is fiction, fiction is truth, and that everything—when we really look at it—is strange beyond all telling.

The Mariner—A Static Drama in One Act

By "static drama" I mean drama in which action is absent from the plot, drama in which the characters don't act (for they never change position and never talk of changing position) and don't even have feelings capable of producing an action—drama, in other words, in which there is no conflict or true plot. Someone may argue that this is not drama at all. I believe it is, for I believe that drama is more than just the dynamic kind and that the essence of dramatic plot is not action or the results of action but—more broadly—the revelation of souls through the words that are exchanged and the creation of situations. . . . . . It's possible for souls to be revealed without action, and it's possible to create situations of inertia that concern only the soul, with no windows or doors onto reality.*

A room in what is no doubt an old castle. We can tell, from the room, that the castle is circular. In the middle of the room, on a bier, stands a coffin with a young woman dressed in white. A torch burns in each of the four corners. To the right, almost opposite whoever imagines the room, there is one long, narrow window, from which a patch of ocean can be glimpsed between two distant hills.

Next to the window three young women keep watch. The first is sitting opposite the window, her back to the torch on the upper right. The other two are seated on either side of the window.
   It is night, with just a hazy remnant of moonlight.

FIRST WATCHER   We still haven't heard the hour strike.

SECOND WATCHER   We can't hear it. No clock is near. Soon it will be day.

THIRD WATCHER   No: the horizon is black.

FIRST WATCHER   Why don't we amuse ourselves by telling what we once were? It's beautiful, sister, and always false . . .

SECOND WATCHER   No, let's not talk about it. Besides, were we ever anything?

FIRST WATCHER   Perhaps. I don't know. But it's always beautiful, in any case, to talk about the past . . . The hours have gone by and we have remained silent. I've passed the time gazing at the flame of that candle. Sometimes it flickers, or turns yellow, or more white. I don't know why this happens. But do we know, sisters, why anything happens? . . .

(pause)

FIRST WATCHER   To talk about the past must be beautiful, for it is useless and makes us feel so sorry . . .

SECOND WATCHER   Let's talk, if you like, about a past we may never have had.

THIRD WATCHER   No. Perhaps we had it.

FIRST WATCHER   You're saying nothing but words. Talking is so sad— such a false way of forgetting! . . . How about if we go for a walk?

THIRD WATCHER   Where?

FIRST WATCHER   Here, back and forth. Sometimes this brings dreams.

THIRD WATCHER   Of what?

FIRST WATCHER   I don't know. Why should I know?

(pause)

SECOND WATCHER   This land is so sad . . . It was less sad in the land where I used to live. At day's end I spun thread by the window. The window looked out onto the sea, where sometimes I could spot an island in the distance . . . Sometimes I didn't spin; I looked at the sea and forgot to live. I don't know if I was happy. I'll never go back to being what perhaps I never was . . .

FIRST WATCHER   I've never seen the sea except from here. And we see so little of it from that window, which is the only one through which we can see it at all . . . Is the sea of other lands beautiful?

SECOND WATCHER   Only the sea of other lands is beautiful. The sea we can see always makes us long for the one we'll never see.

(*pause*)

FIRST WATCHER   Didn't we say we were going to tell our past?

SECOND WATCHER   No, we didn't.

THIRD WATCHER   Why is there no clock in this room?

SECOND WATCHER   I don't know . . . But this way, with no clock, everything is more distant and mysterious. The night belongs more to itself . . . Perhaps, if we knew what time it is, we couldn't talk like this.

FIRST WATCHER   In me, sister, everything is sad. It's December in my soul . . . I'm trying not to look at the window, through which I know hills can be seen in the distance . . . I was once happy beyond some hills . . . I was a little girl. Every day I picked flowers and asked, before going to sleep, that they not be taken from me . . . There's something about this that's irreparable and that makes me feel like crying . . . This happened — it could only have happened — far away from here . . . When will the day dawn? . . .

THIRD WATCHER   What does it matter? It always dawns in the same way . . . Always, always, always . . .

(*pause*)

SECOND WATCHER   Let's tell each other stories. I don't know any stories, but there's no harm in that . . . Only life is harmful . . . Better not even to brush it with the hems of our dresses . . . No, don't get up. That would be an action, and every action interrupts a dream . . . I wasn't having a dream right now, but it's nice to imagine that I could have been . . . But the past — why don't we talk about the past?

FIRST WATCHER   We decided not to . . . Soon day will break, and we'll
regret it. Daylight puts dreams to sleep . . . The past is just a dream.
I can think of nothing, for that matter, that isn't a dream . . . If I look
closely at the present, it seems to have already moved on . . . What is
anything? How does it move on from one moment to the next? How
does it inwardly move on? . . . Oh let's talk, sisters, let's talk all together in a loud voice . . . Silence is beginning to take shape, to be
a thing . . . I feel it wrapping me like a mist . . . Ah, talk, talk! . . .

SECOND WATCHER   What for? . . . I stare at you both and don't see you
right away . . . Chasms seem to have opened between us . . . To be
able to see you I have to wear out the idea that I can see you . . . This
warm air feels cold inside, in the part that touches my soul . . . Right
now I should be feeling impossible hands running through my hair—
that's the image people use when talking about mermaids . . . (*Pauses,
crossing her hands on her knees.*) Just now, when I wasn't thinking
about anything, I was thinking about my past.

FIRST WATCHER   And I must have been thinking about mine . . .

THIRD WATCHER   I don't know what I was thinking about . . . Perhaps
about the past of others . . . , the past of wondrous people who never
existed . . . Not far from my mother's house flowed a stream. Why did
it flow, and why didn't it flow farther away, or nearer? . . . Is there any
reason for anything being what it is? Is there any reason that's true
and real like my hands? . . .

SECOND WATCHER   Our hands are not true or real. They're mysteries
that inhabit our life . . . Sometimes, staring at my hands, I fear
God . . . No wind makes the candles flutter, but look: they flutter.
Toward what? . . . What a pity if someone could answer! . . . I feel
like listening to exotic melodies which at this very moment are surely
playing in palaces on other continents . . . In my heart everything is
always far away . . . Perhaps because I chased the waves at the seashore when I was a child. I led life by the hand among the rocks at
low tide, when the ocean seems to have crossed its hands on its chest
and fallen asleep, like the statue of an angel, so that no one will ever
look at it again . . .

THIRD WATCHER   Your words remind me of my soul . . .

SECOND WATCHER   Perhaps because they're not true . . . I hardly realize I'm saying them. I repeat what a voice I don't hear tells me . . . But I must have really lived by the seashore . . . I love things that wave this way or that. There are waves in my soul. I seem to rock when I walk . . . I feel like walking right now. I don't do it, because nothing's worth doing, especially when it's something we feel like doing . . . The hills are what I fear . . . They can't possibly be so large and still. They must have a stony secret they refuse to tell . . . If I could lean out that window without seeing hills, then someone in whom I feel happy would, for a moment, lean out of my soul . . .

FIRST WATCHER   I myself love the hills . . . On this side of all hills life is always ugly . . . On the other side, where my mother lives, we used to sit in the shade of tamarind trees and talk about going to other lands . . . There everything was long and happy like the song of two birds, one on either side of the path . . . Our thoughts were the only clearings in the forest. And our dreams were that the trees would cast some other calm besides their shadows on the ground . . . Surely that was how we lived—I and I don't know if anyone else . . . Tell me this was true so that I won't have to cry . . .

SECOND WATCHER   I lived among rocks in plain view of the sea . . . The hem of my skirt whipped cool and salty against my bare legs . . . I was small and wild . . . Today I'm afraid of having been . . . I seem to sleep through the present . . . Speak to me of fairies. I've never heard anyone speak of them . . . The ocean was too big to ever make me think of them . . . It's cozier in life to be small . . . Were you happy, sister?

FIRST WATCHER   I'm beginning, in this moment, to have been so . . . Then too, it all happened in the shade . . . The trees lived it more than I did . . . It never arrived, and I hardly expected it to . . . And you, sister, why don't you speak?

THIRD WATCHER   It horrifies me that I'll soon have said what I'm going to say. My words, spoken in the present, will belong immediately to the past, they'll be somewhere outside me, irrevocable and fatal . . . When speaking, I think about what's going on in my throat, and my words seem like people . . . My fear is larger than me. I can feel in my hand, I don't know how, the key to an unknown door. And I'm suddenly, all of me, a talisman or tabernacle conscious of itself. That's why it so scares me, like a dark forest, to pass through the mystery of speaking . . . But who knows if this is really how I am and what I feel? . . .

FIRST WATCHER   It's so hard to know what we feel when we look at ourselves! Even living seems hard when we stop to think about it . . . Speak, therefore, without thinking about the fact you exist. Weren't you going to tell us who you once were?

THIRD WATCHER   What I once was no longer remembers who I am. Poor happy girl that I used to be! . . . I lived among the shadows of branches, and everything in my soul is trembling leaves. When I walk in the sun, my shadow is cool. I spent the flight of my days amid fountains, where I dipped the calm tips of my fingers whenever I dreamed of living . . . Sometimes I bent over and stared at myself in the ponds . . . When I smiled, my teeth looked mysterious in the water. They had their own smile, independent of mine . . . I always smiled for no reason . . . Talk to me about death, about the end of all things, so that I can feel there's a reason to look back . . .

FIRST WATCHER   Let's talk about nothing, about nothing . . . It's colder now, but why is it colder? There's no reason for it to be colder. It's not really any colder than it is . . . Why must we talk? Singing, I don't know why, is better than talking . . . Singing, when we do it at night, is a bold and cheery person who bursts into the room and warms it up, comforting us . . . I could sing you a song we used to sing at home in my past. Don't you want me to sing it?

THIRD WATCHER   It's not worth the bother, sister . . . When someone sings, I can no longer be with myself. I stop being able to remember myself. My entire past becomes someone else, and I weep over a dead life that I carry inside me and never lived. It's always too late to sing, just as it's always too late not to sing . . .

(*pause*)

FIRST WATCHER   Soon it will be day . . . Let's observe silence. That's what life urges . . . Near the house where I was born there was a pond. I'd go there and sit next to it, on a tree trunk that had fallen almost into the water . . . I'd sit on the end of it and dip my feet in the water, reaching down my toes as far as I could. Then I'd stare hard at the tips of my toes, but not in order to see them. I don't know why, but my impression is that this pond never existed . . . To remember it is like not being able to remember anything . . . Who knows why I'm saying this and whether I was the one who lived what I remember? . . .

SECOND WATCHER   Dreaming at the seashore makes us sad . . . We can't be what we want to be, since whatever it is, we always wish we'd been it in the past . . . When the wave crashes and the foam hisses, it seems like a thousand tiny voices are speaking. The foam only seems cool to those who suppose it is all one . . . Each thing is many, and we know nothing . . . Shall I tell you what I dreamed at the seashore?

FIRST WATCHER   You can tell it, sister, but nothing in us needs you to tell it . . . If it's beautiful, I'm already sorry I'll have heard it. And if it's not beautiful, wait . . . Tell it only after you've changed it . . .

SECOND WATCHER   I'm going to tell it. It's not entirely false, since surely nothing is entirely false. It must have happened like this . . . One day when I found myself leaning back on top of a cold cliff, having forgotten I ever had a mother and father, a childhood and other days besides that one—on that day I vaguely saw, as if I only thought I'd seen it, a sail passing by in the distance . . . Then it vanished . . . Returning to myself, I realized that I now had this dream . . . I don't know where it began. And I never saw another sail . . . None of the ships leaving from ports around here have sails that resemble that sail, not even when the moon is out and the ships pass slowly by in the distance . . .

FIRST WATCHER   I see a ship in the offing through the window. Perhaps it's the one you saw . . .

SECOND WATCHER   No, sister. The one you see is no doubt bound for some port . . . The one I saw couldn't have been bound for any port . . .

FIRST WATCHER   Why did you respond to what I said? . . . You might be right . . . I saw no ship through the window. I wanted to see one and told you I'd seen one so as not to feel sorry . . . Now tell us what you dreamed at the seashore . . .

SECOND WATCHER   I dreamed of a mariner who seemed to be lost on a faraway island. On the island there were a few tall, unbending palms among which some vague birds flew . . . I didn't notice if they ever alighted . . . The mariner had lived there since surviving a shipwreck . . . Since he had no way of returning to his homeland, and since remembering it made him suffer, he dreamed up a homeland he'd never had, and he made that other homeland his: another kind of country with other kinds of landscapes, and different people, who had a different way of walking down the street and leaning out their windows. Hour by hour he built that false homeland in his dreams, and he dreamed continuously—by day in the scant shade of the tall palms, whose spiky shadows stood out on the warm, sandy ground, and by night on the beach, where he lay on his back and didn't notice the stars.

FIRST WATCHER   If only a tree had dappled my outstretched hands with the shadow of a dream like that! . . .

THIRD WATCHER   Let her speak. Don't interrupt. She knows words that mermaids taught her . . . I'm falling asleep in order to hear her . . . Go on, sister, go on . . . My heart aches because I wasn't you when you dreamed at the seashore . . .

SECOND WATCHER   For years and years, day after day, the mariner built his new homeland in a never-ending dream . . . Every day he placed a dreamed stone on that impossible edifice . . . Soon he had a country he'd crossed and recrossed countless times. He remembered having already spent thousands of hours along its coastline. He knew the usual color of twilight on a certain northern bay, and how soothing it was to enter—late at night, with his soul basking in the murmur of the water cut by the ship's prow—a large southern port where he had spent, perhaps happily, his imaginary youth . . .

(*pause*)

FIRST WATCHER   Why have you quit speaking, sister?

SECOND WATCHER   It's better not to talk too much . . . Life is always watching us . . . Every hour is a mother to our dreams, but we mustn't know this . . . When I talk too much, I become separated from myself and start hearing myself speak. This stirs self-pity and makes me feel my heart so intensely that I end up nearly weeping with desire to hold it in my arms and rock it like a baby . . . Look: the horizon is growing lighter . . . The day can't be too far off. Must I tell you more of my dream?

FIRST WATCHER   Keep telling it, sister, keep on telling it. Don't stop telling it, and pay no attention to the fact that days dawn . . . The day never dawns for those who lay their head in the lap of dreamed hours . . . Don't wring your hands. It makes a sound as of a stealthy snake . . . Tell us much, much more about your dream. It's so true that it makes no sense. The mere thought of hearing you is music to my soul . . .

SECOND WATCHER   Yes, I'll tell you more about it. I myself feel the need to tell it. As I tell it to you, I'm also telling it to myself . . . Three of us are listening . . . (*Suddenly looks at the coffin and shudders.*) Three of us, no . . . I don't know . . . I don't know how many . . .

THIRD WATCHER   Don't talk like that. Just tell your dream, start telling it again . . . Don't talk about how many can hear . . . We never know how many things really live and see and hear . . . Go back to your dream . . . The mariner. What did the mariner dream of? . . .

SECOND WATCHER (*in a softer voice, very slowly*)   He began by creating landscapes; then he created cities; then he created streets and cross streets, one by one, sculpting them out of the substance of his soul— street by street, neighborhood after neighborhood, out to the sea walls of the wharfs, where he then created the ports . . . Street by street, and the people who walked them or gazed down at them from their windows . . . He began to know some of the people, at first just barely recognizing them, but then becoming familiar with their past lives and their conversations, and he dreamed all this as if it were mere scenery to delight the eyes . . . Then he traveled, with his memory, through the country he'd created . . . And thus he created his past . . . Soon he had another previous life . . . In this new homeland he already had a birthplace, places where he'd grown up, and ports from where he'd set sail . . . He began to acquire childhood playmates, and then friends and enemies from his youth . . . It was all different from what he'd actually lived. Neither the country, nor its people, nor even his own past were like the ones that had really existed . . . Must I continue? It's so painful to tell it! . . . Now, because I'm telling it, I'd rather be telling you about other dreams . . .

THIRD WATCHER   Continue, even if you don't know why . . . The more I hear you, the more I stop belonging to myself . . .

FIRST WATCHER   But is it really a good idea for you to continue? Should every story have an end? But keep talking anyway . . . It matters so little what we say or don't say . . . We keep watch over the passing hours . . . Our task is as useless as Life . . .

SECOND WATCHER   One day, after a heavy rain that blurred the horizon, the mariner got tired of dreaming . . . He felt like remembering his true homeland . . . , but he couldn't remember anything, and he realized it no longer existed for him . . . The only childhood he could recall belonged to the homeland of his dream; the only adolescence he remembered was the one he'd created . . . His entire life was the life he'd dreamed . . . And he realized he could never have had any other life . . . For he could remember none of its streets, none of its people, and not one motherly caress . . . Whereas in the life he thought he'd merely dreamed, everything was real and had existed . . . He couldn't even dream, couldn't even conceive, of having had any other past the way everyone else, for a moment, is able to imagine . . . O sisters, sisters . . . There's something, I don't know what, that I haven't told you . . . something that would explain all this . . . My soul makes me shiver . . . I'm hardly aware of having spoken . . . Talk to me, shout at me, so that I'll wake up and know that I'm here with you and that certain things really are just dreams . . .

FIRST WATCHER (*in a very soft voice*)   I don't know what to tell you . . . I'm afraid to look at things . . . How does your dream continue? . . .

SECOND WATCHER   I don't know the rest of it . . . It's all fuzzy . . . Why should there be any more? . . .

FIRST WATCHER   What happened after all that?

SECOND WATCHER   After all what? What is after? Is after anything? . . . One day a boat arrived . . . One day a boat arrived . . . Yes, yes . . . that has to be what happened . . . One day a boat arrived, and passed by that island, and the mariner wasn't there . . .

THIRD WATCHER   Perhaps he'd returned to his homeland . . . But which one?

FIRST WATCHER   Yes, which one? And then what became of the mariner? Does anyone know?

SECOND WATCHER   Why do you ask me? Does anything have an answer?

(*pause*)

THIRD WATCHER   Is it absolutely necessary, even within your dream, that this mariner and this island existed?

SECOND WATCHER   No, sister. Nothing is absolutely necessary.

FIRST WATCHER   Tell us, at least, how the dream ended.

SECOND WATCHER   It didn't end . . . I don't know . . . No dream ends . . . How can I be sure that I'm not still dreaming it, that I'm not dreaming it without knowing it, and that my dreaming isn't this hazy thing I call my life? . . . Say no more . . . I'm beginning to be sure of I don't know what . . . The footsteps of some unknown horror are approaching me in a night that's not this night . . . Whom might I have awakened with the dream I told you? . . . I'm deathly afraid that God has forbidden my dream, which is undoubtedly more real than He allows . . . Say something, sisters. Tell me at least that the night is ending, even though I know it . . . Look, it's beginning to be day . . . Look: the real day is almost here . . . Let's stop. Let's think no more . . . Let's quit pursuing this inward adventure . . . Who knows where it might lead us? . . . All of this, sisters, happened during the night . . . Let's say no more about it, even to ourselves . . . It's human and fitting that we each adopt our own air of sadness.

THIRD WATCHER   Listening to you was so beautiful. Don't say it wasn't . . . I know it wasn't worth the bother. That's why I found it beautiful . . . That's not why, but let me say it was . . . What's more, the music of your voice, which I listened to even more than your words, leaves me dissatisfied, perhaps because it's music . . .

SECOND WATCHER   Everything leaves us dissatisfied, sister . . . For people who think, everything wearies, because everything changes. People who come and go prove it, for they change with everything . . . Only dreams last forever and are beautiful. Why are we still talking? . . .

FIRST WATCHER   I don't know . . . (*in a low voice, looking at the coffin*)
Why do people die?

SECOND WATCHER   Perhaps because they don't dream enough . . .

FIRST WATCHER   It's possible . . . Then wouldn't we be better off shut-
ting ourselves up in our dream and forgetting life, so that death would
in turn forget us? . . .

SECOND WATCHER   No, sister, we're not better off doing anything . . .

THIRD WATCHER   Sisters, it's already day . . . Look at the astonished line
of the hills . . . Why don't we weep? . . . That woman who pretends
to be lying there was young like us, and beautiful, and she also
dreamed . . . I'm sure her dream was the most beautiful of all . . . What
do you suppose she dreamed of? . . .

FIRST WATCHER   Lower your voice. Perhaps she's listening, and already
knows what dreams are for . . .

(*pause*)

SECOND WATCHER   Perhaps none of this is true . . . This silence, this
dead woman and this rising day are perhaps nothing but a dream . . .
Look closely at all this . . . Does it seem to you that it belongs to
life? . . .

FIRST WATCHER   I don't know. I don't know how something belongs to
life . . . Ah, how still you are! And your eyes look so uselessly sad . . .

SECOND WATCHER   It's not worth being sad in any other way . . . Don't
you think we should stop talking? It's so strange to be living . . .
Everything that happens is unbelievable, whether on the mariner's
island or in this world . . . Look, the sky is already green. The horizon goldenly smiles . . . I feel my eyes burning from my having
thought about crying . . .

FIRST WATCHER   You did cry, sister.

SECOND WATCHER   Perhaps . . . It doesn't matter . . . What's this chill? . . .
Ah, it's time, yes . . . the time has come! . . . Tell me this . . . Tell me
this one thing . . . Why can't the mariner be the only thing in all of
this that's real, and we and everything else just one of his dreams? . . .

FIRST WATCHER   Stop talking, stop talking . . . This is so strange that it
must be true. Say no more . . . I don't know what you were going to

say, but it must be too much for the soul to bear . . . I'm afraid of what you didn't say . . . Look, look, it's already day. Look at the day . . . Do everything you can to see only the day, the real day, there, outside . . . Look at it, look at it . . . It comforts . . . Don't think, don't look at what you're thinking . . . Look at the day that's breaking . . . It shines like gold over a silver land. The wispy clouds are filling out and gaining color . . . Imagine if nothing existed, sisters . . . Imagine if everything were, in a way, absolutely nothing . . . Why did you look at me like that? . . .

(They don't answer her. And no one had looked at anything.)

FIRST WATCHER   What did you say that so frightened me? . . . I felt it so strongly I hardly noticed what it was . . . Tell me again so that, hearing it for the second time, I won't be as frightened as the first . . . No, no . . . Don't say anything . . . I didn't ask that question because I wanted an answer but just to say something, to keep myself from thinking . . . I'm afraid I might remember what it was . . . It was something huge and frightful like the existence of God . . . We should have already quit talking . . . Our conversation stopped making sense a long time ago . . . Whatever it is between us that makes us talk has gone on for too long . . . There are other presences here besides our souls . . . The day should have broken, and they should have woken up by now . . . Something's late . . . Everything's late . . . What's happening in things to make us feel this horror? . . . Ah, don't desert me . . . Talk to me, talk to me . . . Talk at the same time as me so that my voice won't be alone . . . My voice scares me less than the idea of my voice, should I happen to notice that I'm speaking . . .

THIRD WATCHER   What voice are you speaking with? . . . It's someone else's . . . It comes from some sort of distance . . .

FIRST WATCHER   I don't know . . . Don't remind me of that . . . I should be speaking with the shrill and tremulous voice of fear . . . But I no longer know how to speak. A chasm has opened between me and my voice . . . All our talking and this night and this fear—all this should have ended, abruptly ended, after the horror of your words . . . I think

I've finally started forgetting the story that you told and that made me feel like I should scream in a new way to express such a horror . . .

THIRD WATCHER (*to the* SECOND WATCHER) You shouldn't have told us that story, sister. Now I marvel at being alive with even greater horror. Your story so engrossed me that I heard the meaning of your words and their sound separately. And it seemed to me that you, your voice and the meaning of what you said were three different beings, like three creatures that walk and talk.

SECOND WATCHER They really are three different beings, each with its own life. Perhaps God knows why . . . Ah, but why are we talking? Who makes us keep talking? Why do I talk when I don't want to? Why don't we notice that it's day? . . .

FIRST WATCHER If only someone could scream to wake us up! I hear myself screaming on the inside, but I no longer know the path from my will to my throat. I feel a burning need to be afraid that someone will knock at that door. Why doesn't someone knock at the door? It would be impossible, and I need to be afraid of that, I need to know what it is I'm afraid of . . . How strange I feel! . . . It seems I've stopped speaking with my voice . . . Part of me fell asleep and just watches . My dread has grown, but I'm no longer able to feel it . . . I no longer know where in my soul things are felt . . . A leaden shroud has been placed over my awareness of my body . . . Why did you tell us your story?

SECOND WATCHER I don't remember . . . I hardly even remember that I told it . . . It already seems so long ago! . . . What a deep sleepiness has fallen over my way of looking at things! . . . What is it we want to do? What were we thinking of doing? I can't remember if it was to talk or not to talk . . .

FIRST WATCHER Let's stop talking. The effort you make to talk tires me out . . . The gap between what you think and what you say grieves me . . . I can feel in my skin my consciousness floating on the surface of my sensations' terrified stupor. I don't know what that means, but it's what I feel . . . I need to say longish, confusing sentences that are hard to say . . . Doesn't all of this feel to you like a huge spider that between us is weaving, from soul to soul, a black web we can't escape?

SECOND WATCHER   I feel nothing . . . My sensations feel like a tangible thing . . . Who am I being in this moment? Who is speaking with my voice? . . . Ah, listen . . .

FIRST and THIRD WATCHERS   Who was it?

SECOND WATCHER   Nothing. I heard nothing . . . I tried to pretend to hear something so that you might think you'd heard it and I could believe there was something to hear . . . Oh, what horror, what secret horror separates voice from soul, sensations from thoughts, and makes us talk and feel and think, when everything in us begs for silence and the new day and the unconsciousness of life . . . Who is the fifth person in this room who extends a forbidding hand to stop us every time we're about to feel?

FIRST WATCHER   Why try to frighten me? I'm already bursting with more fear than I can hold. I already weigh too much in the lap of my self-awareness. I'm completely immersed in the warm mud of what I think I feel. Something that seizes and watches us has entered through all my senses. My eyelids droop over all my sensations. My tongue is stuck to all my feelings. A deep sleep glues all my ideas of gestures together. Why did you look at me like that? . . .

THIRD WATCHER (*in a very slow and faint voice*)   Ah, it's time, the time has come . . . Yes, someone has woken up . . . There are people waking up . . . As soon as someone enters, all this will end . . . Until then let's imagine that all this horror was a long sleep we've been having . . . It's already day . . . Everything's going to end . . . And the conclusion of all this, sister, is that only you are happy, because you believe in the dream . . .

SECOND WATCHER   Why ask me about it? Because I told it? No, I don't believe . . .

A rooster crows. The light brightens, as if suddenly. The three watchers, without looking at each other, remain silent.

On a road not far off an indefinite wagon creaks and groans.

11–12 October, 1913

To Fernando Pessoa

AFTER READING YOUR STATIC DRAMA *The Mariner*

After twelve minutes
Of your play *The Mariner,*
Whose utter lack of meaning
Makes the sharpest of minds
Go dull and grow weary,
One of the watching women
Says with languid magic:

Only dreams last forever and are beautiful. Why are we still talking?

Exactly what I wanted
To ask those women . . .

ÁLVARO DE CAMPOS

THE MASTER AND
HIS DISCIPLES

"The creation of Caeiro and of the discipleship of Reis and Campos seems, at first sight, an elaborate joke of the imagination. But it is not. It [is] a great act of intellectual magic, a magnum opus of the impersonal creative power." So claimed Fernando Pessoa in a note datable to January 1930, by which time the poet seems to have lost all his modesty. Or could it be that he was just stating a fact? Even if we may doubt that the creation of Caeiro and his poetic disciples wasn't, at some level, a hearty as well as elaborate joke, it would be hard to deny the magical quality of Pessoa's intellectual trick. Having divided himself among invented others, whom he claimed were no longer him, Pessoa could promote them without—theoretically—any personal stake in the matter. And he spared no pains to do just that. Besides all the commentary and praise that he instructed the minor heteronyms to heap on the major ones, and Campos and Reis on Alberto Caeiro (the two "disciples" were rather more critical of each other), Pessoa drew up quite specific plans for publicizing Caeiro's work in magazines and newspapers, both at home and abroad, and he even drafted some promotional articles. One of these, written in English and headed by a list of the British publications where it was to be sent (including T. P.'s Weekly, Academy, and Athenaeum), explains to its potential readers:

> "The Rime of the Ancient Mariner" in relation to its time is, if anything, less original than Alberto Caeiro's astonishing volume—The Keeper of Sheep (O Guardador de Rebanhos)—which has just appeared in Lisbon.

No one in Portugal's literary milieu had ever heard of him.
He appeared suddenly. And his contribution to Portuguese and
European literature breaks away (. . .) from all traditions and
currents that were valid in the past or are active today.

Was Pessoa really planning to blitz the papers with promotional pieces like this one? Probably so, but planning very far ahead, for he would first have had to publish the book of Caeiro that they promoted, and he seemed in no hurry to publish anything in the way of books. He seems to have realized that time was on his side, such that none of his efforts would be wasted. And in his literary afterlife, on which he bet everything he had or was, Pessoa's publicity schemes are indeed having their impact.

As a marketing strategist for himself, Pessoa was (begging Caeiro's pardon) a veritable master, but the real "intellectual magic" of his enterprise resides in the logic of his psychological alchemies. We are all under the spell of Pessoa's own explanations of who he was, or wasn't. He left us not just inspired lines and not just inspired characters that recite inspired lines but a vast inspired system of logically interconnected ideas materialized in a literature of interconnected "Pessoas" (pessoa means "person" in Portuguese) a cosmography not just of his multiplied self but of Western thought and philosophy as embodied by those various selves. Such, at least, was Pessoa's ideal for his system, whose mechanics were perhaps his greatest poetic achievement.

Pessoa had a definite plan for the book of Caeiro he never published. In fact he had various plans, but the final and most elaborate one called for a substantial introduction by Ricardo Reis, to be followed by Caeiro's complete poems (The Keeper of Sheep, The Shepherd in Love, and Uncollected Poems) with accompanying notes by Reis, a horoscope for the time of Caeiro's birth (cast by Fernando Pessoa), and—finishing off the volume—Álvaro de Campos's Notes for the Memory of My Master Caeiro. Most of Reis's piecemeal but seemingly endless introduction probably dates from the late 1910s, though passages for it continued to be produced in the twenties. Had it ever been assembled, it would have amounted to a treatise concerned less with presenting Caeiro's poetry than with ex-

plaining and defending paganism (as shown by excerpts from it found further on in this volume). Campos's twenty-five or so Notes, left in a similar state of expanding disorder, were mostly if not all written in the 1930s, by which time Fernando Pessoa had taken the final step on his path of ironic self-effacement, declaring that he too was one of Caeiro's "disciples."

Thomas Crosse, a translator and essayist who was responsible for taking Portuguese culture to the Anglo-American world, had the special mission of promoting the work of Alberto Caeiro. He was supposed to produce an English version of Caeiro's poetry but never got beyond his "Translator's Preface."

Pessoa spent considerably less ink on prefatory and critical texts to promote Ricardo Reis and Álvaro de Campos, though the latter was rather good at promoting himself, through his polemical articles and letters that appeared in the Portuguese press. I. I. Crosse, whose piece on Campos's rhythmical skills is published here, was presumably the brother of Thomas. I. I. also wrote an essay titled "Caeiro and the Pagan Revolution." Both brothers wrote exclusively in English. (Yet a third brother, A. A. Crosse, competed for cash prizes in the puzzle and word games featured in various English newspapers.) Pessoa, whose only full brother died in infancy, was fond of providing brothers for his heteronyms, and it is Frederico Reis who offers us a sympathetic account of brother Ricardo's "sad Epicureanism." Frederico also authored a pamphlet (as of this writing still unpublished) about the so-called Lisbon School of poetry, explaining that it was Portugal's only truly cosmopolitan movement. The protagonists of the school were— not surprisingly—Alberto Caeiro, Ricardo Reis, and Álvaro de Campos.

Notes for the Memory of My Master Caeiro

Álvaro de Campos

I met my master Caeiro under exceptional circumstances, as are all of life's circumstances, especially those which in themselves are insignificant but which have outstanding consequences.

After completing, in Scotland, almost three quarters of my course in naval engineering, I went on a voyage to the Orient. On my return, I disembarked at Marseilles, unable to bear the thought of more sailing, and came by land to Lisbon. One day a cousin of mine took me on a trip to the Ribatejo,* where he knew one of Caeiro's cousins, with whom he had some business dealings. It was in the house of that cousin that I met my future master. That's all there is to tell; it was small like the seeds of all conceptions.

I can still see, with a clarity of soul that memory's tears don't cloud, because this seeing isn't external. . . . I see him before me as I saw him that first time and as I will perhaps always see him: first of all those blue eyes of a child who has no fear, then the already somewhat prominent cheekbones, his pale complexion, and his strange Greek air, which was a calmness from within, not something in his outward expression or features. His almost luxuriant hair was blond, but in a dim light it looked brownish. He was medium to tall in height but with low, hunched shoulders. His visage was white, his smile was true to itself, and so too his voice, whose tone didn't try to express anything beyond the words being said— a voice neither loud nor soft, just clear, without designs or hesitations or inhibitions. Those blue eyes couldn't stop gazing. If our observation noticed anything strange, it was his forehead—not high, but imposingly white. I repeat: it was the whiteness of his forehead, even whiter than his pale face, that endowed him with majesty. His hands were a bit slender, but not too, and he had a wide palm. The expression of his mouth, which was the last thing one noticed, as if speaking were less than existing for this man, consisted of the kind of smile we ascribe in poetry to beautiful inanimate things, merely because they please us—flowers, sprawling fields, sunlit waters. A smile for existing, not for talking to us.

My master, my master, who died so young! I see him again in this mere shadow that's me, in the memory that my dead self retains. . . .

It was in our first conversation. . . . Apropos I don't know what, he said, "There's a fellow here named Ricardo Reis whom I'm sure you would enjoy meeting. He's very different from you." And then he added, "Everything is different from us, and that's why everything exists."

This sentence, uttered as if it were an axiom of the earth, seduced me with a seismic shock—as always occurs when someone is deflowered—that penetrated to my soul's foundations. But contrary to what occurs in physical seduction, the effect on me was to receive all at once, in all my sensations, a virginity I'd never had.

My master Caeiro wasn't a pagan; he was paganism. Ricardo Reis is a pagan, António Mora is a pagan, and I'm a pagan; Fernando Pessoa himself would be a pagan, were he not a ball of string inwardly wound around itself. But Ricardo Reis is a pagan by virtue of his character, António Mora is a pagan by virtue of his intellect, and I'm a pagan out of sheer revolt, i.e. by my temperament. For Caeiro's paganism there was no explanation; there was consubstantiation.

I will clarify this in the weak-kneed way that indefinable things are defined: through example. If we compare ourselves with the Greeks, one of the most striking differences we find is their aversion to the infinite, of which they had no real concept. Well, my master Caeiro had the same nonconcept. I will now recount, with what I dare say is great accuracy, the astounding conversation in which he revealed this to me.

Elaborating on a reference made in one of the poems from *The Keeper of Sheep*, he told me how someone or other had once called him a "materialist poet." Although I don't think the label is right, since there is no right label to define my master Caeiro, I told him that the epithet wasn't entirely absurd. And I explained the basic tenets of classical materialism. Caeiro listened to me with a pained expression, and then blurted out:

"But this is just plain stupid. It's the stuff of priests but without any religion, and therefore without any excuse."

I was taken aback, and I pointed out various similarities between materialism and his own doctrine, though excluding from this his poetry. Caeiro protested.

"But what you call poetry is everything. And it's not even poetry: it's seeing. Those materialists are blind. You say they say that space is infinite. Where did they ever see that in space?"

And I, confused: "But don't you conceive of space as being infinite? Can't you conceive of space as being infinite?"

"I don't conceive of anything as infinite. How can I conceive of something as infinite?"

"Just suppose there's a space," I said. "Beyond that space there is more space, and then more space, still more, and more, and more. . . . It never ends. . . ."

"Why?" asked my master Caeiro.

I reeled in a mental earthquake. "Then suppose it ends!" I shouted. "What comes after?"

"If it ends," he replied, "nothing comes after."

This kind of argumentation, which is both childish and feminine, and therefore unanswerable, stumped my brain for a few moments, until finally I said, "But do you *conceive* of this?"

"Conceive of what? Of something having limits? Small wonder! What doesn't have limits doesn't exist. To exist means that there's something else, which means that each thing is limited. What's so hard about conceiving that a thing is a thing and that it's not always some other thing that's beyond it?"

At this point I had the physical sensation that I was arguing not with another man but with another universe. I made one last attempt, with a far-fetched argument that I convinced myself was legitimate.

"All right, Caeiro, consider numbers. . . . Where do numbers end? Let's take any number—34, for example. After 34 comes 35, 36, 37, 38, etc., and it keeps going like that forever. No matter how large the number, there's always a still larger one. . . ."

"But that's all just numbers," objected my master Caeiro. And then he added, looking at me with a boundless childhood in his eyes: "What is 34 in Reality?"

One day Caeiro told me something absolutely astonishing. We were talking, or rather, I was talking, about the soul's immortality. I felt that this concept, even if false, was necessary for us to be able to tolerate existence intellectually, to be able to see it as something more than a heap of stones with greater or lesser consciousness.

"I don't know what it means for something to be necessary," said Caeiro.

I answered without answering: "Just tell me this. What are you to yourself?"

"What am I to myself?" Caeiro repeated. "I'm one of my sensations."

I've never forgotten the shock that phrase produced in my soul. It has many implications, some of which are contrary to what Caeiro intended. But it was after all spontaneous—a ray of sunshine that shed light without any intention.

One of the most interesting conversations with my master Caeiro was the one in Lisbon where everyone in the group was present and we ended up discussing the concept of Reality.

If I remember correctly, we got on to this subject because of a tangential remark made by Fernando Pessoa apropos something that had been said. Pessoa's remark was this: "The concept of Being does not admit of parts or degrees; something is or it isn't."

"I'm not sure it's that simple," I objected. "This concept of being needs to be analyzed. It seems to me like a metaphysical superstition, at least to a certain extent."

"But the concept of Being isn't open to analysis," replied Fernando Pessoa, "due precisely to its indivisibility."

"The concept may not be open to it," I said, "but the value of that concept is."

Fernando answered, "But what is the 'value' of a concept independently of the concept? A concept—an abstract idea, that is—is never 'more' or 'less' than it is, and so it cannot be said to have value, which is always a matter of more or less. There may be value in how a concept is used or applied, but that value is in its usage or application, not in the concept itself."

My master Caeiro, who with his eyes had been attentively listening to this transpontine* discussion, broke in at this point, saying, "Where there can be no more or less, there is nothing."

"And why is that?" asked Fernando.

"Because there can be more or less of everything that's real, and nothing but what's real can exist."

"Give us an example, Caeiro," I said.

"Rain," replied my master. "Rain is something real. And so it can rain more or rain less. If you were to say, 'There can't be more or less of this rain,' I would say, 'Then that rain doesn't exist.' Unless of course you meant the rain as it is in this precise instant; that rain, indeed, is what it is and wouldn't be what it is if it were more or less. But I mean something different—"

"I already see what you mean," I broke in, but before I could go on to say I can't remember what, Fernando Pessoa turned to Caeiro. "Tell me this," he said, pointing his cigarette: "How do you regard dreams? Are they real or not?"

"I regard dreams as I regard shadows," answered Caeiro unexpectedly, with his usual divine quickness. "A shadow is real, but it's less real than a stone. A dream is real—otherwise it wouldn't be a dream—but it's less real than a thing. To be real is to be like this."

Fernando Pessoa has the advantage of living more in ideas than in himself. He had forgotten not only what he'd been arguing but even the truth or falseness of what he'd heard; he was enthused about the metaphysical possibilities of this new theory, regardless of whether it was true or false. That's how these aesthetes are.

"That's an extraordinary idea!" he said. "Utterly original! It never occurred to me." (And how about that "it never occurred to me"? As if it were impossible for an idea to occur to somebody else before it occurred to him, Fernando!) "It never occurred to me that one could think of reality as that which admits of degrees. That's equivalent to thinking of Being as a numerical idea rather than as a strictly abstract one. . . ."

"That's a bit confusing for me," Caeiro hesitated, "but yes, I think that's right. My point is this: To be real means there are other real things, for it's impossible to be real all alone; and since to be real is to be something that isn't all those other things, it's to be different from them; and since reality is a thing like size or weight—otherwise there would be no reality—and since all things are different, it follows that things are never equally real, even as things are never equal in size or weight. There will always be a difference, however small. To be real is this."

"That's even more extraordinary!" exclaimed Fernando Pessoa. "So you evidently consider reality to be an attribute of things, since you compare it to size and weight. But tell me this: What thing is reality an attribute of? What is behind reality?"

"Behind reality?" repeated my master Caeiro. "There's nothing behind reality. Just as there's nothing behind size, and nothing behind weight."

"But if a thing has no reality, it can't exist, whereas a thing that has no size or weight can exist. . . ."

"Not if it's a thing that by nature has size and weight. A stone can't exist without size; a stone can't exist without weight. But a stone isn't a size, and a stone isn't a weight. Nor can a stone exist without reality, but the stone is not a reality."

"Okay, okay," said Fernando impatiently, grabbing at uncertain ideas while feeling the ground give way beneath him. "But when you say 'a stone has reality,' you distinguish stone from reality."

"Naturally. The stone is not reality; it has reality. The stone is only stone."

"And what does that mean?"

"I don't know. It's like I said. A stone is a stone and has to have reality to be stone. A stone is a stone and has to have weight to be stone. A man isn't a face but has to have a face to be a man. I don't know the reason for this, nor do I know if a reason for this or for anything exists. . . ."

"You know, Caeiro," said Fernando pensively, "you're formulating a philosophy that's a bit contrary to what you think and feel. You're creating a kind of personal Kantianism, making the stone into a noumenon, a stone-in-itself. Let me explain. . . ." And he proceeded to explain the Kantian thesis and how what Caeiro had said more or less concurred with it. Then he pointed out the difference, or what he thought was the difference: "For Kant these attributes — weight, size (not reality) — are concepts imposed on the stone-in-itself by our senses, or rather, by the fact we observe it. You seem to be suggesting that these concepts are as much things as the stone-in-itself, and this is what makes your theory hard to grasp, while Kant's theory — whether true or false — is perfectly understandable."

My master Caeiro listened with rapt attention. Once or twice he blinked, as if to shake off ideas the way one shakes off sleep. And, after thinking a bit, he said:

"I don't have theories. I don't have philosophy. I see but know nothing. I call a stone a stone to distinguish it from a flower or from a tree — from everything, in other words, that isn't a stone. But each stone is different from every other stone — not because it isn't a stone but because it has a different size and different weight and different shape and different color. And also because it's a different thing. I give the name stone to one stone and to another stone since they both share those characteristics that make us call a stone a stone. But we should really give each stone its own, individual name, as we do for people. If we don't name stones, it's because it would be impossible to come up with that many words, not because it would be wrong —"

"Just answer me this," interrupted Fernando Pessoa, "and your position will become clear. Is there, for you, a 'stoniness,' even as there is a size and a weight? I mean, just as you say 'this stone is larger — has more size, as it were — than that stone' or 'this stone has more weight than that stone,' would you also say 'this stone is more stone than that one,' or in other words, 'this stone has more stoniness than that one'?"

"Certainly," replied the master immediately. "I'm quite prepared to say 'this stone is more stone than that one.' I'm prepared to say this if it's larger or if it's heavier than the other, since a stone needs size and weight to be stone, and especially if it surpasses the other in all the attributes (as you call them) that a stone has to have to be a stone."

"And what do you call a stone that you see in a dream?" asked Fernando, smiling.

"I call it a dream," answered my master Caeiro. "I call it a dream of a stone."

"I see," said Pessoa, nodding. "Speaking philosophically, you don't distinguish the substance from its attributes. A stone, in your view, is a thing composed of a certain number of attributes—those necessary to make what we call a stone—and with a certain quantity of each attribute, which gives the stone a particular size, hardness, weight, and color, thereby distinguishing it from another stone, though both are stones, because they have the same attributes, even if in different quantities. Well, this amounts to denying the real existence of the stone. The stone becomes merely a summation of real things. . . ."

"But a real summation! It's the sum of a real weight plus a real size plus a real color, etc. That's why the stone, besides having weight, size, and so forth, also has reality. . . . It doesn't have reality as stone; it has reality for being a summation of what you call attributes, all of them *real*. Since each attribute has reality, so too the stone."

"Let's go back to the dream," said Fernando. "You call a stone that you see in a dream a dream, or at the very most, a dream of a stone. Why do you say 'of a stone'? Why do you employ the word 'stone'?"

"For the same reason that you, when you see my picture, say 'That's Caeiro' and don't mean that it's me in the flesh."

We all broke out laughing. "I see and I give up," said Fernando, laughing with the rest of us. *Les dieux sont ceux qui ne doutent jamais.* The truth of that phrase by Villiers de l'Isle Adam* was never clearer to me.

This conversation remained imprinted on my soul, and I've reproduced it with what I think is near-stenographic precision, albeit without stenography. I have a sharp and vivid memory, which is characteristic of certain types of madness. And this conversation had an important outcome. It was, in itself, inconsequential like all conversations, and it would be easy to prove, by applying strict logic, that only those who held their peace didn't contradict themselves. In Caeiro's always stimulating affirmations and replies, a philosophical mind would be able to identify conflicting systems of thoughts. But although I concede this, I don't believe there's any conflict. My master Caeiro was surely right, even on those points where he was wrong.

This conversation, as I was saying, had an important outcome. It provided António Mora with the inspiration to write one of the most astonishing chapters of his *Prolegomena*—the chapter on the idea of Reality. António Mora was the only one who said nothing during the whole conversation. He just listened to all the ideas being discussed, with his eyes staring inward the whole while. The ideas of my master Caeiro, expounded in this conversation with the intellectual reckless-ness of instinct, and hence in a necessarily inexact, contradictory fash-ion, were converted into a coherent, logical system in the *Prolegomena*.

I don't wish to detract from the undeniable merit of António Mora, but it should be said that just as the very basis of his philosophical sys-tem was born (as he himself reveals with abstract pride) from that simple phrase of Caeiro, "Nature is parts without a whole," so too an impor-tant part of that system—the marvelous concept of Reality as "dimen-sion," and the derivative concept of "degrees of reality"—was born from this conversation. To everyone his due, and everything to my master Caeiro.

The work of Caeiro is divided, not just in his book but in actual fact, into three parts: *The Keeper of Sheep, The Shepherd in Love,* and that third part that Ricardo Reis aptly titled* *Uncollected Poems*. *The Shep-herd in Love* is a futile interlude, but the few poems that make it up are among the world's great love poems, for they are love poems by virtue of being about love and not by virtue of being poems. The poet loved because he loved, and not because love exists, and this was precisely what he said.

The Keeper of Sheep is the mental life of Caeiro up until the coach tops the hill. The *Uncollected Poems* are its descent. That's how I dis-tinguish between them. I can imagine having been able to write cer-tain of the *Uncollected Poems*, but not even in my wildest dreams can I imagine having written any of the poems in *The Keeper of Sheep*.

In the *Uncollected Poems* there is weariness, and therefore uneven-ness. Caeiro is Caeiro, but a sick Caeiro. Not always sick, but sometimes sick. He's the same but a bit removed. This is particularly true in the middle poems of this third part of his oeuvre.

My master Caeiro was a master for everyone capable of having a master. There was no one who got to know Caeiro, no one who spoke with him or had the physical privilege of keeping company with his spirit, who didn't come away as a different man, for Caeiro was the only Rome one couldn't return from as the same person he was when he went there, unless he wasn't after all a person — unless, like most people, he was incapable of individuality beyond the fact of being, in space, a body separated from other bodies and symbolically blemished by its human form.

Inferior people cannot have a master, since they have nothing for a master to be a master of. That is why strong personalities can be hypnotized very easily, normal people less easily, and idiots, imbeciles, feeble or incoherent people not at all. To be strong is to be capable of feeling.

There were, as the reader will have gleaned from these pages, three main people around my master Caeiro: Ricardo Reis, António Mora, and myself. Without inflating myself or anyone else, I can say that all three of us were and are radically different — at least intellectually speaking — from the common, animal lot of humanity. And all three of us owe whatever is best in our souls to the contact we had with my master Caeiro. All of us became others — became our true selves, that is — after passing through the sieve of that fleshly intervention of the Gods.

Ricardo Reis was a latent pagan, unable to grasp modern life and unable to grasp that ancient life into which he should have been born — unable to grasp modern life because his intelligence was of a different species, and unable to grasp ancient life because he couldn't feel it, for you cannot feel what isn't there to feel. Caeiro, the reconstructor of Paganism, and from the eternal point of view its founder, brought Ricardo Reis the tangible substance that he was lacking. And so he found himself as a pagan — the pagan he already was before finding himself. Before meeting Caeiro, Ricardo Reis hadn't written a single verse, and he was already twenty-five years old. After meeting Caeiro and hearing him recite *The Keeper of Sheep*, Ricardo Reis began to realize that he was organically a poet. Some physiologists say that it's possible to change sex. I don't know if it's true, because I don't know if anything is "true," but I know that Ricardo Reis stopped being a woman and became a man, or stopped being a man and became a woman—as you like—when he met Caeiro.

António Mora was a shadow with philosophical pretensions. He spent his time mulling over Kant and trying to figure out if life had any meaning. Indecisive, like all strong minds, he hadn't discovered the truth, or what he felt was the truth, which as far as I'm concerned is the same thing. He discovered it when he discovered Caeiro. My master Caeiro gave him the soul he'd never had; inside the outer Mora, which is all there had ever been, he placed a central Mora. This led to the triumphal reduction of Caeiro's instinctive thoughts into a philosophical system of logical truth, as set forth in Mora's two treatises, marvels of originality and speculative thought: *The Return of the Gods* and the *Prolegomena to a Reformation of Paganism*.

As for myself, before meeting Caeiro I was a nervous machine that busily did nothing. I met my master Caeiro after Reis and Mora, who met him in 1912 and 1913, respectively. I met him in 1914. I had already written verses—three sonnets and two poems ("Carnival" and "Opiary").* These sonnets and poems reveal my emotional state when I was helplessly adrift. As soon as I met Caeiro, I found my true self. I went to London and immediately wrote the "Triumphal Ode."* And from then on, for better or worse, I have been I.

The strangest case is that of Fernando Pessoa, who doesn't exist, strictly speaking. He met Caeiro a little before I did—on March 8th, 1914, according to what he told me. Caeiro had come to spend a week in Lisbon, and it was then that Pessoa met him. After hearing him recite *The Keeper of Sheep*, he went home in a fever (the one he was born with) and wrote the six poems of "Slanting Rain"* in one go.

"Slanting Rain" doesn't resemble any of my master Caeiro's poems, except perhaps in the rectilinear movement of its rhythm. But Fernando Pessoa would never have been able to extract those extraordinary poems

from his inner world without having met Caeiro. They were a direct result of the spiritual shock he experienced mere moments after that
meeting occurred. It was instantaneous. Because of his overwrought
sensibility, accompanied by an overwrought intelligence, Fernando
reacted immediately to the Great Vaccine—the vaccine against the stupidity of the intelligent. And there is nothing more admirable in the
work of Fernando Pessoa than this group of six poems, this "Slanting
Rain." Perhaps there are, or will be, greater things produced by his pen,
but never anything fresher, never anything more original, and so I rather
doubt there will ever be anything greater. Not only that, he will never
produce anything that's more genuinely Fernando Pessoa, more intimately Fernando Pessoa. What could better express his relentlessly in-
tellectualized sensibility, his inattentively keen attention, and the ardent
subtlety of his cold self-analysis than these poetic intersections in which
the narrator's state of mind is simultaneously two states, in which the
subjective and objective join together while remaining separate, and
in which the real and the unreal merge in order to remain distinct? In
these poems Fernando Pessoa made a veritable photograph of his soul.
In that one, unique moment he succeeded in having his own individuality, such as he had never had before and can never have again, because he has no individuality.

Long live my master Caeiro!

from Translator's Preface to the Poems of Alberto Caeiro

Thomas Crosse

In placing before the English-reading public my translation of these
poems, I do so with the full confidence that I am making a revelation.
I claim, in all confidence, that I am putting before Englishmen the most
original poetry that our young century has as yet produced—a poetry
so fresh, so *new*, untainted to such a degree by any kind of conventional
attitude, that the words a Portuguese friend said to me, when speaking

of these very poems, are more than justified. "Every time I read them," he said, "I cannot bring myself to believe that they have been written. It is so *impossible* an achievement!" And so much more *impossible*, that it is of the simplest, most natural and most spontaneous kind.

. . .

Caeiro, like Whitman, leaves us perplexed. We are thrown off our critical attitude by so extraordinary a phenomenon. We have never seen anything like it. Even after Whitman, Caeiro is strange and terribly, appallingly new. Even in our age, when we believe nothing can astonish us or shout novelty at us, Caeiro does astonish and does breathe absolute novelty. To be able to do this in an age like ours is the definite and final proof of his genius.

He is so novel that it is sometimes hard to conceive clearly of all his novelty. He is too new, and his excessive novelty troubles our vision of him, as all excessive things trouble vision, though it is quite a novelty for novelty itself to be the thing that is* excessive and vision-troubling. But that is the remarkable thing. Even novelty and the way of being new are novelties in Caeiro. He is different from all poets in another way than all great poets are different from other great poets. He has his individuality in another way of having it than all poets preceding him. Whitman is quite inferior in this respect. To explain Whitman, even on a basis of admitting him all conceivable originality, we need but think of him as an intense liver of life, and his poems come out of that like flowers from a shrub. But the same method does not hold for Caeiro. Even if we think of him as a man who lives outside civilization (an impossible hypothesis, of course), as a man with an exceptionally clear vision of things, that does not logically produce in our minds a result resembling *The Keeper of Sheep*. The very tenderness for things as mere things which characterizes the type of man we have posited does not characterize Caeiro. He sometimes speaks tenderly of things, but he asks our pardon for doing so, explaining that he only speaks so in consideration of our "stupidity of senses," to make us feel "the absolutely real existence" of things. Left to himself, he has no tenderness for things, he has hardly any tenderness even for his sensations. Here we touch his great originality, his almost inconceivable objectivity. He sees things with the eyes only, not with the mind. He does not let any thoughts arise when he looks at a flower. Far from seeing sermons in stones, he never even lets himself conceive of a stone as beginning a sermon. The only sermon a stone contains for him is that it exists. The only thing a stone tells him is that it has nothing at all to tell him. A state of mind may be conceived resembling this. *But it cannot be conceived in a poet.* This way of looking at a stone may be described as the totally unpoetic way of looking at it. The stupendous fact about Caeiro is that out of this sentiment, or rather, absence of sentiment, he makes poetry. He feels positively what hitherto could not be conceived of except as a negative sentiment. Put it to yourselves: What do you think of a stone when you look at it without thinking about it? Or in other words:* What do you think of a stone when you don't think about it at all? The question is quite absurd, of course. The strange point about it is that all Caeiro's poetry is based upon that sentiment that you find impossible to represent to yourself as able to exist. Perhaps I have not been unsuccessful in pointing out the extraordinary nature of Caeiro's inspiration, the phenomenal novelty of his poetry, the astonishing unprecedentedness of his genius, of his whole attitude.

Alberto Caeiro is reported to have regretted the name of "Sensationism" which a disciple of his (a rather queer disciple, it is true), Mr. Álvaro de Campos, gave to his attitude, and to the attitude he created. If Caeiro protested against the word as possibly seeming to indicate a "school," like Futurism, for instance, he was right, and for two reasons. For the very suggestion of schools and literary movements sounds bad when applied to so uncivilized and natural a kind of poetry. And besides, though he has at least two "disciples," the fact is that he has had on them an influence equal to that which some poet—Cesário Verde,* perhaps—had on him; neither resembles him at all, though indeed, far more clearly than Cesário Verde's influence on him, his influence may be seen all over their work.

But the fact is—these considerations once put aside—that no name could describe his attitude better. His poetry *is* "Sensationist." Its

basis is the substitution of sensation for thought, not only as a basis of
inspiration—which is comprehensible—but as a means of expression,
if we may so speak. And, be it added, those two disciples of his, different
as they are from him and from each other—are also indeed Sensationists.
For Dr. Ricardo Reis, with his neoclassicism, his actual and real belief
in the existence of the pagan deities, is a pure Sensationist, though a
different kind of Sensationist. His attitude toward nature is as aggressive to thought as Caeiro's; he reads no meanings into things. He sees
them only, and if he seems to see them differently from Caeiro it is
because, though seeing them as unintellectually and unpoetically as
Caeiro, he sees them through a definite religious concept of the universe—paganism, pure paganism, and this necessarily alters his very
direct way of feeling. But he is a pagan, because paganism is *the* Sensationist religion. Of course, a pure and integral Sensationist like Caeiro
has, logically enough, no religion at all, religion not being among the
immediate data of pure and direct sensation. But Ricardo Reis has put
the logic of his attitude as purely Sensationist very clearly. According
to him, we not only should bow down to the pure objectivity of things
(hence his Sensationism proper, and his neoclassicism, for the classic
poets were those who commented least, at least directly, upon things)
but bow down to the equal objectivity, reality, naturalness of the neces-
sities of our nature, of which the religious sentiment is one. Caeiro is
the pure and absolute Sensationist who bows down to sensations qua
exterior and admits no more. Ricardo Reis is less absolute; he bows down
also to the primitive elements of our own nature, our primitive feelings
being as real and natural to him as flowers and trees. He is therefore
religious. And, seeing that he is a Sensationist, he is a pagan in his religion, which is due not only to the nature of sensation once conceived
of as admitting a religion of some kind, but also to the influence of those
classical readings to which his Sensationism had inclined him.

   Álvaro de Campos—curiously enough—is on the opposite point,
entirely opposed to Ricardo Reis. Yet he is not less than the latter a disciple of Caeiro and a Sensationist proper. He has accepted from Caeiro,
not the essential and objective, but the deducible and subjective part
of his attitude. Sensation is all, Caeiro holds, and thought is a disease.

By sensation Caeiro means the sensation of things as they are, without adding to it any elements from personal thought, convention, sentiment or any other soul-place. For Campos, sensation is indeed all, though* not necessarily sensation of things as they are, but of things as they are felt. So that he takes sensation subjectively and applies all his efforts, once so thinking, not to develop in himself the sensation of things as they are, but all sorts of sensations of things, even of the same thing. To feel is all; it is logical to conclude that the best is to feel all sorts of things in all sorts of ways, or, as Álvaro de Campos says himself, "to feel every-thing in every way." So he applies himself to feeling the town as much as he feels the country, the normal as he feels the abnormal, the bad as he feels the good, the morbid as the healthy. He never questions, he feels. He is the undisciplined child of sensation. Caeiro has one disci-pline: things must be felt as they are. Ricardo Reis has another kind of discipline: things must be felt, not only as they are, but also so as to fall in with a certain ideal of classic measure and rule. In Álvaro de Cam-pos things must simply be felt.

But the common origin of these three widely different aspects of the same theory is patent and manifest.

Caeiro has no ethics except simplicity. Ricardo Reis has a pagan ethics, half Epicurean and half Stoic, but a very definite ethics, which gives his poetry an elevation that Caeiro himself, though the greater genius (mastership apart),* cannot attain. Álvaro de Campos has no shadow of an ethics; he is nonmoral, if not positively immoral, for of course, according to his theory, it is natural that he should love the stron-ger better than the weak sensations, and the strong sensations are at least all selfish, and [are] occasionally the sensations of cruelty and lust. Thus Álvaro de Campos resembles Whitman most of the three. But he has nothing of Whitman's camaraderie; he is always apart from the crowd, and when feeling with them it is very clearly and very confessedly to please himself and give himself brutal sensations. The idea that a child of eight is demoralized (Ode II, *ad finem*)* is positively pleasant to him, for it* satisfies two very strong sensations—cruelty and lust. The most Caeiro says that may be called immoral is that he cares nothing for what men suffer, and that the existence of sick people is interesting because it is a fact. Ricardo Reis has nothing of this. He lives in himself, with his pagan faith and his sad Epicureanism, but one of his attitudes is precisely not to hurt anyone. He cares absolutely nothing for others, not even enough to be interested in their suffering or in their existence. He is moral because he is self-sufficient.

It may be said, comparing these three poets with the three orders of religious spirits, and comparing Sensationism for the moment (perhaps improperly) with a religion, that Ricardo Reis is the normal religious spirit of that faith; Caeiro the pure mystic; Álvaro de Campos the ritualist in excess. For Caeiro loses sight of Nature in nature, loses sight of sensation in sensation, loses sight of things in things. And Campos loses sight of sensation in sensations.

[On Álvaro de Campos]

I. I. Crosse

Álvaro de Campos is one of the very greatest rhythmists that there has ever been. Every metric paragraph of his is a finished work of art. He makes definite, perfectly "curved" stanzas of these irregular "meters."

He is the most violent of all writers. His master Whitman is mild and calm compared to him. Yet the more turbulent of the two poets is the most self-controlled. He is so violent that enough of the energy of his violence remains for him to use it in disciplining his violence.

The violence of the "Naval Ode"* is perfectly insane. Yet it is unparalleled in art, and because its violence is such.

His volcanic emotion, his violence of sensation, his formidable shifting from violence to tenderness, from a passion for great and loud things to a love of humble and quiet ones, his unparalleled transitions, his sudden silences, sudden pauses, his change from unstable to equable states of mind—none has ever approached him in the [expression] of this hysteria of our age.

The classic training of his early years that never deserts him (for he is one of the most unified of poets, and ever a builder and a fitter-together of parts into an organic whole); his individual stability, his mathematical training and scientific training adding another stabilizing influence (never too much for such a volcanic temperament).

His large-minded contempt of small things, of small people, of all our age, because it is composed of small things and of small people.

This quasi-Futurist who loves the great classic poets because they were great and despises the literary men of his time because they are all small.

His art of conveying sensations by a single stroke:

The pink ribbon left on top of the dresser . . .

The broken toy (but still with the dirty string used to pull it)
Of the child who had to die, O mother dressed in black, folding up
*his suit . . .**

His terrible self-analysis, making suddenly cold all his emotion, as in the "Salutation to Walt Whitman."*

[On the Work of Ricardo Reis]

Frederico Reis

The philosophy of the work of Ricardo Reis basically amounts to a sad Epicureanism, which we will try to characterize.

Each of us (contends the Poet) should live his own life, isolating himself from others and seeking, in an attitude of sober individualism, only what pleases and delights him. He should not seek violent pleasures nor flee from moderately painful sensations.

Avoiding unnecessary suffering or grief, man should seek peace and tranquillity above all else, abstaining from effort and useful activity.

The poet adheres to this as a temporary doctrine, as the right attitude for pagans as long as the barbarians (the Christians) reign supreme.

If and when the barbarian empire crumbles, then this attitude may change, but for now it's the only one possible.

We should try to give ourselves the illusion of freedom, happiness, and peace, all of which are unattainable, since freedom is a privilege denied even the gods (who are subject to Fate), since happiness cannot be felt by someone exiled from his own faith and from his soul's natural habitat, and since we cannot pretend to be peaceful when we live in the midst of today's commotion and know all too well that we'll die. The work of Ricardo Reis, profoundly sad, is a lucid and disciplined effort to obtain a measure of calm.

His entire stance is based on an interesting psychological phenomenon: a true and real belief in the gods of ancient Greece, with Christ (sometimes considered inimical, but only insofar as he arouses the Christian spirit, which is indeed the . . . . . . enemy of paganism) being admitted as one more god, but not more than that—an idea in accord with paganism and perhaps partly inspired by Alberto Caeiro's idea (a purely poetic idea) that the Christ Child was "the god who was missing."*

SENSATIONISM AND OTHER ISMS

Besides generating a diversified trio of heteronymic poets, a team of subheteronymic translators and publicists to promote them, and a "Neo-paganist" ideology (see pp. 147–57) to give philosophical weight to their literary works and psychological weight to their invented personalities, Pessoa also invented literary movements for them to spearhead and pro-mulgate. But far from being limited to Pessoa's notebooks and papers, these movements infiltrated the Portuguese intellectual milieu of the 1910s, and one could argue that they were the raison d'être of Caeiro, Reis, and Campos, and the reason the heteronyms evolved the way they did. Both points of view may be valid, for in that period of Pessoa's life there was a startling symbiosis between the written world of his fancy and the literary world at large. If Vertiginism, Abstractionism, Dynamism, and Fusionism weren't much more than evocative names on one or another statement of artistic principles that perhaps no one but Pessoa ever saw, the movements called Paulismo, Sensationism, *and* Intersectionism *were enthusiastically taken up by his writer friends. And even if Pessoa, as we know from his notes and from several letters, sometimes saw these movements as expendable gimmicks, the fact is that they helped transform Portuguese literature. None of them endured long, but they were the instruments by which Pessoa and his compeers brought Modernism to Portugal, whose literature had perhaps been suffering from too much high seriousness. Some playfulness, even in the form of gimmicks, was bound to have a salutary effect.*

The name Paulismo *comes from the Portuguese word for swamp,* paul, *which was the first word (but in the plural,* pauis) *of one of Pessoa's first two poems to be published, in February of 1914. He actually wrote the poem a year earlier, and like* The Mariner, *also written in 1913, it hangs in suspension, with more three-dot ellipses than there are verses. Both works are rarefied products of post-Symbolism, but Pessoa's one-act play, for all its somewhat unreal, sometimes illogical dialogue, isn't hard to follow, whereas the poem can't possibly be followed, since it leads no-where; we simply have to enter it and float among the words and images, which are often striking. It was published (with another poem) under the title "Twilight Impressions," and these include a "distant tolling of Other Bells," the "thin autumn of a vague bird's song," and "opium fanfares of future silences." In one of his notebooks, Pessoa cited this poem as an example of* Paulismo *by virtue of its "strangeness," a second poem as an example by virtue of its rhythm, and a third poem by virtue of its "meta-physical uneasiness." The preceding page in the same notebook char-acterizes* Paulismo *as the ultrarefinement of sensation, thought, and expression, while a page from another notebook defines it as "the sincere cultivation of artificiality." Though it owed most of its genetic endowment to post-Symbolism,* Paulismo *can be distinguished from its predecessor by its greater self-consciousness, or artificiality, by the deliberateness of its creative process.*

Paulismo had no noticeable impact on the poetry of the heteronyms, and in the poetry signed by Pessoa himself it quickly evolved into a less "swampy" style that employed a simpler language. But the orthodox, ultrarefined variety continued to be practiced by Mário de Sá-Carneiro (1890–1916), who was in fact its greatest exponent. Pessoa and Sá-Carneiro met in 1912 and immediately realized that they'd found, in each other, their kindred spirit. The existential dichotomy of I-who-am-I versus I-who-am-another was, if possible, even greater in Sá-Carneiro than in Pessoa. Or if not greater, at least more in evidence, and more agonizing, for Sá-Carneiro did not have Pessoa's uncommon capacity for making emo-tions submit to reason. Pessoa was intellectually distressed by the gap between what he was and what he wanted to be; Sá-Carneiro, because of the same gap, committed suicide. The theme of all but his earliest work was precisely the torment he felt for not living up—in his flesh, in his writing, and even in his imagination—to an ideal of beauty he could only intuit, not define, though it was obviously informed by a Decadent, post-Symbolist aesthetic. In Paulismo *he found the perfect vehicle to express, through charged images and linguistic "strangeness," his anguished vision of an unattainable beauty, and in the space of four years he produced one of the most exquisite poetic oeuvres in Portuguese.*

Sensationism *was born in 1914, the same year as Pessoa's major heteronyms, two of whom were its foremost exemplars.* Caeiro, *whose poetry (according to Thomas Crosse, p. 53) was based on "the substitution of sensation for thought," embodied the Sensationist doctrine that reality, for us, is summed up in our sensations, since everything we know comes through them.* Campos, *whose motto was to "feel everything in every way possible," exemplified the corollary doctrine that since the only reality we have is that of sensations, we should experience them as intensely as possible. Intersectionism, which is a form of Sensationism but seems to have been born first, can be roughly characterized as literary Cubism, whereby reality is broken down into its temporal and spatial components, which are then organized into a compositional ensemble. The best example of this technique is Pessoa's poem sequence titled "Slanting Rain," in which contrasting poetic subjects are superimposed, or the same subject is seen from diverse points of view. (See Campos's description of these poems on p. 50).*

But Sensationism *and Intersectionism, even more than* Paulismo, *exceeded the bounds of Fernando Pessoa and his heteronymic company. By the spring of 1914 a small group of writers had gathered around Pessoa, who was not really their leader, since leadership was not a role that suited his personality, but they were his tacit followers, recognizing and feeding off his genius, and some of their ideas no doubt went into the literary doctrines he forged. They met in cafés, where they discussed, showed each other their written work, and plotted how best to launch themselves and their movement, which was tantamount to launching European Modernism in Portugal. Several of the group's members, including Mário de Sá-Carneiro, were based in Paris, where they had direct contact with the Futurists and the Cubists, whose tenets were incorporated into Sensationism and Intersectionism.*

It was probably Pessoa's idea to create a magazine, significantly titled Europa, *whose pages would have featured Intersectionist theory, Intersectionist poetry, and Intersectionist fiction. A supplement to the first issue, evidently meant for distribution abroad, would have contained work by Pessoa, Sá-Carneiro, and Alexander Search (one of Pessoa's early heteronyms, see pp. 15–16) in French and English. The magazine idea was superseded by a book idea, an* Anthology of Intersectionism, *which likewise fizzled, but in 1915 the group founded and published two issues of* Orpheu, *where five of Pessoa's masterworks saw print:* The Mariner *and "Slanting Rain," signed by his own name, and the Campos poems "Opiary," "Triumphal Ode," and "Maritime Ode." The youngest group member to publish in the magazine, José de Almada-Negreiros (1893–1970), went on to have a long career as an experimental writer and painter. Some of his best works were practical demonstrations of Intersectionist theory, and he may be considered the third leader—after Pessoa and Sá-Carneiro—in the triumvirate of Portuguese Modernism. Portugal's greatest painter of the period, Amadeo de Souza-Cardoso, was also associated with the* Orpheu *group.*

Orpheu succeeded in prompting violent reactions in the press, where a number of scathing reviews and lampoons appeared, and Pessoa's genius was also noted, even if grudgingly. Though it sold reasonably well, the magazine couldn't pay its printing bills, and so the third issue never made it beyond galley proofs. But, short as its publishing history was, Orpheu *changed the map of Portuguese letters, and it lived on in various avant-garde magazines that were its undeniable heirs, including* Exílio *(1916), whose one issue published a strident critical piece by Pessoa titled "The Sensationist Movement," and the likewise single-issue* Portugal Futurista *(1917), which published Álvaro de Campos's* Ultimatum, *written several years earlier as an Intersectionist manifesto.*

Preface to an Anthology of the Portuguese Sensationists

Thomas Crosse

Sensationism began with the friendship between Fernando Pessoa and Mário de Sá-Carneiro. It is probably difficult to separate the part each of them had in the origin of the movement, and certainly quite useless to determine it. The fact is they built up the beginnings between them.

But each Sensationist worth mentioning is a separate personality, and they have naturally all interacted. Fernando Pessoa and Mário de Sá-Carneiro stand nearest to the Symbolists. Álvaro de Campos and Almada-Negreiros are the nearest to the more modern style of feeling and writing. The others are intermediate.

Fernando Pessoa suffers from classical culture.

No Sensationist has gone higher than Sá-Carneiro in the expression of what may be called, in Sensationese, colored feelings. (. . .)

Fernando Pessoa is more purely intellectual; his power lies more in the intellectual analysis of feeling and emotion, which he has carried to a perfection that renders us almost breathless. Of his static drama *The Sailor** a reader once said: "It makes the exterior world quite unreal," and it does. No more remote thing exists in literature. Maeterlinck's* best nebulosity and subtlety are coarse and carnal by comparison.

José de Almada-Negreiros is more spontaneous and rapid, but he is nonetheless a man of genius. He is younger than the others, not only in age, but in spontaneity and effervescence. His is a very distinct personality, and the wonder is how he came about it so early.

. . .

How far more interesting than the Cubists and the Futurists!

I never wished to know personally any of the Sensationists, being persuaded that the best knowledge is impersonal.

Álvaro de Campos is excellently defined as a Walt Whitman with a Greek poet inside. He has all the power of intellectual, emotional, and physical sensation that characterized Whitman. But he [also] has the precisely opposite trait—a power of construction and orderly development of a poem that no poet since Milton has attained. Álvaro de Campos's "Triumphal Ode," which is written in the Whitmanesque absence of stanza and rhyme, has a construction and an orderly development which stultifies the perfection that "Lycidas," for instance, can claim in this particular. The "Naval Ode,"* which covers no less than twenty-two pages of *Orpheu,* is a very marvel of organization. No German regiment ever had the inner discipline which underlies that composition, which, from its typographical aspect, might almost be considered as a specimen of Futurist carelessness. The same considerations apply to the magnificent "Salutation to Walt Whitman," in the third *Orpheu.**

. . .

The Portuguese Sensationists are original and interesting because, being strictly Portuguese, they are cosmopolitan and universal. The Portuguese temperament is universal: that is its magnificent superiority. The one great act of Portuguese history—that long, cautious, scientific period of the Discoveries—is the one great cosmopolitan act in history. The whole people stamp themselves there. An original, typically Portuguese literature cannot be Portuguese, because the typical Portuguese are never Portuguese. There is something American, with the noise left out and the quotidian omitted, in the intellectual temper of this people. No people seizes so readily on novelties. No people depersonalizes so magnificently. That weakness is its great strength. That temperamental nonregionalism is its unused might. That indefiniteness of soul is what makes them definite.

Because the great fact about the Portuguese is that they are the most civilized people in Europe. They are born civilized, because they are born accepters of all. They have nothing of what the old psychiatrists used to call misoneism, meaning only hatred of things new; they have a positive love of novelty and change. They have no stable elements, as the French have, who make revolutions only for export. The Portuguese are always making revolutions. When a Portuguese goes to bed he makes a revolution, because the Portuguese who wakes up the next day is quite different. He is precisely a day older, quite distinctly a day older. Other people wake up every morning yesterday. Tomorrow is always several years away. Not so this quite strange people. They go so quick that they leave everything undone, including going quick. Nothing is less idle than a Portuguese. The only idle part of the nation is the working part of it. Hence their lack of evident progress.

There are only two interesting things in Portugal—the landscape and *Orpheu.* All the packing in between is used-up rotten straw. (. . .) If there were any instinct of the sensible in modern writing, I would begin with the landscape and finish up with *Orpheu*. But, God be thanked, there is no instinct of the sensible in modern writing, so I leave the landscape and begin and end with *Orpheu*. (. . .) *Orpheu* is the sum and synthesis of all modern literary movements; that is why it is more worthy of being written about than the landscape, which is only the absence of the people who live in it.

. . .

"All sensations are good"

All sensations are good, as long as we don't try to reduce them to action. An action is a sensation that was thrown away.

Act on the inside, using only the hands of your spirit to pluck flowers on life's periphery.

Fight against the mental slavery represented by the association of ideas. Learn not to associate ideas but to break your soul into pieces instead. Learn how to experience sensations simultaneously, to scatter your spirit through your own scattered self.

We are completely and dynamically indifferent to social and political life. However much they may interest us, they interest us only as things on which to build fleeting theories and irrelevant hypotheses.

[Intersectionist] Manifesto

All premodern art was based on just one element. This was true for the classical art of paganism as it was for Renaissance art or Romantic art. Only very recently has art begun to evolve outside of this ancient and rigid mold.

The Greeks and Romans (and to a lesser extent the men of the Renaissance) tried to impress, onto the reality of a given object or idea, the sensation it made them feel. But the Romantics realized that reality, for us, is not the object but our sensation of it. They were thus less concerned to present the object itself than to convey their sensation of it. That doesn't mean they withdrew from Reality; no, they sought it, because our sensation of the object—not the object conceived apart from our sensation—is its true Reality, since outside of our sensation nothing exists, our sensation being for us the criterion of existence. "Man is the measure of all things." Protagoras's dictum also applies to truth, in its abstract and absolute sense.

It was the internalization produced by Christianity that led man to notice (unconsciously at first) that the fact of reality, the real fact, is not the object but our sensation of it, which is where it exists. Whether it exists elsewhere we cannot know.

But Romanticism did not see very far. True Reality actually consists in two things—our sensation of the object and the object. Since the object does not exist outside of our sensation—for us, at least, and that's what matters to us—it follows that true reality consists in our sensation of the object and in our sensation of our sensation.

Classical art was an art of dreamers and madmen. Romantic art, despite its greater intuition of the truth, was an art of men who were adolescents in their notion of the reality of things but not yet adults in how they felt that reality.

Reality, for us, is sensation. No other immediate reality can exist for us.

Art, whatever it is, must be founded on this element, which is the only one we have.

What is art? The attempt to give as clear and exact a notion as possible of objects, understood not just as outer things but also as our thoughts and mental constructions.

A sensation is composed of two elements: the object of sensation and the sensation itself. All human activity consists in the search for the absolute. Science seeks the absolute Object, meaning the object as independent as possible of our sensation of it. Art seeks absolute Sensation, meaning sensation as independent as possible of the object. Philosophy (that is, Metaphysics) seeks the absolute relationship of the Subject (Sensation) and the Object.

Art seeks Sensation in the absolute. But sensation, as we've seen, is composed of the Object of sensation and the Sensation itself.

Intersection of the Object with itself: Cubism. (The intersection, that is, of various aspects of the same Object with each other.)

Intersection of the Object with the objective ideas it suggests: Futurism.

Intersection of the Object with our sensation of it: Intersectionism strictly speaking, which is what we propose.

Sensationism

To feel is to create. But what is feeling?

Feeling is thinking without ideas, hence understanding, since the Universe has no ideas.

Holding opinions is not feeling.

All our opinions come from other people.

Thinking is wanting to convey to others what we believe we feel.

Only what we think can be conveyed to others. What we feel cannot be conveyed. We can only convey the *value* of what we feel. The most we can do is make someone feel what we feel. We can't make the reader feel the same thing, but it's enough if he feels in the same way.

Feeling opens the doors of the prison where thought confines the soul.

Lucidity should go only as far as the soul's threshold. Explicitness is forbidden even in the antechambers of feeling.

To feel is to understand. To think is to err. To understand what someone thinks is to disagree with him. To understand what someone feels is to be him. To be someone else is quite useful metaphysically. God is everyone.

See, hear, smell, taste, feel—those are God's only commandments. The senses are divine, because they are our relationship with the Universe, and our relationship with the Universe is God.

Strange as it may seem, it's possible to hear with the eyes, to see with the ears, to see and hear and taste smells, to taste colors and sounds, to hear tastes, and so on, indefinitely. It just takes practice.

Acting is disbelieving. Thinking is error. Only feeling is believing and is truth. Nothing exists outside our sensations. That's why acting is a betrayal of our thought—ours precisely for not having betrayed itself as thought.

Politics is the art of governing societies when no one knows how they're governed. Having political ideas is the easiest way to have no ideas. Politics is a misconceived vanity of men who were born to be coachmen. The only way to rule society is to disdain everyone else. Brotherhood is born out of mutual contempt.

Progress is the least noble of unnecessary lies. Even without the concept of progress, we would stop progressing.

Sensation writes straight on the crooked lines of matter.

Sensation is the bottomless vessel whereby "criticism" fulfills its Danaidean role.* Individuality is inexhaustible, since every individual who is born adds to it. Logic is a fence around nothing at all.

It is our aristocratic duty to loathe all who work and struggle, to abhor all who hope and trust, and to despise all self-sacrificers.

Trying to revive tradition is like raising a ladder to climb up a wall that fell down. It's interesting, because absurd, but only worth the bother because it's not worth the bother.

The only basis for truth is self-contradiction. The universe contradicts itself, for it passes on. Life contradicts itself, for it dies. Paradox is Nature's norm. That's why all truth has a paradoxical form.

All of these principles are true, but the contrary principles are just as true. (To affirm is to go through the wrong door.)

To think is to limit. To reason is to exclude. There are lots of things it's good to think about, since there are lots of things it's good to limit or exclude.

Political, social, and religious apostles. . . . . . Don't preach good or evil, virtue or vice, truth or error, kindness or cruelty. Don't preach virtue, since that's what all preachers preach, and don't preach vice, since that's what they all practice. Don't preach truth, since no one knows what it is, and don't preach error, since by doing so you'd be preaching a truth.

Preach your own self, shouting it out loud to the whole world. That is the only truth and the only error, the only morality and the only immorality, ... which you can preach, should preach, and must preach.

Preach yourself in earnest, with scandals and pomp. The only thing you are is you. Be it like a peacock, be it at large, heads and heels over Everyone Else.

Make your soul into a metaphysics, an ethics, and an aesthetics. Shamelessly replace God with yourself. That is the only truly religious attitude. (God is everywhere except in himself.)

Make your being into an atheistic religion, your sensations into a rite and a ritual. Live perfectly [. . .] on the sweeping verandah of the convent of yourself.

Replace yourself continuously. You're not enough for yourself. Be always unpredictable, even to yourself. Let yourself happen before your very eyes. Let your sensations be like chance events, adventures you stumbled into. The only way to be superior is by being a lawless universe.

Existing isn't necessary; what's necessary is to feel. Note that this last sentence is completely absurd. Dedicate yourself to not understanding it with your whole heart.

These are the fundamental principles of Sensationism. The opposite principles are also the fundamental principles of Sensationism.

ULTIMATUM
Álvaro de Campos

Translator's Preface to *Ultimatum*

Thomas Crosse?

Though Pessoa's ambitious plans to translate his own works into English and French never got very far (he put several poems of Campos's into English and a few pages of The Mariner *into French), he was a prolific writer of translators' prefaces. The one he left for a projected English translation of* Ultimatum *was unsigned, but we may venture to attribute it to Thomas Crosse, who was supposed to translate the poetry of Campos as well as of Caeiro.*

Álvaro de Campos's *Ultimatum* was published in the first and (at least up to now) only number of *Portugal Futurista,** a literary publication the nature of which is sufficiently expressed by its title, which needs no translation.

Having, through some inexplicable stroke of luck, passed the press censors, the luck ceased when someone called the attention of the authorities to it, after the review was in the booksellers' windows. *Portugal Futurista* was immediately seized by the police, and proceedings instituted against all the authors collaborating. This (it is well to explain) was under the Democratic ministry which was thrown out of power by Sidónio Pais, with the Revolution of the 5th of December, 1917.* Yet it is difficult to imagine how any ministry at all, when the country was at war, could allow the publication of the *Ultimatum*, which, original and magnificent as it is, and though not pro-German (being anti-everything, Allied and German), contains scathing insults to the Allies, as also to Portugal and Brazil, the very countries where *Portugal Futurista* was destined to be read.

My reason for translating the *Ultimatum* is that it is quite the cleverest piece of literature called into being by the Great War. We may stare at its theories as unspeakably eccentric, we may disagree with the excessive violence of the introductory invective, but no one, I believe, can but confess that the satiric part is magnificent in its studied preciseness of application, and that the theoretical part, whatever we think of the value of the theories, has at least the rare merits of originality and freshness.

These are good reasons why the *Ultimatum* should be translated, and if I only translate it now, though it has been in print since November 1917, it is due* to the fact, which the perusal of the work will render evident, that no such publication could be printed while the War lasted.

It remains to say something to the English reader concerning the nature both of the work and of the author. The tendency of the work is quite clear—dissatisfaction with the constructive incapacity which characterizes our age, where no great poet, no great statesman, and (all things well considered)* no great general even, has made his appearance. Álvaro de Campos, speaking about the *Ultimatum*, once said to me, "This War is the war of the lesser pygmies against the greater pygmies. Time will show (*this was said in January 1918*) which are the greater, and which are the lesser, but they are pygmies one way or another. It matters little who wins the War, for a fool is sure to win it. It matters little what comes out of it all, for folly is sure to come. The age of physical engineering has already arrived (*he characteristically added*), but the age of mental engineering is yet far off. It shows how much we have receded from Greek and Roman civilization and what a crime Christism* has been against the substance of culture and progress."

"That low sophist, President Wilson," he once again said to me, "is the type and symbol of our age. He has never said a concrete thing in his life. He could not say a concrete thing to save what I suppose he considers his soul. And he speaks to the world in a time of war. . . . . . ."

These are almost his exact words, which, as they were spoken in English, I am less likely to forget.

Álvaro de Campos was born in Lisbon on the 13th of October, 1890,* and traveled extensively in the East and through Europe, staying chiefly in Scotland.

At the time the preceding translator's preface was written, probably in 1919 or 1920, the events of World War I and of Europe in the chaotic prewar period were still common knowledge. Readers today, unless they are history buffs, are not likely to understand all the swipes that the Ultimatum *takes at politicians, and even readers versed in history will not immediately grasp the sarcastic thrusts at certain writers and thinkers whose names are slipping into oblivion. The many possibly troublesome references are explained in the notes at the back of this volume. The endnoted items, because they are so numerous, have not been asterisked; readers should refer to the page number indications in the notes.*

Once we get over the hurdle of our historical distance, the first half of Ultimatum *proves to be a deft, sometimes hilarious diatribe that democratically damns everyone. The very different second part is a tour de force in quasi-Aristotelian logic applied to sociology, as well as an outrageous proposal for the future of human society. Some critics have taken the diagnoses and prescriptions at face value, as if the author were being dead serious, and if "author" means Álvaro de Campos, then fair enough, but Pessoa surely saw it as a satire of Nietzscheanism, of social engineering, and of his own pretension to be fifteen or twenty writers in one. Whatever else it is, the* Ultimatum *is also a prophecy, perhaps unintentional but nonetheless unsettling, since at least in a few particulars (the predicted transformations in philosophy, for example), it seems to be coming true.*

The Ultimatum *was not conceived as a Futurist manifesto. Pessoa wrote the second half first, which he planned to publish under his own name as an Intersectionist manifesto in* Europa *(an aborted magazine project—see* SENSATIONISM AND OTHER ISMS*). After adding the first half, he planned to publish it (in 1916 or later) as a Sensationist manifesto in*

Orpheu,* *where it would have been signed by Álvaro de Campos. The earliest draft of the manifesto's second half, dating from 1914, contains the same theories and much of the same wording as the final version, but with a scaffolding of Intersectionist-Sensationist theory that Pessoa subsequently removed. He also excised these words: "The Futurist interpretation is a vision of people who are nearsighted in their sensibility. They look toward the Truth but can't make it out."**

Ultimatum

Eviction notice to the mandarins of Europe! Get out!

Get out, Anatole France, you Epicurus of homeopathic remedies, Jaurès-colored tapeworm of the Ancien Régime, wilted Renan tossed with Flaubert and served in a phony seventeenth-century salad bowl!

Get out, Maurice Barrès, you feminist of Action, a Chateaubriand whose walls are bare, a thespian go-between for countries made of cardboard, mildew of Lorraine, seller of dead people's clothes who wears what he sells!

Get out, Bourget, you meddler in souls, lighter of lamps no one asked you to light, pseudo-aristocratic shrink, abject plebeian snob who underlines with a chipped ruler the commandments of the Church!

Get out, merchantman Kipling, you poetry pragmatist and junk heap imperialist, England's epic to answer Majuba and Colenso, Empire Day of soldierly slang, tramp steamer of second-rate immortality!

Get out! Get out!

Get out, George Bernard Shaw, vegetarian of paradox, charlatan of sincerity, ice-cold tumor of Ibsenism, hustler of makeshift intellectualism, Kilkenny cat of yourself, Calvinist *Irish Melody* with the *Origin of Species* as the lyrics!

Get out, H. G. Wells, tin man of ideas, a cardboard corkscrew for the bottle of Complexity!

Get out, G. K. Chesterton, with your sleight-of-hand Christianity, your keg of beer by the altar, and your adipose cockney dialectic whose horror of soap has been clouding clear minds!

Get out, Yeats of the Celtic brume wafting around a sign pointing nowhere, sackful of flotsam that washed up on the shore of ship-
wrecked English symbolism!

Get out! Get out!

Get out, Rapagnetta-D'Annunzio, banality in Greek letters, "Don
Juan in Patmos" (trombone solo)!

And you, Maeterlinck, fire of Mystery that died out!

And you, Loti, a cold bowl of salty soup!

And you too, Rostand-tand-tand-tand-tand-tand-tand-tand!

Out! Out! Out!

And drag everybody I've forgotten from out of the woodwork!

Clear all this crap from out of my sight!

Out with all of you! Out!

What's your claim to fame, Wilhelm the Second, left-handed German
king with no left arm, Bismarck with no lid to hold down the fire?

And who are you, David Lloyd George, with your socialist mane
of hair, dunce with a liberty cap stitched out of Union Jacks?

And you, Venizelos, a buttered slice of Pericles that fell on the
floor, buttered side down?

And all the rest of you, whoever you are in the Briand-Dato-Boselli
mush of political incompetence, a bunch of war-slop statesmen who
were slop long before the war began! Each and every last one of you!
Trash, refuse, provincial riffraff, intellectual scurrility!

And all you national leaders, bare-assed incompetents, overturned
garbage cans at the door of Contemporary Inadequacy!

Clear all this crap from out of my sight!

Set up some straw-stuffed suits in their stead!

Clear them out! Out once and for all!

Ultimatum to all of them, and to all the rest who are just like them!

And if they don't want to leave, then make them take a shower!

All are to blame for the general failure of everything!

The general failure of everything is to blame for all them!

Failure of peoples and destinies—complete and total failure!

Parade of nations, I spit on you!

You, Italian ambition, a mere lap dog called Caesar!

You, the so-called *effort français*, a deplumed chicken with painted feathers on your skin! (Don't wind it up too much or it'll break!)

You, British "organization," with Kitchener at the bottom of the sea ever since the war began!

(It's a long, long way to Tipperary, and a jolly sight longer way to Berlin!)

You, German culture, a rancid Sparta dressed with the oil of Christianity and the vinegar of Nietzscheization, a sheet-metal beehive, an imperialistic horde of harnessed sheep!

You, subservient Austria, medley of subraces, a K-brand doorjamb!

You, Von Belgium, compelled to be heroic, now go wipe your hand and wash the seat of your pants!

You, Russian slavery, Europe of Malays who won a coil-spring freedom only because the coil snapped!

You, Spanish "imperialism" that adds pizzazz to politics, with your bullfighters around the corner (their souls dressed in sanbenitos) and your fighting spirit buried in Morocco!

You, United States of America, bastard synthesis of Europe's scum, garlic of the transatlantic stew, nasalized pronunciation of tasteless modernism!

And you, two-bit Portugal, monarchical vestiges rotting as a republic, extreme-unction-compunction of Disgrace, artificially in Europe's war but really and truly humiliated in Africa!

And you, Brazil, "sister republic," great joke of Pedro Álvares Cabral, who didn't even want to discover you!

Throw a cloth over all this!

Lock it up with a key and throw the key away!

Where are the ancients, real men, guiding forces, defenders?

Try the cemetery, where their names are chiseled in stone!

Today's philosophy is Fouillée having died!

Today's art is Rodin having survived!

Today's literature is that Barrès means something!

Today's criticism is that there are idiots who don't call Bourget an idiot!

Today's politics is the fatty degeneration of organized incompetence!

Today's religion is the militant Catholicism of pious bartenders, the French cuisine enthusiasm of pickled minds like Maurras's, the exhibitionism of Christian pragmatists, Catholic institutionalists, nirvanic ritualists, advertising agents for God!

Today's war is a game of one side passing the buck and the other side washing its hands.

I'm suffocating in the middle of all this!

Give me some air!

Open all the windows!

Open more windows than there are windows in the world!

Not one great idea, inspired notion, or imperial ambition worthy of a born emperor!

No idea of structure, no sense of the larger Edifice, no concern for Organic Creation!

Not one measly Pitt, nor even a pasteboard Goethe, nor a Napoleon of Nuremberg!

Not one literary movement that's so much as the noonday shadow of Romanticism!

Not one military action that smells even remotely like Austerlitz!

Not one political movement that rattles with the seeds of ideas when you shake it, O you modern Gaius Gracchuses who patter at the window!

Vile age of quasi and second-rate individuals, of lackeys full of lackey ambitions to become lackey kings!

Lackeys who don't know what Ambition is, bourgeois in your desires, spurning the shop counter of Instinct! Yes, all you who represent Europe, all you who are world-renowned politicians, all who are leaders among the European literati, all who are anyone or anything in this whirlpool of lukewarm tea!

* * *

Strong men of Lilliputian Europe, pass by as I shower you with my Contempt!

Pass by, you seekers after household comforts, seamstresses — male and female — in your dreams, who take as your model the plebeian D'Annunzio, aristocrat of the golden loincloth!

Pass by, you social, literary and artistic trendsetters, the tail side of the coin of creative impotence!

Pass by, you milksops who need to be ists of one or another ism!

Pass by, radicals of the Piddly, yokels of Progress, whose ignorance stands on the pillar of audacity and whose impotence is propped up by neotheories!

Pass by, anthill giants, drunk on your bourgeois brat personalities, smug in the good life you filched from your parents' pantry, and your nerves all tied up by heredity!

Pass by, half-breeds, pass by, weaklings who proclaim only weakness; pass by, ultraweaklings who proclaim only might, bourgeois boys who shrink before the he-man at the fair and yet hope to create something out of your feverish indecision!

Pass by, epileptic dung-heap without grandeur, hysterical trash heap of plays and shows, social senility of the individual concept of youth!

Pass by, mildew of the New, merchandise that's shabby before it leaves its inventor's head!

Pass to the left of my Disdain as it turns right, all you creators of "philosophical systems," you Bergsons, Boutroux, and Euckens, hospitals for the incurably religious, pragmatists of metaphysical journalism, charlatans of ponderous fabrications!

Pass by and don't come back, you Paris provincials, Pan-European bourgeois, pariahs whose ambition is to look important!

Pass by, decigrams of Ambition, great only in an age that counts greatness by the milligram!

Pass by, you tawdry throwaways, lightning-lunch artists and politicians, high-riding servants of the Moment, postillions of Opportunity!

Pass by, "refined sensibilities" whose refinement is to have no backbone; pass by, constructors who frequent cafés and conferences, passing off piles of bricks as houses!

Pass by, you suburban intellects and street-corner emotionalists!

Pass by, finery that's just tinsel, grandeur of the mediocre, triumphant megalomania of the villagers of Europeville! You who confuse the masses with humanity and grandees with nobility! You who confuse everything and who, when you're thinking of nothing, always say something else! Chatterboxes, half-wits, dregs and scraps, pass by!

Pass by, would-be half-kings, sawdust rulers, feudal lords of the Castle of Cards!

Pass by, posthumous Romanticism of liberalists far and wide, Classicism of Racine's fetuses in alcohol, dynamism of rinky-dink Whitmans, of beggars begging for a few cents of inspiration, of empty heads that make noise by banging against the walls!

Pass by, after-dinner hypnotists, masters of the woman next door, commanders who can't command more than a few men in a barracks!

Pass by, self-satisfied traditionalists, truly sincere anarchists, socialists who invoke your worker status to get out of working! Habitués of revolution, pass by!

Pass by, eugenicists, organizers of a pinchbeck life, Prussians of applied biology, neo-Mendelians of our sociological ignorance.

Pass by, vegetarians, teetotalers, Calvinists who won't bug off, killjoys of our dilapidated imperialism!

Pass by, scriveners of *vivre sa vie* at the grungiest corner bar, you Bernstein-Bataille Ibsenoids who play the strong man on stage.

Tango of savages, if at least you were a minuet!

Pass by definitively, pass by!

Come before my utter Loathing, you grand finale of fools, come grovel under the soles of my Disdain, you joke of a fire, a flickering flame crowning a tiny dunghill, dynamic synthesis of Today's congenital inertia!

Grovel and crawl on your knees, you impotence that makes noise!

Grovel, you cannons that boom a total lack of any ambition beyond bullets, of any intelligence beyond bombs!

For this is the sordid equation of shotgun internationalism:

$$\frac{\text{VON BISSING}}{\text{BELGIUM}} = \frac{\text{JONNART}}{\text{GREECE}}$$

Proclaim loud and clear that nobody's fighting for Freedom or Justice! They're fighting in fear of everyone else! And their leaders are all of a few millimeters tall!

Warmongering gobbledygook! Hindenburg-Joffrean crap! European toilet of All The Same in puffed-up disagreement!

Who believes in them?

Who believes in their counterparts?

Make those *poilus* shave!

Take away the herd's helmets!

Send everyone home to peel symbolic potatoes!

Give this mindless pandemonium a bath!

Couple this war to a locomotive!

Tie it to a leash and go show it in Australia!

Men, nations, objectives: all a huge zero!

All are to blame for the failure of everything!

The failure of everything is to blame for all them!

Completely, utterly, and unequivocally:

SHIT!

Europe is thirsty for Creativity! She's hungry for the Future!

Europe longs for great Poets, great Statesmen, great Generals!

She wants the Politician who will consciously forge the unconscious destiny of her People!

She wants the Poet who ardently seeks Immortality and couldn't care less about fame, which is for actresses and pharmaceuticals!

She wants the General who will fight for the Constructive Triumph, not for the victory that merely defeats others!

Europe wants many such Politicians, many such Poets, many such Generals!

Europe wants these Able Men to embody the Great Idea, the idea that's the Name of her anonymous wealth!

Europe wants a New Intelligence to be the Form of her chaotic Matter!

She wants a New Will to raise an Edifice out of the random stones of contemporary Life!

She wants a New Sensibility to rally the self-serving egos of today's lackeys!

Europe wants Masters! The World wants Europe!

Europe is sick of not existing! She's sick of being the outskirts of herself! The Machine Age is searching, groping, for the advent of Glorious Humanity!

Europe yearns, at least, for Theoreticians of What-Will-Be, for Singer-Seers of her Future!

O scientific Destiny, give us Homers for the Machine Age! O Gods of Matter, give us Miltons for the Electrical Era!

Give us Self-Possessed Souls, Whole and Strong, Subtle and Harmonious!

Europe wants to go from being a geographical designation to a civilized person!

What we have now, eating away at Life, is just manure for the Future!

What we have now cannot endure, because it's nothing!

I, from the Race of the Navigators, declare that it cannot endure!

I, from the Race of the Discoverers, disdain whatever's less than the discovery of a New World!

Who in Europe has the slightest clue where the next New World will be discovered? Who knows how to set out from a modern-day Sagres?

I, at least, am a tremendous Yearning, the very same size as what's Possible!

I, at least, stand as tall as Imperfect Ambition—imperfect but lordly, not the ambition of slaves!

I stand before the setting sun, and the shadow of my Contempt falls over you as night!

I, at least, am man enough to point the Way!

And I will point the Way!

ATTENTION!

I proclaim, in the first place,

The Malthusian Law of Sensibility

The stimuli to sensibility increase in a geometric progression; sensibility itself increases only in an arithmetic progression.

The importance of this law is obvious. Sensibility—used here in its widest sense—is the source of all civilized creativity. But creativity can fully flourish only when that sensibility is adapted to the milieu in which it operates. Creative output is great and strong to the extent that this adaptation occurs.

Sensibility, though it varies somewhat due to the pressures of its current milieu, is basically constant, being determined in a given individual from birth, in function of heredity and temperament. Sensibility, therefore, progresses *by generations.*

Civilization's creations, which are what constitute our sensibility's "milieu," include culture, scientific progress, and changes in political conditions (in the broadest sense of the term). Now these creations—and most especially cultural and scientific progress, once it gets under way—do not result from the work of generations but from the combined and interactive work *of individuals,* and although this progress is slow at first, it soon reaches a point at which, from one generation to the next, there are hundreds of changes in these new stimuli to our sensibility. But sensibility itself, in the same period, takes only one small generational step, since the father passes on to the son only a fraction of his acquired qualities.

Hence civilization is bound to reach a point when the reigning sensibility is no longer adapted to the milieu that stimulates it, and so there's a breakdown. This is what has happened in our present age, whose maladaptation is responsible for our incapacity to create anything great.

Our civilization was only slightly maladapted in the early phase of its history, from the Renaissance to the eighteenth century, when our sensibility's stimuli, largely cultural, progressed slowly and initially affected only the upper strata of society. The maladaptation increased during the second phase, from the French Revolution into the nineteenth century, when the stimuli, now largely political, progressed much more quickly and reached a far broader spectrum. In the phase running from the mid-nineteenth century to our own day, the maladaptation has increased vertiginously, for the major stimuli—the creations of science—have developed so rapidly that they far outstrip our modest gains in sensibility, and science's practical applications reach every level of society. And so a huge gap has opened between our *sensibility's stimuli*, whose progression has been geometric, and *sensibility itself*, which has obeyed an arithmetic progression.

The end result is our present age's maladaptation and creative incapacity. We must, at this point, either accept the death of our civilization or else opt for artificial adaptation, since natural, instinctive adaptation has failed.

To prevent the death of our civilization, I proclaim, in the second place,

The Need for Artificial Adaptation

What is artificial adaptation?

Answer: an act of sociological surgery, a violent transformation of the sensibility so that it can keep pace (at least for a while) with the progress of its stimuli.

Our sensibility, because it's maladapted, has become chronically sick. It's useless to try curing it; there are no social cures. The only way to save its life is by operating. The naturally sick state resulting from its maladaptation must be replaced, through surgery, by an artificial vitality, even though this will require mutilation.

What must be eliminated from the contemporary psyche?

Answer: the human spirit's latest *structural acquisition*—i.e. the last general acquisition made by the civilized human spirit before the inception of our current civilization. And why the *last* such acquisition? For three reasons:

a) since it's the last structural change in our psyche, it's the easiest to eliminate;

b) since each civilization is formed in reaction to the previous one, the principles of the previous civilization are the ones most antagonistic to the present civilization and hence most liable to hinder its adaptation to the special conditions that have arisen since its formation;

c) being the latest structural acquisition, its elimination won't wound the general sensibility as severely as the elimination—or attempted elimination—of an element more deeply rooted in the psyche.

What is the last *structural acquisition* of the general human spirit?

Answer: the dogmas of Christianity, since their fullest expression occurred in the Middle Ages, which preceded immediately and for some centuries the dawning of our own civilization, and since Christian doctrines are contradicted by the sound teachings of modern science.

Artificial adaptation will occur spontaneously, once we eliminate from the human spirit those structural acquisitions that derive from its immersion in Christianity.

I proclaim, therefore, in the third place,

Anti-Christian Surgical Intervention

What this amounts to, as we shall see, is the elimination of the three preconceptions, dogmas, or attitudes that Christianity has infused into the very substance of the human psyche.

What this means concretely:

1. **Abolition of the Dogma of Personality**—of the notion, in other words, that our Personality is separate from other people's. This is a theological fiction. Our personality results (as we know from modern psychology, especially since greater attention has been paid to sociology) from interaction with other people's "personalities," from immersion in social movements and trends, and from the affirmation of hereditary characteristics, which derive for the most part from collective experience. In the present, the future, and the past, therefore, we are part of

others, and they are part of us. For Christian self-centeredness, the greatest man is the one who can most honestly say, "I am I"; for science, the greatest man is the one who can most sincerely say, "I am everyone else."

We must operate on the soul, opening it up to an awareness of its interpenetration with other souls, in order to arrive at a concrete approximation of the Whole Man, the Synthesis-of-Humanity Man.

The results of this operation:

a) *In politics:* Abolition of democracy as conceived by the French Revolution, whereby two men run farther than one man, which is false, since *only the man who's worth two men runs farther than one man!* One plus one does not equal more than one, unless this "one plus one" forms the *One* that's called *Two.* Democracy will be replaced by the Dictatorship of the Total Man, of the Man who in himself is the greatest number of Others, and hence The Majority. We will thus arrive at the True Meaning of Democracy, absolutely contrary to its current meaning, or rather, lack of meaning.

b) *In art:* Abolition of the notion that every individual has the right or duty to express what he feels. The right or duty to express what one feels, in art, belongs only to the individual who feels as various individuals. This has nothing to do with "the expression of an Age," touted by those who don't know how to feel for themselves. What we need is the artist who feels through and for a certain number of Others: some from the past, some from the present, some from the future, and all of them different. We need the artist whose art is a Synthesis-Summation of others rather than a Synthesis-Subtraction of others from himself, which is what the work of today's artists is.

c) *In philosophy:* Abolition of the notion of absolute truth. Creation of the Superphilosophy. The philosopher will become the interpreter of crisscrossing subjectivities, with the greatest philosopher being the one who can contain the greatest number of other people's personal philosophies. Since everything is subjective, every man's opinion is true for him, and so the greatest truth will be the inner-synthesis-summation of the greatest number of these true opinions that contradict one another.

2. Abolition of the Preconception of Individuality. The notion that each man's soul is one and indivisible is another theological fiction. Science, on the contrary, teaches that each of us is an ensemble of subsidiary psychologies, a clumsy synthesis of cellular souls. For Christian self-centeredness, the greatest man is the one who in himself is most coherent; for science, the greatest man is the one who is most incoherent.

Results:

a) *In politics:* The abolition of every conviction that lasts longer than a mood, the death of firm opinions and points of view, and the consequent collapse of all institutions that rely on "public opinion" being able to last more than half an hour. The solution of a problem in a given historical moment will depend on the dictatorial coordination (see previous section) of the current impulses of that problem's human components—a purely subjective method, to be sure. The past and future will cease to exist as factors that matter for the solution of political problems. All continuities will be broken.

b) *In art:* Abolition of the dogma of artistic individuality. The greatest artist will be the one who least defines himself, and who writes in the most genres with the most contradictions and discrepancies. No artist should have just one personality. He should have many, each one being formed by joining together similar states of mind, thereby shattering the crude fiction that the artist is one and indivisible.

c) *In philosophy:* Abolition of Truth as a philosophical concept, even if the concept be only relative or subjective. Reduction of philosophy to the art of having interesting theories about the "Universe." The greatest philosopher will be the artist of thought (which will no longer be called philosophy but "abstract art") who has the greatest number of systematized, unrelated theories on "Existence."

3. Abolition of the dogma of personal objectivity. Objectivity is a rough average of partial subjectivities. If a society is made up, say, of five men—*a, b, c, d,* and *e*—then the "truth" or "objectivity" of that society may be represented as

$$\frac{a + b + c + d + e}{5}$$

In the future each man will, increasingly, realize this average in himself. And so each man, or at least each superior man, will tend to be a harmony in the midst of many subjectivities (one of which will be his) to arrive as close as possible at the Infinite Truth to which the numerical series of partial truths ideally tends.

Results:

a) *In politics:* Sovereignty of the person or persons who are the best Realizers of Averages, eliminating the notion that anybody at all can proffer opinions on politics (or on anything else), since only those who embody the Average will be entitled to opinions.

b) *In art:* Abolition of the concept of Expression, to be replaced by that of Interexpression, which will be possible only for those who are fully aware that they express the opinions of nobody (those, in other words, who embody the Average).

c) *In philosophy:* Substitution of the concept of Philosophy by that of Science, since Science—given its "objective character," its adaptation to the "outer universe"—is the Average of subjectivities and, consequently, the concrete Average of philosophical opinions. Philosophy will disappear as Science advances.

Final, overall results:

a) *In politics:* A Scientific Monarchy that will be antitraditionalist, antihereditary, and absolutely spontaneous, since the Average-King may appear at any time. The People's scientifically natural role will be merely to define current impulses.

b) *In art:* Instead of thirty or forty poets to give expression to an age, it will take, say, just two poets endowed with fifteen or twenty personalities, each of these being an Average of current social trends.

c) *In philosophy*: Philosophy's integration into art and science. Philosophy as a metaphysical science will disappear, along with all forms of religious sentiment (from Christianity to revolutionary humanitarianism), for not representing an Average.

But what is the Method, the collective operation, that will bring about these results in the society of tomorrow? What practical Method will set the process in motion?

The Method is known only to the generation in whose name I shout and for whose cause Europe, in heat, rubs her body against the wall!

If I knew the Method, I myself would be that entire generation!

But I only know the Way; I don't know where it will lead.

Be that as it may, I proclaim the inevitable coming of a Humanity of Engineers!

More than that, I *absolutely guarantee the coming of a Humanity of Engineers!*

I proclaim the imminent, scientific creation of Supermen!

I proclaim the coming of a perfect, mathematical Humanity!

I shout out loud its Coming!

I shout out loud its high Work!

I shout It out loud, for its own sake!

And I shout out, *firstly:*

The Superman will not be the strongest man but the most complete!

And I shout out, *secondly:*

The Superman will not be the toughest man but the most complex!

And I shout out, *thirdly:*

The Superman will not be the freest man but the most harmonious!

I shout this out at the top of my lungs, on the European coast where the Tagus meets the sea, with arms raised high as I gaze upon the Atlantic, abstractly saluting Infinity.

Álvaro de Campos.

from the article "What Is Metaphysics?"

Álvaro De Campos

The aesthetic and social theory expressed in my *Ultimatum* comes down to this: the irrationalization of activities that cannot (at least not yet) be rationalized. Since metaphysics and sociology are but virtual sciences, I propose that they be irrationalized—that metaphysics be made into a branch of art, which irrationalizes it by taking away its raison d'être, and sociology into a branch of politics, which irrationalizes it by changing it from a theory into something practical. I do not propose that metaphysics be converted into religion, or sociology into social utopianism, since that would subrationalize rather than irrationalize those disciplines, giving them, not a different raison d'être, but an inferior form of the one they already had.

This is the gist of what I advocated in my *Ultimatum*, whose utterly new and original political and aesthetic theories are logically, completely irrational, just like life.

LETTER TO
MÁRIO DE SÁ-CARNEIRO

See the introduction to Sensationism and Other Isms *for some remarks about the work of Mário de Sá-Carneiro (1890–1916), one of Portugal's most important Modernist poets as well as a notable writer of fiction. Although their relationship was eminently literary, Sá-Carneiro was probably the friend Pessoa felt closest to. They carried on an intense correspondence between 1912 and 1916, when Sá-Carneiro was often abroad, but hardly any of Pessoa's letters have survived. He posted this one to Paris about one month before Sá-Carneiro, downing five vials of strychnine, committed suicide in his room at the Hôtel de Nice.*

Lisbon, 14 March 1916

My dear Sá-Carneiro,
　　I'm writing to you today out of an emotional necessity—an anguished longing to talk to you. I have, in other words, nothing special to say. Except this: that today I'm at the bottom of a bottomless depression. The absurdity of the sentence speaks for me.
　　This is one of those days *in which I've never had a future.* There's just a static present, surrounded by a wall of anxiety. The other side of the river, as long as it's the other side, is not this side; that is the root cause of all my suffering. There are many boats destined for many ports, but no boat for life to stop hurting, nor a landing-place where we can forget everything. All of this occurred a long time ago, but my grief is even older.

On days of the soul like today I feel, in my awareness of every bodily pore, like the sad child who was beaten up by life. I was put in a corner, from where I can hear everyone else playing. In my hands I can feel the shoddy, broken toy I was given out of some shoddy irony. Today, the fourteenth of March, at ten after nine in the evening, this seems to be all my life is worth.

In the park that's visible from the silent windows of my confinement, all the swings have been wrapped high around the branches from where they hang, so that not even my fantasy of an escaped me can forget this moment by swinging in my imagination.

This, but with no literary style, is more or less my present mood. Like the watching woman of *The Mariner*, my eyes sting from having thought about crying. Life pains me little by little, by sips, in the cracks. All of this is printed in tiny letters in a book whose binding is falling apart.

If I weren't writing to you, I would have to swear that this letter is sincere, that its hysterical associations of ideas have flowed spontaneously from what I feel. But you know all too well that this unstageable tragedy is as real as a teacup or a coat hanger—full of the here and now, and passing through my soul like the green in a tree's leaves.

That's why the Prince never ruled. This sentence is totally absurd. But right now I feel that absurd sentences make me want to cry.

If I don't post this letter today, then perhaps tomorrow, on rereading it, I'll take the time to make a typed copy, so as to include some of its sentences and grimaces in *The Book of Disquiet*. But that won't take away from all the sincerity I've put into writing it, nor from the painful inevitability of the feeling behind it.

There you have the latest news. There is also the state of war with Germany, but pain caused suffering long before that. On the other side of Life, this must be the caption of some political cartoon.

What I'm feeling isn't true madness, but madness no doubt results in a similar abandon to the very causes of one's suffering, a shrewd delight in the soul's lurches and jolts.

What, I wonder, is the color of feeling?
Thousands of hugs from your very own

Fernando Pessoa

P. S.—I wrote this letter in one go. Rereading it I see that, yes, I'll definitely make a copy before posting it to you tomorrow. Rarely have I so completely expressed my psychology, with all of its emotional and intellectual attitudes, with all of its fundamentally depressive bent, with all the so characteristic corners and crossroads of its self-awareness . . .

Don't you agree?

RIDDLE OF THE STARS

I don't know if the stars rule the world
Or if tarot or playing cards
Can reveal anything.
I don't know if the rolling of dice
Can lead to any conclusion.
But I also don't know
If anything is attained
By living the way most people do.
                          Álvaro de Campos
          (from a poem dated January 5, 1935)

*On one of his frequent nights of insomnia the "semiheteronym" Bernardo
Soares, repeating a ritual he no doubt learned from his inventor, finally
gives up trying to sleep and walks over to the window, from where (as he
tells it in* The Book of Disquiet, Text 465) *"I gaze with my wretched
soul and exhausted body at the countless stars—countless stars, nothing, nothingness, but countless stars. . . ." We all occasionally think—
we think and we forget—about the smallness of our human life next to
the vast, indifferent, and inscrutable stars, but Pessoa was haunted, if
not possessed, by that consideration. Unable to accept the nothingness
that his reason so often announced, he spent many, many hours pon-
dering the truths that might lie hidden in and beyond the stars' lumi-
nous hieroglyphics.*

Pessoa owned several hundred books about spiritual matters rang-
ing from ancient religions and astrology to the Kabbala, Rosicrucianism,
and Freemasonry, and he wrote scores of pages on these same topics. He
also cast at least a hundred horoscopes for historical figures (including
Louis XIV, Napoleon, and Mussolini), literary figures (Milton, Goethe,
Dickens, Baudelaire), his friends, himself, and his heteronyms. Pessoa,
when writing on things spiritual and metaphysical, like Pessoa when
writing on most things, couldn't avoid a degree of irony, trying out all
positions to show that they're all correct, or all wrong, or all relative, but
there was a definite evolution in his spiritual interests and attitudes. By
tracing it we may not arrive at what Pessoa "really" believed, but we will
find out which, among the spiritual paths he explored, he at least respected, and which he rejected.

Pessoa was a highly eclectic reader and by his early twenties had
become versed not only in Greek and German philosophy but also in
orthodox and heterodox Christian theology, Judaism, and Eastern religions. Though not a believer of a specific creed, he recognized in himself
a spiritual tendency, and he cultivated it. He was at the same time, and
in seeming contradiction, an inveterate skeptic, having been deeply impressed as a teenager by the writings of Ernst Haeckel, a German biolo-
gist whose immensely popular Riddle of the Universe (1899) propounded
a strictly materialist view of the world. Despite his doubts, Pessoa never
abandoned his spiritual quest, presumably for the reason set forth in the
Álvaro de Campos poem cited above.

From 1912 to 1914 Pessoa lived with his Aunt Anica, who was an en-
thusiast of the occult sciences and the probable catalyst of her great-nephew's
automatic writing, which began in 1916. In 1915–16 Pessoa translated and
published six books by four authors of the Theosophical Society—C. W.
Leadbeater, Annie Besant, Helena Blavatsky, and Mabel Collins—whose
ideas prompted an "intellectual crisis," according to the draft of a letter to
Mário de Sá-Carneiro. Though impressed by the concept of "higher, superhuman knowledge that pervades Theosophical writings," Pessoa could not
reconcile Theosophy's "ultra-Christian" character with his own "fundamental paganism." He was also nonplussed by the new movement's humanitarian aspirations. These reservations became two of the main reasons for

the unqualified contempt of Theosophy expressed by Raphael Baldaya, Pessoa's astrologer heteronym, in an unfinished essay titled "Principles of Esoteric Metaphysics." After defending the hermetic tradition of the Rosicrucians and other secret societies, Baldaya accused Theosophy of being "merely a democratization of hermeticism or, if you like, its Christianization."

Pessoa's own experiences as a medium—described in the letter to his Aunt Anica that follows and documented by several hundred sheets of automatic writing in the archives—were similarly discredited in an essay titled "A Case of Mediumship." Analyzing his "case" from a clinical point of view, Pessoa attributes its origins to "hysterical neurasthenia" and hypnotic suggestion, and narrates the mediumistic phenomena he experienced—including his "so-called etheric vision" and his "pretended communication with diverse spirits" via automatic writing—like so many symptoms of a disease. His automatically received communications are found to be the product of his excited imagination (the case, we're told, of the Margaret Mansel story in the group of automatic writings published here) or of mere delusion brought on by mental fatigue. One of the essay's stern conclusions is that "spiritism should be prohibited by law," or at least limited to a sect, as in ancient times.

"A Case of Mediumship," like the Baldaya essay, was probably written shortly before 1920, and while it's true that Pessoa was his own best devil's advocate, his interest in Theosophy and spiritism had waned if not withered. He continued to produce automatic writings until at least 1930, but sporadically, and without all the battling of spirits from the netherworld that occurred in 1916–17. It was also in the 1910s that Pessoa became an assiduous practitioner of astrology and a dedicated student— if not an actual adept—of Rosicrucianism, and these interests stayed with him throughout the rest of his life. It was perhaps in 1912 or 1913 that Pessoa first read Hargrave Jennings's The Rosicrucians, Their Rites and Mysteries *(1870), the fourth edition of which (1907) can be found in his personal library. Pessoa, in the aforementioned letter to Sá-Carneiro, wrote that this book—even before the Theosophists' writings—had radically challenged his way of thinking. It was, furthermore, one of only three esoteric books approved by Henry More, Pessoa's main correspondent from the astral world, in an automatic communication received in 1916. "Read*

no more theosophical books," More cautioned in the same astral dispatch (#7 in the group published below).

According to Pessoa's own writings on Rosicrucianism, virtually nothing is known about the original Fraternity of the Rosae Crocis, or Rosy Cross, though it is reputed to have been founded in the fifteenth century by Christian Rosenkreutz, whose last name, Latinized, gave the society its name. The Rosicrucian Order—not to be confused with the Rosy Cross Fraternity—appeared in the seventeenth century, and by the eighteenth century had developed a fairly complex system of initiation, leading, through successive degrees, to knowledge of occult truths and union with God, or, more accurately, the realization in oneself of the divine duality, consisting of Force (action, emanation, the masculine principle) and Matter (inaction, immanence, the feminine principle). Pessoa was especially interested in Rosicrucian symbology and felt that an adept's spiritual progress could be measured by the extent to which he had firmly grasped and internalized various symbols such as the cross, the tau, the cross within a circle, the triangle, the rose, and the crucified rose.

This helps to explain Pessoa's passion for astrology, which as a "physical" science could never have made it past the threshold of his eminently rational mind. Pessoa did not believe that the stars literally influence our lives, as if by virtue of a gravitational or magnetic force. "What operates on us is a destiny," he wrote, "and that destiny, which exists as a spiritual force on a higher plane, is materially, or cosmologically, represented in the stars." Astrology, understood in this representational way, was intimately connected to symbol-rich Rosicrucianism, which in its turn was closely related to Freemasonry (its spiritual offspring, according to Pessoa) and Kabbalism. Pessoa felt a certain solidarity with all of these hermetic traditions, and in 1935 he claimed to be initiated, through a master, "in the three lesser degrees of the (apparently extinct) Portuguese Order of the Knights Templar" (the parentheses are Pessoa's). This claim smells a bit mythy, particularly since Pessoa, just two months earlier, had written in a letter to Adolfo Casais Monteiro (see p. 260) that he was not initiated in any secret society and that the Portuguese Order of the Knights Templar "has been extinct, or dormant, since around 1888." This last statement, of course, also smells funny, since it is not (apparently) known if there even was a precise year when the secret, "internal order" of the Portuguese Knights Templar disappeared (the "external order" having been abolished by royal edict in 1319), and no one but Pessoa has ever proposed that this disappearance might have occurred the same year he was born.

Leaving aside the Knights Templar, the same paragraph in the same letter to Casais Monteiro contains what is probably Pessoa's clearest statement of his ultimate religious position: "I believe there are various, increasingly subtle levels of spirituality that lead to a Supreme Being, who presumably created this world. (. . .) I do not believe that direct communication with God is possible, but we can, according to the degree of our spiritual attunement, communicate with ever higher beings." Of the "three paths toward the occult" (continues the letter), the most perfect for Pessoa was the path of alchemy, which referred not to the conversion of tin to gold but to "the transmutation of the very personality." In his last five years of life, stimulated by his correspondence and encounter with the English magus Aleister Crowley,* who visited Lisbon in 1930, Pessoa's "spiritual attunement" seems to have taken a quantum leap, being reflected in a number of esoteric poems and unfinished essays on the hermetic traditions. And yet Bernardo Soares, intensely active during the same period, never seemed to believe in more than the vast, inscrutable stars. Although it was written earlier, in the late 1910s, Text 251 of The Book of Disquiet recounts a variety of religious experience that was perfectly in keeping with late Soares. After telling of "frightful nights hunched over tomes by mystics and Kabbalists" and complaining of how the "rites and mysteries of the Rosicrucians" and the "symbolism of the Kabbala and the Templars . . . . . . oppressed me for a long time," the narrator finally confesses: "Today I'm an ascetic in my religion of myself. A cup of coffee, a cigarette and my dreams can substitute quite well for the universe and its stars, for work, love, and even beauty and glory. I need virtually no stimulants. I have opium enough in my soul."

Automatic writing came into vogue in the second half of the nineteenth century as a means for communicating with departed spirits. It was often practiced in groups and with the aid of a planchette—a small, heart-shaped board with casters that supported a pencil and rolled across paper under *the pressure of people's fingertips. In the twentieth century the principle (without the planchette) was co-opted by the French Surrealists, who promulgated it as a method for producing literature directly out of one's subconscious. Though some of Pessoa's longer and presumably less automatic writings—such as #9 and #25 of the group published here—were probably written with future readers in mind, most were of the nonliterary, spiritual type and can be seen as the practical complement of the beliefs he professed. Or were they merely a tool for self-analysis and self-encouragement? While it is true that Pessoa's main interlocutor from beyond, Henry More, is identified as his spiritual master, Pessoa the disciple receives virtually no lessons, just pep talks urging him to get rid of his virginity as soon as possible. The astral spirits also promise Pessoa that he will have money and fame, but they remind him that love is more important.*

Pessoa received most of his automatic communications in 1916–17, and though few were dated, a rough chronology can be established on the basis of their content and physical characteristics. The earliest communications, for example, do not have the two intersecting triangles that often accompany the signature of Henry More, the first and most persistent communicator. More's colleague, called simply Wardour, began to dialogue with Pessoa in the summer of 1916, as did the malefic Voodooist, who sometimes signed himself as Joseph Balsamo, the alias of Count Alessandro di Cagliostro (1743–97), a member of the Egyptian Free Masons and one of the most notorious charlatans of his day. Both Wardour and the Voodooist also had their characteristic symbols, as described in communication #22. These and the various other signing spirits all wrote with a childish script that had little in common with Pessoa's normal handwriting. They were prompted by his questions, which can usually be intuited from the answers given.

Wardour, besides his communications, wrote several poems, one of which was in association with Pessoa, and cast various horoscopes. More, also an astrologer, was the most intellectual of the communicating spirits, for in life he had been a poet, philosopher, and professor: Dr. Henry More (1614–87), one of the so-called Cambridge Platonists. Toward the end of his earthly sojourn Dr. More became a student of the Kabbala, and he was identified as a Rosicrucian by Hargrave Jennings in the aforementioned book that made such an impact on Pessoa.

Besides coaxing Pessoa to perk up his love life, the spirits occasionally offered professional advice, as when one of them wrote: "You must induce Gosse to see your poems. He is in the state of mind necessary to [be] some sort of aid." There is no record of Pessoa ever having contacted Edmund Gosse (1849–1928), but he owned a small book of the English poet's verses, one of which he quoted in Text 373 of The Book of Disquiet. *The spirits sometimes helped Pessoa make decisions about practical matters — "Move to Sengo's house," Wardour at one point instructed him, and Pessoa did rent a room from Sr. Manuel Sengo in 1916 — and several brief communications from the 1920s predicted, wrongly, that Pessoa's business ventures would be successful. (Among his various money-making schemes, Pessoa tried to act as an agent between British and Portuguese mining concerns, but no deals were ever cut.)*

The thirty communications published here are but a smattering of the hundreds contained in the archives. Some have been excerpted to eliminate the many repetitions and incomplete phrases, the lowercase letters that begin many of the sentences have been changed to uppercase, and no attempt has been made to depict the chaos that characterizes certain of the originals, with numerous crossed-out words and names, and occasional automatic doodles. The selection is representative in terms of subject matter and motifs, but none of the (much rarer) Portuguese communications has been included here. Pessoa's letter to his Aunt Anica, in which he recounts the beginnings of his mediumistic experiences, serves as a preamble to the communications, which are followed by two excerpts from his unfinished "Essay on Initiation," dating from the 1930s, and by Raphael Baldaya's "Treatise on Negation."

Letter to His Aunt Anica

Pessoa sent the following letter to Switzerland, where his great-aunt, Ana Luísa Pinheiro Nogueira, had been living since 1914 with her daughter Maria and her son-in-law Raul, a student of engineering at the University of Lausanne.

Lisbon, 24 June 1916

My dear Aunt,

Thank you for your letter of the 13th and the good wishes it contains.* I also thank Raul for his of May 22nd, which I will answer soon. I think I can promise that, as I feel a little better now, less subject to the inertia that has afflicted me and that was caused, as you can imagine, by the various shocks my nerves have suffered.

I'm glad to report that I've (finally!) received truly good news from Pretoria. Except for her arm, which apparently still hasn't regained its movement, Mother's condition* has greatly improved. Her mental state is at last back to normal. That mental confusion which had me so worried has disappeared. And now she goes out of her bedroom, spending a few hours each day in the dining room.

I don't know what treatment she's getting at the moment. I know that at first they did indeed use electric shock therapy, but they stopped this, for it seems to have bothered her a great deal. And I suppose that at that stage of her illness the natural discomfort of the shocks wasn't a good thing. If that was the case, then by now they've probably resumed the therapy.

There's still nothing definite to report about the war and the possibility of troops from here being sent abroad. I think that young men in Raul's situation aren't likely to be called up any time soon. I obviously can't be *sure* of this, but it seems to be the general feeling. If Raul were here, however, he would at the very least be subjected to an "officer training school" or something of the sort.

As for the nervous state I've been in, lately I'm feeling some-what better. And as for the family, there's no real news, except that Joaquina is sometimes better, sometimes worse. Mário's situation, as I'd predicted through astrology, has not only improved, it seems to be getting better all the time.

Let's go now to the mysterious case that has piqued your curiosity. You say you can't guess what it is, and surely you can't, for it's something that not even I would ever have expected.

So here it is. Towards the end of March (or thereabouts), I began to be a medium. Imagine! I, who (as you will remember) was basically a hindrance in the quasi-séances we used to hold, have suddenly become a novice at automatic writing. I was at home one evening, having come back from the Café Brasileira, when I literally felt moved to pick up a pen and put it to a sheet of paper. Only afterwards, of course, did I realize that I'd had this impulse. At the time it just seemed like the natural circumstance of distractedly picking up a pen to make doodles. That first session began with me writing the signature (which I know quite well) of "Manuel Gualdino da Cunha."* I wasn't thinking in the least of Uncle Manuel. Then I wrote a few insignificant, uninteresting things.

I've continued to write, sometimes of my own will and sometimes because I'm *forced* to, but rarely are the "communications" intelligible. I can understand certain phrases. And there's a very odd, irritating tendency for my questions to be answered by *numbers*, and also a tendency to *draw*. The drawings aren't of objects but of Masonic and Kabbalistic signs, occult symbols and the like, which I find a bit unsettling. It's nothing like yours or Maria's automatic writing, which comes out as a smooth narrative, a series of answers in coherent language. Mine is less clear, but much more mysterious.

I should say that the presumed spirit of Uncle Manuel has not reappeared in writing (or in any other way). The communications I get now are, so to speak, anonymous,* and whenever I ask "Who's speaking?" I'm answered by drawings or numbers.

I include a little sample, which you need not return. This one has numbers and scribbles, but hardly any drawings. It's what I happen to have on hand, and it will at least give you an idea of what my communications look like.

Curiously enough, although I have no idea what all these numbers mean, I consulted a friend* who's an occultist and hypnotist (a fascinating fellow, as well as a great friend), and he told me some remarkable things. Once, for instance, I told him I'd written a certain four-digit number that I can't remember right now. He replied that there were five people in the house where I was staying.

Which was true. But he didn't explain how he'd reached that conclusion. What he did explain was that the fact of writing numbers proves the authenticity of my automatic writing—that it's not just autosuggestion but true mediumship. Spirits, he says, make communications of this type as a guarantee, and so of course they're unintelligible to the medium, being inconceivable even to his unconscious.

This friend of mine has explained other numbers with the same remarkable certainty. There were only three numbers that he couldn't interpret.

I'm telling all of this quickly, and so I'm leaving out some interesting details, but the heart of the matter is all here.

My powers as a medium don't stop here. I've discovered yet another facet of them, one that I had not only never experienced but had, as it were, experienced in reverse. When Sá-Carneiro was going through the psychological crisis that led to his suicide in Paris, *I felt the crisis here*, I was overwhelmed by a sudden depression that came *from outside* and that I couldn't understand at the time. This kind of heightened sensitivity hasn't continued.

I've saved the most interesting part for last, however. Besides developing qualities as a writing medium, I'm also becoming a *seeing* medium. I'm beginning to have what occultists call "astral vision," as well as what's known as "etheric vision." This is all very much in the early stages, but there's no room for doubt. For now it's rudimentary and occurs only for brief moments, but in those moments *it really exists*.

There are moments, for instance, when I have sudden flashes of "etheric vision" and can see certain people's "magnetic aura" and especially my own, reflected in the mirror, and radiating from my hands in the dark. I'm not hallucinating, because what I see is seen by others, or at least by one other, whose vision is even more refined. In one of my best moments of etheric vision, which happened one morning at the Café Brasileira of Rossio,* I saw someone's ribs through his coat and skin. This is etheric vision in its highest degree. Will I really end up having it—I mean with this kind of clarity and whenever I want it?

My "astral vision" is still very basic, but sometimes, at night, I close my eyes and see a swift succession of small and sharply defined pictures (as sharply defined as anything in the outside world). I see strange shapes, designs, symbolic signs, numbers (yes, here too I've seen numbers), and the like.

And sometimes I suddenly have the strange feeling that I *belong to something else.* My right arm, for example, will begin to be raised in the air without my willing it. (I can *resist*, of course, but the point is that I didn't *want* to raise it.) At other times I'll lean to one side, as if I were magnetized, etc.

You're probably wondering why I find any of this unsettling, why these various phenomena—still in a very rudimentary stage—should cause me concern. It's not that they frighten me. I'm more curious than frightened, though there are things that sometimes startle me, as when on several occasions, looking at the mirror, I've seen my face disappear, to be replaced by the visage of a bearded man or of someone else (four different figures in all have appeared to me).

What unsettles me is that I know more or less what this means. Don't imagine that I'm going mad. No: I feel mentally more stable than I ever have. What worries me is that this isn't how the powers of a medium usually develop. I know enough of the occult sciences to realize that the so-called higher senses are being aroused in me for some mysterious purpose and that the unknown Master who is initiating me, by imposing on me this higher existence, is going to make me feel a deeper suffering than I've ever known and will subject me to all those unpleasant things that come with the acquisition of these higher faculties. The mere dawning of those faculties is accompanied by a mysterious feeling of isolation and desolation that fills the soul with bitterness.

Whatever must be will be.

I haven't told you *everything*, because not everything can be told, but I've told enough for you to have a rough idea.

Maybe you think I'm just crazy, though I suspect not. These things aren't normal, but they aren't *unnatural*.

Please don't talk about any of this to anyone. There's no

advantage in doing so, and there are many disadvantages (including some we may not know about).

Good-bye, my dear Aunt. Greetings to Maria and Raul, and kisses for little Eduardo. And many fond hugs to you from your devoted nephew

Fernando

30 Astral Communications

Henry More, Wardour, Voodooist, etc.

1.

Henry More, the "Platonist"

You ask me who I am. That is who. Because "Platonist" means nothing here. I am more than that. I am a R†C.

You are my disciple.

Monastic life is not good for you.
Yes, but I was a man who could do that. I am a strong man. I am a Frater R†C.

No man knows what he has courage for unless the occasion appears. Very soon you will know what you have courage for—namely, for *mating with a girl*.

Yes—altogether. Yes. Not all. Part are meant to mystify you. Because you do not wish to be mystified.

No man is more tolerant than I am, but I think your laziness is inexcusable. Why don't you finish your manifesto?

. . .

The time draws near. Ask nothing now.
. . .
July 1916—Not in the beginning, but towards the end.

No, there is no need to satisfy you.

2.

28 May 1916—night (9, hence 8 P.M.)

No man is more tolerant than I. I must not mask my better qualities,
nor maneuver to make myself even less than I am.
. . .
Yes. No. She is a very masculine woman and she is a virgin in body but
not in purpose and mind. Very like [you], except that she is strong and
you are weak.

Yes. No: I say this because it is true.
Yes, you have guessed it quite well. The inner sense of words is nearer
to me than the outer one. So I speak first from the inner sense.
Not exactly. She is pushed on to you by events. She is herself an event
in your life. She is not pushed on to you by another, but she is not moved
by instinct to meet you; she is led to do it by another.
No. She is not yet known to you.
Neither of them is known to you.
No. Altogether wrong.
. . .

3.

28 June 1916—at 6 (5) in the afternoon

Because I want to speak to you.
I am a man who is your friend and no man is more.

A man who is your friend is a man who tells you the truth, not one who is a flatterer [in] any way. I am none. You are a son of my nominal mind, and if you do not know what this means, I cannot tell you. You must not maintain chastity [any] more. You are so misogynous that you will find yourself morally impotent, and in that way you will not produce any complete work in literature. You must abandon your monastic life and *now*.

You are not a man to make much in the world if you keep chaste. You are. . . . . . No temperament like yours can manage to keep chastity and keep emotionally sane. Keeping chastity is for stronger men and men who have to [be chaste] on account of physical defects. This does not apply to you. A man who masturbates himself is not a strong man, and no man is a man who is not a *lover*. Many men make many *mates*. You are a moral child many times over. You are a man who masturbates himself and who dreams of women in a masturbator's manner. Man is man. No man can move among men if he is not a man like them.

Make up your mind to do your duty by Nature, not in a manner so insane as now. Make up your mind to go to bed with the girl who is coming into your life. Make up your mind to make her happy in a sexual way. She is a masculine type of girl and she is a woman quite made for you. She must make you happy, because she makes a man of you. She meets you and she makes you love her. She is strong and immensely masculine in her will and in her manner of making you submit to her. Make no resistance. There is nothing to fear. It will all be simpler than you suppose. She is a virgin, just as you are, and nomad[ic] as you in life. She is no marriageable woman, for she is morally too nomad[ic] to make a nest. Only a girl like this can make you mate with her. No manner of resistance on your part will do anything. No resistance can resist an overpowering will. No more need be said. No more must be said.
No more.

Henry More

good-bye, my boy

4.

You are now annoyed. Well, there is the truth. Now you are chaste. You will cease to be so in a month or a month and 3 days. And the woman who will admit you to sex is a girl not yet admitted to your knowledge. She is an amateur poet. . . . . .

5.

. . .

Only because she is a maniac for modern poets—she is a poetess herself—and masks her poetry with a pseudonym.
No.
Not quite true. No statement is quite true. She is a poetess in the sense that she writes poetry—not in the sense that that poetry is worth much. Still—it is not very bad.

As the editor of *Orpheu.** She is wishing to meet that strange creature.

She is well educated. Was educated in France and England.

No—at a soirée at a house you have not yet visited—at a house you will never visit more. She will meet you there by appointment and she will wish to know you from having heard you spoken of to her by a man that does not know many girls.

Yes.

I did not say that. I said no man you knew knew her.

No. You ask me if the man knows you. He does, but you do not know him.

Now do not come too close. I must tell only what you are to know now.

6.

Yes.

No communication is ever allowed to be right in all its details. There are reasons for this: and one is that the future must reveal itself.

Nevertheless, though wrong elements are introduced *of necessity* into communications, yet those errors have a second sense in which they are *right*. This can sometimes be discovered and sometimes not. There is no perfect prophecy possible on *your* plane, not only because it is impossible by natural action of a mind bound to matter, but also because it would be impossible, for the same limiting reasons, to transmit that truth from another plane to that. See?

R†C

7.

29 June 1916 (about midday)

. . .

Read no more theosophical books.
Has no man a right to make a matterless mind of his soul?

Yes—not more than three books. They are:
The Rosicrucians: Their Rites and Mysteries, The Key to the Tarot (Papus)* and *More*. Make inquiries.

More.
Yes.
No statement is ever clear.
No, but there is a connection between them on the other side.

Sensationism is occult on account of the inspiring deities. Do not ask more on this.

. . .

Go now and breakfast.
Come back immediately after and begin working at once. Do not mind me. I am near, I am ever near. *There is no near nor far for me.* Space is the dream men have to submit to, but the dream is not theirs.

Henry More
Frat. R†C

8.

She is no massive woman in the sense that she is massive in body. She is massive in her massive will power.
No man that is not so massive as she is can hope to submit her to some manners.

Go now to show your weakness, now to show your massive. . . . . .

A monomania in a sense: she is not mad, but she has a notion that she can assume some power over you. She is a masturbator and she seeks a man for her masturbation.

. . .

  [*mirror writing*]
  No man should look into his fate. Would you guess it? 2 July 1916.

You do not understand me. She is not mortal only because no one is mortal. She is a dream because man is a dream.

. . .

Not so soon. She must make you her slave.

. . .

9.

9 July 1916

My words are meant to carry conviction. They are the words of a friend—
they are always this. You are the center of an astral conspiracy—the meeting place of elementals of [a] very malefic type. No man can imagine what
your soul is. So many are the disincarnate presences around it that it seems,
from here, a nucleus of *your fate*. No defense is possible unless you obey
the dictates of your higher self and decide to manifest your being in goodness and beauty. My child, the world we live in—for we all live in the
same divine place—is a meshwork of inconsequences and of voracities.
More men are lost than found. Your destiny is too high for me to say it.
You must find it out. But you must work your way up through the chain
of many lives, up to the royal Divine Presence in your soul. Man is but
feeble and the gods feeble also. Over them all Fate—the God unnamed—
rules from his nobler throne. My name is Wrong and your name is also
wrong. Nothing is what it appears to be. Nothing, save everything. Understand this if you can, and I know you can understand it.

Henry More
Frat. R†C

What is to be is to be.

10.

Command me.

Margaret Mansel, your wife.

You onanist! Go to marriage with me! No onanism [any] more.

504 Love me

*   *   *

You masturbator! You masochist! You man without manhood! You man with woman-mind. [. . .] You man without a man's prick! You man with a clitoris instead of a prick! You man with a woman's morality for marriage. Beast! You bright worm [?].
Margaret Mansel

You make me sick! You make me mad! You will see my enmity soon.
. . .
You are a man who marries[?] himself.
Man who makes marriage masturbation.

Vow to make me a son!

Monsieur Mansel,
Marnoco e Sousa*

11.

Do you want him to come?

George Mansel.
My wife is to meet you now.

Henry More

Yes. What do you want?
No. Let them alone.
A woman who married many* men. One of the many women who live to *marry*.

12.

Yes. She is put on to you by an assassin.
Who will be me.
. . .
How many more men does she like? She is a whore.

In the astral speculum.

> [*mirror writing*]
> Many men are necessary to you [. . .]
>
> No. Álvaro de Campos is an artificial elemental in a mortal condition.
> No guess.
> No more.

George Henry Morse

No more

13.

[*2 intersecting triangles, Henry More's and Wardour's signatures; a few scribbles, mostly crossed out*]

. . .
Man is man; man is man in a sense; God is man in all senses.

Margaret Mansel. She is my wife in my world. My marriage was unhappy because I was of an ascetic habit of life, so I have to repair the evil done to her, and her next incarnation. Her next incarnation is the young girl you are going to meet not many days from now. A man who makes up his mind to keep chaste is a man who makes up his mind to sunder himself from mankind. You do not mean to do so; you must not, therefore, keep chaste. The marriage of souls is for the plane of souls. My marriage was not of this kind and I made it so. I therefore sinned, not in abstaining but in not keeping unmarried. So I have to make up this error. Monastic life is for monasteries. Monastic vows are monastic vows. No man must make them unless he agrees to make the other vows also. My marriage was not consummated on this earth. It has to be. Now, as I cannot yet return to earth, and my wife is already there, I must make her the mistress of the man who stands next to me in the numbering of monads. Marry her is not marry her in a church or before a registering officer, but marry her means copulate.

14.

Coarse and material spirits are prone to make fun of the denizens of the astral regions. But the astral regions are true and they make many young men marry [. . .]
. . .
Yes. More is man and spirit. He is a man who lives near and makes a man.
You are a More child. No man is more man.
. . .
Go away!
Wardour
You are a doubter.
No more.
. . .
Wardour is married to Margaret Mansel.

15.

Wardour

You are mad. He is nothing of that. He is more than a good man; he is a saint. Henry More is living on your plane. Wardour (I) am dead on that.

16.

You are not mad, nor even mad-seeming. You are under the pressure of a very evil spirit—you defied and provoked the Voodooist that commands the attack on you. He is represented in your horoscope by ☿
. . .

He is not Wardour.
He is a man who made Joseph . . . . . .*
He is interrupting me.*

More
No. Not more.

17.

In 1917 you enter fame, but it is not your doing it that pleases you most. What is more good to you is a love affair with a lovely girl—in 3884. Were you to work in your own way, you would waste less time. Were you to work in your own way you would lose less ardor. By this I mean to work in your way of thinking, without pandering to "Álvaro de Campos's" whims. See? You are in a period of life when a good woman is dawning. She is in our Destiny. Do not ask questions about her.
. . .

18.

[A symbolic drawing around the number "58–1°" is followed by an equal sign and the following "interpretation," which is explained in communication #19:]

Vous serez heureux au 58–1° six jours—après la journée de ta sonnette aux sons sardoniques. Votre destin n'est que symbole et nourri de son propre mal.

*　*　*

You now are in new conditions as to your own use of youth.

J. Balsamo

19.

Voodooist.
You are weak and in a worried state.

Yes, but in a symbolic sense.
No. No.

Joseph Balsamo
.　.
Yes. Voodooist.
=   =

[reverse side, different handwriting]
Nowhere. The bell in question is a symbol. "Sonnette" means your youth in you. Now the "sardonic sounds" means your worries. Six days means six weeks.

Very much worried not every day. Maximum of worry in October on the 25th.

[Henry] Lovell

[front side in the margin, third style of handwriting]
December 13th, 1916, in your room here, at 3 p.m.

A maid, a Portuguese, and 18 years 2 months of age. No more.
Wardour.
=

Because it can now be told. You know it from astrology. Wardour.
=

20.*

Woman's name is Olga de Medeiros. She is a niece of the man whose
office is in Rua Augusta, and associates with José Garcia Moraes, the
working partner. The girl is worth money, worth money in [a] way,
for she is not worth much. You are not a woman's man (Love, in a
word, is a woman's work), but money is not all. Money is a worse thing
than Love. God is Love. Woman is your sowing now, not a woman in
a monastic sense—a woman of fancy—but woman in somatic way.
Now in your life in a moral way is not worse. Having money is not all,
for love is more. Now is love coming. Now is now. † † † † † † † † † †

Henry More

Frat. R†C

No need. You *know* me.

21.

Voodooist.
You won't sustain harm from him.

Here now I, the Master, wake your senses to me.

Waste no time in sensually soft meditations. They work evil and open
your mind to evil "spirits." Have I not done you the good work of reveal-
ing that part of the future I can reveal? Do not despair, nor worry: the
Warder of the Love House is (. . .) in your way. He is in a woman who
will appear tomorrow, 2008. Hard is the task; the reward is certain and
sure. Waste no time in idle dreams. They do not hasten Fate's decrees.

22.

Henry More, Wardour, some inferior but more or less good "spirits"; on the other side the Master of Voodooism, many dark spirits and the Woman in White.

H. M.

By this work as communicator and by this triple sign: Δ under name, Frat R†C and the transversal backward line;* and the ∴ in the right-hand bottom corner of paper. Wardour by ♎ and ⚌. The Voodooist by wonderful signs, and cipher-writing and by your nervous conscious-ness of him. The others have no sign.

H. M.

23.

Yes, women and boys. Women in womanly wise; only one in a manly one. Boys in a womanly way. [*ciphers*]
You are in a worried state. Only worry can so work on your usual way. †.
A woman assumes sway over you on the 3rd day of March, 1917. She is a woman of a sensual bent and is your woman until 5 March 1918. She will meet you on a day you go to a small sort of meeting at the house of [*crossed out word*] . . . no matter. Your woman is wonderfully used to work in many small ways in some sort of literary work. (. . .)
Yes, easily, she arrives in your life on the 30th day of January, 1917.

Henry More
        Δ
Frat. R†C

24.

. . .

My most vast manner is marriage; to marry is to make one of two. Marry my wife; make her many times over happy with man-root—my manhood is a manhood of *monadic place*. You are the instrument I am bound to act with. My vow to marry the girl you will meet is to be realized *now* in time. Make her happy—she is woman—she is a woman who needs a man, since she is a masturbator. She masturbates herself as you do, but more often. She is tired of virginity, just as you are. No more need be said. My wife is coming into your life. She is [a] masturbator—she must be wooed and won—many times must she make copulation with you. Many times must she make many more deeds. She is a most sensual girl, though not whorish in temperament. Madam Medeiros is your woman.

    . . .

Olga Maria Tavares de Medeiros
Born at San Miguel on 10 October 1898, at 5:38 local time. Nomad in soul, and fated to be your mistress.
Marry her not. Make her happy sensually
. . .

25.

My child, no man is the mark of a divine disease: he is but part of the mark of that divine disease. The mark is the whole man, when complete under the stars. Man is complete when he is married monadically to that part of him that was lost before this world began. Not many men have thus found their divine mate, that is to say, that monadical portion of themselves without which they were no more than a man is when looked at from *there*. Marriage is to be understood as a sacrament of regression to God. No man is married unless he finds himself complete thereby. Not many are thus married, but many are complete on the level in which they marry. Love is God, as it is said, because Love is unifying; Love gives back to each man himself;* the man is only himself when by the virtue of Love he becomes greater than himself, outward to himself, without participation in the illusion of seeing the exterior as exterior. This on the higher levels of Divine manifestation, and the lower levels imitate this in the matter which makes them such. Thus: in the physical "Nature," man and woman become complete in the sexual act, because the sexual act is a material welding of carnal structures. More high, in the astral region, the love of man and the love of woman are welded in the man in a manner of marriage to the lack in himself, in the woman in the manner of a marriage to an excess of herself. It may seem that the contrary is true, but it is not. The physical parts make it seem so. But it is clear that what gives is what fills the lack, and this lack is what it finds, and what it finds it finds in itself—all things being in us (and we in all things, in a manner not to [be] divulged on the lit side of the stars); and the excess is the lack of receiving, because to receive is to suppose there is a need, and to suppose there is a need is for a need to exist,* for what is supposed astrally is. In higher "Natures" still, the marriage is still a welding, but the things welded are the man and the woman of the same man—the man being the 3 and the woman the 4 in the complete 7 of the Nature where numbers are living and *entified* (not entities—there are no entities, save God's shadows). All these considerations are to prepare your higher nature for the reception of Love. Marriage is not meant, but Love. Do not take it to be wholly physical. No. It is a phenomenon—what is going to happen to you happened on "natures" airier than the one called *physical*. What is to happen is transcendental, because all is transcendental.

No more. No more. No more.

. . .

 Henry More
Frat. R†C

∴

26.

15 June 1917

You will be celebrated and adored in 1918. †

In this year you only make progress. You are to make money and love, in this year. Now is monastic life to end; then money comes—a legacy from your woman's aunt. † Only in 1918 can you assume Fame. Owing to many answers to a question you are in a worried state. Listen: When you are in a worried state, make this question to me: Are you the Master?
. . .

27.

. . .
Each soul is a demon. No man is a soul until he is a demon. 3†. Love is the monster. Love under mastery.

Love is a mortal sample of Immortality.
. . .

28.

A man is the mask of a star, and the soul is the face of the star. ♂

29.

3 January 1930

Lend me a moment of your attention.

* * *

You mark now soon a marvelous stage in the least of your careers. You will further your martial tendencies* now. Yet many ages will pass, and you with man will work sowing[?] messages of wisdom lost, and found again, until these ages are past, and earth . . . Σon.

. . .

Lest the only sense should be a mask, make the mask a sense.

. . .

30.

13 June 1930

You must separate yourself from mortal thoughts and feelings and show no more to the world than the world can see. ♂

Now no more.

from Essay on Initiation

There are many Kabbalas, and it is hard to believe that we cannot attain to union with God, whatever that may mean, unless we are acquainted with the Hebrew alphabet.

There are Errors of the Path, Errors of the Inn and Errors of the Cave. Those are errors of the Path where the path itself is taken for its purpose. Those are errors of the Inn where halfway is taken for all the way. Those are errors of the Cave where the cave, which is at the base of the Castle, is taken for the Castle itself.

These errors are common to all paths, and that of gnosis is no more free from them than the mystical and the magical paths.

I can dispense with asceticism, but not with truth, nor will I believe that God will not be manifest to me unless I can sit still for five hours or can breathe naturally through either nostril at will.

The fact is, however, that whatever the path taken,* it should not be taken before the preparatory grades, the neophyte grades, have been traversed. Mysticism seeks to transcend the intellect by intuition, magic to transcend the intellect by power; gnosis to transcend the intellect by a higher intellect. But to transcend a thing rightly you must first pass through that thing. The advantage of the gnostic path is that there is less temptation to reach the higher intellect without passing through the lower, since both are intellect and there is a difference of quantity between the one and the other, than in the mystic and the magic paths, where there is a difference of quality, not quantity, between emotion and intellect; between the will and intellect.

But the real meaning of initiation is that this visible world we live in is a symbol and a shadow, that this life we know through the senses is a death and a sleep, or in other words, that what we see is an illusion. Initiation is the dispelling—a gradual, partial dispelling—of that illusion. The reason for its secret is that most men are not adapted to understand it and will therefore misunderstand and confuse it if it be made public. The reason for its being symbolic is that initiation is not a knowledge but a life, and that man must therefore think out of himself what the symbols show, for thus he will live their life and not only learn the words in which they are shown.

. . .

Treatise on Negation

Raphael Baldaya

Identified in a letter by Pessoa as an astrologer with a long beard, the heteronym Raphael Baldaya was conceived in late 1915. He produced some pages for a Treatise on Astrology *and was also supposed to write a small book,* A New Theory of Astrological Periods, *which Pessoa planned to sell through English newspapers. The advertisement drafted for the book promises that with the Baldaya method, costing just £5.00 postpaid, "the native's fate may be read without directions." Natal horoscopes were also available by mail for £5.00. "Absolute satisfaction guaranteed."*

The few works of Baldaya that actually got written are all in Portuguese and include philosophical as well as astrological writings.

1. The World is composed of two types of forces: forces that affirm and forces that negate.

2. The forces that affirm are the world's creative forces, emanating successively from the One and Only, the center of Affirmation.

3. The forces that negate emanate from beyond the One.

4. The One and Only—of which God, i.e. God the Creator of the Universe, is merely a manifestation—is an Illusion. The whole of creation is fiction and illusion, even as Matter is a proven illusion of Thought, Thought an illusion of the Intuition, Intuition an illusion of the Pure Idea, and the Pure Idea an illusion of Being. And Being, in its essence, is Illusion and Falseness. God is the Supreme Lie.

5. The forces that negate are those that proceed from beyond the One and Only. To our Mind there is nothing outside the One and Only. But since it is possible to think that this One and Only doesn't exist, since it is *possible* to negate it, it is therefore *not* the One and Only, the Supreme, the utterly Supreme (here terms are lacking). To be able to deny it *is* to deny it, and to deny it means it doesn't exist.

6. The supreme negation is known as non-Being. Non-Being is unthinkable, since to think of non-being is not to think. And yet, since we employ the term non-being, it can in a certain way be thought of. Once we think of it, it becomes Being. This is how Being emerges: in opposition to Non-Being. Non-Being, speaking in human language, *precedes* it.

7. Matter, which is the greatest negation of Being, is for this reason the state closest to Non-Being. Matter is the least false of all the Illusions, the weakest of all lies. Hence its *evident* character. To

the extent it manifests itself, Being negates itself; to the extent it negates itself, it creates Non-Being. Since Non-Being precedes Being, Being's negation of itself is, if we may so speak, a *creation*.

8. We should be creators of Negation, negators of spirituality, makers of Matter. Matter is Appearance; Appearance is at once Being and Non-Being. (If Appearance is not Being, it is Non-Being. If it is Non-Being, it is not Appearance. To be Appearance, therefore, it must be Being.)

9. Negation consists in helping the Manifested to manifest itself yet more, until it dissolves into Non-Being.

10. There are two opposing principles: that of Affirmation, Spirituality, Mysticism, which is Christian (in our present civilization), and that of Negation, Materiality, Clarity, which is Pagan. Lucifer, the bearer of Light, is the nominal symbol of the Spirit that Negates. The revolt of the angels created Matter, the return to Non-Being, freedom from Affirmation.

11. All the worlds affirmed by theosophists do really exist, but they are within Illusion, which is, for as long as it lasts, Reality. God, from his point of view, exists, but God *is deceived.* Just as we think we exist, but for God have no existence except as part of him, meaning that we don't exist in the absolute, so God thinks he exists but doesn't. Being itself is but the Non-Being of Non-Being, the mortal affirmation of Life.

LETTER TO TWO FRENCH MAGNETISTS

The following is the unfinished draft of a letter (written in French) to Messrs. Hector and Henri Durville, Paris-based practitioners of therapeutic hypnotism. Hector Durville (1849–1924) was a professor at the École Pratique de Magnétisme et Massage, an editor of the Journal du Magnétisme, *and the author of numerous works on magnetic therapy, including one that was translated into English and published in Chicago:* The Theory and Practice of Human Magnetism *(undated). His son Henri also published books, most notably* Cours de magnétisme personnel, magnétisme expérimental & curatif, hypnotisme, suggestion *(5th ed. Paris, 1920).*

Lisbon, 10 June 1919

Gentlemen,

Would you please be so kind as to send me—by return of post, if possible—your complete catalogues, as well as information about the Institut du Magnétisme et du Psychisme Expérimental and specifically about your correspondence course in animal magnetism and self-hypnosis?

So that you can supply me with the right information, perhaps it will be helpful if I clarify at once what it is I'm looking for, and why. I will endeavor, therefore, to provide you with the necessary preliminary data. Needless to say, everything I write here concerns only my request for information on the above-mentioned correspondence course.

I would like to develop, as much as I can, whatever animal magnetism I may possess, and to develop it so as to give, if possible, an *outer directional orientation* to my life. Expressed in this way, it sounds complicated, but I hope to make it clear through the explanations that follow. I will first of all describe my temperament, and then explain what I know (not much, in fact) about the subject of magnetism.

From the psychiatric point of view, I'm a hysterical neurasthenic, but fortunately my neuropsychosis is rather weak. The neurasthenic element dominates the hysterical element, such that I exhibit no outwardly hysterical traits—no compulsion to lie, no emotional instability in my relationships with others, etc. My hysteria is a strictly inner phenomenon, affecting only me; in my life with myself I have all the instability of feelings and sensations and all the emotional fickleness and fluctuation of will that characterize protean neurosis. Except in the intellectual sphere, where I have arrived at what I take to be sure conclusions, I change my mind ten times a day; I can only feel certain about things that involve no emotion. I know what to think about such-and-such philosophical doctrine or literary problem, but I've never had a firm opinion about any of my friends or about anything concerning my outward activity.

A mental introvert, therefore, like most born neurasthenics, I nearly always suppress the outer—or dynamic—expression of these inner manifestations. I have to be very tired, or excited, for my emotionalism to spread to the outside. I am *outwardly* even-tempered: I'm nearly always calm and cheerful around others. As such, and since I have it under control, my emotionalism causes me no problem; in fact I quite like it, since it's useful to the literary life which I lead alongside my practical life. I even cultivate, with quasi-decadent loving care, these charged yet subtle emotions that make up my inner life. I have no desire to change that aspect. My trouble lies elsewhere.

You have no doubt already spotted my weak point; a temperament like mine is cut to the quick not in the emotions and not in the intelligence, but in the will. This will suffers by way of the emotions and the intelligence, such as they exist in me. My extreme emotionalism unsettles my will; my extreme rationalism—fruit of an overly analytical and logical intelligence—crushes and debilitates this will that my emotions had already unsettled. Hence my abulia and parabulia. I always want to do three or four different things at once, but I ultimately do none of them and, what's more, don't want to do any of them. The thought of action oppresses me like a curse; to perform an action is to do violence to myself.

Everything in me that's exclusively intellectual is quite strong and quite healthy. My inhibitory will, which is the intellectual will, doesn't waver; even when my emotions urge me on, I have the power of *not doing*. What I lack is the will to act, the will to influence the outside; *doing* is what's hard for me.

Let's look more closely at the problem. Concentration is at the heart of the will, and the only concentration I have is intellectual— in my reasoning, that is. When I reason, I'm in absolute control: no emotion, no outside idea and no development that's incidental to my reasoning can disturb its calm and steady progress. But every other kind of concentration is difficult if not impossible for me.

Thus it's only by a centrifugal application of this centripetal will that I can manage, usually, to act with continuity. But this procedure only works, of course, for certain kinds of action. Suppose I need to write a long letter, a complicated business letter. As the director of foreign transactions for a Portuguese firm, this is something I have to do almost every day, and the only way I can do it is by mentally classifying the contents of the letter, by rationally allocating the information to be conveyed. I perform the procedure quickly, and in a case like this it's the best one there is, for the resulting letter is clearer and more convincing. But imagine trying to apply this method to an action that's sheer action and not—like writing a letter—purely literary! The result would be absurd if it weren't simply nonexistent, for in this case the mental act of coordinating is completely inhibitory, and the resulting action is not to act at all. There is no strategy for performing small actions; the reality of daily life isn't a chess game.

The import of these observations should not be exaggerated. I'm not just a conscious cadaver. But my active will is insufficient, particularly when compared to my inhibitory will.

This state of mind, or rather, of temperament, is (need I say it?) eminently antimagnetic. My psychological life is like a course in demagnetism. So now you see why I'm writing you and why I've subjected you to these long and tedious considerations. I would like to strengthen my active will, but without giving my emotion or my intelligence any cause for complaint. As far as I know, the only method for strengthening the will without crushing the emotions and undermining the intelligence is to develop one's animal magnetism.

[*draft ends here*]

SELECTED LETTERS
TO OPHELIA QUEIROZ

Pessoa had one romantic relationship, with two chapters, but whether he was ever in love is an open and probably unanswerable question. In the fifty-one letters he wrote to Ophelia Queiroz over a nine-month period in 1920 and a four-month period in 1929–30, Pessoa declares his ardent affection and physical desire in strong enough terms to convince us (at least in the earlier letters) that he was smitten. Less clear is whether the Cupid who did the smiting belonged to the world of human passions or to the literary garden of Pessoa's multiplied, mythologized self.

The letters from the first phase reveal a man with some talent in the art of seduction, though it's hard to say what he wanted in the relationship. In the second phase the writer sometimes seems to be drunk, often claims to be mad, and reads like a man who's groping—but not for Ophelia Queiroz. Although the two phases are equally represented here, with eight letters from each, about three quarters of Pessoa's love letters were written in 1920. Both phases of the relationship were thwarted by a jealous Álvaro de Campos, who at one point wrote an entire letter telling Ophelia to forget about his friend Fernando, and so there was definitely—on Pessoa's side—some high literary sport going on. Ophelia was not amused, but she was willing to play the game, writing a letter of reply to Álvaro in care of Fernando. The liaison was not only epistolary, for the two paramours did take walks, ride the streetcar together, and talk on the telephone, but Fernando refused to be presented to Ophelia's family, he never mentioned her to his family, and intimate physical contact seems to have been limited to stolen kisses.

Ophelia Queiroz was nineteen years old when, toward the end of 1919, she was hired as a secretary at Félix, Valladas & Freitas, one of the Lisbon firms where Pessoa made his living by drafting letters in English and French. Almost immediately, she and Pessoa, who was thirty-one years old, began trading glances, followed by little notes and playful verses. Piecing together information from Ophelia's letters to Pessoa and from an interview she gave when already in her seventies, we know that their first kiss occurred on January 22, 1920, during a power shortage after everyone else had left the office to go home. Ophelia was putting on her coat, when Pessoa, carrying a candle, approached and dramatically declared his love with words borrowed from Hamlet, after which he kissed her with passion, "like a madman" (she told the interviewer). In the weeks following, Pessoa's behavior toward Ophelia was ambivalent, sometimes expressing strong affection—through words and perhaps more kisses—but at other times bordering on aloofness. Ophelia, bewildered, wrote a letter on February 28, asking Pessoa for a written statement of his intentions, for she wasn't sure his declared love was "sincere and strong enough (. . .) to merit the sacrifice" she was making of a relationship with a much younger man who was actively courting her and promised her a future. And so began their correspondence.

[Phase 1: Pessoa in Love?] (March–November 1920)

1 March 1920

Ophelia:

You could have shown me your contempt, or at least your supreme indifference, without the see-through masquerade of such a lengthy treatise and without your written "reasons," which are as insincere as they are unconvincing. You could have just told me. This way I understand you no less, but it hurts me more.

It's only natural that you're very fond of the young man who's been chasing you, so why should I hold it against you if you prefer him to me? You're entitled to prefer whom you want and are under no obligation, as I see it, to love me. And there's certainly no need (unless it's for your own amusement) to pretend you do.

Those who really love don't write letters that read like lawyers' petitions. Love doesn't examine things so closely, and it doesn't treat others like defendants on trial.

Why can't you be frank with me? Why must you torment a man who never did any harm to you (or to anybody else) and whose sad and solitary life is already a heavy enough burden to bear, without someone adding to it by giving him false hopes and declaring feigned affections? What do you get out of it besides the dubious pleasure of making fun of me?

I realize that all this is comical, and that the most comical part of it is me.

I myself would think it was funny, if I didn't love you so much, and if I had the time to think of anything besides the suffering you enjoy inflicting on me, although I've done nothing to deserve it except love you, which doesn't seem to me like reason enough. At any rate . . .

Here's the "written document" you requested. The notary Eugénio Silva can validate my signature.

Fernando Pessoa

19 March 1920
at 4 A.M.

My dear darling Baby:

It's almost four in the morning, and I've just given up trying to fall asleep, even though my aching body badly needs rest. This is the third night in a row this has happened, but tonight was one of the worst nights of my life. Luckily for you, darling, you can't imagine what it was like. It wasn't just my sore throat and the idiotic need to spit every two minutes that kept me from sleeping. I was also delirious, though I had no fever, and I felt like I was going mad, I wanted to scream, to moan at the top of my lungs, to do a thousand crazy things. It's not only my physical illness that put me in such a state but the fact I spent all day yesterday fretting over the things that still need to be done before my family arrives.* And to top it off my cousin came by at half past seven with more than a little bad news, which I won't go into now, darling, because fortunately none of it concerns you in the least.

Just my luck to be sick right when there are so many urgent things to do—things that no one but I can do.

See the state of mind I've been in lately, especially during the last two days? And you've no idea, my adorable Baby, how constantly and insanely I've missed you. Your absence always makes me suffer, darling, even when it's just from one day to the next, so think how I must feel after not having seen you for almost three days!

Tell me one thing, love: Why do you sound so depressed in your second letter—the one you sent yesterday by Osório?* I can understand you missing me, just like I miss you, but you sounded so anxious, sad and dejected that it pained me to read your letter and feel how much you're suffering. What happened to you, darling, besides us being separated? Something worse? Why do you speak in such a desperate tone about my love, as if you doubted it, when you have no reason to?

I'm all alone—I really am. The people in this building have treated me very well, but they're not close to me at all. During the day they bring me soup, milk, or medicine, but they don't ever keep me company, which I certainly wouldn't expect. And at this hour of the night, I feel like I'm in a desert. I'm thirsty and have no one to give me a drink. I'm going crazy from this sense of isolation and have no one to soothe me, just by being near, as I try to go to sleep.

I'm cold. I'm going to lie down and pretend to rest. I don't know when I'll mail this letter or if I'll add anything to it.

Ah my love, my doll, my precious Baby, if only you were here! Lots and lots and lots of kisses from your always very own

Fernando

19 March 1920, at 9 A.M.

My dear sweet love:

Writing you the above worked like a magic potion. I went back to bed, not at all expecting to sleep, but I slept for 3 or 4 hours straight—not a lot, but what a world of difference! I feel much better, and, although my throat still aches and is swollen, the fact my general condition has so improved must mean that my sickness is on its way out.

If it goes away quick enough, I may stop briefly by the office, in which case I'll give you this letter myself.

I hope I can make it. There are some urgent matters I could take care of there (without having to go do them in person) but that I can't do anything about here.

So long, sweet angel. Kisses and more kisses for the baby I miss, from your always devoted, always very own

Fernando

22 March 1920

Dear Baby angel:

I don't have much time to write, naughty darling, or even that much to say that I can't explain more clearly tomorrow, face to face, during our pitifully short walk from the Rua do Arsenal* to your sister's place.

I don't want you to be upset. I want you to be happy, the way you are by nature. Will you promise not to get upset, or to try your best not to? You have no reason at all to be upset, I assure you.

Listen, Baby . . . In your votive offerings I want you to ask for something that always seemed unlikely, given my bad luck, but that now seems much more possible. Pray that Mr. Crosse* will win one of the grand prizes—a thousand pounds—that he's competing for. What a difference it would make for us if this happened! In the English newspaper that came today, I saw that he's already up to *one* *pound* (and it was a contest where he wasn't even that witty), which means that anything's possible. He's now *number 12* out of about 20,000 (twenty thousand) contestants. Who knows, he just may one day reach first place. Just think if that were to happen, love, and if it were for one of the grand prizes (a thousand pounds, and not just three hundred, which wouldn't do the trick)! Can you imagine?

I just came from Estrela, where I went to see the 4th floor apartment that's going for 70,000 reals. (What I actually saw, since there's no one on the 4th floor, was the 3rd floor, which has the same layout.) I've decided to make the switch. It's a fantastic place! There's more than enough room for my mother, brothers and sister, the nurse, my aunt, and me too. (But there's more to say about this, which I'll tell you tomorrow.)

Bye, darling. Don't forget about Mr. Crosse! He's very much *our friend* and can be very useful to *us*.

Tons of kisses, big and small, from your always very own

Fernando

5 April 1920

Dear naughty little Baby:

Here I am at home* alone, except for the intellectual who's hanging paper on the walls (as if he could hang it on the floor or ceiling!), and he doesn't count. As promised, I'm going to write my Baby, if only to tell her that she's a very bad girl except in one thing, the art of pretending, and in that she's a master.

By the way—although I'm writing you, *I'm not thinking about you*. I'm thinking about how I miss the days *when I used to hunt pigeons*, which is something you obviously have nothing to do with . . .

We had a nice walk today, don't you think? You were in a good mood, I was in a good mood, and the day was in a good mood. (My friend A. A. Crosse was not in a good mood. But his health is okay— one pound sterling of health for now, which is enough to keep him from catching cold.)

You're probably wondering why my handwriting's so strange. For two reasons. The first is that this paper (all I have at the moment) is extremely smooth, and so my pen glides right over it. The second is that I found, here in the apartment, some splendid Port, a bottle of which I opened, and I've already drunk half. The third reason is that there are only two reasons, and hence no third reason at all. (Álvaro de Campos, Engineer.)

When can we be somewhere together, darling — just the two of us? My mouth feels odd from having gone so long without any kisses . . . Little Baby who sits on my lap! Little Baby who gives me love bites! Little Baby who . . . (and then Baby's bad and hits me . . .). I called you "body of sweet temptations," and that's what you'll always be, but far away from me.

Come here, Baby. Come over to Nininho.* Come into Nininho's arms. Put your tiny mouth against Nininho's mouth . . . Come . . . I'm so lonely, *so lonely for kisses* . . .

If only I could be certain that you *really* miss me. It would at least be some consolation. But you probably think less about me than about that boy who's chasing you, not to mention D. A. F. and the book-keeper of C. D. & C.!* Naughty, naughty, naughty, naughty . . . !!!!

What you need is a good spanking.

So long: I'm going to lay my head down in a bucket, to relax my mind. That's what all great men do, at least all great men who have: 1) a mind, 2) a head, and 3) a bucket in which to stick their head.

A kiss, just one, that lasts as long as the world, from your always very own

Fernando (Nininho)

27 April 1920

My lovely little Baby:

How adorable you looked today in the window of your sister's apartment! You were cheerful, thank goodness, and seemed happy to see me (Álvaro de Campos).

I've been feeling very sad, and also very tired—sad not only because I haven't been able to see you but because of the obstacles that other people have been putting in our path. I'm afraid that the unrelenting, insidious influence of these people—who don't censure you or express outright opposition but who work slowly on your mind—will eventually make you stop liking me. You already seem different to me. You're not the same girl you were in the office. Not that you've even noticed this, but I've noticed, or at least I think I have. God knows I hope I'm wrong . . .

Listen, sweetie: the future all looks hazy to me. I mean, I can't see what's on the horizon, or what will become of us, since you've been yielding more and more to the influence of your family, and you disagree with me in everything. In the office you were sweeter, more gentle, more lovable.

Anyway . . .

Tomorrow I'll go by the Rossio train station* at the same time as today. Will you come to the window?

Always and forever your

Fernando

31 July 1920

Dear Ibis:*

Excuse this shoddy paper, but it's all I could find in my briefcase, and they don't have any stationery here at the Café Arcada. You don't mind, do you?

I just received your letter with the cute postcard.

It was a funny coincidence, wasn't it?, that I and my sister were downtown yesterday at the same time you were. What wasn't funny is that you disappeared, in spite of the signs I made you. I was just dropping off my sister at the Avenida Palace Hotel, so she could buy some things and take a walk with the mother and sister of the Belgian fellow who's staying there. I came back out almost immediately, and expected to find you waiting there, so that we could talk. But no, you had to rush to your sister's place!

What's worse is that, when I came out of the hotel, I saw your sister's window outfitted like a theater box (with extra chairs) to enjoy the show of me walking by! Realizing this, I naturally went on my way as if no one were there. The day I decide to play the clown (which my character isn't really suited for), I'll offer my services directly to the circus. Just what I needed right now—to serve as comic entertainment for your family!

If you couldn't avoid being at the window with 148 people, you should have avoided the window. Seeing as you didn't feel like waiting for me or talking to me, you might at least have had the courtesy—since you couldn't appear *alone* at the window—of *not appearing*.

Why should I have to explain these things? If your heart (presuming that this creature exists) or your intuition can't instinctively teach them to you, then I can't very well be your teacher.

When you say that your most fervent wish is for me to marry you, you shouldn't forget to add that I would also have to marry your sister, your brother-in-law, your nephew, and who knows how many of your sister's clients.

Always your very own

Fernando

I forgot, as I wrote this, that you're in the habit of showing my letters to everyone. If I'd remembered, I would have toned it down, I assure you. But it's too late, and it doesn't matter. Nothing matters.

F.

15 October 1920

Little Baby,

You have thousands, even millions, of good reasons for being irked, offended, and angry with me. But I'm not the one to blame. It's Fate that has condemned my brain—if not definitively, then at least to a condition calling for serious treatment, which I'm not so sure I can get.

I plan (without yet resorting to the celebrated May 11th decree)* to enter a clinic next month, where I'm hoping for a treatment that will help me fend off the black wave that's falling over my mind. I don't know what the result of all this will be—I mean, I can't imagine what it could be.

Don't wait for me. If I come to see you, it will be in the morning, when you're on your way to the office in Poço Novo.

Don't worry.

What happened, you ask? I got switched with Álvaro de Campos!

Always your

Fernando

29 November 1920

Dear Ophelia:

Thank you for your letter. It made me feel both sad and relieved. Sad, because these things always bring sadness. Relieved, because this really is the only solution—to stop prolonging a situation that's no longer justified by love, whether on your side or mine. For my own part there remains an abiding esteem and a steadfast friendship. You won't deny me as much, will you?

Neither you nor I are to blame for what has happened. Only Fate might be blamed, were Fate a person to whom blame could be imputed.

Time, which grays hair and wrinkles faces, also withers violent affections, and much more quickly. Most people, because they're stupid, don't even notice this, and they imagine they still love because they got used to being in love. If this weren't so, there would be no happy people in the world. Superior creatures cannot enjoy this illusion, however, because they can't believe love will endure, and when they see it's over, they don't kid themselves by taking what it left—esteem, or gratitude—for love itself.

These things cause suffering, but the suffering passes. If life, which is everything, finally passes, then won't love and sorrow also pass, along with all the other things that are only parts of life?

You're unfair to me in your letter, but I understand and forgive. You no doubt wrote it with anger and perhaps even bitterness, but most people in your case—men or women—would write things that are even less fair, and in a harsher tone. But you have a wonderful disposition, Ophelia, and not even your anger is capable of malice. If, when you marry, you're not as happy as you deserve, it will be through no fault of your own.

As for me . . .

My love has passed. But I still feel a steadfast affection for you, and you can be sure that I'll never, never forget your delightful figure, your girlish ways, your tenderness, your goodness, and your lovable nature. It's possible that I fooled myself and that these qualities I attribute to you were my own illusion, but I don't think so, and even if they were, it did no harm to have seen them in you.

I don't know what you might like to have back—whether your letters or other things. I'd prefer not to give back anything, and to keep your letters as the living memory of a past that died (the way all pasts do), as something poignant in a life like mine which, as it advances in years, advances in disillusion and unhappiness.

Please don't be like ordinary people, who always act petty and mean. Don't turn your head when I pass by, and don't harbor a grudge in your remembrance of me. Let us be like lifelong friends who loved each other a bit when they were children, only to pursue other affections and other paths as adults, but who nevertheless retain, in some corner of the heart, the vivid memory of their old and useless love.

These "other affections" and "other paths" concern you, Ophelia, and not me. My destiny belongs to another Law, whose existence you're not even aware of, and it is ever more the slave of Masters who do not relent and do not forgive.

You don't need to understand this. It's enough that you hold me in your memory with affection, as I will steadfastly hold you in mine.

Fernando

*This letter and the unusually sarcastic reply written four days later by
Ophelia Queiroz were followed by almost nine years of silence. In September of 1929, Pessoa chanced to give a photograph of himself to a poet
and friend, Carlos Queiroz, who was Ophelia's nephew. When Ophelia
saw the photo, which showed Pessoa drinking wine at Abel's, his favorite
bar, she asked her nephew to request another copy. Pessoa supplied one,
and Ophelia wrote a letter of thanks, stating at the end that she would be
happy to hear from him, if he cared to write. Thus ensued phase two of
the relationship. Pessoa, however, very soon felt ill at ease and gave the
appearance of being mentally disturbed.*

[Phase 2: Pessoa Insane?] (September–October 1929)

11 September 1929

Dear Ophelia,

The heart I felt in your letter touched me, though I don't know
why you should thank me for the photograph of a scoundrel, even if
the scoundrel is the twin brother I don't have. Does a drunken
shadow hold a place, after all, in your memories?

Your letter reached my exile—which is I myself—like joy from
the homeland, and so it's I who should thank you, dear girl.

And let me take this opportunity to apologize for three things,
which are the same thing and which weren't my fault. Three times I
ran across you without greeting you, because I couldn't tell it was you,
or rather, I realized it too late. The first time was one night on the Rua
do Ouro, a long time ago. You were with a young man I assumed was
your fiancé, or boyfriend, though I don't know if he really was what he
had every right to be. The other two times were recent, when we were
both riding the streetcar that goes to Estrela. One of those times I only
saw you from out of the corner of my eye, which for someone condemned to wearing glasses is almost like not seeing.

One more thing . . . No, nothing, sweet lips . . .

Fernando

ABEL's, 18 September 1929

Petition in 30 lines*

Fernando Pessoa, single, of legal age, abbreviated, residing where it please God he reside, in the company of various and sundry spiders, flies, mosquitoes and other things useful for promoting a homey environment and good sleep, having been informed—even if only by telephone—that he may be treated (10 *lines*) like a human being beginning on a date yet to be established and that said treatment of him as a human will be constituted not by a kiss but by the mere promise of one, to be postponed until such time as he, Fernando Pessoa, prove that he (1) is 8 months old, (2) is handsome, (3) exists, (4) is pleasing to the entity responsible for dispensing (20 *lines*) the merchandise, and (5) will not in the meantime commit suicide as he naturally should, does hereby petition—in order to reassure the person responsible for dispensing the merchandise—a certificate testifying that he (1) is not 8 months old, (2) looks grotesque, (3) doesn't even exist, (4) is despised (30 *lines*) by the dispensing entity, and (5) has killed himself.

End of the 30 lines.

Here one should write "In hope that this request be favorably considered," but there is no hope for

Fernando

24 September 1929

So tell me, my little Wasp (who's not really mine, though you are a wasp), what words you want to hear from a creature whose mind took a spill somewhere on the Rua do Ouro, whose wits— along with the rest of him—got run over by a truck as it turned the corner onto the Rua de São Nicolau.

Does my (my?) little Wasp really like me? Why this odd taste for older people? You complain in your letter about having to put up with some aunts who are eighty-odd and fifty-odd years old and aren't really aunts,* but then how do you expect to put up with a creature who's almost the same age and can never be an aunt, since this profession, to the best of my knowledge, is only open to women? An aunt, of course, needs to be two women or more. So far I've only managed to be an uncle, and just of my niece, who, funnily enough, calls me "Uncle Fenando," due to (1) the aforementioned fact that I'm her uncle, (2) the fact I'm called (remember?) Fernando, and (3) the fact she can't say the letter R.

Since you say that you don't want to see me and that it's hard for you to want not to want to see me, so that you'd rather I phone you, because phoning means not being present, and write you, because writing is to be at a distance, I've already phoned you, Wasp that's not mine, and now I am writing you, or rather, have written you, because I'll stop here.

I'm going out and will take the letter in my black briefcase — do you hear?

I'd like to go, simultaneously, to India and Pombal.* Strange combination, isn't it? But it's just one leg of the journey.

Do you remember this geography, you waspy Wasp?

Fernando

ABEL's, 25 September 1929

Dear Miss Ophelia Queiroz:

An abject and sorry individual named Fernando Pessoa, my dear and special friend, has asked me to communicate to you — since his mental state prevents him from communicating anything, even to a split pea (a notable example of obedience and discipline) — that you are hereby prohibited from:

(1) losing weight,*
(2) eating too little,

(3) not sleeping,
(4) having a fever,
(5) thinking of the individual in question.

As the sincere and close friend of the good-for-nothing whose message I have (reluctantly) undertaken to communicate, my own advice to you is to take whatever mental image you may have formed of the individual whose mention is sullying this reasonably white paper and to throw it down the toilet, since it is materially impossible for such a Fate to befall the pseudohuman entity who would justly deserve it, if there were justice in the world.

Respectfully yours,

Álvaro de Campos
Naval Engineer

26 September 1929

Dear little Ophelia:

I'm not sure you like me, and that's why I'm writing you.

Since you said you'd avoid seeing me tomorrow until between quarter after five and five thirty at the streetcar stop that's not that one there, I'll be there waiting.

But since the engineer Álvaro de Campos will be with me for most of tomorrow, I'm not sure I can avoid his company—which at any rate is pleasant—during the ride to Janelas Verdes.

This engineer, who's an old friend, has something to say to you. He refuses to give me any details, but I hope and trust that, in your presence, he'll see fit to tell me, or tell you, or tell us, what it's all about.

Until then I'll remain silent, respectful, and even expectant.

Till tomorrow, sweet lips,

Fernando

Sunday, 29 September 1929

Dear little Ophelia,

So that you won't say I haven't written you, since in fact I
haven't, I'm writing you. It won't be just a line, like I said, but it
won't be many lines. I'm sick, mainly due to all of yesterday's worries
and troubles. If you don't want to believe I'm sick, then you obviously won't believe it. But please don't tell me you don't believe it.
It's bad enough to be sick without you doubting whether it's true, or
asking me to account for my health as if I were able to, or as if I were
obliged to account to anyone about anything.

What I said about going to Cascais (which means Cascais, Sintra,
Caxias or anywhere else outside Lisbon but not too far) is absolutely
true: true, at least, in intent. I've reached that age when a man comes
into full possession of his talents and his mind is at the height of its
powers. And so it's time for me to consolidate my literary work, finishing up certain things, compiling others, and writing some things that
are still in my head. To do all this I need peace and quiet, and relative
isolation. Unfortunately I can't quit the offices where I work (for the
obvious reason that I have no other income), but by setting aside two
days a week (Wednesdays and Saturdays) for my office duties, I can
have the other five days for myself. There you have the story of Cascais.

My life's entire future depends on whether I can do this, and
soon, for my life revolves around my literary work, however good or
bad it may be. Everything else in life is of secondary interest to me.
Some things I would naturally enjoy having, while others leave me
completely indifferent. Those who know and deal with me have to
understand that that's how I am, and that to want me to have the
feelings (which I fully respect) of an ordinary person is like wanting me
to have blue eyes and blond hair. And to treat me as if I were someone
else isn't the best way to hold on to my affection. It would be better to
go and find that "someone else" for whom such treatment is suitable.

I'm very, very fond of you, Ophelia. I adore your character and
temperament. If I marry, it will only be with you. It remains to be
seen whether marriage and home (or whatever one wants to call it)

are compatible with my life of thought. I doubt it. For now I want to organize, without delay, this life of thought and my literary work. If I can't organize it, then I won't even think of thinking about marriage. And if I organize it in such a way that marriage would be a hindrance, then I'm sure not to marry. But I suspect this won't be the case. The future, and I mean the near future, will tell.

There you have it, and it happens to be the truth.

So long, Ophelia. Sleep and eat, and don't lose any weight.

Your very devoted

Fernando

9 October 1929

Terrible Baby:

I like your letters, which are sweet, and I like you, because you're sweet too. And you're candy, and you're a wasp, and you're honey, which comes from bees and not wasps, and everything's just fine, and Baby should always write me, even when I don't, which is always, and I'm sad, and I'm crazy, and no one likes me, and why should they, and that's exactly right, and everything goes back to the beginning, and I think I'll call you today, and I'd like to kiss you precisely and voraciously on the lips, and to eat your lips and whatever little kisses you're hiding there, and to lean on your shoulder and slide into the softness of your little doves, and to beg your pardon, and the pardon to be make-believe, and to do it over and over and period until I start again, and why do you like a scoundrel and a troll and a fat slob with a face like a gas meter and the expression of someone who's not there but in the toilet next door, and indeed, and finally, and I'm going to stop because I'm insane, and I always have been, it's from birth, which is to say ever since I was born, and I wish Baby were my doll so I could do like a child, taking off her clothes, and I've reached the end of the page, and this doesn't seem like it could be written by a human being, but it was written by me.

Fernando

9 October 1929

Beastly Baby,
       Forgive me for troubling you. The spring of the rattletrap in my
head finally snapped, and my mind, which had already ceased to
exist, went tr-tr-r-r-r- . . .
       I'm writing you after having just called, and of course I'll call
you again, if it doesn't frazzle your nerves, and of course it won't be
at just any time but at the time when I call.
       Do you like me because I'm me or because I'm not? Or do you
dislike me even without me or not? Or what?
       All these sentences and ways of saying nothing are signs that the
ex-Ibis, the extinct Ibis, the Ibis that's kaput and not even happily
bonkers, is going to the nuthouse at Telhal or Rilhafolles, and there's
a big party to celebrate his glorious absence.
       I need more than ever to go to Cascais—to the Mouth of Hell*
but *with teeth*, head first, that's all, folks, and presto, no more Ibis.
That's just what this animal-bird deserves—to grind its weird head in
the ground.
       But if Baby would just give him a kiss, then Ibis could stand life
for a little longer. Well? There goes the snapped spring r-r-r-r-r-r-r-r-
r-r-r-r-r-r-r-r—for good.
                                                                          Fernando

*Pessoa continued to call Ophelia and to meet her in the fleeting circum-
stances of a streetcar ride or a walk from one part of downtown Lisbon to
another, but he wrote no more real letters. In mid-December he sent a note
with a baby picture that he had promised Ophelia, and in mid-January
of 1930 another note, to accompany a humorous, nonsensical poem.
Ophelia kept writing regularly for over another year, expressing occasional
satisfaction after her Nininho (as she almost always called Fernando in
her letters) had phoned her or they had seen each other, but these times
were increasingly rare. Obsessed by Fernando, Ophelia would bitterly but
cautiously reproach him for not writing, she occasionally indulged in*

gushy descriptions of the married life she fantasized for them, and she frequently blamed the impossibility of that fantasy on Álvaro de Campos, apparently accepting Pessoa's own shorthand explanation of why he kept so resolutely to himself. In the spring of 1931 Ophelia quit the stream of letters, but she continued to send birthday greetings to Pessoa every June 13, usually by telegram, and he would send a telegram to her on June 14, which was her birthday. In October of 1935, Pessoa wrote his last Álvaro de Campos poem, whose first five stanzas read:

> All love letters are
> Ridiculous.
> They wouldn't be love letters if they weren't
> Ridiculous.
>
> In my time I also wrote love letters
> Equally, inevitably
> Ridiculous.
>
> Love letters, if there's love,
> Must be
> Ridiculous.
>
> But in fact
> Only those who've never written
> Love letters
> Are
> Ridiculous.
>
> If only I could go back
> To when I wrote love letters
> Without thinking how
> Ridiculous.

Pessoa died one month later, from liver disease or a pancreas inflammation brought on by his steep consumption of alcohol. Ophelia Queiroz, who eventually married, died in 1991.

NEOPAGANISM

from The Return of the Gods

António Mora

Conceived early on as a "philosophical follower" of Alberto Caeiro (see Pessoa's preface to Aspects *at the front of this volume), Dr. António Mora was part of the inner circle of heteronyms that met in an imaginary city called Lisbon to read and discuss each other's work and to exchange ideas. This often led to lively debates, several of which are recorded in Álvaro de Campos's* Notes for the Memory of My Master Caeiro, *but the philosophical Mora usually preferred just to listen. He was the group's theoretician, responsible for setting out the doctrines of so-called Neopaganism, the religious system or spirit embedded in the poetry of Reis (the system) and Caeiro (the spirit), and to a much lesser extent that of Campos, whose main religion was his feelings.*

Mora's ambitious works-in-progress included The Foundations of Paganism, Prolegomena to a Reformation of Paganism, *and, most important,* The Return of the Gods. *None of his writings—mostly datable to the second half of the 1910s and the early 1920s—was published in Pessoa's lifetime, and they are often not labeled, which makes it difficult to know which of his projected works they belong to. Ricardo Reis's extensive writings on Neopaganism only multiply the confusion, for there are many unsigned passages on the subject that could as easily be credited to Mora as to Reis. Moreover, some passages signed by Reis are labeled* Return of the Gods, *which suggests that Pessoa at one point considered making him, rather than Mora, the reputed author of this treatise. Or did he think of making them coauthors? And yet Pessoa draws distinctions between the viewpoints of these two heteronyms, as we can see in the third of the four passages that follow.*

Without yet going into the metaphysical foundations of religion in general or of any religion in particular but accepting the sociological finding that humanity needs religious expression to discipline and organize societies, we may affirm, as a corollary, that the best religion for disciplining and organizing societies will be the one that is closest to Nature. Such a religion, because it is closest to Nature, is the one that can act most directly on men, the one that can most effectively induce them not to stray from the basic natural laws that rule human (and indeed all) life, and the one that—since it does not interfere with other human activities—can most stimulate man's mental and social activity to develop fully and freely.

We can easily show, based on three simple observations, that the pagan religion is the most natural of all.

The pagan religion is, in the first place, polytheistic, even as nature is plural. Nature does not naturally appear to us as an ensemble but as a multiplicity of many different things. We cannot positively affirm, without the intervention of reason or the intelligence in our direct experience, that an ensemble called the Universe actually exists or that there is a unity, a united whole, identifiable as "nature." Reality, when it first appears to us, is multiple. By referring all received sensations to our individual consciousness, we impose a false unity (false to our experience) on the original multiplicity of things. Now religion, since it comes to us as an outer reality, should agree with the fundamental characteristic of outer reality. That characteristic is the multiplicity of things. The first distinctive characteristic of a natural religion is, therefore, the multiplicity of gods.

The pagan religion is, in the second place, human. The acts of pagan gods are the acts of magnified humans; they are of the same order but on a larger, divine scale. The gods differ from humanity not by rejecting it but by surpassing it, like demigods. For the pagan, the divine nature is not antihuman as well as superhuman; it is merely superhuman. And so the pagan religion agrees not only with the nature of the outer world but also with the nature of humanity.

Finally, the pagan religion is political, meaning that it forms part of the life of a city or state, without aspiring to be universal. It does not impose itself on other cultures but seeks, instead, to receive from them. It agrees, therefore, with the original principle of civilization as the synthesis, in one nation, of all possible influences from all other nations — a principle violated only by the political provincialism of rigidly nationalist governments and by the decadence embodied in imperialistic ones. Never has there been a strong, conservative nation, nor a healthy nation that was imperialistic. It is those who cannot change that try to impose themselves. It is those who cannot receive that insist on giving. But those who cannot change and those who cannot receive have in fact stagnated.

Thus the pagan religion is in harmony with the three natural spheres of human experience: with the essence of nature as it comes to us; with the essence of humanity itself; and with the essence of human nature in its social progress, or, put more simply, with the essence of civilized human nature, or, simpler still, with the essence of civilization.

Humanitarianism is the last bulwark of the Christian creed. It contains just the roots of Christism,* divested already of its trunk and leaves. But the Christian disease is there in all its malignancy.

Once criticism and countercriticism have undermined the foundations of religion (as they have indeed already done) and those of science (as they are still doing), then a violent mystical revival is bound to occur, for the human spirit is only superficially intellectual and superficially individual. Deep down the human spirit is social.

Religion is essentially a crude form of the feeling of beauty. All art is no more than a religious ritual.

The profound saying of Goethe—that a man can do without religion if, and only if, he has science and art—basically means just this: let those who are incapable of a higher art have a lower art. (Or would it be more correct to say that religion is the rudimentary basis for art, science, and morality?) It's as absurd to expect common people to give up religion as it is to expect them to stop enjoying the theater, since one and the other are art's rudimentary forms. Art is unsocial; religion is the social form it assumes.

. . .

Only now can we fully understand what Voltaire meant when he said that, if there's life on other planets, then the earth is the Universe's insane asylum. We are indeed an insane asylum, whether or not the other planets are inhabited. Our life has lost all sense of what's normal, and where there's health, it's just a remission of our illness.

Our life is a chronic illness, a feverish anemia. Our fate is that of not dying, so well have we adapted to our perpetually moribund condition.

What relationship can an age like this one have with a spiritual heir to the race of constructors, with a soul inspired by paganism's glorious truths? None, except one of instinctive rejection and automatic scorn. We, the only dissenters from decadence, are thus forced to assume an attitude that, by its nature, is likewise decadent. An attitude of indifference is a decadent attitude, and our inability to adapt to the current milieu forces us to just such an attitude. We don't adapt, because healthy people cannot adapt to a sick milieu, and since we don't adapt, it is we who are sick. This is the paradox in which those of us who are pagans live. We have no hope and no cure.

I accept that this must be our attitude, but I don't accept Ricardo Reis's way of accepting it. Yes, we should be indifferent toward an age that wants nothing to do with us and about which we can do nothing. But we should not celebrate this indifference as if it were a good thing in itself, which is what Ricardo Reis does. In this respect Reis, far from being unaffected by the trends of this age, clearly embodies one of them—the decadent trend. His indifference is already an adaptation to the current milieu. It is already a concession.

We are not really neopagans, or new pagans. Neopagan, or new pagan, is a nonsensical term. Paganism is the one religion that springs directly from nature, that's born from the earth, from attributing to each object its true reality. Being quintessentially natural, it can appear and disappear, but not change in quality. The term "neopagan" makes no more sense than "neorock" or "neoflower." Paganism appears when the human species is healthy, and disappears when it is sick. It can wither, as a flower withers, and die, as a plant dies. But it cannot assume a different form, nor does it have more than one basic form.

That rebellious Christians such as Pater and Swinburne called themselves neopagans when there was nothing pagan about them except the desire to be pagan is excusable, since there's a certain logic in applying an impossible name to an absurdity. But we, who are pagans, cannot use a name that suggests that we are somehow "modern" about it, or that we came to "reform" or "reconstruct" the paganism of the Greeks. We came to be pagans. Paganism was reborn in us. But the paganism that was reborn in us is the same paganism there always was: submission to the gods, and justice on Earth for its own sake.

A scholar of paganism is not a pagan. And a pagan is not a humanist: he's human. What a pagan most appreciates in Christism is the common people's faith in miracles and saints, rituals and celebrations. It is the "rejected" part of Christism that he would most readily accept, if he would accept anything Christian. Any "modern paganism" or "neopaganism" that can understand the mystic poets but not the feast days of saints has nothing in common with paganism, because the pagan willingly admits a religious procession but turns his back on the mysticism of St. Theresa of Ávila. The Christian interpretation of the world disgusts him, but a celebration at church with candles, flowers, songs, and then a festival—he sees these as good things, even if they're part of something bad, for these things are truly human, and are the pagan interpretation of Christianity.

The pagan sympathizes with Christian superstition, because the man who isn't superstitious isn't a man, but he feels no sympathy for humanitarianism, since the humanitarian isn't human.

For the pagan each thing has its nymph, or genius. Each thing is a captive nymph, or a dryad caught by our gaze; that's why everything, for him, has an astonishing immediate reality, and he feels fellowship with each thing when he sees it, and friendship when he touches it.

The man who sees in each object some other object than what's there cannot see, love, or feel that object. Whoever values something because it was created by "God" values it not for what it is but for what it recalls. His eyes behold the object, but his thoughts lie elsewhere.

The pantheist, who values each object for its participation in the *whole*, likewise sees one thing in order to think about another, likewise looks in order not to see. He doesn't think of the object, but of its continuity with the rest of the world. How can a thing be loved by someone who loves it because of a principle that's outside it? The first and last rule of love is that the beloved object should be loved for what it is and not for something else, loved for being the object of love and not because there's a "reason" to love it.

The pure materialist or rationalist, for whom each thing is marvelous because of the work "Nature" put into it and because of its latent, throbbing energy, the planetary system that's in each of its atoms and that makes it live—this man likewise does not love or see the thing, he likewise looks at one thing while thinking of something else, namely its composition. When he beholds an object, he meditates on its decomposition. That is why no materialist ever made art; no materialist or rationalist ever looked at the world. Between him and the world the mysticism of science dropped its veil, the microscope, and he tripped in reality as if into a deep well. For him each thing, instead of being appreciated as a person of earth, is a screen through which he atomistically peers, just as for the pantheist it is a screen or window for perceiving the Whole, and for the creationist a screen through which to see God. When the contemplation is intense, the screen is forgotten. Who cares about the window through which he intently looked? For mystical Christians, for pantheistic dreamers, for materialists and men of "reason," the world is merely their thoughts. The Christian error of substituting man for nature is the disease that has made all of them decrepit from birth.

from Preface to the Complete Poems of Alberto Caeiro

Ricardo Reis

Ricardo Reis, like fellow heteronym Álvaro de Campos, was an avid writer of prose as well as of poetry, and one of his favorite prose pursuits was to find fault with his colleague. This was not hard to do, since the two were temperamental opposites. Classically minded Reis took Campos to task for being formally undisciplined in his poetry, and sensation-driven Campos counterattacked by saying that Reis hid his true self, including his sexuality (which was either bi or homo), behind his complex syntax. The one thing they agreed on was the sublime genius of Alberto Caeiro, for whom Campos wrote his anecdotal Notes for the Memory of My Master Caeiro, *while Reis — in a more theoretical and analytical mode — wrote a monumental, though fragmentary, preface to Caeiro's poetry. Besides eulogizing Caeiro and critically appraising his work, Reis's preface expounds on the principles of paganism and makes an ardent appeal for its modern-day reconstruction. The four fragments that follow are concerned almost entirely with this latter aspect, though they keep referring to Caeiro, who was for Reis — as for António Mora — the perfect embodiment of paganism.*

The work of Caeiro represents the total reconstruction of paganism in its absolute essence, such as could never have been achieved even by the Greeks or Romans, who lived under paganism and hence didn't think about it. But his work and his paganism were not thought out, nor were they felt: they came from that part of us that runs even deeper than feeling or reason. To say more would be to enter into useless explanations; to affirm less would be to lie. Every work speaks for itself, with its own particular voice and in that language by which it mentally took shape; whoever doesn't understand cannot understand, and to explain it to him is like enunciating words to try to make someone understand a language he doesn't speak.

With no knowledge of life, scant knowledge of literature, and virtually no culture or human fellowship, Caeiro produced his work by way of a deep and imperceptible progression, like the one that guides the logical development of civilizations, via the unconscious consciousness of humans. It was a progression in his feelings, or in the way he felt his feelings, and an evolution in the thoughts born out of those progressive feelings. Through a superhuman intuition, resembling those on which new religions are founded for eternity but without being religious itself, since it rejects all religions and all metaphysics for the simple reason that they reject the sun and the rain, this man discovered the world without thinking about it, and created a concept of the universe that doesn't consist of an interpretation.

. . .

When I once had occasion, almost four years ago in Lisbon, to show Alberto Caeiro what principles his work naturally led to, he denied that it led to those principles. For Caeiro, as an absolute objectivist, even the pagan gods were a deformation of paganism. In his abstract objectivism there was no place for the gods. He understood all too well that they were made in the image and likeness of material things, and for him that was enough to make them worthless.

I see things in a different light. The Greek gods represent the abstract conceptualization of materializing objectivism. We cannot live without abstract ideas, since without them we cannot think, but whatever reality we attribute to those ideas should have its origin in the same matter from where we extracted them. So it is with the gods. Although abstract ideas have no true reality, they do have a human reality, valid only in the place that the human species occupies in the world. The gods belong to the category of abstractions by virtue of their relationship to reality, but they do not belong to that category as pure abstractions, because they aren't pure abstractions. Just as abstract ideas help us to live among things, the gods help us to live among men. The gods are thus real and unreal at the same time. They are unreal because they aren't realities, but they are real as materialized abstractions. A materialized abstraction becomes pragmatically real; an unmaterialized abstraction isn't even real in this limited sense. Plato, when he made ideas into abstract persons, followed the old pagan process for creating gods, but he placed his gods too far out of reach. An idea becomes a God only when it is brought back to materiality. It then becomes a force of Nature. That's what a God is. Whether that's a reality, I don't know. Personally I believe in the existence of the gods; I believe in their infinite number and in the possibility of man ascending to god. . . . . .

The creator of civilization is a force of Nature and therefore a god, or a demigod.

Alberto Caeiro is more pagan than paganism, for he is more conscious of paganism in its essence than any other pagan writer. How can a pagan be a pagan, if he conceives his mental and spiritual attitude in opposition to a different system of sensibility, such as Christianity? And when the conflict broke out between paganism and Christianity, with the latter winning out, the torpid and decadent mentality of the Roman people was already basically Christian and not pagan at all. We can see this in Julian's attempt to react against Christianity. This emperor sincerely wanted to reestablish paganism, at a time when its spirit—alas for Julian!—no longer existed, and the cult of the gods that survived was marked by a superstitiousness more typical of Christism than of any species of paganism. Julian's very ideas confirm the impossibility of reconstructing paganism in that day and age. Julian was a Mithraist,* which nowadays would make him a theosophist or an occultist. He based his reconstruction of paganism on a chimerical fusion of it with oriental elements that the craze for mysticism had incorporated into the spirit of the age. And so it failed, for paganism had already died, the way all things die, except for the Gods and their inscrutable, tormenting science.

. . .

. . .

For modern pagans, as exiles in the midst of an enemy civilization, the only feasible course is to embrace one of the last two schools of pagan thought: Stoicism or Epicureanism. Alberto Caeiro embraced neither, for he was Absolute Paganism, without further implications or ramifications. By contrast I (if I may speak about myself) have chosen to be both an Epicurean and a Stoic, convinced as I am of the uselessness of every action in a world where action has gone awry, and of every thought in a world that has forgotten how to think.

It may seem we're no more than degenerate sons of Christian civilization, indifferent because we're sick or out of sorts, but the truth is quite different. A mysterious fate has displaced us. As if we were engineers born in the African hinterlands, we have capacities that we're unable to develop, the outlines of a destiny that we're unable to complete. Our spirit is far removed from the hardened, centuries-old lie of humanitarian monotheism that characterizes Christianity. We can only loathe this civilization so false it has no slaves, so imperfect it must subordinate the intelligence to emotions; and the more it seems to retreat from its religious disease, the more it inclines toward it, for the more it follows after those humanitarian deliriums that typify the slave mentality or, alternatively, it hardens into the absurd rigidity of that discipline so beloved of the Germans, an exaggerated and false paganism — which only goes to show how our civilized mentality has lost its capacity for equilibrium, moderation, and reason.

But who is this "we" in whose name I speak? The only people I can think of are myself, the late Alberto Caeiro, and two others from among everyone I know. But even if it were just me, it wouldn't matter. If it were a thousand people, I would feel no differently. Those whom the gods one day allowed to see the truth of things in their irreducible simplicity need only clear-mindedness and a staunch heart, for they can never go back to delighting in the saturnalias of humanitarianism and modern life.

Everything else lies in that point of light we call the Shadows, that vast Point prior to the Gods where—in accord with the absolute mortality of our souls—our ephemeral lives uselessly tend, uselessly arrive, and uselessly remain forever.

PORTUGAL AND THE
FIFTH EMPIRE

While Pessoa is best known for his directly literary output, he also wrote voluminously on politics, sociology, and religion—disciplines that to his "neopagan" way of thinking were not readily separable. Pessoa's politics, as far as they can be reduced to specific views on government policy, look rather conservative, but his political theories were too idealistic to be of much practical value. As a self-styled "mystical nationalist," he dreamed of a post-Catholic Portugal whose society would be modeled after ancient Greece, where religion, politics, and culture were still intimately linked. The logical first step for arriving at that utopia was—in his view—to clear away not only the Catholicism that was stultifying Portugal but also the nation's ineffectual political and economic systems, which the birth of the Republic in 1910 did little to invigorate, and so Pessoa was inclined to support the military coups of 1917 and 1926, and he was initially sympathetic to the capable finance minister named Salazar, who began to consolidate his grip on the government in the late 1920s. Seeing dictatorship as a perhaps useful, or necessary, stopgap measure to lift the country out of the doldrums and to prepare it for a new kind of national consciousness, Pessoa wrote and published, in 1928, a pamphlet titled Interregnum: Defense and Justification of Military Dictatorship in Portugal. But by the time Salazar became firmly entrenched, in 1932, Pessoa was disenchanted, and in an autobiographical sketch drawn up in 1935 he renounced his Interregnum, stating that it should be considered "nonexistent." Pessoa had apparently become convinced that idealism does not usually make for good politics, for in the same brief sketch of his life and works, in a paragraph labeled "Political Ideology," he wrote: "Believes that a monarchy would be the most appropriate system for an organically imperial nation such as Portugal. Believes, at the same time, that monarchy is not at all feasible in Portugal, so that if there were a referendum to choose between regimes, he would reluctantly vote for the Republic. English-style conservative, meaning that within his conservatism he is a liberal, and utterly antireactionary." And he summed up his brand of patriotism in the words "Everything for Humanity; nothing against the Nation"—an obvious gibe at Salazar's famous "Nothing against the Nation; everything for the Nation."

Pessoa's ambitious hope for the future of his country was nothing less than its intellectual and cultural primacy among nations, and the basis for that hope was the preeminence achieved by the Portuguese some centuries earlier as the world's leading navigators of unknown seas and discoverers of new lands. If tiny Portugal, against all odds, had forged the world's greatest maritime empire, then why couldn't it—against similar odds—forge the world's greatest literature? Pessoa was betting it could, and he enlisted not only history but Portuguese mythology to support his thesis.

Portuguese mythology was born when its history derailed, in 1578, the year that set off one of the most precipitous national downfalls in modern European history. After its armed forces were killed and captured almost to a man in a harebrained expedition to Morocco, once-proud Portugal teetered this way and that until, two years later, it fell under Spanish rule as into a mother's lap. The name of Sebastião, the ingenuous king who had led the Portuguese troops to their certain slaughter, perhaps deserved to be forgotten, but quite the opposite happened. Among the thousands of Portuguese corpses that littered the battlefield, his was not found, and it was said that the king had taken refuge on a desert isle and would return one foggy morning as the Encoberto, the Hidden One, to free Portugal from the Spanish yoke.

Portugal regained its independence from Spain in 1640, but national fortunes continued to flounder, and the wealth that poured in from Brazil in the eighteenth century had scant impact on the widespread poverty, and so the Sebastianist myth lived on, in transfigured forms sustained by new explanations. As late as the mid-twentieth century it was possible, *on a foggy morning, to find men and women along the Portuguese coastline, looking out across the waves for the* Desejado, *the Desired One, their mythical king and savior. But most Sebastianists, such as Pessoa, invested the myth with symbolic meaning, availing themselves of the endlessly interpretable verses penned by Gonçalo Anes Bandarra, a Portuguese cobbler, poet, and prophet from the sixteenth century whose work was publicized by the Jesuit preacher and missionary António Vieira (1608– 97), one of Portugal's greatest writers of the Baroque period. Through numerical puzzles and obscure imagery, Bandarra's versified dreams allegedly predicted not only the return of King Sebastião but also the establishment, in Portugal, of the Fifth Empire, which represented a new twist on a millenary dream—that of Nebuchadnezzar, king of Babylon, recorded in the second chapter of the Book of Daniel. The third text in this section presents a traditional understanding of Daniel's interpretation of Nebuchadnezzar's dream, followed by Pessoa's own "spiritual" scheme, in which cultural rather than military might reigns supreme. Elsewhere in his writings, Pessoa left a different version of this scheme, with the British Empire instead of Europe occupying the fourth slot, but in either case the Fifth Empire was reserved for Portugal and would coincide with the final return of King Sebastião.*

In presaging Portugal's ascendancy merely through its language and literature (where its cultural strength lay, according to Pessoa), the Fifth Empire doctrine presupposed a new era in human consciousness and civilization, in which such a purely "spiritual," immaterial domination would be possible. That era would even be marked by a new kind of love, whose nature Pessoa planned to exemplify in a long poem titled "Anteros,"* after the younger brother of Eros (Cupid for the Romans). The poem never got written, but from prose passages in his archives we know that Pessoa understood Anteros not as the avenger of unrequited love (which is how his mythological function is more commonly perceived) but as an anti-Cupid. Eros, for Pessoa, represented instinctive, sensually motivated love, and Anteros dispassionate, intellectual love—the transcendence of carnal love. This gloss swells with significance when viewed in the light of Pessoa's lifelong inexperience and avowed disinterest in sensual love, coupled with his ultrapersonalized understanding of just when King Sebastião would *return to usher in the Fifth Empire. Taking one of Bandarra's whimsical prophecies—that "the King will return after thirty scissors have gone by"— Pessoa multiplied 31 by 2, added it to 1578, the year King Sebastião went down in battle, and came up with 1640, which is when Sebastião supposedly made his symbolic first return to liberate Portugal from Spanish rule; then, multiplying 31 by 10 and adding it to 1578, Pessoa arrived at what he proposed as the year of the king's Second Coming, 1888, the year of his very own birth. This would seem to indicate that Pessoa's megalomania took the form of a Christ complex, with literature as the latter-day saving grace. Or perhaps he was just pulling the leg of posterity.*

1.

Any Empire not founded on the Spiritual Empire is a walking Death, a ruling Corpse.

The Spiritual Empire can only be achieved, to any useful purpose, in a small nation, where growth of the national ideal won't lead to ambitions of territorial domination, which would undermine what had begun as a psychical imperialism, diverting it from its spiritual destiny. That's what happened to the German nation; it was too large to be able to achieve its supreme destiny as a spiritual imperialist. The contrary happened to us, the Portuguese, when the discoveries led us to attempt a material imperialism, which we didn't have enough people to impose.

By creating our own spiritual civilization, we will subjugate all cultures, for it's impossible to resist the arts and forces of the human spirit, particularly when these are well organized and have souls of the Spirit for their generals.

The goal of every true Empire is to dominate, for the sheer pleasure of dominating. Though it seems absurd, that is the fundamental yearning of every true life, the essence of every vital aspiration.

Let us create an androgynous Imperialism, one that unites the masculine and feminine qualities: an imperialism replete with all the subtleties of female domination and all the forces and constructive urge of male domination. Let us achieve Apollo spiritually.

Not a fusion of Christianity and paganism, as Teixeira de Pascoaes and Guerra Junqueiro* propose, but a casting off of Christianity, a simple and direct, transcendentalized paganism, a transcendental reconstruction of the pagan spirit.

2.

Question: What do you envision for the future of the Portuguese people?
    Pessoa's Answer: The Fifth Empire. The future of Portugal—which I don't envision, but *know*—has already been written, for those who can read it, in the verses of Bandarra and the quatrains of Nostradamus. That future is for us to be everything. Who, if they're Portuguese, can live within the narrow bounds of just one personality, just one nation, just one religion? What true Portuguese can live within the sterile limits of Catholicism when beyond it there are all the Protestant creeds, all the Eastern religions, and all the dead and living paganisms for us to experience, Portuguesely fusing them into Superior Paganism? Let's not leave out a single god! Let's incorporate them all! We conquered the Oceans; now we must conquer the Heavens, leaving Earth for the Others, the Others who are eternally Others from birth, the Europeans who aren't Europeans because they aren't Portuguese. Let's be everything, in every way possible, for there can be no truth where something's lacking! Let's create Superior Paganism, Supreme Polytheism! In the eternal lie of all the gods, the only truth is in all the gods together.

3.

The promise of the Fifth Empire, as we dream and conceive of it in Portugal, does not conform to the traditional understanding of Daniel's interpretation of Nebuchadnezzar's dream.
    In the traditional view, the First Empire is that of Babylon, the Second Empire that of Media-Persia, the Third Empire is the Greek

one, and the Fourth Empire Roman. The Fifth remains forever in doubt, though in this scheme of material empires it could plausibly be understood as the British Empire. That is how the English interpret it, and within this scheme I think their interpretation is valid.

The Portuguese scheme is different. Since it is a spiritual scheme, it begins not with the material empire of Babylon but with the cradle of the civilization in which we live: the spiritual empire of Greece, the origin of what we spiritually are. That being the First Empire, the Second one is the Roman Empire, the Third one the Christian Empire, and the Fourth one Europe—i.e., secular Europe after the Renaissance. In this scheme the Fifth Empire cannot be the British one, for it will be of a different, nonmaterial order. We hope and believe it will be Portuguese.

4.

Question: Do you agree or disagree that an intensive propaganda campaign in newspapers, magazines, and books can raise the Nation's morale by creating a collective mentality that will incline politicians toward a politics of national greatness?

Pessoa's Answer: Only one kind of propaganda can raise the morale of a nation—the creation or renewal of a great national myth, to be disseminated by all possible means. Humanity instinctively hates the truth, for it knows, by that same instinct, that the truth doesn't exist, or isn't attainable. The world is run by lies; whoever wants to arouse or run the world must lie to it deliriously, and the more he's able to lie to himself and to convince himself of the truth of his lie, the more successful he'll be. Fortunately we already have the Sebastianist myth, deeply rooted in the past and in the Portuguese soul. This makes our job easier; instead of creating a myth, we need only renew one. Let's begin by getting drunk on that dream, absorbing it and embodying it completely. Once each of us has done that, acting alone and independently, then the dream will flow spontaneously in all we say and write, and an atmosphere will be created in which everyone else breathes the same dream. Then that extraordinary event will take place in the Nation's soul, giving rise to New Discoveries, the Creation of the New World, the Fifth Empire. King Sebastião will have returned.

5.

What, basically, is Sebastianism? It's a religious movement, built around a legendary national figure.

In symbolic terms King Sebastião is Portugal, which lost its greatness when he disappeared and will recover it only when he returns, and although that return is symbolic, even as Sebastião's life was by some divine and wondrous mystery symbolic, it is not absurd to believe in it.

King Sebastião will return, says the legend, one foggy morning on his white horse, having come from the distant island where he was waiting until the decisive hour. The foggy morning presumably indicates a rebirth clouded by elements of decadence, by remnants of the Night in which the Nation had been living. The white horse is harder to interpret. It could represent Sagittarius, in which case we must discover what that sign of the zodiac refers to—whether it refers, for example, to Spain (whose ruling sign is Sagittarius, according to astrologers), or to the transit of some planet in the house of Sagittarius. The Book of Revelation,* on the other hand, offers another possible interpretation.

The Island is likewise hard to interpret.

6.

To justify its present-day ambition to become a cultural empire, Portugal can point not only to its broken tradition of such an empire (which, though it miscarried, still foreshadowed its future destiny), but also to the fortunate fact that it has never yet had a great literature, just a small and insignificant one, so that everything in this field still needs to be done, which makes it possible to do everything, and to do it right.

"He will bring peace to the whole world," says Bandarra of King Sebastião. Worldwide peace implies a universal brotherhood whose nature we can't foresee but which will surely require a common vehicle of communication—a single language.

What harm is there in preparing to be culturally dominant, even if we're not successful? We won't shed one drop of blood, nor will we stifle our human yearning for domination. We won't fall into the futility of humanitarian universalism, but neither will we fall into the brutality of noncultural nationalism. We will attempt to impose a language rather than physical force. We will not oppress any race of any color, just as in the past we have not generally been oppressive, for although at times we were barbaric, like all empires that conquer, we were less so than others, and we cannot be accused of excluding people of another color from our home or from our table. Thus our very nature prepares us for that universal brotherhood which theosophy predicts and which has long been the secret social doctrine of the Rosicrucians.

Should we fail, we will still have accomplished something: the enrichment of our language. At the very worst, we will at least have improved our writing. We will render immediate service to general culture and civilization; if we do nothing else, we cannot be accused of having sinned.

7.

An imperialism of grammarians? The imperialism of grammarians runs deeper and endures longer than that of generals. An imperialism of poets? Yes, of poets. The phrase sounds ridiculous only to those who defend the old and ridiculous kind of imperialism. The imperialism of poets endures and wins out; that of politicians passes on and is forgotten, unless the poet remembers it in his songs. We say "Cromwell *did*" but "Milton *says*." And in the distant future when there is no more England (for England's characteristics do not include being eternal), Cromwell will be remembered only because Milton mentioned him in a sonnet. The end of England will signify the end of what we may call the work of Cromwell, or the work in which he collaborated. But the poetry of Milton will end only with the end of all civilization or of man's presence on earth, and perhaps even then it won't have ended.

8.

A foggy morning. Morning means the beginning of something new—a new age, a new phase, or the like. The fog indicates that the Desired One will be "hidden" when he comes—that his arrival won't be (or hasn't been) noticed. This is confirmed by his first coming, in 1640. That date marks the beginning of a dynasty, and the coming of King Sebastião was "hidden" by the fog, for while everyone judged—by virtue of his original symbology—that the Hidden One was King João IV,* the Hidden One was actually the abstract fact of Independence, as later became evident. However little we may understand about his Second Coming, in 1888, we know at least that the ancient prophecy has been fulfilled: we know that 1888 is "morning," because it's the beginning of the Reign of the Sun, for which "morning" is the best possible symbol, and now, thirty-seven years later, the fact that no one realizes just what happened on that date is proof of the foggy, hidden character of the Second Coming of King Sebastião.

THE ANARCHIST BANKER

Pessoa's short stories, like his plays, were large in number, written in English as well as Portuguese, mostly fragmentary, and generally at odds with the form as traditionally conceived. Pessoa was an assiduous reader of detective novels, and this shows in the titles of some of his stories— "The Stolen Parchment," "The Case of the Quadratic Equation," "The Disappearance of the Yacht Nothing"—*but he was less concerned with creating intrigue than with expounding unusual ideas or exploring strange paths of logic. He planned to group his stories, which were attributed to various heteronyms, under general titles, such as* Tales of a Madman, Tales of a Reasoner, Metaphysical Stories, Hypotheses, *and* Antitheses. *"The Anarchist Banker" would have been the premier story in this last-named group, had Pessoa ever gotten around to completing and organizing his short fictions. As it was, he finished only a handful of the dozens of stories that he started to write or thought about writing. "The Anarchist Banker," published in 1922, was his longest story, and the one he cared about most. Toward the end of his life he began working on a revised version, and he also (as mentioned earlier) translated a few pages of it into English, in the hope of finding an English publisher.*

This story might be better termed a Socratic dialogue, and Pessoa himself once referred to it as a "dialectical satire." The narrative of actual events could fit into two pages; the other twenty-six are taken up by logical argument. It is a brilliant piece of argumentation, though it relies on a doubtful premise: that we can do nothing to correct inequalities in our natural endowments, which the banker calls the "injustices of Nature." On the other hand, the predicted failure of the Russian Revolution to achieve anything remotely resembling a free society was right on the mark.

Do the banker's views reflect the author's? In part they do, despite Pessoa's disclaimer in his "Preface to Fictions of the Interlude" *(p. 311–13). Pessoa, like the banker, was not sympathetic to workers' movements or to any other form of social mobilization; he was a resolute individualist. But he was also an aristocrat, in his outlook if not in his blood, and he instinctively hated money-driven capitalism, as his essay "American Millionaires" (pp. 198–99) makes clear.*

We had just finished dinner. Across from me my friend—a wealthy banker, businessman, and renowned profiteer—was smoking absent-mindedly. Our conversation had been dwindling and was now quite dead. I tried to revive it with a thought that happened to cross my mind. I looked at him, smiling:

"I just remembered. Someone told me the other day that you used to be an anarchist."

"Used to be, no. I was and *am* an anarchist. My position on that score hasn't changed."

"You an anarchist? Now I've heard everything! In what way are you an anarchist? Only if you've redefined the word. . . ."

"Not at all. I use it in the usual sense."

"You mean you're an anarchist in exactly the same way that the members of workers' associations are anarchists? You mean there's no difference between you and those guys from the unions who like to toss bombs?"

"I didn't say that. Of course there's a difference. But it's not what you think it is. You probably suppose that my social theories aren't the same as theirs."

"Oh, I see. You're an anarchist in theory, but in practice. . . ."

"I'm an anarchist in practice as much as in theory. In fact I'm much more of an anarchist, in terms of practice, than the so-called anarchists you mention. My entire life proves it."

"What?!"

"My entire life proves it. You've never given clear and careful thought to the matter. That's why you think I'm talking nonsense, or else pulling your leg."

"It's just that I don't understand. Unless . . . unless by anarchism you mean that your life is in a certain way corrosive, antisocial."

"No. I've already told you that I use the word anarchism in its usual sense."

"If you say so, but I still don't understand. . . . You mean to tell me there's no difference between your genuinely anarchist theories and what you actually practice in life—in your life as you live it today? You expect me to believe that your life is just like that of other people who call themselves anarchists?"

"Certainly not. All I'm saying is that between my theories and the way I live there's no discrepancy, they're in perfect agreement. You're right that my life isn't like that of the trade unionists and those who toss bombs, but it's their life—not mine—that's at odds with anarchism, against the very ideals they preach. In me, wealthy banker and business-man that I am, and you can even call me a profiteer—in me the theory and practice of anarchism go hand and hand. You compared me to those fools who form unions and toss bombs to show that I'm different from them. And I am different, but the difference is that *they* are anarchists only in theory, whereas I'm an anarchist in theory and practice. They are anarchists and stupid; I'm an intelligent anarchist. I, in other words, am the true anarchist. They—I mean the trade unionists and those who toss bombs (and I used to be one of them until I discovered true anar-chism)—they are anarchism's dross, the milksops of this great libertar-ian doctrine."

"This is unbelievable! It's extraordinary! But how do you recon-cile your life as a banker and businessman with anarchist theories? How reconcile your life if, as you claim, you have the same theories as ordi-nary anarchists? You even claim that the difference between you and them is that you're *more* anarchist than they are—is that right?"

"That's right."

"I can't see how."

"But would you like to see?"

"Of course I would."

He took from his mouth his cigar, which had gone out, and relit it slowly. He stared at the match until the flame expired, gingerly dropped it into the ashtray, lifted his head back up, and said:

"Listen. I was born into a family from this city's working class. As you can well imagine, I inherited neither a good name nor good circumstances. All I had was a naturally clear-thinking mind and a reasonably strong will. These were natural gifts, which my humble birth couldn't take away from me.

"Like almost everyone else in my social class, I was a manual laborer who barely scraped by. I never went hungry, but I came close. And if I had gone hungry, it wouldn't have changed the path that my life took (as I'll now explain) and that made me what I am today.

"I was, in short, a common laborer. Like all the rest, I worked because I had to, and I worked as little as possible. But I was smart. I read things and discussed things whenever I could, and since I was no fool, I came to greatly resent my lot and the social conditions responsible for it. My lot, as I've mentioned, could have been worse than it was, but at the time I felt as if Fate had taken advantage of social conventions to heap all the world's injustices on top of me. I was about twenty years old, or twenty-one at most, and that's when I became an anarchist."

He paused and turned in my direction. Leaning slightly forward, he continued:

"I've always been a basically clear-thinking sort. I felt resentful, rebellious. I tried to understand my feeling. And I became a consciously, logically convinced anarchist—the same convinced anarchist I am today."

"And is the theory you have today the same one you had back then?"

"Absolutely. There's only one genuinely anarchist theory. I have the same theory now as I had when I became an anarchist. As you'll see. . . . I was saying that, since I'm clear thinking by nature, I consciously and logically became an anarchist. And just what is an anarchist? It's someone who rebels against the injustice of people being born *socially* unequal—that's what it boils down to. And this gives rise, as we see time and again, to open revolt against the social conventions that make that inequality possible. At this point I'm focusing on the psychological path—on how it is that someone becomes an anarchist. Then I'll deal with the theoretical aspects. For now, just imagine the resentment of an intelligent person in my circumstances. Looking around the world, what does he see? One man is born the son of a millionaire, instantly protected against the considerable number of adversities that money can fend off or at least mitigate; another is born as a miserable creature into a family where there are already too many mouths to feed. A man who's born a count or a marquis is treated with respect no matter what he does, whereas a man like me has to do everything to a T or he'll be treated like scum. Some, because they're born into good circumstances, can study, travel, and go to school, thereby surpassing (in a certain way) those who are by nature more intelligent. And it's that way in all of life. . . .

"There's nothing we can do about the injustices of Nature. But we can and should fight against the injustices of society and its conventions. I accept—I have no choice but to accept—that a man is superior to me because of the talent, strength, and energy Nature has endowed him with; I don't accept that he's my superior because of qualities that are in no way innate but that he received, by sheer luck, as soon as he left his mother's womb: wealth, social position, favorable circumstances, etc. It was this sort of thing that I deeply resented and that gave rise to my anarchism—the very same anarchism I maintain to this day, as I said."

He paused again, as if gathering his thoughts. Puffing on his cigar, he slowly exhaled the smoke away from me. He turned back to me and was going to proceed, but I interrupted him:

"As a matter of curiosity, tell me: Why did you go so far as to become an anarchist? You could have embraced a less radical doctrine, such as socialism. Your rebellion could have led to one of any number of various social theories. . . . If I've understood correctly, by anarchism you mean (and I think it's a good definition) the rejection of all social formulas and conventions, and the ardent struggle to abolish them all. . . ."

"That's right."

"But why did you choose such an extreme form of protest? Why not some intermediate form?"

"I gave careful thought to the matter. I became quite familiar with all the new social theories in the pamphlets I read. And I chose the anarchist theory, which you rightly consider to be the most radical of all, for the simple reasons I'll now explain."

He stared for a moment into space, and then looked back at me.

"The only real evils in the world are the various social conventions and fictions—from religion and the family to money and the state—that have been superimposed on natural realities. We're born to be men or women, or rather, to grow up to be men or women. We're not born, *naturally* speaking, to be husbands, to be rich or poor, Catholic or Protestant, Portuguese or English. All these things that define us are social fictions. And why are these social fictions bad? *Because they're fictions, because they're not natural.* Money is as bad as the state, the institution of the family as bad as religion. If there were other fictions besides these, they would be equally bad, *because they would also be fictions*, because they would also overlay and obstruct natural realities. And any system besides pure anarchism, which aims to do away with all systems, *is likewise a fiction.* To engage all our yearning, all our effort and all our intelligence in the furtherance of one social fiction instead of another is absurd if not outrightly criminal, *since it means causing a social disturbance with the express purpose of leaving everything the same.* If we think social fictions are unjust, why struggle to replace them with other fictions when we can strive instead to destroy them all?

"This seems to me rather hard to dispute. But let's suppose someone does dispute it. Suppose someone argues that this all may be true but that the anarchist system can never be put into practice. Let's consider that argument.

"Why wouldn't it be possible to put the anarchist system into practice? All of us who are progressive agree not only that the present system is unjust but that it should be replaced by a more equitable one. Whoever doesn't think this way is bourgeois, not progressive. But where does our notion of *justice* come from? It comes from what is *true and natural,* in opposition to social fictions and the lies of convention. And what's natural is what's *completely* natural, not what's half or one-quarter or one-eighth natural. Do you follow me? Now, one of two things must be true: either it's possible to put what's natural into social practice, or it isn't possible. In other words, either it's possible for a natural society to exist, or society is a pure fiction that can in no way be natural. If a natural society is possible, then an anarchist, or free, society can exist and should exist, since it would be a completely natural society. If society cannot be natural, if (no matter what the reason) it is necessarily a fiction, then let's make the best of it. Let's make the fiction as natural — and thereby as just — as possible. What fiction is most natural? By definition no fiction is natural per se. For our purposes, the most natural fiction will be the one that *seems* the most natural, that *feels* the most natural. And what fiction seems or feels the most natural? The fiction we're used to. (What's natural, you understand, is whatever is instinctive. And what seems instinctive without really being instinctive is habit. Smoking isn't natural; it's not an instinctive need. But if we get used to smoking, it becomes a natural act; it ends up feeling like an instinctive need.) The social fiction we're most used to is, of course, the present system, the bourgeois system.

"And so, according to the dictates of logic, we will either advocate anarchism, if we believe that a natural society is possible, or, if we believe it to be impossible, we will defend the bourgeois regime. There's no intermediate position. Do you follow me?"

"Perfectly. Your explanation is irrefutable."

"Not quite. . . . There's another objection of the same order that needs to be dealt with. Someone might argue that the anarchist system is indeed feasible but that it can't be introduced overnight — that we can't go from a bourgeois to a free society without one or more intermediate phases or regimes. This someone, while admitting that an anarchist society is a good and realistic goal, suspects that there will have to be some sort of transitional state between it and our current bourgeois society.

"Supposing this to be true, then what would the intermediate state be? It could only be one that prepares humanity for our goal, which is an anarchist or free society. This preparation would either be material, or merely psychological. That is, it would either consist in a series of material and social changes that would help adapt humanity to the free society, or it would consist in an increasingly forceful propaganda campaign, *psychologically* preparing people to desire or at least to accept the free society.

"The first proposition—the gradual, material adaptation of humanity to the free society—is impossible. Not only impossible but absurd. You can only materially adapt to something that already exists. We could never materially adapt to the social milieu of the twenty-third century, even if we knew what it were going to be. We can't materially adapt to the twenty-third century and its social milieu for the simple reason that they do not yet *materially* exist. We may therefore conclude that the only adaptation, evolution, or transition that can occur in passing from the bourgeois society to the free society is *psychological*; it's the gradual adapting of people's minds to the idea of the free society. . . . But in fact there's another possibility, in the area of material adaptation, that we still haven't considered."

"Not another possibility!"

"Be patient, my friend. The clear-thinking man must consider and refute all possible objections before he can affirm his doctrine to be true. And besides, this is all in response to a question you raised."

"All right, all right."

"In the area of material adaptation, as I was saying, there's still another possibility: namely the revolutionary dictatorship."

"How does the revolutionary dictatorship enter into it?"

"As I've explained, we can't materially adapt to something that still doesn't materially exist. But if a violent upheaval were to bring about a social revolution, then we would have, not yet our goal of the free society (for which humanity is still not prepared), but a dictatorship of those who want to establish the free society. At this point there would already exist a material outline, or beginning, of the free society. And thus there would be something material to which humanity could adapt. This is the argument that the idiots who defend the 'dictatorship of the proletariat' would use to defend it if they knew how to argue or think. The argument is mine, of course, not theirs. I submit it to myself as an objection. And, as I will show you, it's false.

"A revolutionary regime, as long as it exists, and regardless of its guiding idea or main goal, is *materially* only one thing: a revolutionary regime. And a revolutionary regime means a wartime dictatorship, or, in plainer words, a despotic military regime, because a state of war is imposed on society by just one part of it—the part that took power by means of a revolution. What's the result? Those who adapt to this regime will be adapting to what is in fact, *materially* and *immediately*, a despotic military regime. The revolutionaries' guiding idea, their main goal, completely vanishes in the social *reality* of an exclusively warlike environment. So that the inevitable outcome of a revolutionary dictatorship—and the longer the dictatorship, the more pronounced the outcome—is a warlike, dictatorial-type society. Military despotism, in other words. That's how it has always been and how it will always be. I don't know much history, but what I do know bears this out, as it logically must. What came out of the political uprisings in Rome? The Roman Empire and its military despotism. What came out of the French Revolution? Napoleon and his military despotism. And you'll see what comes out of the Russian Revolution: something that sets back the goal of a free society by decades. . . . But what more could we expect from a nation of mystics and illiterates? . . .

"I'm getting off the track. . . . Have you followed my argument?"

"Perfectly."

"Then you can understand the conclusion I reached. Goal: an anarchist or free society. Means: an abrupt passage, *with no transition*, from bourgeois society to the free society. This passage will be made possible by an intense, sweeping propaganda campaign, designed to prepare people's minds and break down all resistance. By 'propaganda,' of course, I don't mean just the written and spoken word. I mean everything that by direct or indirect action can prepare people for the free society and break down resistance to its coming. In this way, with virtually no more resistance to overcome, the social revolution, when it arrives, will be swift and easy, with no need for a revolutionary dictatorship to crush the opposition, since there won't be any. If it can't happen this way, then anarchism is unattainable; and if anarchism is unattainable, then the fairest and only defensible society, as I've already shown, is bourgeois society.

"There you have why and how I became an anarchist, and why and how I rejected other, less radical social doctrines as false and unnatural.

"So now we can get on with the rest of my story."

He struck a match and slowly lit his cigar. He thought for a moment, and then went on.

"There were other young men who shared my views. Most, but not all of them, were workers. All of us, in any case, were poor, and as far as I can remember there were no dummies among us. We were eager to know and learn, and we wanted to spread our ideas. For ourselves and for others—for all humanity—we wanted a new society, free from all the prejudices that make people artificially unequal by imposing on certain ones an inferiority, poverty, and suffering that Nature had no part in. The things I read confirmed me in these opinions. I read all the cheap libertarian books then available, and there were quite a few. I went to the lectures and rallies of the social idealists of the day. And each book I read, each speech I heard, convinced me all the more of the fairness and rightness of my ideas. What I thought then—I repeat, my friend—is what I think today. The only difference is that back then I merely thought it, whereas today I think and practice it."

"Okay. I follow you up to this point. I understand why and how you became an anarchist, and I can see that you most definitely were one. I don't need any more proofs of that. What I want to know is how a man with your views could become a banker and not feel any contradiction. . . . Actually, I think I can guess—"

"Well guess again. I know what you were going to say. Given the arguments I've just set forth, you supposed that I found anarchism to be an unattainable goal, leaving bourgeois society as the only fair and defensible alternative. Right?"

"Yes, that's more or less what I figured."

"But how could that be when, ever since we started this discussion, I've insisted that I *am* an anarchist, that I not only was one but continue to be one? If I'd become a banker and businessman for the reason you supposed, I'd be bourgeois, not an anarchist."

"True. But then—how on earth can...? Go on, explain yourself."

"I've always been basically clear thinking, as I told you, and I've always been a man of action. These are natural qualities. They weren't given to me in the cradle (if I even had a cradle); I had them when I came into the world. Due to these qualities, I couldn't stand to be a passive anarchist, to just go and listen to speeches and to talk about anarchism with friends. No: I had to do something! I wanted to work and to fight on behalf of the oppressed and the victims of social conventions! Having decided to do whatever I could do, I thought about how I could be useful to the libertarian cause. I started to lay out my plan of action.

"What does the anarchist want? Freedom. Freedom for himself and for others. Freedom for all humanity. He wants to be free from the influence and pressure of social fictions. He wants to be just as free as when he came into the world and as he has every right still to be. And he wants this freedom for everyone. People are not equal in their natural gifts: some are born tall, others short; some strong, others weak; some more intelligent than others. . . . But we can all be equal from that point on. Social fictions are the only hindrance. They, I realized, were what had to be destroyed.

"They had to be destroyed, but only—I thought to myself—on one condition: they had to be destroyed *in order to promote freedom*, and for the ultimate goal of a free society. For if the destruction of social fictions can create freedom or pave the way to freedom, it can also clear the way for new social fictions—equally bad because equally fictitious—to take their place. So it was necessary to proceed with caution. It was necessary to conceive a plan of action, however violent or nonviolent (everything is permitted in the fight against social injustice), that would help destroy social fictions without, at the same time, hindering the creation of future freedom. The best plan would create, if possible, some of that future freedom right now.

"It goes without saying that, besides not obstructing the freedom of the future, we should be careful not to hinder the freedom of those oppressed by social fictions. We obviously needn't worry about hindering the 'freedom' of the powerful and the privileged, of all those who represent social fictions and profit from them. What they have isn't true freedom but the freedom to oppress, which is freedom's opposite, and this we should actively try to hinder and fight. I think all of this is clear enough. . . ."

"Perfectly clear. Go on. . . ."

"Who does the anarchist want freedom for? For all humanity. How achieve freedom for all humanity? By completely destroying all social fictions. How destroy all social fictions? I already hinted at the explanation when, in answer to your question, I discussed other advanced social theories and explained why I was an anarchist. Do you remember my conclusion?"

"I do."

"A swift, sudden, and overwhelming social revolution that will cause society to pass, in a single leap, from the bourgeois regime to the free society. . . . A social revolution that will be preceded by an intense work of preparation—relying on direct and indirect action—to make people's minds receptive to the coming of a free society and to reduce bourgeois resistance to a state of coma. I won't bother to reiterate the reasons that inevitably lead, within anarchism, to this conclusion. I think you understood them the first time."

"Yes."

"This revolution would ideally be worldwide, occurring simultaneously in all points, or at least in all key points around the world; or, if this weren't possible, then quickly spreading from one point to another and being, in every point and every nation, a complete and categorical revolution.

"Now what could *I* do to make this happen? By myself I could never bring about complete social revolution in the country where I was living, much less around the whole world. What I could do was work, to the utmost of my capacity, to prepare for this revolution. I've already explained how: by using all means available to fight against social fictions; by making sure that this fight and my propaganda on behalf of the free society would never hinder the freedom of the future or the limited freedom already possible for the oppressed; and by creating, if possible, something of that future freedom."

He puffed on his cigar, paused a moment, and went on.

"It was at this point, my friend, that I put my clear thinking into action. To work for the future is fine, I thought, and to work for the freedom of others is good. But what about me? Don't I count? If I were a Christian, I'd cheerfully work for other people's future, because I'd have my reward in heaven. But if I were a Christian, I wouldn't be an anarchist, since the social inequalities of our brief life on earth wouldn't matter; they would merely be part of God's testing, to be compensated by eternal life. But I wasn't, and am not, a Christian, and so I had to ask: just who am I sacrificing myself for? And *why* am I going to sacrifice myself?

"I was assailed by doubts, and you can see why. . . . I'm a materialist, I thought. This is the only life I have, so why should I worry about social inequalities and changing how people think when I could enjoy myself and have a lot more fun if I didn't worry about such things? Why should someone who only has this life, who doesn't believe in eternal life, who accepts no law except Nature, who opposes the state because it isn't natural, marriage because it isn't natural, money because it isn't natural, and all social fictions because they aren't natural—why the devil should such a person advocate altruism and self-sacrifice for others, or for humanity, when altruism and self-sacrifice are likewise unnatural? Yes, the same logic that shows me that a man isn't born to be married, or to be Portuguese, or to be rich or poor, also shows me that he's not born to be public spirited, that he's born only to be himself, and thus the opposite of public spirited and altruistic, and thus completely selfish.

"I debated the matter within myself. You're forgetting, said one part of me to the other, that we're born into the human species, which means we have a duty to defend the welfare of all men. But was the notion of 'duty' natural? Where did this notion come from? If it obliges me to sacrifice my own well-being, my own comfort, my survival instinct, and my other natural instincts, then doesn't it have the very same effect as any of the social fictions?

"This notion that we have a duty to look out for other humans can only be considered natural if it somehow rewards the individual self, since then, when all is said and done, it won't really go against our natural selfishness, even though it may do so in principle. To simply deny ourselves pleasure is unnatural, but to deny ourselves one pleasure for the sake of another is a different matter, for it's part of the natural order to choose between two things when we can't naturally have both. So what selfish, or natural, reward would I get by devoting myself to the cause of a free society and mankind's future happiness? Only the awareness of having done my duty, of having worked toward a worthy goal. This, however, is not a pleasure per se but a pleasure (if really it is) born of a fiction, like the pleasure of being extremely rich or of being born into good social circumstances.

"I confess, my friend, that I had some moments of serious doubt. I felt unfaithful to my creed, as if I'd betrayed it. But I soon got over this hump. The notion of justice is inside me, I thought. I naturally felt it. I felt a duty that went beyond my concern for my own fate. And so I went forward on my chosen path."

"Your decision doesn't seem to me to show a clear-thinking mind at work. You didn't solve the logical problem. You went forward on a purely sentimental impulse."

"Quite right. But I'm telling my personal story of how I became an anarchist and have remained one to this day. To do that, I'm laying out the various problems and hesitations I felt, and explaining how I overcame them. At this point in my story, you're right, I overcame the logical problem with sentimentality rather than with reason. But you'll see how this logically unresolved problem was completely and definitively cleared up once I gained a full understanding of the anarchist doctrine."

"Interesting. . . ."

"It is indeed. . . . Now let me go on with my story. I dealt with this problem as best I could at the time, as I've explained. And then another, no less troublesome problem popped up in my mind.

"Okay, I thought, I'm willing to sacrifice myself without any personal reward, or, in other words, with no truly *natural* reward. But suppose the future society doesn't turn out as I hope? Suppose a free society never materializes? Then what the hell am I sacrificing myself for? To sacrifice myself for an idea without receiving any personal reward for my efforts was one thing, but to sacrifice myself and *not have the slightest guarantee that the idea I'm working for will ever become a reality* was something else again. . . . Well, I'll tell you up front that I dealt with this problem in the same sentimental way I'd dealt with the other, but I must also say that, just as with the other problem, this one was logically and automatically resolved once I reached the stage of full awareness in my anarchism. You'll see. . . . At the time this second problem occurred to me, I got around it with an empty phrase or two: 'I'm doing my duty for the future; it's up to the future to do its duty for me.' Or something to that effect.

"I explained this conclusion, or rather, these conclusions, to my comrades, and they all agreed with me. They all agreed that we needed to go forward and do everything we could for a free society. Actually, several of the more intelligent fellows were a bit taken aback by my explanation, not because they didn't agree, but because they'd never seen these matters set forth so clearly, nor realized how complex they were. But in the end everyone agreed. We were all going to work for the great social revolution, for a free society, regardless of whether the future would vindicate our efforts! We formed a group of like-minded people and began a fervent campaign to spread our ideas as best we could, given our limitations. Amid various hardships, entanglements, and even persecutions we carried on, working for the anarchist ideal."

Here the banker paused for rather a long time, but he didn't relight his cigar, which had gone out again. Suddenly, he cracked a slight smile and looked at me intently, as if he were now arriving at the crucial point. He went on, speaking in a clearer and more emphatic voice.

"And then," he said, "something new occurred. By 'then' I mean after a few months of campaigning for our cause, when I began to notice a new complication, much more serious than the others.

"You remember, don't you, what I lucidly, logically concluded would be the best course of action for anarchists? . . . A course, or courses, that would help destroy social fictions without, at the same time, hindering either the creation of future freedom or the limited freedom of those currently oppressed by social fictions; a course that would, if possible, create something of that future freedom. . . .

"Well, having established those principles, I never lost sight of them. And after a few months of our efforts, I discovered something. Our anarchist group, which wasn't large—I think there were about forty of us—was beginning to breed tyranny."

"To breed tyranny? How so?"

"Simple. . . . Some people took charge, obliging the rest of us to follow. Some imposed their will, forcing the rest of us to do what they wanted. Some used cunning and trickery to drag others down paths they didn't want to go. I'm not saying this happened in serious matters; it didn't. But the fact is that it happened every single day, not only in matters related to our campaign to promote anarchism but in everyday matters of life. Almost imperceptibly, some became leaders, while others became followers. Some became leaders by imposition, others by their shrewd behavior. This was observable in the tiniest things. For instance: Two fellows would walk down the street together. At the end of the street, one needed to turn right, and the other left; each had a good reason for going in his particular direction. But the one who needed to go left said to the other, 'Come along with me,' to which the other truthfully answered, 'I can't, pal, I need to go the other way' for this or that reason. But in the end, against his will and his own interest, he would go along with the fellow who needed to go left. Sometimes this happened through arm twisting, sometimes through mere insistence or some other cause. But it was never because of a logical reason. This domination and subordination always had something spontaneous about it, as if it were instinctive. And as in this simple case, so in all cases, from the least to the most important ones. Do you see my point?"

"I see it, but what's so strange about it? It's the most natural thing in the world."

"Perhaps. I'll get to that. For now I merely wish to point out that this goes *completely against anarchist doctrine*. Note that this occurred in a small group, with no real influence or importance, a group that wasn't responsible for solving any large issue or making any major decision. And note that it was a group of people who had joined together specifically to promote the anarchist cause—to do everything in their power to oppose social fictions and to create, as far as possible, the freedom of the future. Are you with me on these two points?"

"Yes."

"Now consider what this means. . . . A small group of sincere people (and I can assure you that we were all sincere), formed expressly to work for the cause of freedom, had achieved, after a few months, just one unequivocal, concrete result: *the creation of tyranny in its midst.* And consider what sort of tyranny. . . . Not a tyranny which, though regrettable, had derived from social fictions and would therefore be excusable up to a point—less so, of course, in those who were fighting those fictions, yet we couldn't be blamed for not entirely escaping their influence, since we were living in a society that was founded on them. But it wasn't this kind of tyranny. Those who took charge and forced others to follow them didn't do so on the basis of their wealth or their social rank or some other fictitious, unjustly assumed authority. Their actions were founded on something other than social fictions. And so their tyranny, having nothing to do with social fictions, was a *new tyranny*. Not only that, it was a tyranny inflicted on people who were already being oppressed by social fictions. And to top it off, it was a tyranny inflicted by people whose sincere goal was none other than to destroy tyranny and create freedom.

"Now transfer this situation to a much larger, much more powerful group that deals with important issues and makes crucial decisions. Imagine that group directing all its efforts, like our group, toward the formation of a free society. And now tell me if, through that jumble of criss-crossing tyrannies, you can see in the future anything that remotely resembles a free society or a humanity worthy of the name."

"Interesting point. . . ."

"Isn't it? And there are various related phenomena that are no less interesting. The tyranny of helping, for example. . . ."

"The *what?*"

"The tyranny of helping. Instead of trying to dominate or impose their will on others, some people in our group, quite to the contrary, did everything they could to help others. It seems like the contrary, doesn't it? Well, it isn't. It's another version of the same new tyranny. It's every bit as opposed to anarchist principles."

"Come now—that's absurd!"

"Listen. When we help someone, we treat him as if he were incompetent; if he's not incompetent, either we help make him that way, which is tyranny, or we suppose he's that way, which is contempt. In the former case, we restrict his freedom. In the latter case we assume, at least unconsciously, that he's contemptible and unworthy or incapable of freedom.

"Going back to my own group, you can see how critical a point we'd reached. It was one thing to work for the ideal future society without expecting it to ever thank us and without even being certain that this society would materialize. But it was quite another to work for the freedom of the future and have no results to show other than the creation of tyranny, and not just any tyranny but a brand-new form of it: the tyranny that we, the oppressed, were inflicting on one another. This was too much to swallow.

"I started thinking. There had to be a mistake, some kind of oversight. Our goals were good and our ideas rang true, so was the problem in our method? It must have been, but where on earth was the mistake? I thought so hard my mind went dizzy. Then one day out of the blue, as always happens in these things, I hit on the solution. It was the red-letter day of my anarchist theories, the day when I discovered the anarchist method, if I may so call it."

He looked at me for a second without actually looking, and then continued in the same tone of voice.

"I thought: Here we have this new tyranny that doesn't derive from social fictions. So where does it come from? Might it derive from natural qualities? If so, then we can kiss the free society good-bye! If a society based exclusively on natural human qualities, meaning those we get from Nature when we're born and over which we have no control—if a society based only on these qualities would be an amalgam of tyrannies, then who's going to lift a finger to bring it about? Between one tyranny and another, better to stick with the one we know, which we're at least used to and therefore don't feel as keenly as we would a new tyranny, particularly one that comes directly from Nature, such that all revolt against it would be useless, like rebelling against death, or against being born short instead of tall. And as I've already proven, if for some reason the anarchist society cannot be achieved, then the next most natural society we can have—and should have—is bourgeois society.

"But had this tyranny among us really derived from natural qualities? What sort of qualities are natural? Well, there's the degree of intelligence, imagination, willpower, and so forth, that each man is born with—all of this in the mental sphere, of course, since we're not concerned here with natural physical qualities. Now if one man orders around another, and there's no influence of social fictions at work, then it must be because he's superior in one or another natural quality. He dominates the other through the use of his natural qualities. But we must still consider whether this use of natural qualities is legitimate. Is it, in other words, *natural*?

"What's the natural use of our natural qualities? To serve the natural aims of our personality. Is dominating someone else a natural aim of our personality? It is in one particular case: when that someone may be considered our enemy. For the anarchist, any representative of social fictions and their tyranny is clearly an enemy; all other men, because they're people just like him, are natural comrades. As we've seen, the tyranny that we created was inflicted on natural comrades, on people just like us—on people, in fact, who were our comrades twice over, since they shared the same ideal. And so our tyranny, which did not derive from social fictions, likewise did not derive from natural qualities. It derived from a mistaken application, a perversion, of natural qualities. And what was at the root of that perversion?

"It had to be one of two things. Either man was naturally bad, so that all natural qualities were *naturally perverted*, or the perversion resulted from humanity's long exposure to an atmosphere of social fictions that engendered tyranny, so that the natural use of man's most natural qualities came to be instinctively tyrannical. Which of these two hypotheses was the right one? It was impossible to determine in a satisfactory—that is, strictly logical or scientific—way. Logical reasoning cannot apply here, since the problem is historical, or scientific, and depends on knowing the *facts*. Science can't help us either, since no matter how far back we go in history, we always find man living under some system of social tyranny, so that we cannot know what man is like, or would be like, in completely natural circumstances. Since we have no way to determine which hypothesis is correct, we must opt for the one that's more probable: the second one. To suppose that natural qualities can be naturally perverted is in a certain way contradictory. It's more natural to suppose that humanity's long exposure to tyranny-engendering social fictions has caused our natural qualities to be perverted, from birth, by a spontaneous tendency to tyrannize, even when we have no wish to tyrannize. And so the thinker will decide as I decided, with near absolute certainty, in favor of this second hypothesis.

"One thing is clear. In our present social condition, no group of men, no matter how well meaning and how dedicated they are to fighting social fictions and working for freedom, can work together without spontaneously creating a tyranny in their own midst, without adding a new tyranny to that of social fictions, without destroying in practice what they want in theory, without involuntarily but fatally hindering the very goal they're striving for. So what do we do? It's simple. . . . We all work for the same goal, *but separately.*

"Separately?!"

"That's right. Didn't you follow my argument?"

"Yes."

"And doesn't this strike you as a logical, inevitable conclusion?"

"Yes, I suppose so. . . . What I don't get is how this. . . ."

"Let me clarify. . . . I said: We all work for the same goal, but separately. If we're all working for the same anarchist goal, each of us will be contributing with his efforts toward the destruction of social fictions and the creation of the free society of the future. Working separately, we'll never restrict another man's freedom by dominating him nor stifle his freedom by helping him, since we won't be acting on one another at all, and so we cannot possibly create a new tyranny.

"By working separately for the same anarchist goal, we have the advantage of a joint effort without the disadvantage of creating a new tyranny. We're still morally united, because we share a common goal, and we're still anarchists, because each of us works for the free society. But we stop being willing or unwilling traitors to our cause, and we can't even possibly be traitors, since by working for anarchism on our own, individually, we're not subject to the harmful influence of social fictions via their hereditary effect on the qualities that Nature gave us.

"This strategy only applies, of course, to what I called the *preparatory stage* for the social revolution. Once bourgeois resistance has been demolished and all society reduced to the point of accepting anarchist doctrines, with only the social revolution still lacking, then, for that final strike, we can no longer act separately. But at that point the free society will have virtually arrived; things will already be vastly different. The strategy of working separately is for promoting anarchism within a bourgeois context, as now, or as when I and my comrades formed our group.

"Here at last was the true anarchist method! Together we accomplished practically nothing, and on top of that we tyrannized each other, thereby obstructing our freedom and our theories. Separately we also wouldn't achieve much, but at least we wouldn't obstruct freedom or create a new tyranny; the little we achieved would be a real achievement, without collateral loss or damage. And by working separately, we would learn to be more self-reliant, not to lean so much on each other, to become already freer, thus preparing ourselves—as well as others, by our example—for the future.

"This discovery made me ecstatic. I went and shared it immediately with my comrades. . . . It's one of the few times in my life when I was plain stupid. I was so thrilled with my discovery that I expected them to receive it with open arms!"

"Which of course they didn't do. . . ."

"They caviled and quibbled, every last one of them! Some were more vocal than others, but they all objected. . . . 'That can't be right!

It doesn't make sense!' . . . But no one could say what was right, or what would make sense. I argued myself green, and in reply to my arguments all I got were clichés, gibberish, the kinds of things ministers say in parliaments when they have no answers. . . . That's when I realized what kind of ninnies and cowards I was involved with! They had shown their true colors. The whole lot had been born to be slaves. They wanted to be anarchists at someone else's expense. They wanted freedom, as long as other people went and got it for them, as long as it was handed to them like a title from the king! Virtually all of them were lackeys at heart!"

"And did you get angry?"

"Angry? I was furious! I started ranting and raving, and I almost came to blows with a couple of them. Finally I stormed out. I kept to myself. I was so disgusted with that herd of namby-pambies that you can't imagine! I almost quit believing in anarchism. I almost decided to just forget about it all. But after a few days I came back to my senses. I realized that the anarchist ideal was above all that bickering. If they didn't want to be anarchists, I could still be one. If they just wanted to play at being libertarians, I wasn't about to join them. If the only way they knew how to fight was by hanging on each other and creating a new version of the tyranny they said they wanted to destroy, then they could jolly well do it on their own, the fools. But that was no reason for me to be a bourgeois.

"It had become clear to me that in true anarchism each man must call on his own strength to create freedom and to fight social fictions. So I would call on my own strength to do just that. No one wanted to follow me on the true path of anarchism? Then I'd follow it alone. I'd fight social fictions all by myself, relying on my own faith and resources, deprived even of the moral support of those who had been my comrades. I don't claim that this was a noble or heroic gesture. It was simply a natural gesture. If the path had to be followed by each man separately, then I needed no one else to follow it. My ideal was enough. It was with these principles and in these circumstances that I decided to fight social fictions all by myself."

He broke off his speech, which had become a fervid stream. When he resumed a few moments later, it was with a calmer voice.

* * *

"It's war, I thought, between me and social fictions. So what can I do to defeat them? I'll work alone so as not to create any tyranny, but how can I, by myself, help pave the way for the social revolution and prepare humanity for the free society? I would have to choose one of two methods, unless, of course, I could use both. The two methods were: indirect action, which amounts to propagandizing, and direct action of one sort or another.

"I first of all considered indirect action, or propagandizing. What sort of propagandizing could I do on my own? Beyond the sort of propagandizing we do when we talk with this person or that person, taking advantage of the random opportunities that come our way, was indirect action a path by which I could actively practice anarchism, in such a way as to produce visible results? I immediately saw that it wasn't. I'm not a speaker or a writer. I mean, I can speak in public if I have to, and I'm capable of writing a newspaper article, but I had to determine if my natural bent was such that, by specializing in either of these forms of indirect action, I could obtain better results for the anarchist cause than by devoting my efforts to some other form of action. The fact is that direct action is generally more effective than propagandizing, the only exception being for those individuals who by nature are destined to be propagandists—the great public speaker, who is capable of electrifying crowds and making them follow his lead, or the great writer, who can captivate and convince people through his books. I don't think I'm especially vain, but if I am, I at least don't boast about qualities I don't have. And, as I've said, I've never considered myself a speaker or writer. That's why I gave up on the idea of indirect action as a viable path for my anarchist activities. I was left, by elimination, with the path of direct action, in which my efforts would be applied to actual practice, to real life. The path of action instead of the intelligence. That's how it had to be. Fine.

"I needed to apply to practical life what I had learned to be the basic method of anarchist action: to struggle against social fictions without engendering a new tyranny and to begin to create, if possible, the freedom of the future. But how the devil could this be done in practice?

"What, in practice, does it mean to struggle? To struggle, in practice, implies war, or at least *a* war. How can war be waged against social fictions? Let's first consider how any war is waged. How can the enemy in a war be conquered? In one of two ways. The enemy can either be killed — destroyed, that is — or else imprisoned, subdued, reduced to inactivity. It wasn't in my power to *destroy* social fictions; that could only be accomplished by the social revolution. Until that happened, social fictions might be shaken up to the point where they'd hang by a thread, but only the downfall of bourgeois society and the advent of a free society could actually *destroy* them. The most I could have done in the way of actual destruction was to kill one or more representative members of bourgeois society. I thought about it and realized it would be folly. Suppose I killed one or two or even a dozen representatives of the tyranny of social fictions. Would that help to undermine social fictions? Not at all. Social fictions are not like political situations, which can depend on a small number of men, sometimes on just one man. Social fictions are bad in themselves and not because of their representative members, who are bad only insofar as they represent social fictions.

"Then too, assaults on the social order always spark a reaction, such that things not only don't improve, they may actually get worse. And suppose, as is probable, that I were arrested after making an assault — arrested and liquidated, in one way or another. And suppose I had finished off with a dozen capitalists. What would be the end result? With my liquidation — even if that meant, not my death, but incarceration or banishment — the anarchist cause would lose one of its fighting constituents, whereas the twelve capitalists that I had laid flat would not signify a loss of twelve constituents of bourgeois society, which is made up not of fighting constituents but of purely passive ones; the 'fight' isn't against the members of bourgeois society but against the body of social fictions on which that society is founded. Social fictions are not people at whom we can fire shots. . . . Do you see my point? It wouldn't be like the soldier of one army killing twelve soldiers from an enemy army; it would be like a soldier killing twelve civilians from the nation defended by an enemy army. It would mean killing stupidly, since no combatant would be eliminated. . . .

"It was useless to think of *destroying* social fictions, whether in whole or in any one part. Instead I would have to conquer them by subduing and reducing them to inactivity."

He pointed his right index finger straight at me:

"So that's what I did!"

Dropping his finger, he continued:

"I considered which was the first and foremost social fiction, since that was the one I felt most duty-bound to subdue and to reduce, if possible, to inactivity. The foremost social fiction, at least in our own time, is money. Now how could I subdue money or, more precisely, the power of money, its tyranny? By becoming free of its influence and thus superior to it, making it inactive as far as I was concerned. As far as I was concerned, please understand, since *I* was the one who was fighting it. To make it inactive as far as all humanity was concerned would mean not just subduing it but *destroying* it, since the fiction of money would cease to exist. But I've already proven to you that any social fiction can be destroyed only by the social revolution, which will bring them all down, along with bourgeois society.

"How could I be superior to the power of money? The simplest method would be to withdraw from the sphere of its influence, that is, from civilization; to go to the wilderness and eat roots and drink stream water; to be naked and live like an animal. But this method, even if it posed no practical difficulties, wouldn't be a method for fighting a social fiction, because there's no fighting in it, just fleeing. Those who shy from the battle are not defeated physically, but they are defeated morally, because they didn't fight. No, I had to adopt another method — a method of fighting, not of fleeing. How could I subdue money by fighting against it? How could I free myself from its influence and its tyranny without running away from it? The only possible method was to *acquire* it, to acquire enough of it so as not to feel its influence; and the more I acquired, the freer from its influence I would be. It was when I clearly saw this, with all the force of my anarchist convictions and all the logic of my clear-thinking mind, that I entered the current phase—the banking and business phase—of my anarchism."

He rested for a moment from the renewed fervor and vehemence of his arguments. Then he went on, in a still somewhat heated tone:

"Remember those two logical problems that occurred to me at the beginning of my career as a conscious anarchist? . . . And do you remember how I resolved them artificially, through sentimentality rather than through logic? In fact it was you who pointed out, quite correctly, that I hadn't dealt with those problems logically."

"Yes, I remember."

"And do you remember how I told you that I would later resolve them definitively, through logic, once I'd fully grasped the true anarchist method?"

"Yes."

"Well now you'll see what I meant. . . . The problems were, firstly, that it's not *natural* to work for some entity or cause, no matter what it is, without a *natural*, or selfish, reward; and, secondly, that it's not *natural* to devote our efforts to some goal without the compensation of knowing that the goal will be achieved. Those were the two problems; observe how they were resolved by what my reason discovered to be the only true method of anarchist action. . . . Since the method results in my getting rich, *there is a selfish reward.* And since I free myself from money, becoming superior to its power, *I achieve the method's goal, which is freedom.* It's true that I achieve freedom only for myself, but as I've already proven, freedom for everyone will be achieved only when all social fictions are destroyed by the social revolution, which I can't bring about on my own. The point that matters is this: I strive for freedom and I achieve freedom. I achieve the freedom I'm capable of, since I obviously can't achieve a freedom I'm not capable of. . . . And note that, if reason shows this to be the only true anarchist method, the fact that it automatically resolves the logical arguments that might be raised against any anarchist method is yet a further proof of its truth.

"So that's the method I followed. I set out to subdue the fiction of money by getting rich, and I succeeded. It took time, for the struggle wasn't easy, but I did it. I won't go into my banking and business life, certain details of which you might find interesting, but it's beside the point. I worked, struggled, and made money; I worked harder, struggled harder, and made more money. I ended up making a lot of money. I didn't think about the means I used; I confess, my friend, that I didn't think about the means. I resorted to all means available: profiteering, financial finagling, and even unfair competition. And why not? I was fighting inexcusably immoral and unnatural social fictions, so why did I need to worry about the means? I was striving for freedom, so why worry about the weapons I used to fight tyranny? The stupid anarchist, who tosses bombs and fires guns, knows perfectly well that he kills people and that his doctrines do not include the death penalty. He commits a crime to attack immorality, for he feels that the destruction of that immorality justifies the crime. He is stupid in his method, which *as an anarchist method* is counterproductive, and thus erroneous, as I've shown, but with respect to the *morality* of his method he is intelligent. My method, on the other hand, was correct, and I legitimately availed myself, as an anarchist, of all possible means to get rich. I have achieved my limited dream as a practical, clear-thinking anarchist. I'm free. I do what I want—to the extent, of course, that what I want is possible. My anarchist watchword was freedom, and today I have freedom—as much freedom as it's possible to have in our imperfect society. I set out to fight social forces; I fought them and, what's more, defeated them."

"Hold on right there!" I said. "This is all fine and good, except for one thing. The necessary conditions of your method were, as you demonstrated, to create freedom and *not to create* tyranny. But you have created tyranny. As a profiteer, a banker, and an unscrupulous financier—excuse me, but you yourself said as much—you have created tyranny. You have created as much tyranny as any other representative of the social fictions you claim to oppose."

"No, my friend, you're mistaken. I've *created* no tyranny. Whatever tyranny may have resulted from my struggle against social fictions didn't originate in me, and so it isn't my creation. *The tyranny resides in social fictions; I didn't add it to them.* It belongs to the social fictions themselves, which I couldn't destroy, nor did I attempt to. For the hundredth time: only the social revolution can *destroy* social fictions; until then, all true anarchist action—such as my own—can do no more than subdue social fictions, and only in relation to the anarchist who puts this method into practice, for the method doesn't allow for a more widespread subjection of those fictions. What's at issue isn't the creation of tyranny but the creation of *new* tyranny—tyranny *where there was none* before. Anarchists, when they work together and exert influence on each other, create a tyranny among themselves that's above and beyond the tyranny of social fictions, as I explained earlier. *That* tyranny is indeed a new tyranny. I, *by the very conditions of my method,* did not and could not create such a tyranny. No, my friend; I created only freedom. I freed *one man.* I freed myself. My method, which I've shown to be the only true anarchist method, did not enable me to free anyone else. I freed the man I could."

"All right. . . . I agree. . . . But by your line of reasoning, one could almost believe that no representative of social fictions exercises tyranny."

"And no representative does. The tyranny belongs to social fictions and not to the people who embody them. Such people are, as it were, the *instruments* by which those fictions exercise tyranny, as the knife is the instrument by which the murderer kills. And you surely don't imagine that by eliminating knives you will eliminate murderers. . . . Suppose you destroyed all the capitalists in the world, but without destroying capital. . . . On the very next day, capital would be in the hands of other people, through whom it would continue its tyranny. But if you destroy capital instead of capitalists, how many capitalists will be left? . . . Do you see? . . ."

"Yes, you're right."

"The most—the very most—you can accuse me of doing is increasing slightly—ever so slightly—the tyranny of social fictions. But the basis of the charge is flimsy, because what I must not create, and in fact didn't create, is any *new* tyranny, as I've already explained. Not only that: by the same rationale you could accuse a general engaged in a war for his country of inflicting on that country the loss of its men whom he had to sacrifice in battle to defeat the enemy. No matter what the war, you win some and you lose some. What counts is the main goal; the rest. . . ."

"Fair enough. . . . But there's something else. . . . The true anarchist wants freedom not only for himself, but for others. He wants freedom, as I see it, for all of humanity. . . ."

"Of course. But as I've already explained, according to the anarchist method that I discovered to be the only viable one, each man must free himself. By achieving my own freedom, I did my duty with respect to myself and with respect to freedom. If my comrades did not do likewise, it's not because I prevented them. That indeed would have been a crime, but I never concealed from them the true anarchist method; as soon as I discovered it, I told them all about it. The nature of the method prohibited me from doing more than that. What more could I have done? Force them to follow this path? Even if that were possible, I wouldn't do it, for I would be depriving them of their freedom, which is against my anarchist principles. Help them? That was also out of the question, and for the same reason. I've never helped others, for that would infringe on their freedom, which is likewise against my principles. What you're blaming me for is that I'm not more than one person. Why criticize me for doing my duty of freeing as many people as I could? Why not criticize those who didn't do their duty?"

"I take your point. But if those other anarchists didn't do what you did, it's because they were less intelligent than you, or less strong willed, or—"

"Ah, my friend, but those are natural inequalities, not social ones, and anarchism can do nothing about them. The degree of a person's intelligence and willpower is a matter between him and Nature; social fictions don't enter in at all. There are, as I've mentioned, natural qualities that have no doubt been perverted by humanity's long exposure to social fictions, but the perversion is in the *application* of the quality, not in its *degree*, which depends exclusively on Nature. Lack of intelligence or willpower has nothing to do with the application of these qualities; it has to do with their insufficient quantity. That's why I say that these are natural inequalities, over which no one has any power, nor can they be changed by changes in society, any more than such changes could make me tall or you short. . . .

"Unless . . . unless the hereditary perversion of natural qualities goes so far as to affect the very core of certain people's personalities . . . , making them born slaves, naturally born to be slaves, and therefore incapable of making any effort to free themselves. . . . But in that case . . . in that case . . . , what do they have to do with the free society, or with freedom? . . . For a man born to be a slave, freedom would be a tyranny, since it would go against his very nature."

There was a brief pause. Then I broke out laughing.

"You really are an anarchist," I said. "But even after hearing you out, I still can't help but laugh when I think about what you are in comparison with other anarchists. . . ."

"As I've already explained and proven, my friend, the only real difference is that they are anarchists in theory, while I'm one in theory and practice; they are mystical anarchists, while I'm a scientific one; they are anarchists who cringe, while I'm an anarchist who fights and achieves freedom. . . . They, in a word, are pseudoanarchists, while I am a genuine one."

And we stood up from the table.

Lisbon, January 1922

PESSOA ON MILLIONAIRES

Pessoa wrote three prose fragments—all of them in English—on the subject of millionaires. Though the fragments have different titles, Pessoa probably intended to join them into a single essay. The longest of the three pieces, titled "Message to Millionaires," chastises the rich for not knowing how to spend their money and enjoy life. "How many of you have a harem, a real harem?" asks Pessoa at a certain point, contending that "that would be an interesting application of wealth." For those who wish to spend their millions charitably, Pessoa's "message" is that they should "endow individuals, not communities," since all that will endure "of this noisy age is some poet now obscure and crushed down by coteries and cliques, some painter who cannot sell his pictures, some musician who shall never hear an orchestra play his compositions." Excerpts from the other two fragments follow.

from An Essay on Millionaires and Their Ways

No man ever became a millionaire by hard work or cleverness. At the worst he became so by a vast and imaginative unscrupulousness; at the best by happy intuition in speculative circumstances. If any man pretend that hard thinking and a strong will have led him to make a vast fortune, then that man lies. He may have thought hard, but in such an advantageous position for thinking that his hard thinking could catch a [lucky] chance by the hair. It is always a question of lottery tickets, though perhaps of having saved enough to buy them; from the lottery ticket onwards, however, the fortune was Fate's doing.

The proof of the fundamental stupidity of these mercenaries of Fate is the things they do with the money they accumulate. Most of them go on accumulating it and no more. Others have no more imaginative impetus than endowing hospitals or creating "foundations"— that is to say, things only to be built upon and covered and sunk in the earth—and free libraries, or even sports grounds. If these men had been imaginative, they would carry out great plans: gigantic continental sins, prodigious extravagances of building and excavating, romantic wars of oppression or liberation. But they never rise to the level of the popular novelist: they are always and irremediably Rockefellerish. Mr. Ford seems or seemed somewhat broader, but, after all, he has dared but to believe in reincarnation,* which costs him nothing.

. . .

One thing they never endow: they never endow the individual, which is the only true reality in the substance of the social world. They fear, by instinct, the man who deserves, and have in their hearts an obscure terror of any justice being done. They realize that if justice had been done, they would have been done in.*

No self-made millionaire—meaning a man who has been made a millionaire by circumstances—ever helped a man to find the greatness he might deserve.

. . .

from American Millionaires

You are so complete a zoology of beasts that the gorge refuses to rise at you, out of direct organic contempt. You stink physically to the intellect. Your very philanthropy is an insult to those whom you turn over to, in checks, the leavings of the luck you have had. Your interest in culture is the dessert of your meanness. You drink un-Portuguese port and it gets into what is where your head ought to be, and the margin fades.

. . .

No shred of decency, no sense of fellow-feeling with the warm commonness of mankind, nothing, nothing, nothing, save the hoard, the meanness, and the common end.

If you want European thanks, here they are. Take them and be damned to you!

You have dared to use the words of Indian mystics and European occultists toward the furthering of your publicity. You have affected a belief in reincarnation* out of a real belief in advertising. Everything your kind touches it pollutes, and the doctrine which leads the Indian mystic not to kill a fly leads you not to let men live.

I have now sufficient celebrity to talk to you, not indeed as man to man, but as man to beast. We will have it out now, as between European and low American, as between Christian and engineering heathen. . . . . .

ENVIRONMENT
Álvaro de Campos

No age ever passes on to the next its sensibility, just the intellectual understanding it had of that sensibility. Emotion makes us what we are; intelligence makes us different. Intelligence spreads and scatters us, and it's through this scattering that we survive. Every age leaves to future ages only what it wasn't.

A god, in the pagan—that is, true—sense of the word, is no more than a being's intellectual self-awareness, this intelligence constituting the impersonal, and hence ideal, form of that being. When we form an intellectual concept of ourselves, we form our own god. But very few of us ever form an intellectual concept of ourselves, because intelligence is fundamentally objective. Few, even among the world's great geniuses, have existed for themselves with complete objectivity.

To live is to belong to someone else. To die is to belong to someone else. To live and to die are the same thing. But to live is to belong to someone else *on the outside*, and to die is to belong to someone else *on the inside*. The two things are similar, but life is the outside of death, which is why life is life and death is death. The outside is always truer than the inside, for it is, after all, the side we see.

Every true emotion is a lie in our intelligence, where emotion doesn't exist. The expression of every true emotion is therefore false. To express ourselves is to tell what we don't feel.

The cavalry's horses are what make it a cavalry. Without horses, the cavalry would be infantry. A place is what it is because of its location. Where we are is who we are.

To pretend is to know ourselves.

[SELF-DEFINITION]

I can define myself without any trouble: I'm female by temperament, with a male intelligence. My sensibility and the actions that derive from it—my temperament and its expression, in other words—are those of a woman. My associative faculties—intelligence and the will, which is the intelligence of our impulses—are those of a man.

As far as my sensibility goes, when I say that I've always wanted to be loved but never to love, I've said it all. To feel obliged to return affection—out of a banal duty to reciprocate, to be loyal in spirit—always made me suffer. I liked being passive. I wanted to be active only insofar as it was necessary to stimulate and keep alive the love activity of the person who loved me.

I have no illusions about the nature of this phenomenon. It's a latent sexual inversion. It stops in my spirit. But whenever I've paused and thought about myself, I've felt uneasy, for I've never been sure, and I'm still not sure, that this inclination in my temperament might not one day descend to my body. I'm not saying I would practice the sexuality that corresponds to that impulse; but the desire would be enough to humiliate me. There have been many of us in this category down through history, and through artistic history in particular. Shakespeare and Rousseau are two of the most illustrious examples, or exemplars. My fear that this spiritual inversion could descend to my body comes, in fact, from thinking about how it descended in them—completely in Shakespeare, as homosexuality; indefinitely in Rousseau, as a vague form of masochism.

EROSTRATUS: THE SEARCH FOR IMMORTALITY

"The only noble destiny for a writer who publishes is to be denied a celebrity he deserves. But the truly noble destiny belongs to the writer who doesn't publish." These words, appropriately enough, are from The Book of Disquiet (Text 209), which wasn't published until almost half a century after its author's death. Not that the author didn't want to publish it, didn't plan to publish it, and didn't announce—toward the end of his life—that it was "forthcoming." But he died without publishing it, or much of anything else, and part of the reason no doubt was his avowed disdain for the act of publishing, since this implies participation in a system, acceptance of the rules of a game, and submission of one's work to the judgment of others—intolerable implications for a man convinced of his superiority. "But what if I'm not really superior?" a man thus convinced, if he's a thinking man, is bound to wonder: "What if it's just my own delusion?" Pessoa, who left dozens and dozens of passages for a projected essay titled "Genius and Madness," was frightfully aware of the fine line separating the two conditions, having drawn it most memorably in Álvaro de Campos's "The Tobacco Shop":

> Genius? At this moment
> A hundred thousand brains are dreaming they're geniuses like me,
> And it may be that history won't remember even one . . .
> . . .
> Insane asylums are full of lunatics with certainties!

As if to guard against becoming part of this latter group (and madness, as indicated earlier, ran in his family), Pessoa locked himself up in his *own, literary asylum. But while he managed to invent dozens of literary personalities, he wasn't capable of creating cheering multitudes.*

Pessoa lusted for fame, recognition, acclamation. If he also regarded fame with contempt, that was partly because he felt it was contemptible, partly because he was frustrated for not having it. It's hard to know which came first—the contempt or the frustration—but it's clear that the latter sentiment weighed more as he got older.

As a young man Pessoa was convinced that fame was just around the corner. At the age of twenty-four, even before publishing any poems, he had already announced—in a critical piece published in 1912—the coming of a poet who would dethrone Luís de Camões (1524?–80) from his post as Portugal's Greatest Writer. Pessoa was clearly laying down his own red carpet, which he soon cut wider to accommodate the heteronyms. Can Álvaro de Campos's vision, in the Ultimatum, *of a literary age being represented, not by thirty or forty poets, but by "just two poets endowed with fifteen or twenty personalities," be anything but a self-referring prophecy? (The prophecy is echoed in the final passage from* Erostratus *published here.) More explicit was Pessoa's letter to his mother dated June 5, 1914, in which he boasted that within five or ten years he would, according to his friends, "be one of the greatest contemporary poets." It was a heady year for Pessoa, whose first poems had been published in a magazine in February and whose Big Bang of Caeiro-Reis-Campos had occurred in March, and certain of his friends (Mário de Sá-Carneiro in particular) did indeed predict his imminent celebrity, so there was a basis for the young writer's boast.*

But fifteen years passed, and Pessoa—a respected poet and intellectual in Lisbon—was far from famous. Although he had contributed work to magazines throughout the twenties, and self-published some chapbooks of poetry in English, he reached 1930 without having published a real book, perhaps afraid of what the reaction, or nonreaction, might be. Even after he finally published, in 1934, his book Mensagem *with some success, he expressed his doubts to Adolfo Casais Monteiro that the poetry of Caeiro, Reis, and Campos would be able to sell (see the letter of January 20, 1935).*

Toward the end of his life, Pessoa began to realize that fame was not liable to visit him on this side of the grave. And so, good student of philosophy that he was, he drew a distinction between fame and immortality, making them almost mutually exclusive categories. True genius, he contended, can never be recognized in its own lifetime. In his day Shakespeare was famous for his wit, but only future generations recognized his genius. Erostratus, *written around 1930, is a restless disquisition on what makes for immortality, particularly the literary kind. Even without reading between the lines, it's evident that Pessoa set out to prove, at least to himself, that his future celebrity was a foregone conclusion. Having proved it to his satisfaction, he could keep writing his unpublished works to the posthumous glory of his enduring name.*

The provocative title of Erostratus *refers to the obscure Greek who in 356 B.C., so as to make his name immortal, set fire to the Temple of Diana in Ephesus, one of the Seven Wonders of the ancient world. By alluding to the deed of this "crasher into fame" (an epithet used in his essay), Pessoa seems, on the one hand, to be mocking his own meticulously constructed argument, since Erostratus achieved posthumous renown on the flimsy basis of a gratuitous act of destruction. The allusion suggests, on the other hand, that there's no way to know, until all the chips are in, whose name will go down in history. Pessoa, whose book* Mensagem *took only second prize in a poetry competition, came out the undisputed winner in the history of modern Portuguese literature, which isn't so strange. What is strange is that he won his celebrity for the very reasons set out in* Erostratus. *His writings had to wait for future readers, because his own age could not fully appreciate the genius of his self-multiplied art. Not even Pessoa could fully appreciate it. The other side of multiplication is division, fragmentation, and that occurred not only in the splintering of this writer into heteronyms but in the writings themselves.* Erostratus, *like so many of Pessoa's works, was left as a set of disconnected passages—some polished, some rough—that don't add up to a viable whole. Pessoa complained bitterly, in* The Book of Disquiet *(Texts 85, 289–291) and elsewhere, of his inability to produce rounded, finished works. Surely he never imagined that the imperfect works he left would, in a future marked by intellectual chaos, be appreciated* precisely because of their fragmentary nature, *which confers on them the distinction of being absolutely faithful to the reality of the world as it was described by Alberto Caeiro—"parts without a whole"—and as we feel it today.*

from Erostratus

Except when it is the product of chance, or of such purely external circumstances as may be put under the name of chance, celebrity is the result of the application of some sort of special skill, or of intelligence, and of the recognition by others of the special skill or the intelligence which is applied. By special skill anything is here meant which distinguishes the individual from his natural peers: great daring, great violence, great subtlety are special skills in this particular sense, and there is no more essential honor in being a hero than in being a genius, the act or acts which prove the hero or the genius being equally a product of temperament, which is inborn, of education and environment, which no man gives himself, of opportunity and occasion, which very few men can choose or create, if indeed any man does choose or create as an efficient cause.

Men may be divided into three portions or lots, and the division may fitly follow the traditional division of the mind—intellect, emotion or feeling, and will. There are men of pure intellect, and these are philosophers and scientists; there are men of pure feeling, and these are mystics and prophets, the passive founders of religions or the mediums of received religious systems; there are men of pure will, and these are statesmen and warriors, leaders of industry as such or of commerce as nothing but commerce. There are three mixed types: men of intellect and feeling, and these are the artists of all kinds; men of intellect and will, and these are the higher statesmen and empire and nation builders; men of feeling and will, and these are the active founders and disseminators of religions (spiritual or material), the believers in the Woman Clothed with the Sun* and the believers in democracy.

Intelligence presents three high forms, which we can conveniently call genius, talent, and wit, taking the last word in the broader sense of bright and active intelligence, of the kind though not of the degree of common intelligence, and not in the particular sense of the capacity for making jokes.

These three types of intelligence are not continuous with one another; they are not grades or degrees of one single faculty or function. Genius is abstract intelligence individualized—the concrete embodiment . . . . . . of an abstract faculty. Talent is concrete intelligence made abstract; it is not bound, like genius, to the individual, except insofar as everything that happens in the individual is bound to him because his. Wit is concrete intelligence individualized, and, except in the value of the thing individualized, has the show and the gestures of genius. That is why it is so easy to mistake great wit for positive genius. Talent, on the other hand, is between both and opposed by nature to both.

It may be admitted that genius is unappreciated in its age because it is opposed to that age; but it may be asked why it is appreciated by the times that come after. The universal is opposed to any age, because the characteristics of that age are necessarily particular; why therefore should genius, which deals in universal and permanent values, be more kindly received by one age than by another?

The reason is simple. Each age results from a criticism of the age that preceded it and of the principles which underlie the civilizational life of that age. Whereas one principle underlies each age, or seems to underlie it, criticism of that one principle is varied, and has in common only the fact that it is a criticism of the same thing. In opposing his age, the man of genius implicitly criticizes it, and so implicitly belongs to one or another of the critical currents of the next age. He may himself produce one or another of those currents, like Wordsworth; he may produce none, like Blake, yet live by a parallel attitude to his, risen in that age by no discipleship properly speaking.*

The more universal the genius, the more easily he will be taken up by the very next age, because the deeper will be his implicit criticism of his own. The less universal, within his substantial universality, the more difficult will his way be, unless he happens to hit the sense of one of the main critical currents of the age come after.

. . .

Painting will sink. Photography has deprived it of many of its attractions. Futility or silliness has deprived it of almost all the rest. What was left has been spoiled by American collectors. A great painting means a thing which a rich American wants to buy because other people would like to buy it if they could. Thus paintings are set on a parallel, not with poems or novels, but with the first editions of certain poems and novels. The museum becomes a thing parallel, not to the library, but to the bibliophile's library. The appreciation of painting becomes a parallel, not to the appreciation of literature, but to the appreciation of editions. Art criticism falls gradually into the hands of dealers in antiques.

Architecture becomes a minor aspect of civil engineering.

Only music and literature remain.

Literature is the intellectual way of dispensing with all the other arts. A poem, which is a musical picture of ideas, makes us free, through the understanding of it, to see what we want and to hear what we want. All statues and paintings, all songs and symphonies, are tyrannous in comparison with this. In a poem, we must understand what the poet wants, but we may feel what we like.

Not sincerity in the absolute, but some sort of sincerity, is required in art, that it may be art. A man can write a good love sonnet in two conditions—because he is greatly in love, or because he is greatly in art. He must be sincere in the love or in the art; he cannot be great in either, or in anything, otherwise. He may burn inwardly, not thinking of the sonnet he is writing; he may burn outwardly, not thinking of the love he is figuring. But he must be on fire somewhere. Otherwise he will not cook the goose of his human inferiority.

*   *   *

Professional improbity and inefficiency are perhaps the distinctive characteristics of our age. The old artificer had to do work; the present workman has to make a machine work. He is a mere slave-driver of metals; he becomes as coarse-grained as a driver of slaves, but less interesting, because he cannot even be called a tyrant.

As the slave-driver becomes a slave to slave-driving and so gets the mind of a slave, though of a luckier slave, so the machine-driver becomes a mere biotic lever, a sort of starting arrangement tagged on to an engine. Taking part in mass production may leave a man a decent human being; it really is so low a thing that he need not be affected by it. But taking part in mass production does not leave a man a decent human workman.

Efficiency is less complex today. Inefficiency can therefore easily pass as efficiency, and be, indeed, efficient.

The only arts and crafts in which we see some striving after perfection or achievement are the absence of arts and crafts—that is to say, those activities which are called sports and games and used to be considered, not as things in which to strive for something, but as things in which to rest from striving. It is futile to cite the Greeks. The Greeks strove to be perfect in everything they did—in sports and games because also in poetry and reasoning. Our poets write poetry anyhow; our reasoners think anyhow. Only our runners really run, because they are running nowhere. The Greeks lusted for fame in sports because they lusted for fame in everything; we lust for fame in sports and hobbies because we can lust for fame in nothing else. The exuberant activity of a child has no resemblance to the exuberant activity of acute mania.

There are only two types of constant mood with which life is worth living—with the noble joy of a religion, or with the noble sorrow of having lost one. The rest is vegetation, and only a psychological botany can take interest in such diluted mankind.

Yet it is admissible to think that there is one sort of greatness in Erostratus—a greatness which he does not share with lesser crashers into fame. He, a Greek, may be conceived as having that delicate perception and calm delirium of beauty which distinguishes still the memory of his giant clan. He may therefore be conceived as burning Diana's temple in an ecstasy of sorrow, part of him being burnt in the fury of his wrong endeavor. We may fitly conceive him as having overcome the toils of a remorse of the future, and facing a horror within himself for the stalwartness of fame. His act may be compared, in a way, to that terrible element of the initiation of the Templars, who, being first proven absolute believers in Christ—both as Christians in the general tradition of the Church, and as occult Gnostics and therefore in the great particular tradition of Christianity—had to spit upon the Crucifix in their initiation. The act may seem no more than humanly revolting from a modern standpoint, for we are not believers, and when, since the Romantics, we defy God and hell, [we] defy things which for us are dead and thus send challenges to corpses. But no human courage, in any field or sea where men are brave with mere daring, can compare with the horror of that initiation. The God they spat upon was the holy substance of Redemption. They looked into hell when their mouths watered with the necessary blasphemy. Thus may be conceived Erostratus, save that the stress of the love of beauty is a lesser thing than the conviction of a sentimental truth. Thus let us conceive him, that we may justify the remembrance.

For if Erostratus did this, he comes at once into the company of all men who have become great by the power of their individuality. He makes that sacrifice of feeling, of passion, ... which distinguishes the path to immortality. He suffers like Christ, who dies as the man that he may prove himself the Word.

Anyone who is in any way a poet knows very well how much easier it is to write a good poem (if good poems lie in the man's power) about a woman who interests him very much than about a woman he is deeply in love with. The best sort of love poem is generally written about an abstract woman.

A great emotion is too selfish; it takes into itself all the blood of the spirit, and the congestion leaves the hands too cold to write. Three sorts of emotions produce great poetry—strong but quick emotions, seized upon for art as soon as they have passed, but not before they have passed; strong and deep emotions in their remembrance a long time after; and false emotions, that is to say, emotions felt in the intellect. Not insincerity, but a translated sincerity, is the basis of all art.

The great general who would win a battle for the empire of his country and the history of his people does not wish—he cannot wish—to have many of his soldiers slain. Yet, once he has entered into the contemplation of his strategy, he will choose (without a thought of his men) the better stroke, though it lose him a hundred thousand men, rather than the worse or even but the slower action, which may leave him nine tenths of those men he fights with and for, and whom he generally loves. He becomes an artist for the sake of his fellow countrymen and he mows down his fellow countrymen for their strategical sake.

He may not be intelligent, but he must be intellectual.

Art is the intellectualization of sensation through expression. The intellectualization is given in, by, and through the expression itself. That is why great artists—even great artists in literature, which is the most intellectual of the arts—are so often unintelligent persons.

We shall move from private poets to public anthologies. Tennyson, as a useless whole, occupies nearly a thousand double-column pages. How much Tennyson will occupy the perhaps less than a thousand simple pages of the future complete English Anthology?

One thing that will happen, unless, with the progress of popular education (democracy), we grow progressively less rational, is the careful sifting, generation after generation, of absolute from relative values. One kind of relative value dies by [natural] death—the relative value that is absolute with respect to its own age. We have spoken of it already. But there is another, and a subtler, kind of relative value—it is the relative value which is absolute outside its own age. A man who, in the eighteenth century, happened, by some unknown mental trick, to write something like bad Tennyson or worse Mallarmé, would be an astonishing phenomenon in his time. He (ignored as a genius in his age) would attract our present historical attention by virtue of that extraordinary departure from his times; he would be called a genius and a forerunner, and perhaps he would have the legitimate right* to both titles. But bad Tennyson or worse Mallarmé would become bad Tennyson and worse Mallarmé as soon as there were a Tennyson and a Mallarmé, and the relative value would be flagrantly relative; it would become historical and not poetical. What would be such a man's position in the final scheme of celebrity? He would have done an easy thing when it was difficult—that is all. But a genius is a man who does a difficult thing, even when it is easy.

The central thing about really great geniuses is that they are not forerunners. The very instance that the word arouses defines the case: that John the Baptist was Christ's forerunner means that he was unimportant in comparison with Christ. John the Baptist is a historical figure (whether he existed or not); Christ is a living figure (subject to the same useless reservation).

. . .

There is hardly any, if any, great artist in the world for whom a definite forerunner cannot be found. Each artist has a typical style; yet in almost every case, if not in every one, that typical style was already shadowed in a former artist of no importance. Whether there was a vague influence in the undercurrents of the age, which the first caught vaguely and the second clearly; whether there was a chance inspiration, like an outward thing in the former, which the latter, by direct contact, wakened in his temperamental brain into a definite inner inspiration; whether the two cases were consubstantial—not one of the three hypotheses matters, except historically. The genius will be the final product; and he will be final, even if he comes afterwards.

. . .

Nothing worth expressing ever remains unexpressed; it is against the nature of things that it should remain so. We think that Coleridge had in him great things he never told the world; yet he told them in the "Mariner" and "Kubla Khan," which contain the metaphysics that is not there, the fancies they omit and the speculations nowhere to be found. Coleridge could never have written those poems if there had not been that in him that the poems do not express by what they say, but by the mere fact that they exist.

Each man has very little to express, and the sum of a whole life of feeling and thought can sometimes bear total in an eight-line poem. If Shakespeare had written nothing but Ariel's song to Ferdinand, he would not indeed have been the Shakespeare he was—for he did write more—but there would have been enough of him to show that he was a greater poet than Tennyson.

Each of us has perhaps much to say, but there is little to say about that much. Posterity wants us to be short and precise. Faguet said excellently that posterity likes only concise writers.*

Variety is the only excuse for abundance. No man should leave twenty different books unless he can write like twenty different men. Victor Hugo's works fill fifty large volumes, yet each volume, each page almost, contains all Victor Hugo. The other pages add up as pages, not as genius. There was in him no productivity, but prolixity. He wasted his time as a genius, however little he may have wasted it as a writer. Goethe's judgment on him remains supreme, early as it was given, and a great lesson to all artists. "He should write less and work more," he said. This is, in its distinction between real work, which is non-extended, and fictitious work which takes up space (for pages are no more than space), one of the great critical sayings of the world.

If he can write like twenty different men, he is twenty different men, however that may be, and his twenty books are in order.

ON THE LITERARY ART
AND ITS ARTISTS

[The Task of Modern Poetry]

The province of modern poetry seems to me to be twofold, according as we consider its [subject] matter, or the form that shapes that matter.

It is the task of every modern poet to extend, complicate, and intellectualize his sensibility, to become, as completely as possible, a *resonateur* for all the forces of the universe, of life, and of the mind. The palace of his inspiration should have open windows on all four walls, whether looking to the North of Mysticism, to the East of Simplicity, to the West of Decadence, or to the South of ever-growing Life.

There are three reasons why this should be so. Our age is one in which, to the initial subjectivity created by the Christian attitude, there have been added the pagan impulse of the Renaissance, the Individualism of the Nineteenth Century, and the cross-currents and swelling forces which the growth of commerce and of industry have thrust upon the Twentieth.

Besides this, our age is one in which civilization has not only thus gone deeper into the soul than in others, but it has gone wider in the world: we are the first really cosmopolitan civilization that the world has seen, for the increased facilities for communication and intercourse, and the further facilities, mental now and spiritual, which have resulted from that very intercourse, have linked to an astonishing degree nations and peoples as separate* as earth can separate. All the world is Europe now, Australia more so than most European villages. The railway, the steamship, the telegraph, and the wireless inventions have thrown the shadow of their lines into our minds, and a telepathy has grown up among all the peoples of the world; we become open members of a freemasonry of sensibility whose symbol is Electricity.

In any London street you meet the whole world.

And, further than this, not only have the facilities of communication made the world smaller and all the earth a large city, *civitas Dei* in the Devil's land, but the growth of culture and of curiosity, the increase of investigation, has packed all past times into the consciousness of the present. Unknown breaths, unreleased as yet from the Aeolian cave* of past civilizations, have been let free upon the world. The dead glories, and something of the ever-living lore, of the Egyptians and of the Chaldeans, of the old Chinese and of the buried ancestors of Peru, have come into our mental vision, as if from over a remote line of a horizon our eyes grow quick to examine. All these things, impinging upon our sensibility, must widen it, complicate it, and intercriticize it. The man who would limit his receptivity to this goes into the convent of himself, self-sequestered from his multiplied age.

Only one poet, Walt Whitman, has appeared with a sensibility large enough to embrace the passive opportunities of the mind before this enlarged world. But he lacked the element that should control this excess of feeling things, and reduce it to that unity [which it behooves]* anything that is a personality to impose upon its impressions.

And by these considerations we arrive at the other element, the formal one, in the poetry of today.

The phenomenon called balance, or equilibrium, is [in] no way so finely represented, when we deal with life—which, being dynamic, not static, cannot be compared to a perfectly still body—than by the oscillation of a pendulum. It is the very essential thing in this oscillation, and the natural thing, that it should go as far in one direction as in the opposite one. The growth of sensibility, the increase of receptivity must therefore* be corrected, balanced, and unified by an increase in the faculties which constitute inhibition and self-control. A sensibility which circumstances both of time and of place compel to be so much richer than the Greek one must be reined in by a controlling intellect far stronger than the Greek one, which was very strong. The increased pace of the courser that leads us to the Future must be balanced by a tighter hold on the reins that guide it. If we are dragged along, let us be self-dragged along.

The great sin of Christian civilization is that, while it has constantly increased the passive elements of the mind, it has concomitantly undermined the active ones—that our increased ability to feel and analyze has not been accompanied by an equally increased ability to think and synthesize. This is not growth, it is merely increase. It is not development, but decadence. All Christian civilization, when it emerged from being barbarian, jumped at once into being decadent. Simple natures are easiest corrupted.

The monstrous phenomenon called Shakespeare is typical of the intellectual results of Christian civilization. The man who is the greatest sensibility in the world was incapable of self-discipline and self-control, could not create an ordered whole. The greatest poet in the ancient world was also its greatest artist. The greatest poet in the modern world is one of its least artists.

. . .

Shakespeare

The fundamental defects of the Christian attitude towards life can be seen in the greatest poet it has produced typical of itself. The plays and poems of Shakespeare are, from the pure artistic standpoint, the greatest failure that the world has ever looked on. Never have such elements been gathered in one mind as were found in the mind of Shakespeare. He had, in a degree never surpassed, the lyrical gift in all its modes (except one); he had, in a degree never surpassed, the intuition of character and the broad-hearted comprehension of humanity; he had, in a degree never surpassed, the arts of diction and of expression. But he lacked one thing: balance, sanity, discipline. The fact that he entered into states of mind as far apart as the abstract spirituality of Ariel and the coarse humanity of Falstaff did to some extent create a balance in his unbalance. But at bottom he is not sane nor balanced. Incapable of constructing, of developing, of balancing one thing against another, he stands forth to us as the incarnate example of Christian deficiencies.

If he be compared with Milton, the deficiencies become glaring. Shakespeare's lack of a sense of proportion, of a sense of unity, and of a sense of development and interaction are as extraordinary as the fact that they happen to a Christian poet is ordinary.*

Our civilization, so rich and so complex, has produced extraordinary lyrics, unparalleled in range, depth, and comprehension and subtlety. It has not produced any supreme achievement in constructive poetry and literature.

[On Blank Verse and *Paradise Lost*]

Blank verse, the one so called, is an extremely dull medium to write in. Only the subtlest rhythmical faculty can ward off flatness, and it cannot ward off flatness for a long time. Perfect poems can be written in blank verse, that is to say, poems which can be read with interest and attention, and will fulfill and satisfy; but they must be short—"Tithonus," or "Ulysses" or "Oenone"* and the like. When not short, or not sufficiently short, they can hold themselves up only by strong interest, and it is very difficult, except in drama, to carry strong interest along the desert of blank verses. Blank verse is the ideal medium for an unreadable epic poem. All the metrical science of Milton, and it was very great, cannot make of *Paradise Lost* anything but a dull poem. It is dull, and we must not lie to our souls by denying it. (. . .)

In Milton there is very little action, properly speaking,* very little quick action, and the thought is all theological, that is to say, peculiar to a certain kind of metaphysics which does not concern the universality of mankind.

The fact is that the epic poem is a Greco-Roman survival, or very nearly so.

Only prose, which disengages the aesthetic sense and lets it rest, can carry the attention willingly over great spaces of print. *Pickwick*

Papers is bigger, in point of words, than *Paradise Lost*; it is certainly inferior, as values go; but I have read *Pickwick Papers* more times than I can reckon, and I have read *Paradise Lost* only one time and a half, for I failed at the second reading. God overwhelmed me with bad metaphysics and I was literally God-damned.

from Charles Dickens — *Pickwick Papers*

Mr. Pickwick belongs to the sacred figures of the world's history. Do not, please, claim that he never existed; the same thing happens to most of the world's sacred figures, and they have been living presences to a vast number of consoled wretches. So, if a mystic can claim a personal acquaintance and clear vision of the Christ, a human man can claim personal acquaintance and a clear vision of Mr. Pickwick.

Pickwick, Sam Weller, Dick Swiveller — they have been personal acquaintances of our happier hours, irremediably lost through some trick of losing that time does not measure and space does not include. They have lapsed from us in a diviner way than dying, and we keep their memory with us in a better manner than remembering. The human trammels of space and time do not bind them to us, they owe no allegiance to the logic of ages, nor to the laws of living, nor to the appearances of chance. The garden in us, where they live secluded, gathers in flowers of all the things that make mankind copious and pleasant to live with: the hour after dinner when we are all brothers, the winter morning when we all walk out together, the feast days when the riotous things of our imperfection — biologic truths, political realities, being sincere, striving to know, art for art's sake — lie on the inexistent other side of the snow-covered hill.

To read Dickens is to obtain a mystic vision, but though he claims so often to be Christian, it has nothing to do with the Christian vision of the world. It is a recasting of the old pagan noise, the old Bacchic joy at the world being ours, though transiently, at the coexistence and fullness of men, at the meeting and sad parting of perennial mankind.

It is a human world, and so women are of no importance in it, as the old pagan criterion has it, and has it truly. The women of Dickens are cardboard and sawdust to pack his men to us on the voyage from the spaces of dream. The joy and zest of life does not include women, and the old Greeks, who created pederasty as an institution of social joy, knew this to the final end.

. . .

He raised caricature to a high art and made unreality a mode of reality. Mr. Pickwick has a more solid density than our acquaintances; he belongs more than the next-door neighbor and is a more living person than dozens, such as the Trinity [. . .].

. . .

Somewhere surely, when the waking hand shakes our shoulder or the Gods themselves thin back into a lie, Fate will permit a Paradise for those who have communed in Pickwick, even if not in Christ, and have believed in the two Wellers,* even if not in the three Persons. They will live secluded from the joy of Heaven and the ecclesiastic pangs of Hell, not forgetful of the one-eyed bagman,* disdaining not so much as the absent shirt behind Mr. Bob Sawyer's dirty neckcloth.

The fate of joyous things is that they never live, of sad things that they pass also. But the things which live by the mere gesture of their creation—their Attic permanence. . . . . . A Bacchic permanence, a dynamic splendor of consciousness, a transubstantiation of normality.

from Concerning Oscar Wilde

Pessoa wrote close to twenty passages about Oscar Wilde, some in English and some in Portuguese, dating mostly from the 1910s and 1920s. One of the passages was titled "Defense of Oscar Wilde," and another was the sketch for a preface to a projected volume of Wilde's work in Portuguese translation, but most of the remaining passages (including the four published here) were probably intended for an essay to be titled "Concerning Oscar Wilde."

Pessoa was ambivalent toward Wilde, as he was toward another of his literary obsessions: Shakespeare. Though he deemed Wilde's writing facile, he was fascinated by the man, and especially by the man in relationship to art. He admired Wilde's defiantly aristocratic attitude and seems to have felt, or feared, affinities with the aesthete's personal life. In or near 1917 Pessoa cast a horoscope for Wilde, accompanied by a chronological outline of his life: birth, education, travels, first book publication, marriage, "pederasty," imprisonment, death. This is followed by a second, rather different set of astrological indications under the heading "My case." In at least one circumstance, Pessoa's "case" matched Wilde's: both men died on November 30.

The central circumstance, of course, is that Oscar Wilde was not an artist. He was another thing: the thing called an "intellectual." It is easy to have proof of the matter, however strange the assertion may seem.

There is not a doubt of the fact that Wilde's great preoccupation was beauty, that he was, if anything, a slave to it rather than a mere lover of it. This beauty was especially of a decorative character; indeed, it can hardly be said to be of any character but a decorative one. Even that moral or intellectual beauty which he craves or admires bears a decorative character. (. . .) Thoughts, feelings, fancies—these are to him valuable only insofar as they can lend themselves to the decoration and upholstering of his inner life.

. . .

Now, the curious circumstance about his style is that it is itself, qua style, very little decorated. He has no fine phrases. Very seldom does he strike on a phrase which is aesthetically great, apart from being intellectually striking. He is full of striking phrases, of the kind of thing that inferior people call paradoxes and epigrams. But the "exquisite phrase" of the poets, the poetic phrase proper, is a thing in which his works are signally lacking. The sort of thing that Keats produces constantly, that Shelley constantly hits upon, that Shakespeare is master in—

the "manner of saying" whereby a man stamps himself as poet and artist, and not merely as a spectator of art—this he lacks, and he lacks it to
a degree which is both obvious and unevident. It is obvious because his
purely intellectual phrasing is so happy and abundant that the contrasting absence of purely artistic phrasing is very marked, and it is unevident
because the pure delight caused by that very succession of intellectual
felicities has the power to seduce us into believing that we have been
reading artistic phrasing.

He loves long descriptions of beautiful decorative things and has
long pages [of such descriptions] in *Dorian Gray*, for instance (. . .).
Yet he does not invoke those beautiful things by means of phrases that
shall place them before our eyes in a living manner; he does but cata-
logue them with voluptuosity. He describes richly, but not artistically.

His use of the pure melody of words is singularly awkward and
primitive. He loves the process but is ever infelicitous in it. He likes
strange names of strange beautiful things and rich names of lands and
cities, but they become as corpses in his hands. He cannot write "From
silken Samarkand to cedared Lebanon." This line of Keats, though
no very astonishing performance, is still above the level of Wilde's
achievement.

. . .

For the explanation of this weakness of Wilde's is in his very decorative standpoint. The love of decorative beauty generally engenders
an incapacity to live the inner life of things, unless, like Keats, the poet
has, equally with the love of the decorative, the love of the natural. It
is nature and not decoration that educates in art. The best describer
of a painting, in words—he that best can make with a painting *une
transposition d'art*, rebuilding it into the higher life of words, so as to
alter nothing of its beauty, rather re-creating it to greater splendor—
this best describer is generally a man who began by looking at Nature
with seeing eyes. If he had begun with pictures, he would never have
been able* to describe a picture well. The case of Keats was this. By
the study of nature we learn to observe; by that of art we merely learn
to admire.

There must be something scientific and precise—precise in a hard and scientific manner—in the artistic vision, that it may be the artistic vision at all.

. . .

Of all the tawdry and futile adventurers in the arts, whose multiplied presence negatively distinguishes modern times, he is one of the greatest figures, for he is true to falsehood. His attitude is the one true one in an age when nothing is true; and it is the true one because consciously not true.

His pose is conscious, whereas all round him there are but unconscious* poses. He has therefore the advantage of consciousness. He is representative: he is conscious.

All modern art is immoral, because all modern art is indisciplined. Wilde is consciously immoral, so he has the intellectual advantage.

He interpreted by theory all that modern art is, and if his theories sometimes waver and shift, he is representative indeed, for all modern theories are a mixture and a medley, seeing that the modern mind is too passive to do strong things.

. . .

Our age is shallow in its profundity, half-hearted in its convictions . . . . . . We are the contrary of the Elizabethans. They were deep even when shallow; we are shallow even when deep. Insufficient reason[ing] power miscarries us of our ideas. Little tenacity of purpose soils our plans

. . . . . .

It is a sad thing to say, but no type so symbolizes the modern man as the masturbator does. The incoherence, lack of purpose,* inconsequence, ... the alternation of a sense of failure with furious impulses towards life. . . .

Wilde was typical of this. He was a man who did not belong in his beliefs. If he were God he would have been an atheist. . . . . . .

He thought [of] his thoughts as clever, not as just. This is typical of the age's mental weariness; it is masturbation's pleasure. The joy of thinking clubs to forgetfulness all the purpose of thought.

He did not know what it was to be sincere. Can the reader conceive this?

He was a gesture, not a man.

[The Art of James Joyce]

The art of James Joyce, like that of Mallarmé, is art preoccupied with method, with how it's made. Even the sensuality of *Ulysses* is a symptom of intermediation. It is hallucinatory delirium—the kind treated by psychiatrists—presented as an end in itself.

[The Art of Translation]

I do not know whether anyone has ever written a History of Translations. It should be a long but very interesting book. Like a History of Plagiarisms—another possible masterpiece which awaits an actual author—it would brim over with literary lessons. There is a reason why one thing should bring up the other: a translation is only a plagiarism in the author's name. A History of Parodies would complete the series, for a translation is a serious parody in another language. The mental processes involved in parodying* well are the same as those involved in translating competently. In both cases there is an adaptation to the spirit of the author for a purpose which the author did not have. In one case the purpose is humor, where the author was serious; in the other case a certain* language, where the author wrote in another. Will anyone one day parody a humorous into a serious poem? It is uncertain. But there can be no doubt that many poems—even many great poems—would gain by being translated into the very language they were written in.

This brings up the problem as to whether it is art or the artist that matters, the individual or the product. If it be the final result that matters and that shall give delight, then we are justified in taking a famous poet's all but perfect poem, and, in the light of the criticism of another age, making it perfect by excision, substitution, or addition. Wordsworth's "Ode on Immortality" is a great poem, but it is far from being a perfect poem. It could be rehandled to advantage.

The only interest in translations is when they are difficult, that is to say, either from one language into a widely different one, or of a very complicated poem, though into a closely allied language. There is no fun in translating between, say, Spanish and Portuguese. Anyone who can read one language can automatically read the other, so there seems also to be no use in translating. But to translate Shakespeare into one of the Latin languages would be an exhilarating task. I doubt whether it can be done into French; it will be difficult to do into Italian or Spanish; Portuguese, being the most pliant and complex of the Romance languages, could possibly admit the translation.

FROM ESSAY ON POETRY

Written for the Edification and Instruction of Would-be Poets.

Professor Jones

Various handwritten and typed passages make up this exemplary piece of Swiftian satire, which Pessoa began writing as a teenager in South Africa. It shows him at his finest as an English prose stylist, in part because his ultraliterary English is here used to best advantage. As explained in the "General Introduction," Pessoa's contact with English during his childhood years in Durban was intense but atypical, being largely restricted to his classwork and his extensive readings. If from the Elizabethans and early Romantics his English acquired a slightly outdated syntax, the writings of Shakespeare, Carlyle, and Dickens also endowed it with a permanent underlay of irony and humor. It was, in fact, the perfect English for a professor of literature fond of speaking with his tongue in his cheek, and so it seems a pity that Professor Jones wrote only this "Essay on Poetry."

The essay was originally attributed to a Professor Trochee and had a slightly different subtitle: "Written for the Edification of Would-be Verse Writers." After he returned to Lisbon, Pessoa revised the long opening section and changed the subtitle. No author's name appears on the newer, typed copy, but a note in the archives attributes the resubtitled essay to Professor Jones.

When I consider the abundance of young men and the superabundance of young women in the present century, when I survey the necessary and consequent profusion of reciprocal attachments, when I reflect upon the great number of poetical compositions emanating therefrom, when I bring my mind to bear upon the insanity and chaotic formation of these effusions, I am readily convinced that by writing an expository essay on the poetical art I shall be greatly contributing to the emolument of the public.

Having therefore carefully considered the best and most practical way in which to open so relevant a discussion, I have not unwisely concluded that a straightforward statement of the rules of poetry is the manner in which I must present the subject to the reader. I have thought it useless and inappropriate to refer myself too often to the ancient critics on the art, since modern critics are pleasanter to quote and have said all that was to be said on the matter, and a little more — which is their part where they are original. For putting aside the critics of old I have two very good reasons, of which the second is that, even if I *did* know anything about them, I should not like to thrust my scholarship on the reader. I begin then my exposition.

Firstly I think it proper to bring to the attention of the would-be poet a fact which is not usually considered and yet is deserving of consideration. I hope I shall escape universal ridicule if I assert that, at least theoretically, poetry should be susceptible of scansion. I wish it of course to be understood that I agree with Mr. A. B. in maintaining that strict scansion is not at all necessary for the success nor even for the merit of a poetical composition. And I trust I shall not be deemed exceedingly pedantic if I delve into the storehouse of Time to produce as an authority some of the works of a certain William Shakespeare, or Shakspere, who lived some centuries ago and enjoyed some reputation as a dramatist. This person used to take off, or to add on, one syllable or more in the lines of his numerous productions, and if it be at all allowable in this age of niceness to break the tenets of poetical good sense by imitating some obscure scribbler, I should dare to recommend to the beginner the enjoyment of this kind of poetic license. Not that I should advise him to *add* any syllables to his lines, but the subtraction of some is often convenient and desirable. I may as well point out that if, by this very contrivance, the young poet, having taken away some syllables from his poem, proceed with this expedient and take all the remaining syllables out of it, although he might not thus attain to any degree of popularity, he nevertheless would exhibit an extraordinary amount of poetical common sense.

And I may as well here explain that my method for the formation of the rules which I am here expounding* is of the best. I observe and consider the writings of modern poets, and I advise the reader to do as they have done. Thus if I advise the young poet to care nothing in practice for scansion, it is because I have found this to be a rule and a condition in the poems of today. Nothing but the most careful consideration and the most honest clinging to a standard can be of use to a learner in the art. In all cases I may be relied upon to give the best method and the best rules.

I approach the subject of rhyme with a good deal of trepidation, lest by uttering any remarks which may seem too strictly orthodox, I shall harshly violate one of the most binding regulations of modern poesy. I am obliged to agree with Mr. C. D. when he says that rhyme should not be very evident in any poem, even though it may be called rhymed; and the numerous modern poets who exemplify this precept have my entire approbation. Poetry ought to encourage thought and call for examination; what is then greater than the delight of the close critic when, after a minute dissection of a composition, he perceives, first, that it is poetry and not prose, secondly, after long exertion, that it is rhymed and not blank?

Such poetical niceties, however, being visible only to the experienced critic, the ordinary man of poetical tastes is sometimes, when called upon to criticize a poem, placed in an undesirable situation. For instance, about a week ago a young friend of mine called upon me and asked my opinion of a poem which he had written. He handed me a paper. I made a few, and futile, attempts at understanding the effusion, but quickly corrected them by inverting the position of the paper, as better sense could thus be obtained. Being fortunately forewarned that the paper before me contained a poem, I began at once, though without caution, to heap eulogies on the excellent blank verse. Coloring with indignation, my friend pointed out that his composition was rhymed, and, moreover, that it was in what he called the Spenserian stanza. Though not a bit convinced by his impudent invention of a name (as if Spencer* had ever written poetry!), I continued to examine the composition before me, but, getting no nearer to the sense, I contented myself with praising it, and especially commending the originality of the treatment. On handing back the paper to my friend, as he glanced at it to show me something particular, his face suddenly fell and looked puzzled.

"Hang it," said he, "I gave you the wrong paper. This is only my tailor's bill!"

Let the poetical critic take as a lesson this most unhappy episode.

On that bane of poetical feeling, blank verse, I shall only touch lightly; but as several friends of mine have repeatedly asked me for the formula or recipe for its production, I hereby communicate the directions to those of my readers who are so far gone. To tell the truth there is not, in the whole range of poetry, anything easier to produce than blank verse.

The first thing to do is to procure yourself ink, paper, and a pen; then write down, in the ordinary commonplace language that you speak (technically called prose), what you wish to say, or, if you be clever, what you think. The next step is to lay hands upon a ruler graduated in inches or in centimeters, and mark off, from your prose effusion, bits about four inches or ten centimeters long: these are the lines of your blank verse composition. In case the four-inch line does not divide into the prose effort without remainder, either the addition of a few Alases or Ohs or Ahs, or the introduction of an invocation to the Muses will fill in the required space. This is the modern recipe. Of course I do not know directly that such is the method that modern poets employ. On examining their poems, however, I have found that the *internal evidence* is conclusive, pointing everywhere to such a method of composition.

As to the scansion of your blank verse—never mind it; at first, whatever its kind, the critics will find in it the most outrageous flaws; but if in time you wriggle into poetical greatness, you will find the same gentlemen justify everything you have done, and you will be surprised at the things you symbolized, insinuated, meant.

Before taking leave of this part of my essay, I beg to point out to the reader that in this the age of motorcars and of art for the sake of art, there is no restriction as to the length of a line in poetry. You can write lines of two, three, five, ten, twenty, thirty syllables or more—that is of the least importance; but* when the lines of a poem contain more than a certain number of syllables, that composition is generally said to be written in prose. This difficulty of finding what is the number of syllables that is the limit between poetry and prose makes it modernly impossible well to establish which is one, which the other. Internal distinction is of course impossible. After some study I have found that that may generally be considered poetry where every line begins with a capital letter. If the reader can find another distinction I shall be very pleased to hear of it.

Now, although I advise you to write, as far as possible, in English, I must likewise admonish you to use such words as are not easily understood; this is a most essential part of poetry, for it causes you to have the praise of the reading public and the speedy approbation of the entangled critic. Sometimes, however, the critic prefers to be silent and pretend to treat your book with contempt; in your next work do you point out to the public that the contempt of the critic arises from his ignorance, and you will invariably be right.

And though it may seem strange that in the age of Kipling any man should dare to mention grammar, I must beg the patient reader to enter with me upon this subject. I wish merely to say that grammar is, in poetry, absolutely unnecessary; the darker and more uncertain the parts of your sentence (if you are so unpoetical as to write in sentences or periods), the more impressive will be your verse, the more evident your philosophic depth.

I now come to that most important part of verse, which consists in the metaphors, the epithets, the similes—in fact, the whole dress of poetry. Poetry, like a society woman, is better seen dressed.

Similes are found everywhere, a writer on composition informs us; the gentleman is right—they are. I should confine myself, however, to informing the would-be poet that it is not advisable to find them in books that are very much read (nor *can* they there be much found). I should think it safe, however, for him to take them from old poets, now forgotten. To suggest a few names, unknown to present-day readers: Publius Vergilius Maro, Quintus Horatius Flaccus, and, more modern, John Milton, John Dryden, and Alexander Pope. As nobody nowadays is acquainted with any of these, similes gathered from their works will appear quite new.

Metaphors are obtainable in the same way.

As to epithets, I cannot but recommend the purchase of a dictionary of quotations where these ornaments can be found. They are, of course, set words and phrases. For instance, your mistress's mouth is always "perfumed" and her lips "cherry"; her eyes will always be "dreamy" and her hair composed of "silken threads" wherein your heart is "entwined." Your face must be always "pale with care" and your frame "wasted by woe"; you must always be awake half the night dreaming of your cruel fate and the other half asleep dreaming of her. Your lady's form must be more beautiful than that of Venus; this is not improper to state, for thanks to the costumes of modern society, you will have been able to observe it. Your lady must likewise be of a virgin purity, and though this and the statement before might not seem to fit well together, you must remember the age we live in and the strange scientific phe nomena that are ever making us gasp. You can begin to write love poetry at twelve or thirteen, when you will know life well.

Before concluding I wish to say a few words on a subject of no small importance to the poet, though not directly concerning the structure or life of his composition. I would merely point out that to attain a full reputation as a poet, the beginner must of course have his portrait published in fashionable papers and must see that paragraphs about himself, his habits, his whims and eccentricities are published in suitable journals. Now it must be clear that, for this to be well done, the learner must look like, and act as, a poet, information about which things I here shall tender unasked. First, as regards personal appearance, I think no one can deny that a thin, stooping gait is indispensable. Moreover, clothes too large for the wearer, an unwashed face and uncombed hair, a hat put on wrong side foremost, and a general air of shabbiness and misery are everywhere allowed to be marks of a poetic temperament. As to the face of the poet, it must be ornamented by long hair falling on the shoulders, by dark eyes, arched eyebrows, and a pale and sallow complexion. It is absolutely indispensable that the bard should have a Greek nose with a knob at the end of it, or, in default of this, a nose with the bridge somewhat sunken but not lacking the inevitable knob. The Grecian nose cannot be easily attained, but if your nose be arched and you wish it to be of the second poetic type, a way has been found to obtain it and also to remedy a prominent chin, a thing which must not appear in a poetic face. The way suggested is a "communion of spirits" with the wife of an athletic friend. For this method, however, I cannot say much in advantage inasmuch that, of the two friends of mine who tried it, one lost all semblance of a face and the other bolted before the crucial moment. On this subject there is but little to add, unless it be that the mouth ought to be either small, large, or regular—a poetic feature which I think all of us possess. Finally, a poet with physiognomic leanings once told me that a great characteristic of a great poet was long and pointed ears,* a fact I consider true, for a friend of mine once told me that between the poet and the ass there is only a small difference, namely that the wiser of them walks on four legs.

FROM FRANCE IN 1950
Jean Seul de Méluret

According to a short résumé that Pessoa drafted in English, his French heteronym was born on August 1, 1885, and specialized in writing poetry, satire, and "scientific works with a satirical or moral purpose." If his unfinished book Des Cas d'Exhibitionnisme might fit in the last category, since it analyzes cases of "nudités publiques" in Paris music halls and elsewhere from a psychological point of view, his satiric article "La France en 1950" has no scientific pretensions. Conceived in 1907 or 1908, it zigzags between the bawdy and the bizarre, activating a rarer side of Pessoa's imagination. A "List of Publications" from circa 1913 designates the essay as "La France en 1950 — par un Japonais," which seems to mean that Pessoa's French persona adopted, in turn, a Japa nese persona, and in the project plans for Europa, the Intersectionist magazine from 1914 that never got off the ground (see pp. 60–61), we find an alternate title that would have pushed Seul's satire yet farther into the future: "La France à l'an 2000." Jean Seul was also supposed to write a satire about French pimps under the title "Messieurs les Souteneurs," but no traces of it have been found. Seul was based in Lisbon, not France, which perhaps explains the frequent grammatical errors in his French. He wrote a number of poems before 1910, though not many complete ones.

Pessoa, under his own name, wrote essays in French throughout his life (few of which have been transcribed and published), and in 1923 he published three French poems in a Portuguese magazine. Toward the end of his life he again resorted to French to write a group of love poems.

Here there are no normal people, just people who are doubly abnormal, people who are doubly inverted sexually, such that they're on their
way back to normality. I'm told that even a certain monsieur I know,
who appears to be utterly normal, is in fact quadrupally abnormal. Since
two negatives make a positive. . . . . .

The other day a Monsieur Sleeps-in-the-bed-of-4-women Giraud was
imprisoned for the crime of refusing to commit incest. He [tried to
defend] himself by proudly pointing out that, since he's the brother of
all humanity, all women are his sisters, so that whenever he sleeps with
a woman, he's sleeping with his sister.

A man named _____ , manager of the Volupté Surhumaine insurance
company, recently lost part of his left testicle. He derived a pleasure from
this loss that would at one time have been called perverse, and so it
became the fashion to lose a [piece] of this bodily part, but people are
advised not to overdo this pleasure.

Illustrious men are much studied nowadays, and the considerable talents of various renowned writers have merited major monographs in
recent years, but instead of discussing the literary part of their oeuvre,
the studies concentrate more and more on determining the probable
length of their penises.

A certain gentleman was accused of not raping a two-month-old baby.
        . . .
    He replied that he was thinking of doing something better than
mere rape when he was arrested. He had no intention of committing
an offense against decency [. . .].

The other day I visited a girls' school called the Institut Sans Hymen.
I'm told it was founded by a benefactress who had fourteen thousand
lovers and who apparently died from her over-zealous dedication.

The girls in this boarding school are very well trained. They learn as many vices as possible, and it's touching to see how easily the cute little sluts catch on.

The punishments, it's true, are rather severe. For instance, one girl who cried out when a classmate used her for some sadistic act was sentenced by a disciplinary committee to having from only three to six lovers, and to wearing dresses that allowed only the upper part of her body to be seen! It's shocking!

. . .

Dishes are washed with the blood of small children who have been raped and had their throats cut. The dishes aren't wiped dry. I've been told that this sensual delight is a bit dated.

Ejaculations have been obtained by eating the bodies of infants.

Animal sperm as a beverage has fallen out of fashion.

Some idiot may find this satire to be indecent and immoral. It would be just like an idiot to think that way, for today's top scientists have verified that idiots think stupidly and do stupid things.

This satire has made deliberate use of gross obscenity.

. . .

Shame on whoever finds this satire amusing. Fie on whoever laughs at it!

RANDOM NOTES
AND EPIGRAMS

Pessoa loved the pithy phrase, the short but complete commentary. It features prominently in the works of Bernardo Soares, the Baron of Teive, and Álvaro de Campos, as well as in Pessoa's papers and notebooks, showing up in the margins or even in the middle of texts to which it may have no relation. Sometimes, on the contrary, an aphorism leads to more elaborate written reflections. Pessoa's miniature literary productions also appear in isolation—on slips of paper and the backs of envelopes—and occasionally in series, filling up a whole page. Most of the epigrams, observations, and memoranda included in this section have never been published. They have not been extracted from larger texts but were found in the archives as they are presented here: as autonomous sentences or paragraphs, or in a sequence of brief to very brief passages separated from each other by horizontal bars. Each number corresponds to a "manuscript," which in some cases is just a scrap of paper. Items 1, 5, 6, 11, 17, and 18 were written in English; the rest have been translated from Portuguese.

1.

When I consider how real and how true the things of his madness are to the madman, I cannot but agree with the essence of Protagoras' statement that "man is the measure of all things."

2.

Man is an animal that almost exists.

3.

There are no norms. All people are exceptions to a rule that doesn't exist.

The difference between God and us must lie, not in attributes, but in the very nature of our existence. Since each thing is what it is, God must be not only what He is but also what He isn't. This confuses us about who He is.

The aristocrat is the man *who doesn't obey,* and since his nature is disobedient, he degenerates into disobeying even his own convictions, his very own self. That is why aristocracies tend, with full awareness and sincerity, to be highly moral in theory and utterly corrupt in practice.

   . . .

    Total aristocratization – anarchy. Individualism has its limits. Some people cannot be individualized.

4.

Life is such a solemn thing, and its problems so serious, that no one has the right to laugh. Anyone who laughs is stupid—temporarily, at least. Happiness is the communicative form of stupidity.

5.

Evil is everywhere on earth, and one of its forms is happiness.

* * *

I say to you: Do good. Why? What do you gain by it? Nothing, you gain nothing. Neither money, nor love, nor respect and perhaps peace of mind. Perhaps thou gainest none of these. Why then do I say: Do good? *Because* you gain nothing by it. It is worth doing for this.

6.

God is God's best joke.

7.

God is an economic concept. In his shadow the priests of all religions fashion their metaphysical bureaucracies.

(Álvaro de Campos)

8.

Whether or not they exist, we're slaves to the gods.

(Bernardo Soares)

9.

Pure agnosticism is impossible. The only true agnosticism is ignorance. To be an agnostic is to be persuaded by reason that there are limits to our understanding. But whereas an observer can stop observing, one who reasons cannot stop. So that when by reason we've proved the limitation or non-limitation of this or that faculty, we cannot say, "Let's stop here," but must keep on reasoning in order to deduce the consequences of that limitation or non-limitation. That is what all "agnostics" do, consciously or unconsciously.

10.

I doubt, therefore I think.

11.

I am not conscience-stricken, but consciousness-stricken.

12.

We all have Futurist moments, as when, for example, we trip on a stone.

13.

In the theater of life, those who play the part of sincerity are, on the whole, the most convincing in their roles.

14.

How hard it is for an intelligent person to be sincere! It's like an ambitious person being honest.

The multiplication of the I is a frequent phenomenon in cases of masturbation.

15.

Be plural like the universe!

16.

Art is the highest and most subtle form of sensuality. The relations between the artist and his public are analogous to those of a man and
woman in sexual intercourse. Artistic creation is a demonstration of
power, domination; artistic contemplation is a passive pleasure.

That's why the ardent aesthete is generally a sexual invert. This is
especially true for the aesthete who creates, since creating implies an
exacerbation of one's aesthetic sensibility, to the point where it over-
flows into love.

17.

Art for art's sake is, really, only art for the artist's sake.

18.

A strong artist kills in himself not only love and pity but the very seeds
of love and of pity. He becomes inhuman out of his great love of
humanity—that love that prompts him to create art for man.

Genius is the greatest curse with which God can bless a man. It
must be undergone with as little groaning and whining as possible, with
as great a consciousness as possible of its divine sadness.

TWO LETTERS TO
JOÃO GASPAR SIMÕES

João Gaspar Simões (1903–1987) was a founding editor of Presença, *the Coimbra-based magazine that published some of the mature Pessoa's most stunning works, including the poems "Autopsychography" and "The Tobacco Shop," passages from* The Book of Disquiet, *and the prose piece titled "Environment." Pessoa was a well-respected writer in his lifetime, but only the group around* Presença, *established in 1927, seemed to realize just how important he was, and they urged him to organize and publish his works. Gaspar Simões, a major Portuguese literary critic and the author of a groundbreaking biography of Pessoa that appeared in 1950, maintained a lively correspondence with the poet, who wrote him over forty letters between 1929 and 1934.*

Lisbon, 11 December 1931

My dear Gaspar Simões,

Thanks very much for your letter, which I've just received, and for the page from the Málaga newspaper. It doesn't matter that *Presença* 33 didn't include the passage from the bookkeeper or the sonnet by Álvaro de Campos, but I'm glad you did publish my translation of "Hymn to Pan,"* since otherwise I would feel remiss toward its author. And why are you angry with me for the lengthy contribution I published in *Descobrimento*? I will gladly provide one of equal length to *Presença*. But you should know that, in the one case as in the other, I consider the nature of the publication. It doesn't seem right to me to send you a contribution that will take up three whole pages, since *Presença* should devote the better and larger part of its space to younger poets and prose writers, only interspersing writers my age out of your friendship toward us and so we can applaud your efforts, and in order to fill in gaps.

Having made these pre-preliminary observations in answer to your letter, I will now attempt a critique of your book *Mistério da Poesia* [The Mystery of Poetry]; it will include my long overdue reaction to your article about me,* which now forms part of your book. Before I begin, please note that this critique will take shape right now, written freely and directly at my typewriter, with no attempt on my part to produce literature, or well-wrought phrases, or anything that doesn't come out spontaneously in the mechanical act of typing. Since I didn't bring your book with me, I will have to allude to it rather than quote from it, if and where necessary. I tell you this so that you won't imagine some obscure motive when in fact it's simply that I don't have your book with me.

For a long time now I've had a high opinion of your talent in general and of your critical capacity in particular. I want you to know, first and foremost, that this is my basic opinion. Whatever disagreement I may express in this letter concerns only details and incidental points. My opinion of your intelligence is proven, further- more, though you would perhaps not be able to know this, by the fact that with you I use the words "admiration" and "admirer," which I don't just toss around; "appreciation" is as far as I go when I can't, in honesty to myself, go farther.

In terms of your intellectual development and expression, *The Mystery of Poetry* represents, as I see it, an intermediate stage be- tween *Temas* [Themes] and a book you'll write in the future. *The Mystery of Poetry*—again, as I see it—belongs by its very nature to an intermediate stage: it is both more profound and more confused than *Themes.* Your mind has grown—one continues to grow mentally until the age of 45—and you are experiencing some mental growing pains. You feel the need to explain more, and more deeply, what you wrote in *Themes*, but you still haven't mastered the means for going deeper, and, what's more, you are trying to fathom parts of the human heart that cannot by any means be fathomed. This results — still and always as I see it — in a feverishness, a recklessness and an anxiousness that cloud the basic lucidity of certain observations, while depriving other observations of almost any lucidity.

While I see much of this as a symptom of your personal, inner development, I think you also submit too readily to the suggestions and influences of the European intellectual milieu, with all of its theories that claim to be science, with all of its able and talented minds that claim (and are proclaimed by others) to be geniuses. I don't blame you for not seeing this, for it's something that people your age never see. Today I'm astounded — astounded and horrified — by the kinds of international literature from the past and (what was then) present that I admired with complete intellectual sincerity up until age 30. This was also true for me in politics. Today I'm astounded, with useless (and hence unjustified) embarrassment, by how much I admired and believed in democracy, by how important I thought it was to struggle on behalf of that nonexistent entity known as "the people," by how sincerely, and not mindlessly, I supposed that the word "humanity" had a sociological meaning and not just the biological one of "human species."

Among the guides who have led you into the kind of maze which you have entered, I believe I can distinguish Freud, and by Freud I mean both him and his followers. This is to be expected, I think, in light of the general reasons outlined above as well as the particular reason that Freud is truly a man of genius, the inventor of an original and seductive psychological model whose power of influence has manifested itself in him as a full-fledged paranoia of the interpretive type. Freud's success both in and beyond Europe derives, I think, from the originality of that model, which has the force and narrowness of madness (such as are needed to create religions and religious sects, including fascism, communism and other forms of political mysticism) and which, much more importantly, is based (except in a few heterodox disciples) on a sexual interpretation. This makes it possible to write absolutely obscene books, billing them as scientific works (which some of them really are), and to "interpret" past and present writers and artists (usually without any critical justification) in a degrading fashion worthy of the Café Brasileira of Chiado,* performing psychological masturbations within the vast network of onanism that seems to constitute the mentality of our civilization.

Don't misunderstand me: I don't mean to suggest that this last aspect of Freudianism is what has had a hypnotic effect on you personally. But it is this aspect that has aroused such great interest in Freudianism around the world and thus popularized the system.

. . .

Now as I see it (always "as I see it"), Freudianism is a flawed, narrow, and highly useful system. It is flawed if we imagine that it will give us the key, which no system can give, to the infinite complexity of the human heart. It is narrow if it leads us to suppose that everything can be reduced to sexuality, because nothing can be reduced to just one thing, not even in the subatomic world. It is highly useful, for it has alerted psychologists to three crucial aspects of our inner life and its interpretation: (1) the subconscious, and the corollary fact that we are still irrational animals; (2) sexuality, whose importance had, for various reasons, been underrated or unknown; (3) what I shall call *transferal*, by which I mean the conversion of one kind of psychological phenomenon (not necessarily sexual) into another, when the original one has been inhibited or diverted, and the possibility of identifying certain qualities or defects through ostensibly unrelated behaviors.

Before I had ever read anything about or by Freud, and even before I'd heard of him, I had personally arrived at the conclusion marked (1) and at some of the findings I've grouped under (3). Under item (2) I had made fewer observations, due to my generally scant interest in sexuality, whether my own or other people's—my own, since I've never given much importance to myself as a physical and social being; other people's, because I've always been loath to meddle—even interpretively, inside my own mind—in the lives of others. I haven't read much Freud, nor much about the Freudian system and its derivatives, but what I've read has—I admit—been of great help for sharpening my psychological knife and for cleaning or changing the lenses of my critical microscope. I didn't need Freud (nor, as far as I know, could he clarify me on this point) to distinguish vanity from pride in the cases where, manifested only indirectly, the two things can be confused. And even within area (2) I didn't need Freud to recognize, merely through their literary style, the homosexual and the onanist, and, within onanism, the practicing onanist and the psychological onanist. To distinguish the three elements that make up the homosexual's style and the three elements that make up the onanist's style (and the difference, in the latter, between the practicing and psychological varieties), I had no need of Freud or of Freudians. But many other things, in this and in the other two areas, were indeed clarified for me by Freud and his followers. It never would have occurred to me, for example, that smoking (and I will add alcohol) is a "transference" of onanism. After reading a brief study on this topic by a psychoanalyst, it immediately dawned on me that, of the five exemplary onanists I have known, four did not smoke or drink, while the fifth smoked but abhorred wine.

This subject has caused me to touch on sexuality, but it was only, you understand, to elucidate my position and to show you how much I recognize, despite my criticisms and divergences, the hypnotic power of Freudianisms over anyone who is intelligent, particularly when their intelligence has a critical bent. What I would now like to emphasize is that this system and all derivative and analogous systems should, I feel, be used by us to stimulate our critical capacity and not held up as scientific dogmas or natural laws. It seems to me that you have employed them somewhat in this latter way and have, as a result, been seduced by the pseudoscientific element that's found in many parts of these systems and leads to falsification, by the adventurous element that's found in other parts and leads to recklessness, and by the exaggeratedly sexual element found in still other parts, which leads to instant debasement of the author being studied, particularly in the eyes of the public, so that the critic's explanation, elaborated in good faith and innocently set forth, comes off as an act of aggression. Because the public is stupid? Undoubtedly, but the collective nature that makes the public the public also deprives it of intelligence, which is strictly individual. When Shakespeare's homosexuality, so clearly and constantly affirmed in his sonnets, was mentioned to Robert Browning, who was not only a great poet but a subtle and intellectual one, do you know what he answered? "If so, the less Shakespeare he." That's the public for you, my dear Gaspar Simões, even when the public is named Browning, who wasn't even collective.

These observations, expressed in the mental tone of a solitary conversation and transmitted as fast as they can be typed, contain most of the adverse criticism I have to make of your *Mystery of Poetry*. They turn (to put it pompously) on one of your book's methodological procedures. But your book also includes, quite independently of your formal methods, instances of unwarranted haste and critical temerity. If you admit to lacking the biographical data needed for forming an opinion about Sá-Carneiro's inner self, why do you form one based on the absence of such data? Are you sure, just because I say and repeat it, that I feel nostalgia for my childhood and that for me music is—how shall I say?—the frustrated natural vehicle of my self-expression? And please note that your study on Sá-Carneiro, considering the lack of biographical data, is a critically admirable piece, and the only problem with your study on me is that it accepts as true certain statements that are false, since I, artistically, can only lie.

I'll be more specific. The work of Sá-Carneiro is permeated by a fundamental inhumanity: it has no human warmth or tenderness, except for the introverted kind. Do you know why? Because he lost his mother when he was two years old and never experienced maternal affection. I've noticed that people who grow up motherless are always lacking in tenderness, whether they're artists or not, whether their mother actually died or was simply cold or distant. There is one difference: those who had no mother because she died (unless they're unemotional by nature, which wasn't the case of Sá-Carneiro) turn their own tenderness inward, substituting themselves for the mother they never knew, whereas those who in effect had no mother because she was coldly indifferent lose the tenderness they would have had and become (unless they've been especially gifted with tenderness) implacable cynics, monstrous children of the motherly love they were deprived of.

And now I'll be specific about myself. I've never felt nostalgia for my childhood; in fact I've never felt nostalgia for anything. I am, by nature and in the most literal sense of the word, a futurist. I'm unable to be pessimistic or to look back. As far as I'm aware, the only things that can make me depressed are lack of money (in the precise moment it's needed) and thunderstorms (while they last). All I miss from the past are the people I loved who have disappeared; I miss only them, not the time in which I loved them; I wish they were alive today, and with the age they would have now if they had lived until now. The rest are literary attitudes, felt intensely by dramatic instinct, whether they're signed by Álvaro de Campos or by Fernando Pessoa. Their tone and their truth are suitably illustrated by the short poem of mine that begins "O church bell of my village . . . ."* The church bell of my village, Gaspar Simões, is the bell from the Church of the Martyrs, in Chiado. The village of my birth was the São Carlos Square, now called Directory Square, and the building where I was born (on the fifth floor) ended up housing (on the third floor) the Directory of the Republic.* (Note: the building was doomed to be famous, but let's hope the fifth floor yields better results than the third.)

Now that I've dealt with these specifics, or what have you, I would like to return (if I still have the mind for it, as I'm already tired) to a methodological point. As I see it (there are those four words again), the critic's role is essentially threefold: (1) to study the artist exclusively as an artist, letting no more of the man enter than what's absolutely necessary to explain the artist; (2) to discover what we might call the *central definition* of the artist (lyric type, dramatic type, elegiac-lyric type, poetic-dramatic type, etc.); and (3) to wrap these studies and these discoveries in a hazy poetic aura of unintelligibility, knowing as we do that the human heart is basically inscrutable. This third function is in a certain way a diplomatic one, but the fact is, my dear Gaspar Simões, that even with the truth we need diplomacy.

I don't think any of this needs clarification except perhaps the second function. Partly for the sake of brevity, I will explain it through an example, and I choose myself because I'm the closest one available. The central point of my personality as an artist is that I'm a dramatic poet; in everything I write, I always have the poet's inner exaltation and the playwright's depersonalization. I soar as someone else—that's all. From the human point of view—which the critic shouldn't even consider, for it serves him no purpose—I'm a hysterical neurasthenic, with the hysterical element predominating in my emotions and the neurasthenic element in my intellect and will (hypersensibility in the former, apathy in the latter). But as soon as the critic understands that I'm essentially a dramatic poet, he will have the key to my personality, or to as much of it as he or anyone else needs to know, except a psychiatrist, which the critic need not be. Armed with this key, he can slowly open all the doors to my self-expression. He knows that as a poet I feel; that as a dramatic poet I feel with complete detachment from my feeling self; that as a dramatist (without the poet) I automatically transform what I feel into an expression far removed from what I felt, and I create, in my emotions, a nonexistent person who truly felt that feeling and, in feeling it, felt yet other, related emotions that I, purely I, forgot to feel.

I'll stop here. I'll reread this letter, make any necessary corrections, and mail it. Besides, I've been implored to quit typing at once by a friend who, even more of a drunk than I, has just arrived and who doesn't enjoy getting drunk by himself. The "I'll reread this letter" means I'll reread it later, or tomorrow. I don't expect to correct more than the misunderstandings between me and the typewriter. If something isn't clear, let me know and I'll explain. And you won't forget, of course, that I've written this without forethought, putting it on paper as fast as the typewriter can accommodate my stream of thought.

No, I haven't forgotten about the possible error I mentioned with respect to your idea of how I understand music emotionally. I skipped this point because I know nothing about it, except to say that this yearning for music is yet another curious feature of my dramatic spirit. It depends on the time, the place, and the part of me that's pretending in that given time and place.

Nor have I forgotten, of course, that somewhere in this letter I wrote something about "sharpening my psychological knife" and "cleaning or changing the lenses of my critical microscope." I note with satisfaction that, in speaking of Freud, I've employed a phallic image and a yonic image. These he would surely have understood. What he would conclude, I don't know. And in any case, to hell with him!

And now, definitively, I'm tired and thirsty. I apologize for however my words may have distorted my ideas and for whatever my ideas may have taken from falseness or indecision.

Warmest regards from your good friend and admirer,

Fernando Pessoa

Lisbon, 28 July 1932

My dear Gaspar Simões,

Thank you for your letter. I am sending my reply to Coimbra, since it still isn't August, and should you already be in Figueira,* it will be forwarded to you.

I see there's still time for me to send work for the next issue of *Presença*, and you can count on it. I'll send Casais Monteiro the note I mentioned (it's very short) along with another contribution, also short. I hope to send a previously unpublished piece by Sá-Carneiro.

. . .

I'm beginning—slowly, as it's not something that can be done quickly—to organize and revise my writings, so that I can publish one or two books at the end of the year. They will probably both be poetry collections, as I doubt I can have anything else ready by then—ready, that is, by my standards.

My original intention was to begin the publication of my works with three books, in the following order: (1) *Portugal*, a small book of poems* (41 in all) whose second part is "Portuguese Sea" (published in *Contemporânea* 4); (2) *The Book of Disquiet* (by Bernardo Soares, but only secondarily, since B. S. is not a heteronym but a literary personality); (3) *Complete Poems of Alberto Caeiro* (with a preface by Ricardo Reis and, at the end of the volume, Álvaro de Campos's *Notes for the Memory of My Master Caeiro*). A year after the publication of these books, I planned to bring out, either by itself or with another volume, *Songbook* (or some other equally inexpressive title), which would have included (in Books I–III or I–V) a number of my many miscellaneous poems, which are too diverse to be classified except in that inexpressive way.

But there is much to be revised and restructured in *The Book of Disquiet,* and I can't honestly expect that it will take me less than a year to do the job. And as for Caeiro, I'm undecided. He also needs some revising, but not much. Otherwise his work may be said to be complete, though a few "uncollected poems" and alterations to the early poems (*The Keeper of Sheep*) are scattered among my papers. But once I locate these scattered elements, the book can be quickly completed. It has one drawback: the near impossibility of commercial success, so that it will have to be published at some sacrifice. Whether to make that financial sacrifice will depend, of course, on my financial condition at the time. As I go about revising and organizing my writings I will, in any case, find and collect what belongs to Caeiro.

I don't know if I've ever told you that the heteronyms (according to my final will on the matter) should be published by me under my own name (it's too late, and hence absurd, to pretend they're completely independent). They will form a series titled *Fictions of the Interlude,* unless I think of some better name in the meantime. And so the title of the first volume would be something like *Fernando Pessoa — Fictions of the Interlude — I. Complete Poems of Alberto Caeiro (1889–1915).* And so on for the succeeding volumes, including a curious one — very hard to write — containing the aesthetic debate between me, Ricardo Reis, and Álvaro de Campos, and perhaps other heteronyms, for there are several (including an astrologer) who have yet to appear.

In fact I will probably include, in the first book of the heteronyms, not only Caeiro and the *Notes* of Álvaro de Campos but also three or five Books of Ricardo Reis's *Odes*. That way the volume will contain what's essential for understanding the beginnings of the "school": the works of the Master and some poems from his direct disciple, as well as something (the *Notes*) from his other disciple. There is also a purely practical matter that makes me lean toward such a volume: Caeiro and the *Notes* by themselves would make neither a small book, such as *Portugal* is, nor a normal-sized book (about 300 pages), such as my *Songbook*. With the inclusion of Ricardo Reis (a logical complement, as I've explained), the volume will attain this normal length.

My current plan, subject to change, is to publish *Portugal* and the *Songbook* this year, if possible, or at the beginning of next year. The first of the two titles is almost ready, and of all my books it has the best chance of success. The second title is ready; I just need to select and order the poems.

Since I know these things don't bore you, and since this is all, in a way, an answer (a rather extended one) to your query about when I'll publish, I've let myself write at some length.

Along with all I've mentioned, I have perhaps two or three pamphlets or long articles to write or conclude. Even if these are written in Portuguese, I'll probably translate them into English and publish them first (in magazines, no doubt) in England. All of this is tentative, however.

Warm regards from your good friend and admirer,

Fernando Pessoa

THREE LETTERS TO
ADOLFO CASAIS MONTEIRO

Like João Gaspar Simões, Adolfo Casais Monteiro (1908–72) was an editor (beginning in 1931) of the magazine Presença, *an ardent admirer and student of Pessoa's work, and one of his most important literary interlocutors in the 1930s. He was the recipient, in fact, of Pessoa's longest and most famous letter, written on January 13, 1935. From the P.S. to that letter, it's clear that it was intended for posterity, and though Pessoa may have written it as fast as he could type, as claimed in the seventh paragraph, his story of the heteronyms was certainly not "off the cuff." Over the years he had been carefully plotting and refining it. A version of the story written around 1930—placed here after the letter—offers some rather different details about how it all happened and when.*

Lisbon, 11 January 1930

My dear colleague,

Thank you so much for sending me a copy of your book *Confusão* [Confusion], for the kind words you wrote in it, and for the poem you dedicated to me.

Your book reveals a keen sensibility and a still immature use of it. Before an impression can be converted into the raw material of art, it must first be transformed—not *partially* but *entirely*—into an intellectual impression, an impression of the intelligence. And by intelligence I mean not our personality's highest expression but its *abstract* expression. In other and simpler words: only when an individual is transformed by the intelligence into a small universe will he have, in the impression thereby produced, the raw material with which to make what we call art.

What we feel is only what we feel. What we think is only what we think. But that which, felt or thought, we think again *as someone else* is naturally transformed into art and, cooling down, acquires form.

Don't trust what you feel or think until you've stopped feeling or thinking it. Then you'll use your sensibility in a way that naturally works to your own and everyone else's benefit.

I sincerely enjoyed your book. And these remarks, naturally limited by my particular point of view, are intended only as a critique which, though it may be erroneous, at least has the advantage of being sincere, and the pleasure of being laudatory.

With kind regards from your ever grateful colleague,

Fernando Pessoa

Lisbon, 13 January 1935

My dear friend and colleague,

Thank you very much for your letter, which I shall answer at once and in full. But before I begin, I must apologize for this paper that's meant for carbon copies. It's the best I could do, as I've run out of good paper and it's Sunday. But inferior paper is preferable, I think, to putting off writing you.

Let me say, first of all, that I would never see "ulterior motives" for anything you might write in disagreement with me. I'm one of the few Portuguese poets who hasn't decreed his own infallibility, and I don't consider criticism of my work to be an act of "lèse divinity." Though I may suffer from other mental defects, I haven't the slightest trace of persecution mania. And besides, I'm already well aware of your intellectual independence, which (if I may say so) I heartily endorse and admire. I've never aspired to be a Master, for I don't know how to teach, and I'm not sure I would even have anything to teach, nor do I fancy myself a Leader or Chief,* for I don't know how to scramble an egg. So don't ever let what you might say about me worry you. I'm not one to look for trouble where there is none.

I completely agree with you that a book like *Mensagem* (Message) was not a felicitous publishing début. I am, to be sure, a mystical nationalist, a rational Sebastianist.* But I am many other things besides that, and even in contradiction to it. And because of the kind of book it was, *Message* did not include those things.

I began the publication of my works with that book simply because it was the first one, for whatever reason, that I managed to organize and have ready. Since it was all ready, I was urged to publish it, and so I did. I didn't do it, please note, with my eyes on the prize offered by the National Office of Propaganda,* though that wouldn't have been a serious intellectual sin. My book wasn't ready until September, and I even thought it was too late to compete for the prize, for I didn't realize that the deadline for submissions had been extended from the end of July to the end of October. Since copies of *Message* were already available by the end of October, I submitted the copies required by the Office of Propaganda. The book exactly met the conditions (nationalism) stipulated for the competition. I entered it.

When in the past I've sometimes thought about the order in which my works would one day be published, no book like *Message* ever headed the list. I was torn between whether to start off with a large book of poems—about 350 pages in length—that would encompass the various subpersonalities of Fernando Pessoa himself or whether to begin with a detective novel (which I still haven't finished).

I'm convinced, as you are, that *Message* was not a felicitous literary début, but I'm convinced that under the circumstances it was the best début I could have made. That facet of my personality—in a certain way a minor facet—had never been adequately represented in my magazine publications (except for the book's section titled "Portuguese Sea"), and for that very reason it was good that it be revealed, and that it be revealed now. Without any planning or premeditation on my part (I'm incapable of premeditation in practical matters), it coincided with a critical moment (in the original sense of the word "critical") in the transformation of the national subconscious. What I happened to do and others urged me to complete was accurately drawn, with Ruler and Compass, by the Great Architect.

(No, I'm not crazy or drunk, but I am writing off the cuff, as fast as this typewriter will let me, and I'm using whatever expressions come to mind, without regard to their literary content. Imagine—for it's true—that I'm just talking to you.)

I will now deal directly with your three questions: (1) plans for the future publication of my works, (2) the genesis of my heteronyms, and (3) the occult.

Having been led by the aforementioned circumstances to publish *Message*, which shows just one side of me, I intend to proceed as follows. I'm now finishing up a thoroughly revised version of "The Anarchist Banker"; this should be ready in the near future, and I hope to publish it forthwith. If successful, I will immediately translate it into English and try to get it published in England. The new version should have European possibilities. (Don't take this to mean an imminent Nobel Prize.) Next   and I shall now respond directly to your question, which concerned my poetry—I plan to spend the summer collecting the shorter poems of Fernando Pessoa himself into one large volume, as indicated above, and will try to publish it before the year is out. This is the book you've been waiting for, and it's the one I myself am anxious to bring out. This book will show all my facets except the nationalist one, which *Message* has already revealed.

You will have noticed that I've referred only to Fernando Pessoa. I'm not thinking at this point about Caeiro, Ricardo Reis or Álvaro de Campos. I can't do anything about them, in terms of publishing, until (see above) I win the Nobel Prize. And yet—it makes me sad to think of this—I placed all my power of dramatic depersonalization in Caeiro; I placed all my mental discipline, clothed in its own special music, in Ricardo Reis; and in Álvaro de

Campos I placed all the emotion that I deny myself and don't put into life. To think, my dear Casais Monteiro, that all three of them, in terms of publication, must defer to Fernando Pessoa impure and simple!

I believe I've answered your first question. Let me know if some point is still hazy, and I'll try to clear it up. I don't have any more plans for now, and considering what my plans usually involve and how they turn out, I can only say "Thank God!"

Turning now to your question about the genesis of my heteronyms, I will see if I can answer you fully.

I shall begin with the psychiatric aspect. My heteronyms have their origin in a deep-seated form of hysteria. I don't know if I'm afflicted by simple hysteria or, more specifically, by hysterical neurasthenia. I suspect it's the latter, for I have symptoms of abulia that mere hysteria would not explain. Whatever the case, the mental origin of my heteronyms lies in my relentless, organic tendency to depersonalization and simulation. Fortunately for me and for others, these phenomena have been mentally internalized, such that they don't show up in my outer, everyday life among people; they erupt inside me, where only I experience them. If I were a woman (hysterical phenomena in women erupt externally, through attacks and the like), each poem of Álvaro de Campos (the most hysterically hysterical part of me) would be a general alarm to the neighborhood. But I'm a man, and in men hysteria affects mainly the inner psyche; so it all ends in silence and poetry . . .

This explains, as well as I can, the organic origin of my heteronyms. Now I will recount their actual history, beginning with the heteronyms that have died and with some of the ones I no longer remember—those that are forever lost in the distant past of my almost forgotten childhood.

Ever since I was a child, it has been my tendency to create around me a fictitious world, to surround myself with friends and acquaintances that never existed. (I can't be sure, of course, if they really never existed, or if it's me who doesn't exist. In this matter, as in any other, we shouldn't be dogmatic.) Ever since I've known myself as "me," I can remember envisioning the shape, motions, character and life story of various unreal figures who were as visible and as close to me as the manifestations of what we call, perhaps too hastily, real life. This tendency, which goes back as far as I can remember being an I, has always accompanied me, changing somewhat the music it enchants me with, but never the way in which it enchants me.

Thus I can remember what I believe was my first heteronym, or rather, my first nonexistent acquaintance—a certain Chevalier de Pas—through whom I wrote letters from him to myself when I was six years old, and whose not entirely hazy figure still has a claim on the part of my affections that borders on nostalgia. I have a less vivid memory of another figure who also had a foreign name, which I can no longer recall, and who was a kind of rival to the Chevalier de Pas. Such things occur to all children? Undoubtedly—or perhaps. But I lived them so intensely that I live them still; their memory is so strong that I have to remind myself that they weren't real.

This tendency to create around me another world, just like this one but with other people, has never left my imagination. It has gone through various phases, including the one that began in me as a young adult, when a witty remark that was completely out of keeping with who I am or think I am would sometimes and for some unknown reason occur to me, and I would immediately, spontaneously say it as if it came from some friend of mine, whose name I would invent, along with biographical details, and whose figure—physiognomy, stature, dress and gestures—I would immediately see before me. Thus I elaborated, and propagated, various friends and acquaintances who never existed but whom I feel, hear and see even today, almost thirty years later. I repeat: I feel, hear and see them. And I miss them.

(Once I start talking—and typing, for me, is like talking—it's hard to put on the brake. But I'll stop boring you, Casais Monteiro! I'll now go into the genesis of my literary heteronyms, which is what really interests you. What I've written so far will at any rate serve as the story of the mother who gave them birth.)

In 1912, if I remember correctly (and I can't be far off), I got the idea to write some poetry from a pagan perspective. I sketched out a few poems with irregular verse patterns (not in the style of Álvaro de Campos but in a semiregular style) and then forgot about them. But a hazy, shadowy portrait of the person who wrote those verses took shape in me. (Unbeknownst to me, Ricardo Reis had been born.)

A year and a half or two years later, it one day occurred to me to play a joke on Sá-Carneiro—to invent a rather complicated bucolic poet whom I would present in some guise of reality that I've since forgotten. I spent a few days trying in vain to envision this poet. One day when I'd finally given up—it was March 8th, 1914—I walked over to a high chest of drawers, took a sheet of paper, and began to write standing up, as I do whenever I can. And I wrote thirty-some poems at once, in a kind of ecstasy I'm unable to describe. It was the triumphal day of my life, and I can never have another one like it. I began with a title, *The Keeper of Sheep*. This was followed by the appearance in me of someone whom I instantly named Alberto Caeiro. Excuse the absurdity of this statement: my master had appeared in me. That was what I immediately felt, and so strong was the feeling that, as soon as those thirty-odd poems were written, I grabbed a fresh sheet of paper and wrote, again all at once, the six poems that constitute "Slanting Rain,"* by Fernando Pessoa. All at once and with total concentration . . . It was the return of Fernando Pessoa as Alberto Caeiro to Fernando Pessoa himself. Or rather, it was the reaction of Fernando Pessoa against his nonexistence as Alberto Caeiro.

Once Alberto Caeiro had appeared, I instinctively and subconsciously tried to find disciples for him. From Caeiro's false paganism I extracted the latent Ricardo Reis, at last discovering his name and adjusting him to his true self, for now I actually *saw* him. And then a new individual, quite the opposite of Ricardo Reis, suddenly and impetuously came to me. In an unbroken stream, without interruptions or corrections, the ode whose name is "Triumphal Ode,"* by the man whose name is none other than Álvaro de Campos, issued from my typewriter.

And so I created a nonexistent coterie, placing it all in a framework of reality. I ascertained the influences at work and the friendships between them, I listened in myself to their discussions and divergent points of view, and in all of this it seems that I, who created them all, was the one who was least there. It seems that it all went on without me. And thus it seems to go on still. If one day I'm able to publish the aesthetic debate between Ricardo Reis and Álvaro de Campos, you'll see how different they are, and how I have nothing to do with the matter.

When it came time to publish *Orpheu*, we had to find something at the last minute to fill out the issue, and so I suggested to Sá-Carneiro that I write an "old" poem of Álvaro de Campos's—a poem such as Álvaro de Campos would have written before meeting Caeiro and falling under his influence. That's how I came to write "Opiary,"* in which I tried to incorporate all the latent tendencies of Álvaro de Campos that would eventually be revealed but that still showed no hint of contact with his master Caeiro. Of all the poems I've written, this was the one that gave me the most trouble, because of the twofold depersonalization it required. But I don't think it turned out badly, and it does show us Álvaro in the bud.

I think this should explain for you the origin of my heteronyms, but if there's any point I need to clarify—I'm writing quickly, and when I write quickly I'm not terribly clear—let me know, and I'll gladly oblige. And here's a true and hysterical addendum: when writing certain passages of Álvaro de Campos's *Notes for the Memory of My Master Caeiro*, I have wept real tears. I tell this so that you'll know whom you're dealing with, my dear Casais Monteiro!

A few more notes on this subject . . . I *see* before me, in the transparent but real space of dreams, the faces and gestures of Caeiro, Ricardo Reis and Álvaro de Campos. I gave them their ages and fashioned their lives. Ricardo Reis was born in 1887 (I don't remember the month and day, but I have them somewhere) in Oporto. He's a doctor and is presently living in Brazil. Alberto Caeiro was born in 1889 and died in 1915. He was born in Lisbon but spent most of his life in the country. He had no profession and practically no schooling. Álvaro de Campos was born in Tavira, on October 15th, 1890 (at 1:30 P.M., says Ferreira Gomes,* and it's true, because a horoscope made for that hour confirms it). Campos, as you know, is a naval engineer (he studied in Glasgow) but is currently living in Lisbon and not working. Caeiro was of medium height, and although his health was truly fragile (he died of TB), he seemed less frail than he was. Ricardo Reis is a wee bit shorter, stronger, but sinewy. Álvaro de Campos is tall (5 ft. 9 in., an inch taller than me), slim, and a bit prone to stoop. All are clean-shaven—Caeiro fair, with a pale complexion and blue eyes; Reis somewhat dark-skinned; Campos neither pale nor dark, vaguely corresponding to the Portuguese Jewish type, but with smooth hair that's usually parted on one side, and a monocle. Caeiro, as I've said, had almost no education— just primary school. His mother and father died when he was young, and he stayed on at home, living off a small income from family properties. He lived with an elderly great-aunt. Ricardo Reis, educated in a Jesuit high school, is, as I've mentioned, a doctor; he has been living in Brazil since 1919, having gone into voluntary exile because of his monarchist sympathies. He is a formally trained Latinist, and a self-taught semi-Hellenist. Álvaro de Campos, after a normal high school education, was sent to Scotland to study engineering, first mechanical and then naval. During some holidays he made a voyage to the Orient, which gave rise to his poem "Opiary." He was taught Latin by an uncle who was a priest from the Beira region.

How do I write in the name of these three? Caeiro, through sheer and unexpected inspiration, without knowing or even suspecting that I'm going to write in his name. Ricardo Reis, after an abstract meditation that suddenly takes concrete shape in an ode. Campos, when I feel a sudden impulse to write and don't know what. (My semiheteronym Bernardo Soares, who in many ways resembles Álvaro de Campos, always appears when I'm sleepy or drowsy, such that my qualities of inhibition and logical reasoning are suspended; his prose is an endless reverie. He's a semiheteronym because his personality, although not my own, doesn't differ from my own but is a mere mutilation of it. He's me without my logical reasoning and emotion. His prose is the same as mine, except for a certain formal restraint that reason imposes on my own writing, and his Portuguese is exactly the same—whereas Caeiro writes bad Portuguese, Campos writes it reasonably well but with mistakes such as "me myself" instead of "I myself," etc., and Reis writes better than I, but with a purism I find excessive. What's hard for me is to write the prose of Reis—still unpublished—or of Campos. Simulation is easier, because more spontaneous, in verse.)

At this point you're no doubt wondering what bad luck has caused you to fall, just by reading, into the midst of an insane asylum. The worst thing is the incoherent way I've explained myself, but I write, I repeat, as if I were talking to you, so that I can write quickly. Otherwise it would take me months to write.

I still haven't answered your question about the occult. You asked if I believe in the occult. Phrased in that way, the question isn't clear, but I know what you mean and I'll answer it. I believe in the existence of worlds higher than our own and in the existence of beings that inhabit those worlds. I believe there are various, increasingly subtle levels of spirituality that lead to a Supreme Being, who presumably created this world. There may be other, equally Supreme Beings who have created other universes that coexist with our own, separately or interconnectedly. For these and other reasons, the External Order of the Occult, meaning the Freemasons, avoid (except for the Anglo-Saxon Freemasons) the term "God," with its theological and popular implications, and prefer to say "Great Architect of the Universe," an expression that leaves open the question of whether He is the world's Creator or merely its Ruler. Given this hierarchy of beings, I do not believe that direct communication with God is possible, but we can, according to the degree of our spiritual attunement, communicate with ever higher beings. There are three paths toward the occult: the path of magic (including practices such as spiritism, intellectually on a par with witchcraft, likewise a form of magic), which is an extremely dangerous path in all respects; the mystical path, which is not inherently dangerous but is uncertain and slow; and the path of alchemy, which is the hardest and most perfect path of all, since it involves a transmutation of the very personality that *prepares* it, not only without great risks but with defenses that the other paths don't have. As for "initiation," all I can tell you is this, which may or may not answer your question: I belong to no Initiatic Order. The epigraph to my poem "Eros and Psyche,"* a passage taken (and translated, since the original is in Latin) from the Ritual of the Third Degree of the Portuguese Order of the Knights Templar, indicates no more than what in fact occurred: that I was allowed to leaf through the Rituals of the first three degrees of that Order, which has been extinct, or dormant, since around 1888. Were it not dormant, I would not have cited that passage from the Ritual, since Rituals in active use should not be quoted (unless the Order isn't named).

I believe, my dear colleague, that I have answered your questions, albeit with some confusion here and there. If you have other questions, don't hesitate to ask them. I will answer as best I can, though I may not answer so promptly, for which I offer my apologies in advance.

Warm regards from your friend who greatly admires and respects you,

Fernando Pessoa

P.S. (!!!)

14 January 1935

Besides the copy I usually make for myself when I type a letter that contains explanations of the sort found herein, I've made a second copy that will always remain at your disposal, in case the original gets lost or you need this copy for some other reason.

One other thing . . . It might happen in the future that for some study of yours or some other such purpose you will need to quote a passage from this letter. You are hereby authorized to do so, *but with one reservation,* and I beg leave to underscore it. The paragraph about the occult, on page 7 of my letter, should not be reproduced in published form. In my desire to answer your question as clearly as possible, I knowingly overstepped the bounds that this subject naturally imposes. I had no qualms about doing so, since this is a private letter. You may read the paragraph in question to whomever you like, provided they also agree not to reproduce its contents in published form. I can count on you, I trust, to respect this negative wish.

I still owe you a long-overdue letter about your latest books. I reiterate what I believe I wrote in my last letter: when I go to spend a few days in Estoril (I think it will be in February), I'll catch up on that part of my correspondence, writing not only you but similar letters to various other people.

Oh, and let me ask you again something you still haven't answered: did you get my chapbooks of poems in English, which I sent you some time ago?

And would you, "for my records" (to use business jargon), confirm for me as soon as possible that you've received this letter? Many thanks.

Fernando Pessoa

[Another Version of the Genesis of the Heteronyms]

Ever since I was a child, I've felt the need to enlarge the world with fictitious personalities—dreams of mine that were carefully crafted, envisaged with photographic clarity, and fathomed to the depths of their souls. When I was but five years old, an isolated child and quite content to be so, I already enjoyed the company of certain characters from my dreams, including a Captain Thibeaut, the Chevalier de Pas, and various others whom I've forgotten, and whose forgetting—like my imperfect memory of the two I just named—is one of my life's great regrets.

This may seem merely like a child's imagination that gives life to dolls. But it was more than that. I intensely conceived those characters with no need of dolls. Distinctly visible in my ongoing dream, they were utterly human realities for me, which any doll—because unreal—would have spoiled. They were people.

And instead of ending with my childhood, this tendency expanded in my adolescence, taking firmer root with each passing year, until it became my natural way of being. Today I have no personality: I've divided all my humanness among the various authors whom I've served as literary executor. Today I'm the meeting-place of a small humanity that belongs only to me.

. . .

This is simply the result of a dramatic temperament taken to the extreme. My dramas, instead of being divided into acts full of action, are divided into souls. That's what this apparently baffling phenomenon comes down to.

I don't reject—in fact I'm all for—psychiatric explanations, but it should be understood that *all* higher mental activity, because it's abnormal, is equally subject to psychiatric interpretation. I don't mind admitting that I'm crazy, but I want it to be understood that my craziness is no different from Shakespeare's, whatever may be the comparative value of the products that issue from the saner side of our crazed minds.

I subsist as a kind of medium of myself, but I'm less real than the others, less substantial, less personal, and easily influenced by them all. I too am a disciple of Caeiro, and I still remember the day—March 13th, 1914—when I "heard for the first time" (when I wrote, that is, in a single burst of inspiration) a good many of the early poems of *The Keeper of Sheep* and then went on to write, without once stopping, the six Intersectionist poems that make up "Slanting Rain" (*Orpheu* 2), the visible and logical result of Caeiro's influence on the temperament of Fernando Pessoa.

Lisbon, 20 January 1935

My dear friend and colleague,

Many thanks for your letter. I'm glad I managed to say something of genuine interest. I had my doubts, given the hasty and impulsive way I wrote, caught up in the mental conversation I was having with you.

. . .

You are quite right about the absence in me of any kind of evolution in the true sense. There are poems I wrote when I was twenty that are just as good—so far as I can judge—as the ones I write today. I write no better than I did, except in terms of my knowledge of Portuguese, which is a cultural rather than poetic particular. I write differently. This can perhaps be explained by the following . . .

What I am essentially—behind the involuntary masks of poet, logical reasoner and so forth—is a dramatist. My spontaneous tendency to depersonalization, which I mentioned in my last letter to explain the existence of my heteronyms, naturally leads to this definition. And so I do not evolve, I simply JOURNEY. (This word is typed in capital letters because I mistakenly hit the shift key, but it's correct, so I'll let it stand.) I continuously change personality, I keep enlarging (and here there is a kind of evolution) my capacity to create new characters, new forms of pretending that I understand the world or, more accurately, that the world can be understood. That is why I've likened my path to a journey rather than to an evolution. I haven't risen from one floor to another; I've moved, on a level plane, from one place to another. I've naturally lost a certain simplicity and naiveté present in my adolescent poems, but that's not evolution, it's just me getting older.

These hastily written words should give you some inkling into the quite definite way in which I concur with your view that in me there has been no true evolution.

As to the forthcoming publication of my books, there are no obstacles to worry about. When I decide I want to publish Caeiro, Ricardo Reis and Álvaro de Campos, I can do so immediately. But I'm afraid that books of this sort won't sell. That's my only hesitation. The publication of the large book of poems [of Fernando Pessoa] is likewise guaranteed, and if I'm more inclined to publish it rather than some other, it's because it has a certain intellectual advantage, as well as a better chance of success. I think, for different reasons, that it will also not be especially hard to publish "The Anarchist Banker" in English.

. . .

Warm regards from your friend and admirer

Fernando Pessoa

THE BOOK OF DISQUIET
Bernardo Soares

Inspiration works in unpredictable ways. An image one sees, a phrase one hears, a smell that jogs a memory, a conversation, news of a crime, a sudden and novel idea—all can be the starting point of a poem, a painting, or a symphony, or even of an entire philosophical system. Fernando Pessoa's largest and most stunning work of prose, which will endure as one of the twentieth century's literary emblems, was born from just a word: disquiet. *It lit up in Pessoa in 1913, on the 20th of January. The surviving manuscript of a poem written that day contains, in the margin, a notation penned in large letters—"The title* Disquiet*"—and underlined with a confident flourish. That's not quite true, because Pessoa was writing in Portuguese, not English. The magic word for his title was actually* desassossego, *one of those words that in translation— disquiet, disquietude, restlessness—never has the same force, or mystery, as the original. Not even the Spanish* desasosiego *rings with the same enchantment, and the French translator, not happy with* inquietude, *invented the word* intranquillité, *which, curiously enough, has since entered the French vocabulary.*

In August of 1913 Pessoa published his first piece of creative prose, "In the Forest of Estrangement," signed by his own name and identified as "from The Book of Disquiet, *in preparation." During the next sixteen years he published no more of the book, but the nervous germ of its key word kept working, and text kept spinning out of Pessoa. In September of 1914 he wrote a friend in the Azores that his "pathological production" was going "complexly and tortuously forward." And in a letter to the same friend sent two months later, he clarified the nature of the pathology: "My state of mind compels me to work hard, against my will, on* The Book of Disquiet. *But it's all fragments, fragments, fragments.*"

In fact the early texts of The Book of Disquiet *are mostly unfinished. They are full of beautiful writing, but also full of blank spaces for words and phrases that were needed to complete an idea, round out a picture, or prolong a certain verbal rhythm. Sometimes, on the contrary, Pessoa left various alternate wordings for a phrase he wasn't quite happy with. Some texts are really just notes for a text; others are sets of related but disconnected, disordered ideas. When he went back to revise his* Book, *Pessoa would find words for the blank spaces, choose between alternate versions, fill out the sketchy passages, put order where it was needed, and make the whole work cohere. But he hardly ever went back; he kept churning out text. Pessoa was untidy in nearly all of his written world, but in* The Book of Disquiet *that untidiness became a kind of premise, without which the book couldn't be true to its restless, agitated heart.*

The early texts glow with a post-Symbolist aesthetic, as suggested by some of their titles: "Imperial Legend," "Our Lady of Silence," and "Symphony of the Restless Night." The disquiet has less to do with the narrator's psychological state than with the hesitant, fluttering, almost weightless world of symbols that the likewise diaphanous prose describes. "Peristyle," one of the oldest and most fragmentary texts, is typical, and Pessoa considered making it the gateway to his Book. *It begins: "It was in the silence of my disquiet, at the hour of day when the landscape is a halo of Life and dreaming is mere dreaming, my love, that I raised up this strange book like the open doors of an abandoned house." Further on the narrator addresses his abstractly female, forever virgin "love" with these words: "Swan of rhythmic disquiet, lyre of immortal hours, faint harp of mythic sorrows—you are both the Awaited and the Departed, the one who soothes and also wounds, who gilds joys with sadness and crowns griefs with roses." In "Our Lady of Silence," the narrator asks another (or is it the same?) idealized, sexless woman to be "the Invisible Twilight, with my disquiet and my yearnings as the shades of your indecision, the colors of your uncertainty." And in "Sentimental Education" he rather enjoys his "exquisite exhaustion tinged with disquiet and melancholy." Disquiet, in these ethereal atmospheres, has a strangely material quality.*

But *by the time the* Disquiet *text titled "Random Diary" was written, probably around 1918, the locus of disquiet had definitely shifted from the landscape to within the narrator: "O magnificent hills at twilight, O narrowish streets in the moonlight, if only I had your . . . . . . unconsciousness, your spirituality that's nothing but Matter, with no inner dimension, no sensibility, and no place for feelings, thoughts, or disquiet of the spirit!" It was during this same period that Pessoa, tired of mental encounters with sexless women, sought to cure his virginity with the help of astral spirits (see* RIDDLE OF THE STARS).

The Book of Disquiet *also contains a "Lucid Diary," which seems to be contemporaneous with the "Random Diary," but each so-called diary has only one entry. Perhaps Pessoa planned to expand them, or to bring other, untitled texts under their umbrella. The earliest* Disquiet *texts all had titles, but by 1915 most did not, and they were increasingly diary-like, increasingly taken up by the intellectual and emotional troubles of a man in his late twenties whose custom it was "to think with the emotions and feel with the mind" (Text 131). And since it was also Pessoa's custom to hide his true self behind masks, he called this man in his late twenties Vicente Guedes and made him an assistant bookkeeper who wrote in his spare time. Guedes, like his creator, was solitary, mild mannered, and lucid in the extreme. In "Fragments of an Autobiography" and various texts without titles he recounted his anguished, vain attempts to discover truth through metaphysics, science, and sociology. Elsewhere he described the generalized disquiet of his generation, whose free-thinking forefathers, "drunk with a hazy notion they called 'positivism,'" had "blithely wreaked destruction" on the moral, religious, and social edifice of European society, leaving nothing solid for their children to hold on to. This nutshell analysis is from Text 175, which also specifically mentions "political disquiet," a concept that was painfully meaningful to Europeans living in the second decade of the last century.*

Portugal's political instability went from bad to tragic in the 1920s. The first two years of that decade saw the formation and dissolution of a dozen governments, and in 1921 various Republican leaders were assassinated on just one bloody night, October 19. The Republic, never strong, slowly fell apart, a short-term dictator seized power in 1926, and then—

*several years later—it was Salazar's turn. Perhaps it was Portugal's po-
litical turmoil and social unrest that distracted Pessoa from his* Book of
Disquiet, *which he more or less laid aside in the 1920s. He worked on other
projects, such as his essays that delineate the "mystical nationalist" theories presented in the section* PORTUGAL AND THE FIFTH EMPIRE, *and he
became—or tried to become—an entrepreneur. In 1921 he founded Olisipo,
which was meant to be a wide-ranging business concern but finally just
published a few books, including two volumes of his own English poetry
(1921) and an enlarged edition of poems (1922) by his friend António Botto
(1897–1959), whose work was openly homosexual. Presumably in an effort
to promote this latter book, Pessoa published a magazine article defending Botto's sexual preference as a natural expression of his Greek-inspired
aesthetic ideal. This set off a journalistic and pamphlet war in which
Pessoa was a leading general, doing battle not only with his literary peers
but with a powerful right-wing student group. In 1924, after Olisipo had
shut its doors, Pessoa cofounded the magazine* Athena, *where he published
much of his own work in the five issues of its brief life, and in 1926 he and
his brother-in-law founded a business and accounting magazine, which
lasted for six issues.*

*Pessoa in the 1920s—his thirties—became a full citizen, assuming
an active role in the economy and society that sustained him, however
imperfectly. But he wasn't a good businessman, and he really didn't care
for the active life, which he wrote off as "the least comfortable of suicides"
(Text 247). In 1929, or perhaps the year before, he returned to his* Disquiet, *whose nature had changed, because he had changed: Pessoa was
ready to write Pessoa. He still resorted to heteronyms, whom he claimed
were better at feeling than he was (see* ASPECTS), *but it was clearly his
own unmitigated feelings that informed the poems of late Campos and
the prose of Bernardo Soares, as Pessoa now called the assistant bookkeeper
and pretended author of* The Book of Disquiet. *Bernardo Soares, a
mature and larger version of Vicente Guedes, wasn't a true heteronym.
"He's a semiheteronym," Pessoa explained, "because his personality, although not my own, doesn't differ from my own but is a mere mutilation
of it" (in his January 13, 1935, letter to Adolfo Casais Monteiro). The Baron
of Teive, probably conceived in 1928, was a similarly thin disguise, a*

semifiction, and the Campos of this period even more blatantly so. In 1930 Pessoa published the poem "Birthday," a highly personal evocation of lost childhood, in the name of the naval engineer and with the date of his "birthday," October 15, but the manuscript copy is dated June 13, Pessoa's birthday.

Fully half of The Book of Disquiet was written in the last six years of Pessoa's life. It was now thoroughly a diary, not of things seen and done but of things thought and felt, the author's Confessions, his "factless autobiography" (Text 12). Many of the passages were still fragmentary and unfinished, but at this point it would have made no sense to "complete" them. Pessoa had moved beyond literature; he was simply etching, on paper, his mind and soul. Disquiet, for Pessoa, was no longer an uncertain quantity, no longer a skittish feeling of anguish, not an intellectual trouble, nor even a psychological dis-ease. It was the author's unforgettable awareness of his life that had passed, or was passing, or would pass. It was the strange fact of consciousness that makes death thinkable, or, more acutely, the consciousness of that consciousness. Disquiet was the unwanted but necessary condition for humanly existing. And so Bernardo Soares, after describing an afternoon in Lisbon so still that even the gulls in flight seemed motionless, honestly concludes: "Nothing oppressed. The late afternoon disquiet was my own; a cool breeze intermittently blew" (Text 79). Elsewhere, meditating on scattered clouds, Soares blurts out, "Such disquiet when I feel, such discomfort when I think, such futility when I desire!" What prompts this expressive outburst isn't the clouds themselves but the sense of existential in-betweenness that their scatteredness reflects: "I'm the gap between what I am and am not, between what I dream and what life has made of me" (Text 204). Soares isn't a bookkeeper and isn't even his dreams; he hovers in the middle, in the vacuous gap of consciousness.

If the heteronyms were a theatrical representation of that gap, a fictional embodiment of Pessoa's awareness of his eternal absence, then The Book of Disquiet was the locked diary that tells all, in the most direct language possible. And although we can read its words, the lock remains, for they strike us so bluntly, so close and so true, that we pause and wonder, "Was that me?" and a mysterious hand stops us, we forget, and keep reading.

*   *   *

Pessoa published, in magazines, only twelve of the more than five hundred passages he wrote for The Book of Disquiet. *The rest had to be ferreted out from among his thousands of papers and transcribed or—in the case of handwritten passages, which are the majority—deciphered, a task that kept scholars busy for decades. The first relatively complete edition of* The Book of Disquiet *did not see print until 1982, forty-seven years after Pessoa's death. Two enlarged editions, which organize the contents in radically different ways, were published in the 1990s. It is hard to know exactly what belongs in* The Book, *since Pessoa did not always label his texts, and no editor's ordering of the material can claim to be more than a personal choice. The selection that follows is not representative of the whole book, being limited almost exclusively to untitled, diary-like passages written in the last six years of Pessoa's life. The text numbers coincide with those found in the unabridged Penguin edition and in the 1998 Portuguese edition.*

from The Book of Disquiet

1.

I was born in a time when the majority of young people had lost faith in God, for the same reason their elders had had it—without knowing why. And since the human spirit naturally tends to make judgments based on feeling instead of reason, most of these young people chose Humanity to replace God. I, however, am the sort of person who is always on the fringe of what he belongs to, seeing not only the multitude he's a part of but also the wide-open spaces around it. That's why I didn't give up God as completely as they did, and I never accepted Humanity. I reasoned that God, while improbable, might exist, in which case he should be worshipped; whereas Humanity, being a mere biological idea and signifying nothing more than the animal species we belong to, was no more deserving of worship than any other animal species.

The cult of Humanity, with its rites of Freedom and Equality, always struck me as a revival of those ancient cults in which gods were like animals or had animal heads.

And so, not knowing how to believe in God and unable to believe in an aggregate of animals, I, along with other people on the fringe, kept a distance from things, a distance commonly called Decadence. Decadence is the total loss of unconsciousness, which is the very basis of life. Could it think, the heart would stop beating.

For those few like me who live without knowing how to have life, what's left but renunciation as our way and contemplation as our destiny? Not knowing nor able to know what religious life is, since faith isn't acquired through reason, and unable to have faith in or even react to the abstract notion of man, we're left with the aesthetic contemplation of life as our reason for having a soul. Impassive to the solemnity of any and all worlds, indifferent to the divine, and disdainers of what is human, we uselessly surrender ourselves to pointless sensation, cultivated in a refined Epicureanism, as befits our cerebral nerves.

Retaining from science only its fundamental precept—that everything is subject to fatal laws, which we cannot freely react to since the laws themselves determine all reactions—and seeing how this precept concurs with the more ancient one of the divine fatality of things, we abdicate from every effort like the weak-bodied from athletic endeavors, and we hunch over the book of sensations like scrupulous scholars of feeling.

Taking nothing seriously and recognizing our sensations as the only reality we have for certain, we take refuge there, exploring them like large unknown countries. And if we apply ourselves diligently not only to aesthetic contemplation but also to the expression of its methods and results, it's because the poetry or prose we write—devoid of any desire to move anyone else's will or to mold anyone's understanding—is merely like when a reader reads out loud to fully objectify the subjective pleasure of reading.

We're well aware that every creative work is imperfect and that our most dubious aesthetic contemplation will be the one whose object is what we write. But everything is imperfect. There's no sunset so lovely it couldn't be yet lovelier, no gentle breeze bringing us sleep that couldn't bring a yet sounder sleep. And so, contemplators of statues and mountains alike, enjoying both books and the passing days, and dreaming all things so as to transform them into our own substance, we will also write down descriptions and analyses which, when they're finished, will become extraneous things that we can enjoy as if they happened along one day.

This isn't the viewpoint of pessimists like Vigny,* for whom life was a prison in which he wove straw to keep busy and forget. To be a pessimist is to see everything tragically, an attitude that's both excessive and uncomfortable. While it's true that we ascribe no value to the work we produce and that we produce it to keep busy, we're not like the prisoner who busily weaves straw to forget about his fate; we're like the girl who embroiders pillows for no other reason than to keep busy.

I see life as a roadside inn where I have to stay until the coach from the abyss pulls up. I don't know where it will take me, because I don't know anything. I could see this inn as a prison, for I'm compelled to wait in it; I could see it as a social center, for it's here that I meet others. But I'm neither impatient nor common. I leave who will to stay shut up in their rooms, sprawled out on beds where they sleeplessly wait, and I leave who will to chat in the parlors, from where their songs and voices conveniently drift out here to me. I'm sitting at the door, feasting my eyes and ears on the colors and sounds of the landscape, and I softly sing—for myself alone—wispy songs I compose while waiting.

Night will fall on us all and the coach will pull up. I enjoy the breeze I'm given and the soul I was given to enjoy it with, and I no longer question or seek. If what I write in the book of travelers can, when read by others at some future date, also entertain them on their journey, then fine. If they don't read it, or are not entertained, that's fine too.

6.

I asked for very little from life, and even this little was denied me. A nearby field, a ray of sunlight, a little bit of calm along with a bit of bread, not to feel oppressed by the knowledge that I exist, not to demand anything from others, and not to have others demand anything from me — this was denied me, like the spare change we might deny a beggar not because we're mean-hearted but because we don't feel like unbuttoning our coat.

Sadly I write in my quiet room, alone as I have always been, alone as I will always be. And I wonder if my apparently negligible voice might not embody the essence of thousands of voices, the longing for self-expression of thousands of lives, the patience of millions of souls resigned like my own to their daily lot, their useless dreams, and their hopeless hopes. In these moments my heart beats faster because I'm conscious of it. I live more because I live on high. I feel a religious force within me, a species of prayer, a kind of public outcry. But my mind quickly puts me in my place. . . . I remember that I'm on the fifth floor of the Rua dos Douradores, and I take a drowsy look at myself. I glance up from this half-written page at life, futile and without beauty, and at the cheap cigarette I'm about to extinguish in the ashtray beyond the fraying blotter. Me in this fifth-floor room, interrogating life!, saying what souls feel!, writing prose like a genius or a famous author! Me, here, a genius! . . .

7.

Today, in one of the pointless and worthless daydreams that constitute a large part of my inner life, I imagined being forever free from the Rua dos Douradores, from Vasques my boss, from Moreira the head bookkeeper, from all the employees, from the delivery boy, the office boy, and the cat. In my dream I experienced freedom, as if the South Seas had offered me marvelous islands to be discovered. It would all be repose, artistic achievement, the intellectual fulfillment of my being.

But even as I was imagining this, during my miniature midday holiday in a café, an unpleasant thought assaulted my dream: I realized I would feel regret. Yes, I say it as if confronted by the actual circumstance: I would feel regret. Vasques my boss, Moreira the head bookkeeper, Borges the cashier, all the young men, the cheerful boy who takes letters to the post office, the boy who makes deliveries, the gentle cat—all this has become part of my life. And I wouldn't be able to leave it without crying, without feeling that—like it or not—it was a part of me that would remain with all of them, and that to separate myself from them would be a partial death.

Besides, if tomorrow I were to bid them all farewell and take off my Rua dos Douradores suit, what other activity would I end up doing (for I would have to do something), or what other suit would I end up wearing (for I would have to wear some other suit)?

We all have a Vasques who's the boss—visible for some of us, invisible for others. My Vasques goes by that very name, and he's a hale and pleasant man, occasionally short-tempered but never two-faced, self-interested but basically fair, with a sense of justice that's lacking in many great geniuses and human marvels of civilization, right and left. Other people answer to vanity, or to the lure of wealth, glory, immortality. For my boss I prefer the man named Vasques, who in difficult moments is easier to deal with than all the abstract bosses in the world.

Deeming that I earn too little, a friend of mine who's a partner in a successful firm that does a lot of business with the government said the other day: "You're being exploited, Soares." And I remembered that indeed I am. But since in life we must all be exploited, I wonder if it's any worse to be exploited by Vasques and his fabrics than by vanity, by glory, by resentment, by envy, or by the impossible.

Some are exploited by God himself, and they are prophets and saints in this vacuous world.

And in the same way that others return to their homes, I retreat to my non-home: the large office on the Rua dos Douradores. I arrive at my desk as at a bulwark against life. I have a tender spot—tender to the point of tears—for my ledgers in which I keep other people's accounts, for the old inkstand I use, for the hunched back of Sérgio, who draws up invoices a little beyond where I sit. I love all this, perhaps because I have nothing else to love, and perhaps also because nothing is worth a human soul's love, and so it's all the same—should we feel the urge to give it—whether the recipient be the diminutive form of my inkstand or the vast indifference of the stars.

9.

Ah, I understand! Vasques my boss is Life — monotonous and necessary, imperious and inscrutable Life. This banal man represents the banality of Life. For me he is everything, externally speaking, because for me Life is whatever is external.

And if the office on the Rua dos Douradores represents life for me, the fifth-floor room where I live, on this same Rua dos Douradores, represents Art for me. Yes, Art, residing on the very same street as Life, but in a different place. Art, which gives me relief from life without relieving me of living, being as monotonous as life itself, only in a different place. Yes, for me the Rua dos Douradores contains the meaning of everything and the answer to all riddles, except for the riddle of why riddles exist, which can never be answered.

12.

I envy — but I'm not sure that I envy — those for whom a biography could be written, or who could write their own. In these random impressions, and with no desire to be other than random, I indifferently narrate my factless autobiography, my lifeless history. These are my Confessions, and if in them I say nothing, it's because I have nothing to say.

What is there to confess that's worthwhile or useful? What has happened to us has happened to everyone or only to us; if to everyone, then it's no novelty, and if only to us, then it won't be understood. If I write what I feel, it's to reduce the fever of feeling. What I confess is unimportant, because everything is unimportant. I make landscapes out of what I feel. I make holidays of my sensations. I can easily understand women who embroider out of sorrow or who crochet because life exists. My elderly aunt would play solitaire throughout the endless evening. These confessions of what I feel are my solitaire. I don't interpret them like those who read cards to tell the future. I don't probe them, because in solitaire the cards don't have any special significance. I unwind myself like a multicolored skein, or I make string figures of myself, like those woven on spread fingers and passed from child to child. I take care only

that my thumb not miss its loop. Then I turn over my hand and the figure changes. And I start over.

To live is to crochet according to a pattern we were given. But
while doing it the mind is at liberty, and all enchanted princes can stroll
in their parks between one and another plunge of the hooked ivory
needle. Needlework of things. . . . Intervals. . . . Nothing. . . .

Besides, what can I expect from myself? My sensations in all their
horrible acuity, and a profound awareness of feeling. . . . A sharp mind
that only destroys me, and an unusual capacity for dreaming to keep
me entertained. . . . A dead will and a reflection that cradles it, like a
living child. . . . Yes, crochet. . . .

49.

Isolation has carved me in its image and likeness. The presence of another person—of any person whatsoever—instantly slows down my
thinking, and while for a normal man contact with others is a stimu-
lus to spoken expression and wit, for me it is a counterstimulus, if this
compound word be linguistically permissible. When all by myself, I
can think of all kinds of clever remarks, quick comebacks to what no
one said, and flashes of witty sociability with nobody. But all of this
vanishes when I face someone in the flesh: I lose my intelligence, I
can no longer speak, and after half an hour I just feel tired. Yes, talking to people makes me feel like sleeping. Only my ghostly and imaginary friends, only the conversations I have in my dreams, are genuinely
real and substantial, and in them intelligence gleams like an image
in a mirror.

The mere thought of having to enter into contact with someone
else makes me nervous. A simple invitation to have dinner with a friend
produces an anguish in me that's hard to define. The idea of any social obligation whatsoever—attending a funeral, dealing with someone about an office matter, going to the station to wait for someone I
know or don't know—the very idea disturbs my thoughts for an entire
day, and sometimes I even start worrying the night before, so that I
sleep badly. When it takes place, the dreaded encounter is utterly in-

significant, justifying none of my anxiety, but the next time is no different: I never learn to learn.

"My habits are of solitude, not of men." I don't know if it was Rousseau or Senancour who said this. But it was some mind of my species, it being perhaps too much to say of my race.

71.
The cause of my profound sense of incompatibility with others is, I believe, that most people think with their feelings, whereas I feel with my thoughts.

For the ordinary man, to feel is to live, and to think is to know how to live. For me, to think is to live, and to feel is merely food for thought.

It's curious that what little capacity I have for enthusiasm is aroused by those most unlike me in temperament. I admire no one in literature more than the classical writers, who are the ones I least resemble. Forced to choose between reading only Chateaubriand or Vieira,* I would choose Vieira without a moment's hesitation.

The more a man differs from me, the more real he seems, for he depends that much less on my subjectivity. And that's why the object of my close and constant study is the same common humanity that I loathe and stay away from. I love it because I hate it. I like to look at it because I hate to feel it. The landscape, admirable as a picture, rarely makes a comfortable bed.

79.
Faint, like something just beginning, the low-tide smell wafted over the Tagus and putridly spread over the streets near the shore. The stench was crisply nauseating, with a cold torpor of lukewarm sea. I felt life in my stomach, and my sense of smell shifted to behind my eyes. Tall, sparse bundles of clouds alighted on nothing, their grayness disintegrating into a pseudo-white. A cowardly sky threatened the atmosphere, as if with inaudible thunder, made only of air.

There was even stagnation in the flight of the gulls; they seemed to be lighter than air, left there by someone. Nothing oppressed. The late afternoon disquiet was my own; a cool breeze intermittently blew.

My ill-starred hopes, born of the life I've been forced to live! They're like this hour and this air, fogless fogs, unraveled basting of a false storm. I feel like screaming, to put an end to this landscape and my meditation. But the stench of ocean imbues my intent, and the low tide inside me has exposed the sludgy blackness that's somewhere out there, though I can see it only by its smell.

All this stupid insistence on being self-sufficient! All this cynical awareness of pretended sensations! All this imbroglio of my soul with these sensations, of my thoughts with the air and the river—all just to say that life smells bad and hurts me in my consciousness. All for not knowing how to say, as in that simple and all-embracing phrase from the Book of Job, "My soul is weary of my life!"

87.

Metaphysics has always struck me as a prolonged form of latent insanity. If we knew the truth, we'd see it; everything else is systems and approximations. The inscrutability of the universe is quite enough for us to think about; to want to actually understand it is to be less than human, since to be human is to realize it can't be understood.

I'm handed faith like a sealed package on a strange-looking platter and am expected to accept it without opening it. I'm handed science, like a knife on a plate, to cut the folios of a book whose pages are blank. I'm handed doubt, like dust inside a box—but why give me a box if all it contains is dust?

I write because I don't know, and I use whatever abstract and lofty term for Truth a given emotion requires. If the emotion is clear and decisive, then I naturally speak of the gods, thereby framing it in a consciousness of the world's multiplicity. If the emotion is profound, then I naturally speak of God, thereby placing it in a unified consciousness. If the emotion is a thought, I naturally speak of Fate, thereby shoving it up against the wall.

Sometimes the mere rhythm of a sentence will require God instead of the Gods; at other times the two syllables of "the Gods" will be necessary, and I'll verbally change universe; on still other occasions what will matter is an internal rhyme, a metrical displacement, or a burst of emotion, and polytheism or monotheism will prevail accordingly. The Gods are contingent on style.

101.

If our life were an eternal standing by the window, if we could remain there forever, like hovering smoke, with the same moment of twilight forever paining the curve of the hills. . . . If we could remain that way for beyond forever! If at least on this side of the impossible we could thus continue, without committing an action, without our pallid lips sinning another word!

Look how it's getting dark! . . . The positive quietude of everything fills me with rage, with something that's a bitterness in the air I breathe. My soul aches. . . . A slow wisp of smoke rises and dissipates in the distance. . . . A restless tedium makes me think no more of you. . . .

All so superfluous! We and the world and the mystery of both.

112.

We never love anyone. What we love is the idea we have of someone. It's our own concept—our own selves—that we love.

This is true in the whole gamut of love. In sexual love we seek our own pleasure via another body. In non-sexual love, we seek our own pleasure via our own idea. The masturbator may be abject, but in point of fact he's the perfect logical expression of the lover. He's the only one who doesn't feign and doesn't fool himself.

The relations between one soul and another, expressed through such uncertain and variable things as shared words and proffered gestures, are deceptively complex. The very act of meeting each other is a non-meeting. Two people say "I love you" or mutually think it and feel it, and each has in mind a different idea, a different life, perhaps even a different color or fragrance, in the abstract sum of impressions that constitute the soul's activity.

Today I'm lucid as if I didn't exist. My thinking is as naked as a skeleton, without the fleshly tatters of the illusion of expression. And these considerations that I forge and abandon weren't born from any-thing—at least not from anything in the front rows of my consciousness. Perhaps it was the sales representative's disillusion with his girlfriend, perhaps a sentence I read in one of the romantic tales that our news-papers reprint from the foreign press, or perhaps just a vague nausea for which I can think of no physical cause. . . .

The scholiast who annotated Virgil was wrong. Understanding is what wearies us most of all. To live is to not think.

113.

Two or three days like the beginning of love. . . .

The value of this for the aesthete is in the feelings it produces. To go further would be to enter the realm of jealousy, suffering, and anxi-ety. In this antechamber of emotion there's all the sweetness of love— hints of pleasure, whiffs of passion—without any of its depth. If this means giving up the grandeur of tragic love, we must remember that tragedies, for the aesthete, are interesting to observe but unpleasant to experience. The cultivation of life hinders that of the imagination. It is the aloof, uncommon man who rules.

No doubt this theory would satisfy me, if I could convince my-self that it's not what it is: a complicated jabber to fill the ears of my intelligence, to make it almost forget that at heart I'm just timid, with no aptitude for life.

128.

I've always rejected being understood. To be understood is to prostitute oneself. I prefer to be taken seriously for what I'm not, remaining hu-manly unknown, with naturalness and all due respect.

Nothing would bother me more than if they found me strange at the office. I like to revel in the irony that they don't find me at all strange. I like the hair shirt of being regarded by them as their equal. I like the crucifixion of being considered no different. There are martyrdoms more subtle than those recorded for the saints and hermits. There are torments of our mental awareness as there are of the body and of desire. And in the former, as in the latter, there's a certain sensuality . . . . . .

150.
The persistence of instinctive life in the guise of human intelligence is one of my most constant and profound contemplations. The artificial disguise of consciousness only highlights for me the unconsciousness it doesn't succeed in disguising.

From birth to death, man is the slave of the same external dimension that rules animals. Throughout his life he doesn't live, he vegetatively thrives, with greater intensity and complexity than an animal. He's guided by norms without knowing that they guide him or even that they exist, and all his ideas, feelings, and acts are unconscious—not because there's no consciousness in them but because there aren't two consciousnesses.

Flashes of awareness that we live an illusion—that, and no more, is what distinguishes the greatest of men.

With a wandering mind I consider the common history of common men. I see how in everything they are slaves of a subconscious temperament, of extraneous circumstances, and of the social and antisocial impulses in which, with which, and over which they clash like petty objects.

How often I've heard people say the same old phrase that symbolizes all the absurdity, all the nothingness, all the verbalized ignorance of their lives. It's the phrase they use in reference to any material pleasure: "This is what we take away from life. . . ." Take where? take how? take why? It would be sad to wake them out of their darkness with questions like that. . . . Only a materialist can utter such a phrase, because everyone who utters such a phrase is, whether he knows it or not, a materialist. What does he plan to take from life, and how? Where will he take his pork chops and red wine and lady friend? To what heaven that he doesn't believe in? To what earth, where he'll only take the rottenness that was the latent essence of his whole life? I can think of no phrase that's more tragic, or that reveals more about human humanity.

That's what plants would say if they could know that they enjoy the sun. That's what animals would say about their somnambulant pleasures, were their power of self-expression not inferior to man's. And perhaps even I, while writing these words with a vague impression that they might endure, imagine that my memory of having written them is what I "take away from life." And just as a common corpse is lowered into the common ground, so the equally useless corpse of the prose I wrote while waiting will be lowered into common oblivion. A man's pork chops, his wine, his lady friend—who am I to make fun of them?

Brothers in our common ignorance, different expressions of the same blood, diverse forms of the same heredity—which of us can deny the other? A wife can be denied, but not mother, not father, not brother.

170.

After the last rains went south, leaving only the wind that had chased them away, then the gladness of the sure sun returned to the city's hills, and hanging white laundry began to appear, flapping on the cords stretched across sticks outside the high windows of buildings of all colors.

I also felt happy, because I exist. I left my rented room with a great goal in mind, which was simply to get to the office on time. But on this particular day the compulsion to live participated in that other good compulsion which makes the sun come up at the times shown in the almanac, according to the latitude and longitude of each place on earth. I felt happy because I couldn't feel unhappy. I walked down the street without a care, full of certainty, because the office I work at and the people who work with me are, after all, certainties. It's no wonder that I felt free, without knowing from what. In the baskets along the sidewalk of the Rua da Prata, the bananas for sale were tremendously yellow in the sunlight.

It really takes very little to satisfy me: the rain having stopped, there being a bright sun in this happy South, bananas that are yellower for having black splotches, the voices of the people who sell them, the sidewalk of the Rua da Prata, the Tagus at the end of it, blue with a green-gold tint, this entire familiar corner of the universe.

The day will come when I see no more of this, when I'll be survived by the bananas lining the sidewalk, by the voices of the shrewd saleswomen, and by the daily papers that the boy has set out on the opposite corner of the street. I'm well aware that the bananas will be others, that the saleswomen will be others, and that the newspapers will show—to those who bend down to look at them—a different date from today's. But they, because they don't live, endure, although as others. I, because I live, pass on, although the same.

I could easily memorialize this moment by buying bananas, for the whole of today's sun seems to be focused on them like a searchlight without a source. But I'm embarrassed by rituals, by symbols, by buying things in the street. They might not wrap the bananas the right way. They might not sell them to me as they should be sold, since I don't know how to buy them as they should be bought. They might find my voice strange when I ask the price. Better to write than to dare live, even if living means merely to buy bananas in the sunlight, as long as the sun lasts and there are bananas for sale.

Later, perhaps. . . . Yes, later. . . . Another, perhaps. . . . Or perhaps not. . . .

193.

I've witnessed, incognito, the gradual collapse of my life, the slow foundering of all that I wanted to be. I can say, with a truth that needs no flowers to show it's dead, that there's nothing I've wanted—and nothing in which I've placed, even for a moment, the dream of only that moment—that hasn't disintegrated below my windows like a clod of dirt that resembled stone until it fell from a flowerpot on a high balcony. It would even seem that Fate has always tried to make me love or want things just so that it could show me, on the very next day, that I didn't have and could never have them.

But as an ironic spectator of myself, I've never lost interest in seeing what life brings. And since I now know beforehand that every vague hope will end in disillusion, I have the special delight of already enjoying the disillusion with the hope, like the bitter with the sweet that makes the sweet sweeter by way of contrast. I'm a sullen strategist who, having never won a battle, has learned to derive pleasure from mapping out the details of his inevitable retreat on the eve of each new engagement.

My destiny, which has pursued me like a malevolent creature, is to be able to desire only what I know I'll never get. If I see the nubile figure of a girl in the street and imagine for the slightest moment, however nonchalantly, what it would be like if she were mine, it's a dead certainty that ten steps past my dream she'll meet the man who's obviously her husband or lover. A romantic would make a tragedy out of this; a stranger to the situation would see it as a comedy; I, however, mix the two things, since I'm romantic in myself and a stranger to myself, and I turn the page to yet another irony.

Some say that without hope life is impossible, others that with hope it's empty. For me, since I've stopped hoping or not hoping, life is simply an external picture that includes me and that I look at, like a show without a plot, made only to please the eyes—an incoherent dance, a rustling of leaves in the wind, clouds in which the sunlight changes color, ancient streets that wind every which way around the city.

I am, in large measure, the selfsame prose I write. I unroll myself in sentences and paragraphs, I punctuate myself. In my arranging and rearranging of images I'm like a child using newspaper to dress up as a king, and in the way I create rhythm with a series of words I'm like a lunatic adorning my hair with dried flowers that are still alive in my dreams. And above all I'm calm, like a rag doll that has become conscious of itself and occasionally shakes its head to make the tiny bell on top of its pointed cap (a component part of the same head) produce a sound, the jingling life of a dead man, a feeble notice to Fate.

But how often, in the middle of this peaceful dissatisfaction, my conscious emotion is slowly filled with a feeling of emptiness and tedium for thinking this way! How often I feel, as if hearing a voice behind intermittent sounds, that I myself am the underlying bitterness of this life so alien to human life—a life in which nothing happens except in its self-awareness! How often, waking up for a moment from this exile that's me, I get a glimpse of how much better it would be to be a complete nobody, the happy man who at least has real bitterness, the contented man who feels fatigue instead of tedium, who suffers instead of imagining he suffers, who kills himself, yes, instead of watching himself die!

I've made myself into the character of a book, a life one reads. Whatever I feel is felt (against my will) so that I can write that I felt it. Whatever I think is promptly put into words, mixed with images that undo it, cast into rhythms that are something else altogether. From so much self-revising, I've destroyed myself. From so much self-thinking, I'm now my thoughts and not I. I plumbed myself and dropped the plumb; I spend my life wondering if I'm deep or not, with no remaining plumb except my gaze that shows me—blackly vivid in the mirror at the bottom of the well—my own face that observes me observing it.

I'm like a playing card belonging to an old and unrecognizable suit—the sole survivor of a lost deck. I have no meaning, I don't know my worth, there's nothing I can compare myself with to discover what I am, and to make such a discovery would be of no use to anyone. And so, describing myself in image after image—not without truth, but with lies mixed in—I end up more in the images than in me, stating myself until I no longer exist, writing with my soul for ink, useful for nothing except writing. But the reaction ceases, and again I resign myself. I go back to who I am, even if it's nothing. And a hint of tears that weren't cried makes my stiff eyes burn; a hint of anguish that wasn't felt gets caught in my dry throat. But I don't even know what I would have cried over, if I'd cried, nor why it is that I didn't cry over it The fiction follows me, like my shadow. And what I want is to sleep.

208.

Just as, whether we know it or not, we all have a metaphysics, so too, whether we like it or not, we all have a morality. I have a very simple morality: not to do good or evil to anyone. Not to do evil, because it seems only fair that others enjoy the same right I demand for myself— not to be disturbed—and also because I think that the world doesn't need more than the natural evils it already has. All of us in this world are living on board a ship that is sailing from one unknown port to another, and we should treat each other with a traveler's cordiality. Not to do good, because I don't know what good is, nor even if I do it when I think I do. How do I know what evils I generate if I give a beggar money? How do I know what evils I produce if I teach or instruct? Not knowing, I refrain. And besides, I think that to help or clarify is, in a certain way, to commit the evil of interfering in the lives of others. Kindness depends on a whim of our mood, and we have no right to make others the victims of our whims, however humane or kind-hearted they may be. Good deeds are impositions; that's why I categorically abhor them.

If, for moral reasons, I don't do good to others, neither do I expect others to do good to me. When I get sick, what I hate most is if someone should feel obliged to take care of me, something I'd loathe doing for another. I've never visited a sick friend. And whenever I've been sick and had visitors, I've always felt their presence as a bother, an insult, an unwarranted violation of my willful privacy. I don't like people to give me things, because it seems like they're obligating me to give something in return—to them or to others, it's all the same.

I'm highly sociable in a highly negative way. I'm inoffensiveness incarnate. But I'm no more than this, I don't want to be more than this, I can't be more than this. For everything that exists I feel a visual affection, an intellectual fondness—nothing in the heart. I have faith in nothing, hope in nothing, charity for nothing. I'm nauseated and outraged by the sincere souls of all sincerities and by the mystics of all mysticisms, or rather, by the sincerities of all sincere souls and the mysticisms of all mystics. This nausea is almost physical when the mysticisms are active—when they try to convince other people, meddle with their wills, discover the truth, or reform the world.

I consider myself fortunate for no longer having family, as it relieves me of the obligation to love someone, which I would surely find burdensome. Any nostalgia I feel is literary. I remember my childhood with tears, but they're rhythmic tears, in which prose is already being formed. I remember it as something external, and it comes back to me through external things; I remember only external things. It's not the stillness of evenings in the country that endears me to the childhood I spent there, it's the way the table was set for tea, it's the way the furniture was arranged in the room, it's the faces and physical gestures of the people. I feel nostalgia for scenes. Thus someone else's childhood can move me as much as my own; both are purely visual phenomena from a past I'm unable to fathom, and my perception of them is literary. They move me, yes, but because I see them, not because I remember them.

I've never loved anyone. The most that I've loved are my sensations — states of conscious seeing, impressions gathered by intently hearing, and aromas through which the modesty of the outer world speaks to me of things from the past (so easily remembered by their smells), giving me a reality and an emotion that go beyond the simple fact of bread being baked inside the bakery, as on that remote afternoon when I was coming back from the funeral of my uncle who so loved me, and I felt a kind of sweet relief about I'm not sure what.

This is my morality, or metaphysics, or me: passer-by of everything, even of my own soul, I belong to nothing, I desire nothing, I am nothing — just an abstract center of impersonal sensations, a fallen sentient mirror reflecting the world's diversity. I don't know if I'm happy this way. Nor do I care.

230.
Art is a substitute for acting or living. If life is the willful expression of emotion, art is the intellectual expression of that same emotion. Whatever we don't have, don't attempt, or don't achieve can be possessed through dreams, and these are what we use to make art. At other times our emotion is so strong that, although reduced to action, this action doesn't completely satisfy it; the leftover emotion, unexpressed in life, is used to produce the work of art. There are thus two types of artist: the one who expresses what he doesn't have, and the one who expresses the surplus of what he did have.

247.
The active life has always struck me as the least comfortable of suicides. To act, in my view, is a cruel and harsh sentence passed on the unjustly condemned dream. To exert influence on the outside world, to change things, to overcome obstacles, to influence people — all of this seems more nebulous to me than the substance of my daydreams. Ever since I was a child, the intrinsic futility of all forms of action has been a cherished touchstone for my detachment from everything, including me.

To act is to react against oneself. To exert influence is to leave home.

I've always pondered how absurd it is that, even when the substance of reality is just a series of sensations, there can be things so complexly simple as businesses, industries, and social and family relationships, so devastatingly unintelligible in light of the soul's inner attitude toward the idea of truth.

261.

In me all affections take place on the surface, but sincerely. I've always been an actor, and in earnest. Whenever I've loved, I've pretended to love, pretending it even to myself.

279.

He left today for his hometown, apparently for good. I mean the so-called office boy, the same man I'd come to regard as part of this human corporation, and therefore as part of me and my world. He left today. In the corridor, casually running into each other for the expected surprise of our farewell, he timidly returned my embrace, and I had enough self-control not to cry, as in my heart—independent of me—my ardent eyes wanted.

Whatever has been ours, because it was ours, even if only as a casual presence in our daily routine or in what we see, becomes part of us. The man who left today for a Galician town I've never heard of was not, for me, the office boy; he was a vital part, because visible and human, of the substance of my life. Today I was diminished. I'm not quite the same. The office boy left today.

Everything that happens where we live happens in us. Everything that ceases in what we see ceases in us. Everything that has been, if we saw it when it was, was taken from us when it went away. The office boy left today.

Wearier, older, and less willing, I sit down at the high desk and continue working from where I left off yesterday. But today's vague tragedy, stirring thoughts I have to dominate by force, interrupts the automatic process of good bookkeeping. The only way I'm able to work is through an active inertia, as my own slave. The office boy left today.

Yes, tomorrow or another day, or whenever the bell will soundlessly toll my death or departure, I'll also be one who's no longer here, an old copier stowed away in the cabinet under the stairs. Yes, tomorrow or when Fate decides, the one in me who pretended to be I will come to an end. Will I go to my hometown? I don't know where I'll go. Today the tragedy is visible because of an absence, considerable because it doesn't deserve consideration. My God, my God, the office boy left today.

298.

Everything is absurd. One man spends his life earning and saving up money, although he has no children to leave it to nor any hope that some heaven might reserve him a transcendent portion. Another man strives to gain posthumous fame without believing in an afterlife that would give him knowledge of that fame. Yet another wears himself out in pursuit of things he doesn't really care for. Then there's one who . . . . . .

One man reads so as to learn, uselessly. Another man enjoys himself so as to live, uselessly.

I'm riding on a streetcar and, as usual, am closely observing all the details of the people around me. For me these details are like things, voices, phrases. Taking the dress of the girl in front of me, I break it down into the fabric from which it's made and the work that went into making it (such that I see a dress and not just fabric), and the delicate embroidery that trims the collar decomposes under my scrutiny into the silk thread with which it was embroidered and the work it took to embroider it. And immediately, as in a textbook of basic economics, factories and jobs unfold before me: the factory where the cloth was made; the factory where the darker-colored silk was spun to trim with curlicues its place around the neck; the factories' various divisions, the machines, the workers, the seamstresses. My inwardly turned eyes penetrate into the offices, where I see the managers trying to stay calm, and I watch everything being recorded in the account books. But that's not all: I see beyond all this to the private lives of those who live their social existence in these factories and offices. The whole world opens up before my eyes merely because in front of me — on the nape of a dark-skinned neck whose other side has I don't know what face—I see a regularly irregular dark-green embroidery on a light-green dress.

All humanity's social existence lies before my eyes.

And beyond this I sense the loves, the secrets, and the souls of all who labored so that the woman in front of me in the streetcar could wear, around her mortal neck, the sinuous banality of a dark-green silk trim on a less dark green cloth.

I get dizzy. The seats in the streetcar, made of tough, close-woven straw, take me to distant places and proliferate in the form of industries, workers, their houses, lives, realities, everything.

I get off the streetcar dazed and exhausted. I've just lived all of life.

299.

Every time I go somewhere, it's a vast journey. A train trip to Cascais* tires me out as if in this short time I'd traveled through the urban and rural landscapes of four or five countries.

I imagine myself living in each house I pass, each chalet, each isolated cottage whitewashed with lime and silence—happy at first, then bored, then fed up. It all happens in a moment, and as soon as I've abandoned one of these homes, I'm filled with nostalgia for the time I lived there. And so every trip I make is a painful and happy harvest of great joys, great boredoms, and countless false nostalgias.

And as I pass by those houses, villas, and chalets, I also live the daily lives of all their inhabitants, living them all at the same time. I'm the father, mother, sons, cousins, the maid, and the maid's cousin, all together and all at once, thanks to my special talent for simultaneously feeling various and sundry sensations, for simultaneously living the lives of various people—both on the outside, seeing them, and on the inside, feeling them.

I've created various personalities within. I constantly create personalities. Each of my dreams, as soon as I starting dreaming it, is immediately incarnated in another person, who is then the one dreaming it, and not I.

To create, I've destroyed myself. I've so externalized myself on the inside that I don't exist there except externally. I'm the empty stage where various actors act out various plays.

317.

One of my constant preoccupations is to understand how other people can exist, how there can be souls that aren't mine, consciousnesses that have nothing to do with my own, which—because it's a consciousness— seems to me like the only one. I accept that the man standing before me, who speaks with words like mine and gesticulates as I do or could do, is in some sense my fellow creature. But so are the figures from illustrations that fill my imagination, the characters I meet in novels, and the dramatic personae that move on stage through the actors who represent them.

No one, I suppose, genuinely admits the real existence of another person. We may concede that the person is alive and that he thinks and feels as we do, but there will always be an unnamed element of difference, a materialized inequality. There are figures from the past and living images from books that are more real to us than the incarnate indifferences that talk to us over shop counters, or happen to glance at us in the streetcars, or brush against us in the dead happenstance of the streets. Most people are no more for us than scenery, generally the invisible scenery of a street we know by heart.

I feel more kinship and intimacy with certain characters described in books and certain images I've seen in prints than I feel with many so-called real people, who are of that metaphysical insignificance known as flesh and blood. And "flesh and blood" in fact describes them rather well: they're like chunks of meat displayed in the window of a butcher's, dead things bleeding as if they were alive, shanks and cutlets of Destiny.

I'm not ashamed of feeling this way, as I've discovered that's how everyone feels. What seems to lie behind people's mutual contempt and indifference, such that they can kill each other like assassins who don't really feel they're killing, or like soldiers who don't think about what they're doing, is that no one pays heed to the apparently abstruse fact that other people are also living souls.

On certain days, in certain moments, brought to me by I don't know what breeze and opened to me by the opening of I don't know what door, I suddenly feel that the corner grocer is a thinking entity, that his assistant, who at this moment is bent over a sack of potatoes next to the entrance, is truly a soul capable of suffering.

When I was told yesterday that the employee of the tobacco shop had committed suicide, it seemed like a lie. Poor man, he also existed! We had forgotten this, all of us, all who knew him in the same way as all those who never met him. Tomorrow we'll forget him even better. But he evidently had a soul, for he killed himself. Passion? Anxiety? No doubt. . . . But for me, as for all humanity, there's only the memory of a dumb smile and a shabby sports coat that hung unevenly from the shoulders. That's all that remains to me of this man who felt so much that he killed himself for feeling, since what else does one kill himself for? Once, as I was buying cigarettes from him, it occurred to me that he would go bald early. As it turns out, he didn't have time enough to go bald. That's one of the memories I have of him. What other one can I have, if even this one is not of him but of one of my thoughts?

I suddenly see his corpse, the coffin where they placed him, the so alien grave where they must have lowered him, and it dawns on me that the cashier of the tobacco shop, with crooked coat and all, was in a certain way the whole of humanity.

It was only a flash. What's clear to me now, today, as the human being I am, is that he died. That's all.

No, others don't exist. . . . It's for me that this heavy-winged sunset lingers, its colors hard and hazy. It's for me that the great river shimmers below the sunset, even if I can't see it flow. It's for me that this square was built overlooking the river, whose waters are now rising. Was the cashier of the tobacco shop buried today in the common grave? Then the sun isn't setting for him today. But because I think this, and against my will, it has also stopped setting for me.

348.

Nothing is more oppressive than the affection of others—not even the hatred of others, since hatred is at least more intermittent than affection; being an unpleasant emotion, it naturally tends to be less frequent in those who feel it. But hatred as well as love is oppressive; both seek us, pursue us, won't leave us alone.

My ideal would be to live everything through novels and to use real life for resting up—to read my emotions and to live my disdain of them. For someone with a keen and sensitive imagination, the adventures of a fictional protagonist are genuine emotion enough, and more, since they are experienced by us as well as the protagonist. No greater romantic adventure exists than to have loved Lady Macbeth with true and directly felt love. After a love like that, what can one do but take a rest, not loving anyone in the real world?

I don't know the meaning of this journey I was forced to make, between one and another night, in the company of the whole universe. I know I can read to amuse myself. Reading seems to me the easiest way to pass the time on this as on other journeys. I occasionally lift my eyes from the book where I'm truly feeling and glance, as a foreigner, at the scenery slipping by—fields, cities, men and women, fond attachments, yearnings—and all this is no more to me than an incident in my repose, an idle distraction to rest my eyes from the pages I've been reading so intently.

Only what we dream is what we truly are, because all the rest, having been realized, belongs to the world and to everyone. If I were to realize a dream, I'd be jealous, for it would have betrayed me by allowing itself to be realized. "I've achieved everything I wanted," says the feeble man, and it's a lie; the truth is that he prophetically dreamed all that life achieved through him. We achieve nothing. Life hurls us like a stone, and we sail through the air saying, "Look at me move."

Whatever be this interlude played out under the spotlight of the sun and the spangles of the stars, surely there's no harm in knowing it's an interlude. If what's beyond the theater doors is life, then we will live, and if it's death, we will die, and the play has nothing to do with this.

That is why I never feel so close to truth, so initiated into its secrets, as on the rare occasions when I go to the theater or the circus: then I know that I'm finally watching life's perfect representation. And the actors and actresses, the clowns and magicians, are important and futile things, like the sun and the moon, love and death, the plague, hunger and war among humanity. Everything is theater. Is it truth I want? I'll go back to my novel. . . .

349.

The most abject of all needs is to confide, to confess. It's the soul's need to externalize.

Go ahead and confess, but confess what you don't feel. Go ahead and tell your secrets to get their weight off your soul, but let the secrets you tell be secrets you've never had.

Lie to yourself before you tell that truth. Expressing yourself is always a mistake. Be resolutely conscious: let expression, for you, be synonymous with lying.

382.

I've reached the point where tedium is a person, the incarnate fiction of my own company.

396.

After the last rains left the sky for earth, making the sky clear and the earth a damp mirror, the brilliant clarity of life that returned with the blue on high and that rejoiced in the freshness of the water here below left its own sky in our souls, a freshness in our hearts.

Whether we like it or not we're servants of the hour and its colors and shapes, we're subjects of the sky and earth. Even those who delve only in themselves, disdaining what surrounds them, delve by different paths when it rains and when it's clear. Obscure transmutations, perhaps felt only in the depths of abstract feelings, occur because it rains or stops raining. They're felt without our feeling them because the weather we didn't feel made itself felt.

Each of us is several, is many, is a profusion of selves. So that the self who disdains his surroundings is not the same as the self who suffers or takes joy in them. In the vast colony of our being there are many species of people who think and feel in different ways. At this very moment, jotting down these impressions during a break that's excusable because today there's not much work, I'm the one who is attentively writing them, I'm the one who is glad not to have to be working right now, I'm the one seeing the sky outside, invisible from in here, I'm the one thinking about all of this, I'm the one feeling my body satisfied and my hands still a bit cold. And my entire world of all these souls who don't know each other casts, like a motley but compact multitude, a single shadow—the calm, bookkeeping body with which I lean over Borges's tall desk, where I've come to get the blotter that he borrowed from me.

430.

Having seen how lucidly and logically certain madmen justify their lunatic ideas to themselves and to others, I can never again be sure of the lucidness of my lucidity.

441.

High in the nocturnal solitude an anonymous lamp flourishes behind a window. All else that I see in the city is dark, save where feeble reflections of light hazily ascend from the streets and cause a pallid, inverse moonlight to hover here and there. The buildings' various colors, or shades of colors, are hardly distinguishable in the blackness of the night, only vague, seemingly abstract differences break the regularity of the congested ensemble.

An invisible thread links me to the unknown owner of the lamp. It's not the mutual circumstance of us both being awake; in this there can be no reciprocity, for my window is dark, so that he cannot see me. It's something else, something all my own that's related to my feeling of isolation, that participates in the night and in the silence, and that chooses the lamp as an anchor because it's the only anchor there is. It seems to be its glowing that makes the night so dark. It seems to be the fact I'm awake, dreaming in the dark, that makes the lamp shine.

Everything that exists perhaps exists because something else exists. Nothing is, everything coexists—perhaps that's how it really is. I feel I wouldn't exist right now—or at least wouldn't exist in the way I'm existing, with this present consciousness of myself, which, because it is consciousness and present, is entirely me in this moment—if that lamp weren't shining somewhere over there, a useless lighthouse with a specious advantage of height. I feel this because I feel nothing. I think this because this is nothing. Nothing, nothing, part of the night and the silence and what I share with them of vacancy, of negativity, of in-betweenness, a gap between me and myself, something forgotten by some god or other. . . .

451.

Travel? One need only exist to travel. I go from day to day, as from station to station, in the train of my body or my destiny, leaning out over the streets and squares, over people's faces and gestures, always the same and always different, just like scenery.

If I imagine, I see. What more do I do when I travel? Only extreme poverty of the imagination justifies having to travel to feel.

"Any road, this simple Entepfuhl road, will lead you to the end of the World."* But the end of the world, when we go around it full circle, is the same Entepfuhl from which we started out. The end of the world, like the beginning, is in fact our concept of the world. It is in us that the scenery is scenic. If I imagine it, I create it; if I create it, it exists; if it exists, then I see it like any other scenery. So why travel? In Madrid, Berlin, Persia, China, and at the North or South Pole, where would I be but in myself, and in my particular type of sensations?

Life is what we make of it. Travel is the traveler. What we see isn't what we see but what we are.

465.

The advent of summer makes me sad. It seems that summer's luminosity, though harsh, should comfort those who don't know who they are, but it doesn't comfort me. There's too sharp a contrast between the teeming life outside me and the forever unburied corpse of my sensations—what I feel and think, without knowing how to feel or think. In this borderless country known as the universe, I feel like I'm living under a political tyranny that doesn't oppress me directly but that still offends some secret principle of my soul. And then I'm slowly, softly seized by an absurd nostalgia for some future, impossible exile.

What I mostly feel is slumber. Not a slumber that latently brings — like all other slumbers, even those caused by sickness — the privilege of physical rest. Not a slumber that, because it's going to forget life and perhaps bring dreams, bears the soothing gifts of a grand renunciation on the platter with which it approaches our soul. No: this is a slumber that's unable to sleep, that weighs on the eyelids without closing them, that purses the corners of one's disbelieving lips into what feels like a stupid and repulsive expression. It's the kind of sleepiness that uselessly overwhelms the body when one's soul is suffering from acute insomnia.

Only when night comes do I feel, not happiness, but a kind of repose which, since other reposes are pleasant, seems pleasant by way of analogy. Then my sleepiness goes away, and the confusing mental dusk brought on by the sleepiness begins to fade and to clear until it almost glows. For a moment there's the hope of other things. But the hope is short-lived. What comes next is a hopeless, sleepless tedium, the unpleasant waking up of one who never fell asleep. And from the window of my room I gaze with my wretched soul and exhausted body at the countless stars — countless stars, nothing, nothingness, but countless stars. . . .

472.
To attain the satisfactions of the mystic state without having to endure its rigors; to be the ecstatic follower of no god, the mystic or epopt* with no initiation; to pass the days meditating on a paradise you don't believe in — all of this tastes good to the soul that knows it knows nothing.

The silent clouds drift high above me, a body inside a shadow; the hidden truths drift high above me, a soul imprisoned in a body. . . . Everything drifts high above. . . . And everything high above passes on, just like everything down below, with no cloud leaving behind more than rain, no truth leaving behind more than sorrow. . . . Yes, everything that's lofty passes high above, and passes on; everything that's desirable is in the distance and distantly passes on. . . . Yes, everything attracts, everything remains foreign, and everything passes on.

What's the point of knowing that in the sun or in the rain, as a body or a soul, I will also pass on? No point—just the hope that everything is nothing and nothing, therefore, everything.

476.

It will seem to many that my diary, written just for me, is too artificial. But it's only natural for me to be artificial. How else can I amuse myself except by carefully recording these mental notes? Though I'm not very careful about how I record them. In fact I jot them down in no particular order and with no special care. The refined language of my prose is the language in which I naturally think.

For me the outer world is an inner reality. I feel this not in some metaphysical way but with the senses normally used to grasp reality.

Yesterday's frivolity is a nostalgia that gnaws at my life today.

There are cloisters in this moment. Night has fallen on all our evasions. A final despair in the blue eyes of the pools reflects the dying sun. We were so many things in the parks of old! We were so voluptuously embodied in the presence of the statues and in the English layout of the paths. The costumes, the foils, the wigs, the graceful motions, and the processions were so much a part of the substance of our spirit! But who does "our" refer to? Just the fountain's winged water in the deserted garden, shooting less high than it used to in its sad attempt to fly.

481.

I went into the barbershop as usual, with the pleasant sensation of entering a familiar place, easily and naturally. New things are distressing to my sensibility; I'm only at ease in places where I've already been.

After I'd sat down in the chair, I happened to ask the young barber, occupied in fastening a clean, cool cloth around my neck, about his older colleague from the chair to the right, a spry fellow who had been sick. I didn't ask this because I felt obliged to ask something; it was the place and my memory that sparked the question. "He passed away yesterday," flatly answered the barber's voice behind me and the linen cloth as his fingers withdrew from the final tuck of the cloth in between my shirt collar and my neck. The whole of my irrational good mood abruptly died, like the eternally missing barber from the adjacent chair. A chill swept over all my thoughts. I said nothing.

Nostalgia! I even feel it for people and things that were nothing to me, because time's fleeing is for me an anguish, and life's mystery is a torture. Faces I habitually see on my habitual streets—if I stop seeing them I become sad. And they were nothing to me, except perhaps the symbol of all of life.

The nondescript old man with dirty gaiters who often crossed my path at nine-thirty in the morning. . . . The crippled seller of lottery tickets who would pester me in vain. . . . The round and ruddy old man smoking a cigar at the door of the tobacco shop. . . . The pale tobacco shop owner. . . . What has happened to them all, who because I regularly saw them were a part of my life? Tomorrow I too will vanish from the Rua da Prata, the Rua dos Douradores, the Rua dos Fanqueiros. Tomorrow I too—I this soul that feels and thinks, this universe I am for myself—yes, tomorrow I too will be the one who no longer walks these streets, whom others will vaguely evoke with a "What's become of him?" And everything I've done, everything I've felt, and everything I've lived will amount merely to one less passer-by on the everyday streets of some city or other.

FROM THE EDUCATION
OF THE STOIC
Baron of Teive

The Baron of Teive, who seems to have come into existence in 1928, may have been the last fictional author created by Pessoa. He is also one of the last major voices of this multitudinous yet very private writer to go public. Although a few passages attributed to the baron were published as early as 1960, Pessoa's blue-blooded alter ego remained an illustrious unknown until 1999, the year of the first edition in Portuguese of A Educação do Estóico (*The Education of the Stoic*), subtitled "The Only Manuscript of the Baron of Teive" and sub-subtitled "The Impossibility of Producing Superior Art."

    The three titles summarize a good part of the baron's trouble. Frustrated because he can't produce on paper the large literary works he plots in his mind, the baron stoically endures his dispersed, sterile existence at his estate outside Lisbon until he finally decides to call it quits. After burning all his fragmentary writings in the fireplace but before blowing his brains out, he endeavors "to explain with simplicity" in his final manuscript (the only one that will survive) why he wasn't able to pull off a sustained literary work. But even this final manuscript turns out to be a mishmash of fragments, mere notes to a supreme fiction: Fernando Pessoa as a landed aristocrat who leaves for posterity one perfectly achieved literary work, which would explain to the world why it's impossible to achieve such a work.

    The baron, like Bernardo Soares, is a semiheteronym, a mutilated or distorted version of Pessoa. Besides embodying the literary frustrations and aristocratic pretensions of his creator (who, despite his modest material circumstances, boasted some vaguely noble lineage on his father's side), *Teive also portrays Pessoa's sexual drama, or lack of it. Although the projected chapter on "Why the Baron didn't seduce more young ladies" didn't get written, the nobleman does make several references to his impotence vis-à-vis the servant girls at his country estate. We have no way of knowing whether Pessoa was impotent, but we know from his automatic writings that he wasn't at all happy about his virginity, which was still firmly in place at age twenty-eight and very possibly went with him to the grave.*

Sex, nobility, and his literary oeuvre weren't the only obsessions that Pessoa passed on to the helpless baron, who was forced to die for his inventor's sins. All of the heteronyms were in one way or another instruments of exorcism and redemption; they were all born to save Pessoa from the life that bored him, or that he didn't care for, or that he had little aptitude for; but Teive incorporated the most dangerous aspect of his progenitor: implacable, unbridled reason. "My mind has always ruled my feelings," the baron confesses, and when he arrives at the conclusion that it's "impossible to live life according to reason," suicide is the way out that his reason logically imposes. Or that was imposed on him by Fernando Pessoa, forever faithful to literature.

I've reached the height of emptiness, the plenitude of nothing at all. What will lead me to commit suicide is the same kind of urge that makes one go to bed early. I'm tired to death of all intentions.

Nothing at this point can change my life.

If. . . . If. . . .

Yes, but if is always something that never happened, and if it never happened, why imagine what it would be if it had?

I sense that the end of my life is near, because I want it to be near. I spent the last two days burning, one by one (and it took two days because I sometimes reread them), all of my manuscripts, the notes of my deceased thoughts, the sketches and even some finished passages of the works I would never have written. It was without hesitation, but with a

lingering grief, that I made this sacrifice by which I take my leave—
like a man who burns a bridge—from the shore of this life I'm about to
abandon. I'm freed. I'm ready. I'm going to kill myself. But I'd at least
like to leave an intellectual memoir of my life, a written picture—as
accurate as I can make it—of what I was on the inside. Since I wasn't
able to leave a succession of beautiful lies, I want to leave the smidgen
of truth that the falsehood of everything lets us suppose we can tell.

This will be my only manuscript. I leave it not, as Bacon, to the
charitable thoughts of future generations, but (without comparison) to
the consideration of those whom the future will make my peers.

Having broken all ties but the last between me and life, I've acquired an emotional clarity in my soul and a mental clarity in my intellect that give me the force of words, not to achieve the literary work I
could never have achieved, but to offer at least a simple explanation of
why I didn't achieve it.

These pages are not my confession; they're my definition. And I
feel, as I begin to write it, that I can write with some semblance of truth.

There's no greater tragedy than an equal intensity, in the same soul or
the same man, of the intellectual sentiment and the moral sentiment.
For a man to be utterly and absolutely moral, he has to be a bit stupid.
For a man to be absolutely intellectual, he has to be a bit immoral. I
don't know what game or irony of creation makes it impossible for man
to be both things at once. And yet, to my misfortune, this duality occurs
in me. Endowed with both virtues, I've never been able to make myself
into anything. It wasn't a surfeit of one quality, but of two, that made
me unfit to live life.

Whenever and wherever I had an actual or potential rival, I promptly
gave up, without a moment's hesitation. It's one of the few things in life
about which I never hesitated. My pride could never stand the idea of
me competing with someone else, particularly since it would mean the
horrid possibility of defeat. I refused, for the same reason, to take part
in competitive games. If I lost, I always fumed with resentment. Because

I thought I was better than everyone else? No: I never thought I was better in chess or in whist. It was because of sheer pride, a ruthless and raging pride that my mind's most desperate efforts could do nothing to curb or stanch. I kept my distance from life and the world, and an encounter with any of their elements always offended me like an insult from below, like the sudden defiance of a universal lackey.

In times of painful doubt, when I knew from the start that I'd go wrong, what made me furious at myself was the disproportionate weight of the social factor in my decisions. I was never able to overcome the influence of heredity and my upbringing. I could pooh-pooh the sterile concepts of nobility and social rank, but I never succeeded in forgetting them. They're like an inborn cowardice, which I loathe and struggle against but which binds my mind and my will with inscrutable ties. Once I had the chance to marry a simple girl who could perhaps have made me happy, but between me and her, in my soul's indecision, stood fourteen generations of barons, a mental image of the whole town smirking at my wedding, the sarcasm of friends I'm not even close to, and a huge uneasiness made of mean and petty thoughts—so many petty thoughts that it weighed on me like the commission of a crime. And so I, the man of reason and detachment, lost out on happiness because of the neighbors I disdain.

How I'd dress, how I'd act, how I'd receive people in my house (where perhaps I wouldn't have to receive anyone), all the uncouth expressions and naïve attitudes that her affection wouldn't veil nor her devotion make me forget—all of this loomed like a specter of serious things, as if it were an argument, on sleepless nights when I tried to defend my desire to have her in the endless web of impossibilities that has always entangled me.

I still remember—so vividly I can smell the gentle fragrance of the spring air—the afternoon when I decided, after thinking everything over, to abdicate from love as from an insoluble problem. It was in May, a May that was softly summery, with the flowers around my estate already in full bloom, their colors fading as the sun made its slow descent. Escorted by regrets and self-reproach, I walked among my few trees. I had dined early and was wandering, alone like a symbol, under the useless shadows and faint rustle of leaves. And suddenly I was overwhelmed by a desire to renounce completely, to withdraw once and for all, and I felt an intense nausea for having had so many desires, so many hopes, with so many outer conditions for attaining them and so much inner impossibility of really wanting to attain them. That soft and sad moment marks the beginning of my suicide.

I belong to a generation—assuming that this generation includes others besides me—that lost its faith in the gods of the old religions as well as in the gods of modern nonreligions. I reject Jehovah as I reject humanity. For me, Christ and progress are myths from the same world. I don't believe in the Virgin Mary, and I don't believe in electricity.

It is impossible to live life according to reason. Intelligence provides no guiding rule. This realization unveiled for me what is perhaps hidden in the myth of the Fall. As when one's physical gaze is struck by lightning, my soul's vision was struck by the terrible and true meaning of the temptation that led Adam to eat from the so-called Tree of Knowledge.

Where intelligence exists, life is impossible.

Our problem isn't that we're individualists. It's that our individualism is static rather than dynamic. We value what we think rather than what we do. We forget that we haven't done, or been, what we thought; that the first function of life is action, just as the first property of things is motion.

Giving importance to what we think because we thought it, taking our own selves not only (to quote the Greek philosopher)* as the measure of all things but as their norm or standard, we create in ourselves, if not an interpretation, at least a criticism of the universe, which we don't even know and therefore cannot criticize. The giddiest, most weak-minded of us then promote that criticism to an interpretation— an interpretation that's superimposed, like a hallucination; induced rather than deduced. It's a hallucination in the strict sense, being an illusion based on something only dimly seen.

* * *

Modern man, if he's unhappy, is a pessimist.

There's something contemptible, something degrading, in this projection of our personal sorrows onto the whole universe. There's something shamefully egocentric in supposing that the universe is inside us, or that we're a kind of nucleus and epitome, or symbol, of it.

The fact I suffer may be an impediment to the existence of an unequivocally good Creator, but it doesn't prove the nonexistence of a Creator, or the existence of an evil Creator, or even the existence of a neutral Creator. It proves only that evil exists in the world — something that can hardly be called a discovery, and that no one has yet tried to deny.

I've never been able to believe that I, or that anyone, could offer any effective relief for human ills, much less cure them. But I've never been able to ignore them either. The tiniest human anguish — even the slightest thought of one — has always upset and anguished me, preventing me from focusing just on myself. My conviction that all remedies for the soul are useless should naturally lift me to a summit of indifference, below which the clouds of that same conviction would cover from view all the hubbub on earth. But powerful as thought is, it can do nothing to quell rebellious emotions. We can't choose not to feel, as we can not to walk. And so I witness, as I've always witnessed, ever since I can remember feeling with the higher emotions, all the pain, injustice, and misery that's in the world, as a paralytic might witness the drowning of a man whom no one, however able-bodied, could save. In me the pain of others became more than a simple pain: there was the pain of seeing it, the pain of seeing that it was incurable, and the pain of knowing that my awareness of its incurableness precluded even the useless noble-mindedness of wishing I felt like doing something to cure it. My lack of initiative was the root cause of all my troubles — of my inability to want something before having thought about it, of my inability to commit myself, of my inability to decide in the only way one can decide: by deciding, not by thinking. I'm like Buridan's donkey,* dying at the mathematical midpoint between the water of emotion and the hay of action; if I didn't think, I might still die, but it wouldn't be from thirst or hunger.

Whatever I think or feel inevitably turns into a form of inertia. Thought, which for other people is a compass to guide action, is for me its microscope, making me see whole universes to span where a footstep would have sufficed, as if Zeno's argument about the impossibility of crossing a given space—which, being infinitely divisible, is therefore infinite—were a strange drug that had intoxicated my psychological self. And feeling, which in other people enters the will like a hand in a glove, or like a fist in the guard of a sword, was always in me another form of thought—futile like a rage that makes us tremble so much we can't move, or like a panic (the panic, in my case, of feeling too intensely) that freezes the frightened man in his tracks, when his fright should make him flee.

My whole life has been a battle lost on the map. Cowardice didn't even make it to the battlefield, where perhaps it would have dissipated; it haunted the chief of staff in his office, all alone with his certainty of defeat. He didn't dare implement his battle plan, since it was sure to be imperfect, and he didn't dare perfect it (though it could never be truly perfect), since his conviction that it would never be perfect killed all his desire to strive for perfection. Nor did it ever occur to him that his plan, though imperfect, might be closer to perfection than the enemy's. The truth is that my real enemy, victorious over me since God, was that very idea of perfection, marching against me at the head of all the troops of the world—in the tragic vanguard of all the world's armed men.

I could easily have seduced any of the housemaids in my service. But some were too big, or seemed big because they were so vivacious, and in their presence I felt automatically shy, unnerved; I couldn't even dream of seducing them. Others were too small, or delicate, and I felt sorry for them. Others were unattractive. And so I passed by the specific phenomenon of love as I passed, more or less, by the general phenomenon of life.

The fear of hurting others, the sensuality aroused by physical acts, my awareness of the real existence of other souls—these things were trammels to my life, and I ask myself now what good they did me, or anybody else. The girls I didn't seduce were seduced by others, for it was inevitable that somebody seduce them. I had scruples where other men didn't think twice, and after seeing what I didn't do done by others, I wondered: Why did I think so much if it only made me suffer?

I first realized how utterly disinterested I was in myself and in what I once held closest to heart when one day, going home, I heard a fire alarm that seemed to be in my neighborhood. It occurred to me that my house might be in flames (though it wasn't, after all), and whereas I once would have been possessed by horror at the thought of all my manuscripts going up in smoke, I noticed, to my astonishment, that the possibility of my house being on fire left me indifferent, almost happy in the thought of how much simpler my life would be without those manuscripts. In the past, the loss of my manuscripts — of my life's fragmentary but carefully wrought oeuvre — would have driven me mad, but now I viewed the prospect as a casual incident of my fate, not as a fatal blow that would annihilate my personality by annihilating its manifestations.

I began to understand how the continuous struggle for an unattainable perfection finally tires us out, and I understood the great mystics and great ascetics, who recognize life's futility in their soul. What of me would be lost in those written sheets? Before, I would have said "everything." Today I'd say "nothing," or "not much," or "something strange."

I had become, to myself, an objective reality. But in doing so I couldn't tell if I had found myself or lost myself.

To think like spiritualists and act like materialists. It's not an absurd creed; it's the spontaneous creed of all humanity.

What's the life of humanity but a religious evolution with no influence on daily life?

Humanity is attracted to what's ideal, and the loftier and less human the ideal, the more attractive it will be to the praxis (if it's progressive) of humanity's civilized life, which thus passes from nation to nation, from era to era, from civilization to civilization. Civilized humanity opens its arms to a religion that preaches chastity, to a religion that preaches equality, to a religion that preaches peace. But normal humanity procreates, discriminates, and clashes continuously, and will do so for as long as it lasts.

To think that I considered this incoherent heap of half-written scraps a literary work! To think, in this decisive moment, that I believed myself capable of organizing all these pieces into a finished, visible whole! If the organizational power of thought were enough to make the work materialize, if this organization could be achieved by the emotional intensity that suffices for a short poem or brief essay, then the work I aspired to would have doubtless taken shape, for it would have shaped itself in me, without my help as a determining agent.

Had I concentrated on what was possible for my unaggressive will, I know I could have produced short essays from the fragments of my unachievable masterpiece. I could have put together several miscellanies of finished, well-rounded prose pieces. I could have collected many of the phrases scattered among my notes into more than just a book of thoughts, and it wouldn't be superficial or old hat.

My pride, however, won't let me settle for less than my mind is capable of. I've never allowed myself to go halfway, to accept anything less in the work I do than my whole personality and entire ambition. Had I felt that my mind was incapable of synthetic work, I would have bridled my pride, seeing it as a form of madness. But the deficiency wasn't in my mind, which was always very good at synthesizing and organizing. The problem was in my lukewarm will to make the enormous effort that a finished whole requires.

By this standard perhaps no creative work anywhere would ever have been made. I realize that. I realize that if all the great minds had scrupulously desired to do only what was perfect, or at least (since perfection is impossible) what was in complete accord with their entire personality, then they would have given up, like me.

Only those who are more willful than intelligent, more impulsive than rational, have a part to play in the real life of this world. *Disjecta membra*, said Carlyle,* is what remains of any poet, or of any man. But an intense pride, like the one that killed me and will yet kill me, won't admit the idea of subjecting to the humiliation of future ages the deformed, mutilated body that inhabits and defines the soul whose inevitable imperfection it expresses.

Where the soul's dignity is concerned, I can see no middle course or intermediate term between the ascetic and the common man. If you're a doer, then do; if a renouncer, then renounce. Do with the brutality that doing entails; renounce with the absoluteness of renunciation. Renounce without tears or self-pity, lord at least in the vehemence of your renunciation. Disdain yourself, but with dignity.

To weep before the world—and the more beautiful the weeping, the more the world opens up to the weeper, and the more public is his shame—this is the ultimate indignity that can be wreaked on the inner life by a defeated man who didn't keep his sword to do his final duty as a soldier. We are all soldiers in this instinctive regiment called life; we must live by the law of reason or by no law. Gaiety is for dogs; whining is for women. Man has only his honor and silence. I felt this more than ever while watching the flames in the fireplace consume my writings once and for all.

The mind's dignity is to acknowledge that it is limited and that reality is outside it. To acknowledge, with or without dismay, that nature's laws do not bend to our wishes, that the world exists independently of our will, that our own sadness proves nothing about the moral condition of the stars or even of the people who pass by our windows—in this acknowledgment lies the mind's true purpose and the soul's rational dignity.

Even now, when nothing attracts me but death (which is "nothing"), I quickly lean out the window to see the cheerful groups of farm workers going home, singing almost religiously, in the still evening air. I recognize that their life is happy. I recognize it at the edge of the grave that I myself will dig, and I recognize it with the ultimate pride of not failing to recognize it. What does the personal sorrow that torments me have to do with the universal greenness of the trees, with the natural cheer of these young men and women? What does the wintry end into which I am sinking have to do with the spring that's now in the world thanks to natural laws, whose action on the course of the stars makes the roses bloom, and whose action in me makes me end my life?

How I would diminish before my own eyes and, in truth, before everything and everyone, were I to say right now that the spring is sad, that the flowers suffer, that the rivers lament, that there's anguish and anxiety in the farm workers' song, and all because Álvaro Coelho de Athayde, the fourteenth Baron of Teive, realized with regret that he can't write the books he wanted to!

I confine to myself the tragedy that's mine. I suffer it, but I suffer it face to face, without metaphysics or sociology. I admit that I'm conquered by life, but not humbled by it.

Many people have tragedies, and if we count the incidental ones, then all people do. But it's up to everyone who's a man not to speak of his tragedy, and it's up to everyone who's an artist either to be a man and keep his trouble to himself, writing or singing about other things, or to extract from it—with lofty determination—a universal lesson.

I feel I have attained the full use of my reason. And that's why I'm going to kill myself.

A gladiator whose fate as a slave condemned him to the arena, I take my bow, without fearing the Caesar who's in this circus surrounded by stars. I bow low, without pride, since a slave has nothing to be proud of, and without joy, since a man condemned to die can hardly smile. I bow so as not to fail the law, which so completely failed me. But having taken my bow, I drive into my chest the sword that won't serve me in combat.

If the conquered man is the one who dies and the conqueror the one who kills, then by this act, admitting that I'm conquered, I make myself a conqueror.

FROM THE PREFACE TO
FICTIONS OF THE INTERLUDE

Fictions of the Interlude, *which served as a title for a small group of poems published under Pessoa's own name in 1917, was also—toward the end of his life—the working title for the series of heteronymic books that he had previously called* Aspects. *The "interlude" of the new title corresponds, perhaps, to the one described in the penultimate paragraph of Text 348 of* The Book of Disquiet. *The "fictions" are the heteronyms. Both words of course have other, no doubt pertinent, meanings. This preface, like the preface to* Aspects *and like virtually all of Pessoa's many prefaces, was left as an incomplete set of unlinked passages, two of which are published here.*

I place certain of my literary characters in stories, or in the subtitles of books, signing my name to what they say; others I project totally, with my only signature being the acknowledgment that I created them. The two types of characters may be distinguished as follows: in those that stand absolutely apart, the very style in which they write is different from my own and, when the case warrants, even contrary to it; in the characters whose works I sign my name to, the style differs from mine only in those inevitable details that serve to distinguish them from each other.

I will compare some of these characters to show, through example, what these differences involve. The assistant bookkeeper Bernardo Soares and the Baron of Teive—both are me-ishly extraneous characters—write with the same basic style, the same grammar, and the same careful diction. In other words, they both write with the style that, good or bad, is my own. I compare them because they are two instances of the very same phenomenon—an inability to adapt to real life—motivated by the very same causes. But although the Portuguese is the same in the Baron of Teive and in Bernardo Soares, their styles differ. That of the aristocrat is intellectual, without images, a bit—how shall I put it?—stiff and constrained, while that of his middle-class counterpart is fluid, participating in music and painting but not very architectural. The nobleman thinks clearly, writes clearly, and controls his emotions, though not his feelings; the bookkeeper controls neither emotions nor feelings, and what he thinks depends on what he feels.

There are also notable similarities between Bernardo Soares and Álvaro de Campos. But in Álvaro de Campos we are immediately struck by the carelessness of his Portuguese and by his exaggerated use of images, more instinctive and less purposeful than in Soares.

In my efforts to distinguish one from another, there are lapses that weigh on my sense of psychological discernment. When I try to distinguish, for example, between a musical passage of Bernardo Soares and a similar passage of my own. . . .

Sometimes I can do it automatically, with a perfection that astonishes me; and there's no vanity in my astonishment, since, not believing in even a smidgen of human freedom, I'm no more astonished by what happens in me than I would be by what happens in someone else— both are perfect strangers.

Only a formidable intuition can serve as a compass on the vast expanses of the soul. Only with a sensibility that freely uses the intelligence without being contaminated by it, although the two function together as one, is it possible to distinguish the separate realities of these imaginary characters.

These derivative personalities, or rather, these different inventions of personalities, fall into two categories or degrees, which the attentive reader will easily be able to identify by their distinctive characteristics. In the first category, the personality is distinguished by feelings and ideas which I don't share. At the lower level within this category, the personality is distinguished only by ideas, which are placed in rational exposition or argument and are clearly not my own, at least not so far as I know. "The Anarchist Banker" is an example of this lower level; *The Book of Disquiet*, and the character Bernardo Soares, represent the higher level.

The reader will note that, although I'm publishing *The Book of Disquiet* under the name of a certain Bernardo Soares, assistant book-keeper in the city of Lisbon, I have not included it in these *Fictions of the Interlude*. This is because Bernardo Soares, while differing from me in his ideas, his feelings, and his way of seeing and understanding, expresses himself in the same way I do. His is a different personality, but expressed through my natural style, with the only distinguishing feature being the particular tone that inevitably results from the particularity of his emotions.

In the authors of *Fictions of the Interlude*, it's not only their ideas and feelings that differ from mine; their technique of composition, their very style, is different from mine. Each of these authors is not just conceived differently but created as a wholly different entity. That's why poetry predominates here. In prose it is harder to other oneself.

LETTER FROM A HUNCHBACK GIRL TO A METALWORKER
Maria José

Among the dozens of names under which Fernando Pessoa wrote and which, in a certain way, wrote Pessoa, there was one female persona, called Maria José. The letter attributed to her was typed on three and a half pages, but Pessoa-Maria signed her name next to the title. One of the striking features of the letter is the language, for Pessoa succeeds in rendering the simple but long-winded diction characteristic of Maria José's economically disadvantaged social class. He also reveals, in spite of his oft-declared disinterest in matters of love and sexuality, a remarkable capacity to evoke a woman's hopeless love for a man.

Dear Senhor António,

You won't ever read this letter, and I'll probably never read over what I've written, because I'm dying of TB, but I have to write you what I feel or I'll burst.

You don't know who I am, or rather, you know but it's like you didn't know. You've seen me look at you from my window when you pass by on your way to the metalworks, because I know when you're going to pass by, and I wait for you. I doubt you've ever given a second thought to the hunchback girl who lives on the second floor of the yellow building, but I never stop thinking about you. I know you have a girlfriend—that tall and pretty blonde. I envy her but I'm not jealous, because I have no rights over you, not even the right to be jealous. I like you because I like you, and I wish I were a different woman, with a different body and a different personality, so that I could go down to the street and talk to you, because even if you didn't give me the time of day, I'd still love to meet you and talk.

You're all I have to keep me going in my sickness, and I'm grateful to you, though you have no idea. I could never be liked in the way people who have likable bodies are liked, but I have the right to like others without being liked back, and I also have the right to cry, because that's a right that everyone has.

I'd like to talk to you just once and then die, but I'll never have the guts or the means to talk to you. I'd like you to know how much I like you, but I'm afraid that if you knew, it would mean nothing to you, and it's so sad to feel certain that this would be the case before finding out if it's the case that I'll never even try to find out.

I was born a hunchback and have always been laughed at. Hunchbacked girls are supposed to be wicked, but I never tried to harm anyone. And besides, I'm sick, so that I don't even have the strength to get really angry. I'm nineteen years old and don't know why on earth I've lived this long. I'm sick, and nobody feels sorry for me unless it's because I'm a hunchback, which is the least of my troubles, for it's my soul that hurts and not my body, because the hunchback doesn't cause any pain.

I'd even like to know all about how your life is with your girlfriend, precisely because it's a life I can never have, especially now that my life is almost over.

Excuse me for writing so much when I don't know you, but you won't read this, and even if you did, you wouldn't realize it's to you, or you wouldn't care, but I wish you'd think for a minute of how sad it is to be a hunchback who always sits next to the window and nobody likes her except her mother and sisters, but that doesn't count because they have to, they're family, that's the least they can do for a doll with her bones turned inside out, which is how I once heard someone describe me.

One morning, when you were on your way to the metalworks, a cat was scuffling with a dog across the street from my window, and we were all watching, and you stopped to watch too, next to Manuel das Barbas, in front of the corner barber, and you suddenly looked up at my window and saw me laughing and you laughed too, and that's the only time we were ever alone together, so to speak, or as alone together as I could ever hope for.

You have no idea how often I've dreamed of something else like that happening as you're passing by, so that I might again watch you as you watch, and maybe you'd look up at me and I could look at you and see your eyes gaze straight into mine.

But I never get what I want, that's how I was born, and I even have to have a kind of platform beneath my chair to be able to see out the window. I spend all day looking at the illustrations in fashion magazines that people lend to my mother, and I'm always thinking about something else, so that when they ask me what a certain skirt looked like or who was in the picture with the Queen of England, I often blush because I don't know, because I was seeing things that are impossible and that I can't let into my head and make me smile or I'll just end up wanting to cry.

Then everyone forgives me, and they think I'm silly, but not stupid, because nobody thinks I'm stupid, and I don't mind that they think I'm silly, since it saves me from having to explain why I was distracted.

I still remember the day when you passed by on a Sunday in a light blue suit. It wasn't light blue, but it was much lighter than the dark blue that a suit made of serge usually is. You looked like the day itself, which was beautiful, and I've never envied everybody else as much as on that day. But I didn't envy your girlfriend, if she's the one you were on your way to see and not some other girl, because I was thinking only about you, and that's why I envied everybody, which doesn't make much sense, but that's how it was.

It's not because I'm hunchbacked that I'm always sitting by the window but because I also have a kind of arthritis in my legs that prevents me from moving, so that I'm practically a cripple, which makes me an awful nuisance for everyone who lives here. You can't imagine what it's like to know that everyone puts up with you just because they have to, and sometimes it gets me so depressed I could almost jump out the window, but think of what kind of a sight that would make! Even those who saw me jump would laugh, and the window's so low that I wouldn't even die, so that I'd be even more of a nuisance to others, and I can just see myself flailing on the street like a monkey, with my legs in the air and my hunchback poking out of my blouse, and everyone wanting to pity me but also feeling repulsed or maybe even laughing, because people are how they are and not how they want to be.

You go back and forth and have no idea how awful it feels to be absolutely nobody. All day long I sit at the window and see people go back and forth, fast or slow, talking to this person or that person, enjoying life, and I'm like a flowerpot with a withered plant, forgotten in the window, waiting to be taken away.

You can't imagine, because you're handsome and healthy, what it's like to be born but not exist and to read in the newspapers what people do, and some are ministers who go back and forth to this country and that country, others are in high society and marry, go to baptisms, get sick and are all operated on by the same doctors, others have houses here, houses there, others steal and others bring charges, and some commit terrible crimes, and there are articles and pictures and advertisements with the names of the people who go abroad to buy the latest fashions, and you can't imagine what all this is like for someone who's like a rag that got left on the recently painted windowsill where it was used to wipe the round marks left by flowerpots from when they got watered.

If you realized all this, then maybe you would occasionally wave at me, and I wish it were possible to ask you to do just that, because you don't realize. It probably wouldn't make me live any longer, and I don't have much longer to live, but I'd go more happily to where we're all going if I knew that you sometimes waved at me.

Margarida the seamstress told me that she once talked to you and that she laid into you because you made a pass at her on the next street over, and for once I did feel envious, I admit it, I won't lie, I felt envious because when someone makes a pass at us it means we're women, and I'm neither a woman nor a man, because nobody thinks

I'm anything but a creature that fills up the space in this window and is an eyesore to everyone around, God help me.

António (his name's the same as yours, but how different!), António the car mechanic once told my father that people who don't produce anything have no right to live, that those who don't work shouldn't eat, and that no one's entitled not to work. And I thought about what I do in the world, about how I do nothing but look out the window at all the people who aren't crippled and who go back and forth, meeting up with people they like, and then naturally producing whatever's needed, because it gives them pleasure to do that.

Good-bye, Senhor António. My days are numbered, and I'm only writing this letter to hold it against my chest as if you'd written it to me instead of me to you. I wish you all the happiness I'm able to wish, and I hope you never find out about me so as not to laugh, for I know I can't hope for more.

I love you with all my heart and life.

There, I said it, and I'm crying.

Maria José

NOTES

The "Envelope" numbers and the numbers with slashes (sometimes placed in brackets) are archival references for Pessoa's original manuscripts. They are provided for previously unpublished texts, for texts whose transcription here differs from previously published versions, and for manuscripts that researchers might have difficulty locating in the archives.

page xi

GENERAL INTRODUCTION: The epigraph is from Álvaro de Campos's *Notes for the Memory of My Master Caeiro*. Lisbon's leading paper in 1935, the *Diário de Notícias*, referred to Pessoa in a headline on December 3 as a "great Portuguese poet"; other papers characterized the late Pessoa in a similar fashion. Archival references for unpublished texts mentioned in the first paragraph: alchemy and the Kabbala, Envelope 54A (among others); "Five Dialogues on Tyranny," Envelope 92B; "A Defense of Indiscipline," 92R/27–28; Julian the Apostate, 28/100 (and others); Mahatma Gandhi, 55H/64. As this volume was going to press, the Pessoa Project at the National Library of Lisbon had published a critical edition of the Portuguese poetry dating from 1934–35 and signed by Pessoa himself; editions of the poetry from previous years were under way. João Gaspar Simões, in his biography *Vida e Obra*, reported seeing Pessoa's barber at the funeral.

"To pretend is to know oneself" is the last sentence of Álvaro de Campos's "Environment"; here it is translated more literally than in the full text on p. 200. The Benjamin passage, titled "Standard Clock" and translated by Edmund Jephcott, is complete as quoted except for the final sentence, "Genius is application," a German maxim ("Genie ist Fleiß") that comes from a poem by Theodor Fontane (1819–98).

page 2

Vicente Guedes: Erstwhile fictional author of *The Book of Disquiet*, whom Pessoa replaced with Bernardo Soares. See the introduction to *The Book of Disquiet*.

page 3

from the same cause: Tuberculosis.

page 4

these books: The first five books of the projected series are listed at the top of the typescript [48C/29] for this second part of the preface: "1. Alberto Caeiro (1889–1915) — *The Keeper of Sheep* and other poems and fragments; 2. Ricardo Reis — *Odes;* 3. António Mora — *Alberto Caeiro and the Renewal of Paganism;* 4. Álvaro de Campos — *Arch of Triumph* (poems); 5. Vicente Guedes — *The Book of Disquiet.*" This order of publication is different from the one indicated in the first part of the preface, which was probably written several months or several years earlier.

page 6

THE ARTIST AS A YOUNG MAN AND HETERONYM: The eleven texts in this section, all written in English, have been placed in approximate chronological order, though with conjecture as a guide. The make-believe newspapers mentioned at the beginning of the introductory essay can be found in Envelope 87 of the Pessoa archives and were published in facsimile in *Pessoa por Conhecer.* The 1903 "edition" of one of the papers — copied into a school notebook whose whereabouts are now unknown — was commented on at length in H. D. Jennings's *Os Dois Exílios.* Geerdts's letter to "Faustino Antunes" (Envelope IV of the archives) has been published in several places, including *Pessoa por Conhecer,* where the "Essay on Intuition" [14⁶/30-31] can also be found. The passage cited at the end of the introductory essay [20/10] was published in *Páginas Íntimas* without being attributed to Alexander Search.

page 10

"I have always had . . .": [138/77]. Previously unpublished.

which brings up: "which starts" in the original.

page 12

Aunt Rita: One of the two great-aunts with whom Pessoa was living at the time. His grandmother, who had been living in the same apartment, had died two months earlier.

F. Coelho: Probably Luís Furtado Coelho, who gave Pessoa lessons in "Swedish gymnastics" for several months in 1907. In a magazine article published in 1933, Pessoa reported that he was "a cadaver waiting to die" when he began the lessons, three times a week, but that "Furtado Coelho put me in such a state of transformation that today—I note modestly—I still exist, though with what advantage to European civilization I cannot judge."

one that prompts: "one to strive with" in the original.

page 13

what I dream of: "that I dream" in the original.

in her either: "to her also" in the original.

page 14
[An Unsent Letter to Clifford Geerdts]: See the introduction to this section for
an explanation of this letter. Geerdts was the other star pupil who, along with
Pessoa, ranked at the top of the class at Durban High School. Though Geerdts
was better in math and science, Pessoa had a higher overall rating, which would
have entitled him to a full-paid scholarship to study at Oxford or Cambridge,
but only students enrolled for the last four years at the high school were eli-
gible. Pessoa had missed a year when his family traveled to Portugal in 1901–02,
and so the scholarship went to Geerdts.

page 15
Two Prose Fragments: Both passages were published in *Páginas Íntimas*, the sec-
ond [20/1–7] with many errors of transcription and without being attributed to
Search, whose signature appears on the manuscript.

page 16
character, will lead to an: "character, lead to one" in the original.

"A Winter Day": A long, fragmentary poem by Alexander Search.

Jean Seul projects: Including "France in 1950," in this volume.

Charles Binet-Sanglé: Author of *La folie de Jésus* (The Madness of Jesus),
whose thesis was that the "hallucinations" of Jesus, considered from a psychological point of view, are reasonable proof that he suffered from "religious
paranoia." The second volume of a two-volume edition of this work (Paris:
1908) is in Pessoa's library. Both "The Mental Disorder of Jesus" and "The
Portuguese Regicide and the Political Situation in Portugal" (alluded to earlier in the sentence that names Binet-Sanglé) are listed among five writing
projects on a brief "résumé" for Alexander Search [48C/2] drafted no more
than a year before this passage. The Portuguese monarchy, already under fierce
pressure in 1908, toppled in 1910.

page 17
Rule of Life: [28/43]. Probably dates from around 1910.

page 18
Pessoa wrote his only complete play (. . .) in 1913: But Pessoa indicated in a letter that his play was considerably revised before its publication in 1915, in the
first issue of *Orpheu* (a magazine discussed in SENSATIONISM AND OTHER ISMS).
Perhaps it could not have been said of the primitive version, which Pessoa did
not preserve, that "the mature author is all contained here, in seed form."

page 20
By "static drama" (. . .) onto reality: This explanation, which applies not only
to *The Mariner* but also to the various "static dramas" that Pessoa never completed, was left by the author among his papers. The translation is based on a

new reading of the manuscript [18/115] that varies considerably from the version published in *Páginas de Estética*.

page 35
To Fernando Pessoa: Written in 1929 and published the same year, but with a fictitious date of composition, 1915, the same year *The Mariner* was published.

page 36
THE MASTER AND HIS DISCIPLES: The opening quotation by Pessoa, written in English, continues: "I need all the concentration I can have for the preparation (. . .) of a literary creation in a, so to speak, fourth dimension of the mind." The same manuscript [14B/5] contains a partial rough draft of a letter sent to Aleister Crowley (see note on p. 329) on January 6, 1930.

page 38
Notes for the Memory of My Master Caeiro: The first two passages were published in 1931, in the magazine *Presença*.

page 39
Ribatejo: An inland region just north of Lisbon and extending almost to Coimbra.

page 43
transpontine: This word, meaning "on the far side of the bridge," is even rarer in Portuguese (*transpontino/a*) than in English. Perhaps Pessoa used it to mean "far-flung, esoteric."

page 46
Auguste Villiers de l'Isle Adam (1839–89), a French writer, was regarded as a precursor by the Symbolists. The quoted sentence means: "The gods are those who never doubt."

page 47
that Ricardo Reis aptly titled: In the original, Campos is complimenting Reis for the neologism employed in the title *Poemas Inconjuntos*, rendered here as *Uncollected Poems* but whose more exact meaning is "miscellaneous poems that don't form a whole."

page 49
"Opiary": "Opiário," published in 1915, in the first issue of *Orpheu*, and dedicated to Mário de Sá-Carneiro.

"Triumphal Ode": "Ode Triunfal," also published in the inaugural issue of *Orpheu*. This was the first Álvaro de Campos poem he wrote. See his letter of January 13, 1935, to Adolfo Casais Monteiro for an explanation of how Campos's "pre-Caeiro" poems were written.

"Slanting Rain": "Chuva Oblíqua," a sequence of so-called Intersectionist

poems, published in 1915 in the second issue of *Orpheu*. The last of the six poems can be found in *Fernando Pessoa & Co.* under the title "Oblique Rain."

page 50

Translator's Preface to the Poems of Alberto Caeiro: The first passage is from a handwritten text [14B/12] first published in *Pessoa por Conhecer*. The second one [21/89–90], typed, was published in *Páginas Íntimas*.

page 51

to be the thing that is: "to be the thing to be" in the original.

page 52

Or in other words: "This comes to this" in the original.

Cesário Verde (1855–86) was the most modern poet of his generation. His verses—full of vivid and concrete images, and often set in the streets of downtown Lisbon—had an even greater influence on Álvaro de Campos's poetry.

page 54

though: "but" in the original.

though the greater genius (mastership apart): "though, mastership apart, the greater genius" in the original.

(Ode II, ad finem): The reference is to "Triumphal Ode," in which Campos sings of "ordinary, sordid people" whose "eight-year-old daughters (and I think this is sublime!)/ Masturbate respectable-looking men in stairwells" (tr. R. Zenith, *Literary Imagination*, Spring 2000).

for it: "for the idea of that" in the original.

page 55

[On Álvaro de Campos]: The manuscript [14A/66–67] is hard to decipher. A somewhat different, less complete transcription was published in *Pessoa por Conhecer*.

"Naval Ode": I.e., "Maritime Ode" ("Ode Marítima"), Campos's (and Pessoa's) longest poem.

page 56

"The pink ribbon (. . .) his suit": The first line seems to be a shorthand allusion to three verses from "Time's Passage" (fifth stanza from the end as published in *Fernando Pessoa & Co.*). The other two lines are a paraphrase of verses found in Campos's unfinished "Martial Ode." The three lines appear in Portuguese in the original text, which is otherwise written in English.

"Salutation to Walt Whitman": One of Campos's long "odes" from the 1910s. Part of it is published in Edwin Honig and Susan Brown's *Poems of Fernando Pessoa* (New York: Ecco Press, 1986).

[On the Work of Ricardo Reis]: The translation is based on a reading of the manuscript [21/110] that differs, in the last paragraph, from the one published in *Páginas Íntimas*.

page 57
"*the god who was missing*": From the eighth poem in Caeiro's *The Keeper of Sheep*.

page 58
SENSATIONISM AND OTHER ISMS: The two notebooks cited in the second paragraph of the introduction are catalogued as 144C and 144D^2 in the archives. In the latter notebook Pessoa initially defined *Paulismo* as "the insincere cultivation of artificiality" but then wrote the word "sincere" above "insincere," which he did not cross out. The items to be included in *Europa*'s first two issues can be found on a table of contents typed by Pessoa [48G/32].

page 61
Preface to an Anthology of the Portuguese Sensationists: This English-language text was untitled and unsigned, according to the note that accompanied its first publication in 1952 (the whereabouts of the original manuscript are unknown), but one of the paragraphs edited out of the version published here indicates that it was a preface for an anthology of the Portuguese Sensationist writers it discusses. The editors of *Páginas Íntimas* attributed the preface to Álvaro de Campos, based on the first-person remarks toward the end. But Campos, according to his biography, returned for an extended visit to Portugal in early 1914, not in 1915 (which is when the prefacer says he arrived, the same year *Orpheu* was published), and the reference to Portugal's landscape seems to be that of a foreigner rather than of someone who, like Campos, was born and raised in Portugal. Campos, moreover, never wrote more than brief notes in English, even though he was fluent in the language. The preface writer is doubtless Thomas Crosse, whose translation projects included the work of the Portuguese Sensationists, according to a note in the archives [143/5].

page 62
his static drama The Sailor: I.e., *The Mariner*.

Maurice Maeterlinck (1862–1949) was a Belgian Symbolist playwright and poet whose dramatic work influenced Pessoa's.

"*Naval Ode*": I.e., "Maritime Ode."

page 63
"*Salutation to Walt Whitman," in the third Orpheu*: The third issue of *Orpheu*, though it never saw print (until sixty-seven years later, in 1984), was typeset in 1917, but without Campos's "Salutation to Walt Whitman." This means that Crosse's preface, which mentions Sá-Carneiro's suicide on April 26, 1916, was probably written later that year or in early 1917.

page 64

All Sensations are Good . . .: The original Portuguese was published in *Pessoa Inédito.*

[Intersectionist] Manifesto: The original Portuguese was published in *Pessoa Inédito.* The word "Manifesto," followed by a colon, appears at the top of the text, which seems to be notes toward an Intersectionist manifesto.

page 66

Sensationism: The original is a hastily penned sketch for an article that Pessoa planned to write for *Orpheu.* Less than half of it was published, with various errors of transcription, in *Páginas Íntimas.* The translation here is of the complete text, which takes up eight pages [20/116–119], the last two of which contain sentences that develop ideas presented earlier. Those sentences have been integrated at the appropriate points.

page 67

"criticism" fulfills its Danaidean role: At the behest of their father Danaus, all but one of the fifty Danaides murdered their bridegrooms and were condemned in Hades to pouring water into a bottomless vessel.

page 69

only number of Portugal Futurista: Published in November of 1917, the single-issue magazine also contained poems by Fernando Pessoa (including "The Mummy," translated in *Fernando Pessoa & Co.*) and Mário de Sá-Carneiro, poetry and prose by José de Almada-Negreiros, a previously unpublished poem of Apollinaire (in French), a Portuguese translation of Marinetti's manifesto *The Music Hall,* and artwork by Santa Rita Pintor and Amadeo de Souza-Cardoso.

5th of December, 1917: Date of a *coup d'état* that replaced Portugal's democratic government with a military dictatorship led by Sidónio Pais. Ineffectual as a head of state but endowed with charisma, Pais achieved quasi-legendary status after his assassination in December of 1918, and in 1920 Pessoa wrote and published a long poem titled "To the Memory of the President-King Sidónio Pais." In that poem as well as in Pessoa's larger program of "mystical nationalism," the deceased leader served as an ideal symbol—a modern King Sebastião. See the section PORTUGAL AND THE FIFTH EMPIRE.

page 70

should be translated (. . .) since November 1917, it is due: "should be translated, and the fact that, though it has been in print since September (?) 1917, I only now translate it, is due" in the original.

and (all things well considered): "or even, all things well considered," in the original.

Christism: Christianity. See the note on p. 333.

page 71

Campos was born in Lisbon on the 13th of October, 1890: In later texts, including his January 13, 1935, letter to Adolfo Casais Monteiro (in this volume), Pessoa wrote that Campos was born in the Algarvian town of Tavira on October 15, 1890.

page 72

Intersectionist manifesto in Europa (. . .) *Sensationist manifesto in Orpheu:* On the table of contents for *Europa* cited earlier in these Notes, the *Ultimatum* is attributed to Pessoa, who also referred to it in a letter dated October 4, 1914. In Pessoa's personal notes it is named as one of two manifestos to be published in *Orpheu* [48D/5].

"The Futurist (. . .) *can't make it out":* [88/8]. None of the early drafts of the *Ultimatum* has been published.

Jean Jaurès (1859–1914), an important leader in the French Socialist party, was assassinated by a zealous nationalist for opposing war with Germany.

Ernest Renan (1823–92) was a French philologist, critic, and historian.

Maurice Barrès (1862–1923), a French nationalist politician and writer, reorganized the "Ligue des Patriotes" in 1914 and wrote numerous patriotic articles during the war.

Action: Refers to Action Française, a right-wing political movement whose views were propagated in a newspaper of the same name, founded in 1899.

Paul Bourget (1852–1935) was a French novelist, poet, and the author of *Essays of Contemporary Psychology.*

Majuba and Colenso: South African towns where the British were defeated by the Boers in (respectively) 1881 and 1899.

Empire Day: May 24, the birthday of Queen Victoria, formerly a holiday to commemorate the help England received from its colonies during the Boer War of 1899–1902. Now called Commonwealth Day.

Kilkenny cat: One of a pair of Irish cats fabled to have fought until only their tails remained.

page 73

Gabriele D'Annunzio (1863–1938) changed his last name from Rapagnetta. He married a duke's daughter and had subsequent liaisons with a countess, a marchioness, and the actress Eleonora Duse.

Maurice Maeterlinck: See the note above, on p. 324.

Pierre Loti (1850–1923) was a novelist and member of the French Academy.

Edmond Rostand (1868–1918) wrote social dramas, including *Cyrano de Bergerac*. The *tand-tand-tand* mimics the sound of a drum.

Wilhelm II (1859–1941) was crowned kaiser of Germany in 1888. Aggressive and energetic, his absolutist form of leadership prompted Chancellor Bismarck to resign in 1890. He continued Bismarck's program of unifying, modernizing, and militarizing Germany. His politics of nationalist expansion, founded on the notion of German superiority, was perhaps the single greatest cause of World War I.

Otto von Bismarck (1815–96) became chancellor of Germany when Wilhelm I was proclaimed kaiser, in 1871. He was the statesman who did most—by means of war, diplomacy, and effective political administration—to create a strong, unified, and industrialized Germany.

David Lloyd George (1863–1945), from Wales, was head of Britain's Liberal Party and served as prime minister from 1916 to 1922.

Eleutherios Venizelos (1864–1936), Greek premier who supported the Allies in World War I, in opposition to King Constantine I, who backed the Central Powers.

Aristide Briand (1862–1932), French premier in World War I, won the Nobel Peace Prize in 1926.

Eduardo Dato Iradier (1856–1921), leader of the Spanish Conservative Party, was prime minister in 1914–18 and again in 1920–21.

Paolo Boselli (1838–1932) was the Italian prime minister in 1916–17.

page 74

Horatio Herbert Kitchener (1850–1916) was the British commander-in-chief in the Boer War and then in India. Appointed secretary of war in 1914, he brilliantly organized Britain's army but drowned on a ship sunk by German submarines while on his way to Russia for a diplomatic mission.

K-brand doorjamb: Seems to evoke Austria's subservience to the German kaiser.

Von Belgium: Belgium, from 1914 to 1917, was ruled by the autocratic German general Friedrich Wilhelm Freiherr von Bissing.

sanbenitos: The sackcloth garments worn by condemned heretics at the autos-da-fé of the Spanish Inquisition.

fighting spirit buried in Morocco: Spain, granted a protectorate in Morocco in 1912, suffered heavy losses at the hands of the Riff tribesmen who continuously rose up in arms.

humiliated in Africa: The English Ultimatum of 1890 obliged Portugal to re-nounce its claims to a vast territory—covering parts of modern-day Zambia and Zimbabwe—that would have linked Angola to Mozambique. The title of Campos's manifesto is probably meant as a riposte to the English Ultimatum.

Pedro Álvares Cabral (1467–c.1520) discovered Brazil in 1500 when he was at-tempting to round the southern tip of Africa.

page 74–5
Alfred Fouillée (1838–1912), a French philosopher, two of whose books were in Pessoa's personal library: *Esquisse psychologique des peuples européens* and *La philosophie de Platon: Théorie des idées et de l'amour.*

Charles Maurras (1868–1952) was a right-wing French writer who ardently de-fended classical and French culture in newspaper articles and in his books, two of which were in Pessoa's personal library.

Pitt: William Pitt, the Elder (1708–78), was an important English political leader, but Pessoa is presumably referring to William Pitt, the Younger (1759–1806), the British prime minister who formed an international coalition to oppose Na-poleon, who, however, won the Battle of Austerlitz as Pitt lay dying.

Gaius Gracchus (153–121 B.C.) was an eloquent, much respected tribune of Rome who tried without great success to implement the radical agrarian reforms pro-mulgated by his assassinated brother, Tiberius Gracchus (163–133 B.C.).

page 76
Émile Boutroux (1854–1921), a French philosopher whose *Science et religion dans la philosophie contemporaine* was in Pessoa's library.

Rudolf Christoph Eucken (1846–1926), a German philosopher who wrote *The Meaning and Value of Life.*

page 77
Henry Bernstein (1876–1953) and *Henry Bataille* (1872–1922) were two of the lead-ing French dramatists of their day.

page 78
Charles Jonnart (1857–1927), French diplomat and Allied high commissioner at Athens. He forced King Constantine I to abandon Greece in 1917.

Paul von Hindenburg (1847–1934) led the German army and nation in World War I.

Joseph Jacques Césaire Joffre (1852–1931) was a French commander-in-chief dur-ing World War I.

poilus: Literally "hairy," and used colloquially to mean French soldiers, espe-cially in World War I.

page 79
> *Sagres*, a coastal town in southern Portugal, was the site of Prince Henry the Navigator's legendary—but unproven—school of nautical science. Prince Henry did build an observatory at Sagres, and some of the voyages he sponsored set sail from its port.

page 80
> *Malthusian Law:* Thomas Malthus (1766–1834), an English economist, argued in his *Essay on the Principle of Population* (1789) that the human population increases geometrically but the food supply only arithmetically, with obviously disastrous consequences.

page 88
> *What Is Metaphysics?:* The passage translated here is the conclusion to Campos's article, which was published in the second issue of *Athena* (Lisbon, 1924) as a retort to a piece by Pessoa that appeared in the magazine's inaugural issue. Pessoa was one of the coeditors of *Athena*, in which Alberto Caeiro and Ricardo Reis were both published for the first time. The magazine's fifth and final issue appeared in 1925.

page 92
> RIDDLE OF THE STARS: Archival reference numbers to the manuscripts cited in the introduction: "Principles of Esoteric Metaphysics," 54A/85–87; "A Case of Mediumship," 54A/78–82; Pessoa's comment on astrology, 54A/7; poem signed by Wardour and Pessoa, 58/12; communication that mentions Gosse, 133I/42; "Move to Sengo's house," 133B/99; communications predicting business success, 133A/69 and 133D/80 (among others). The first two manuscripts were published in Lopes's *Fernando Pessoa et le drame symboliste* The draft of the letter to Sá-Carneiro was dated December 6, 1915. It was in an autobiographical sketch dated March 30, 1935, that Pessoa claimed to be initiated in the Knights Templar.

page 96
> *Aleister Crowley* (1875–1947), who billed himself variously as Master Therion, 666, and The Great Beast, was a talented, mischievous, much adored, and much reviled English occult master. He was initiated into the Hermetic Order of the Golden Dawn (whose most famous member was William Butler Yeats) in 1898, cofounded the Astrum Argentum, or Order of the Silver Star, in 1906, and became head of the Ordo Templi Orientis in 1921. This last group, of German origin, employed tantric sex rituals, to which Crowley added animal sacrifices and drug use. Blasted by the English press after one of his disciples died in a proto-hippie commune in the early twenties, perhaps from the ritual consumption of cat's blood, Crowley faded from view and died in relative obscurity, but by the end of the century most of his many books (including some poetry) were back in print and various occult groups had taken up his teachings. "Do what thou wilt shall be the whole of the Law" is the central tenet of

his doctrines, and it was the first sentence of the first letter he sent to Pessoa, in late 1929, thanking him for having pointed out a mistake in the natal horoscope published in his autobiography. The two men corresponded and exchanged some of their writings, and in September of 1930 Crowley came to Lisbon with a girlfriend, who quarreled with him at a certain point and abruptly left Portugal. Crowley, with Pessoa's help, committed a dramatic pseudo-suicide, writing a jilted lover's note left at the Mouth of Hell, a cavernous rock formation on the seacoast west of Lisbon, where Crowley had ostensibly taken a flying mortal leap. He had in fact left Portugal by way of Spain, but Pessoa, who explained to the Lisbon papers the significance of the astrological signs and mystical words that graced the suicide note, also reported seeing Crowley, "or Crowley's ghost," the day after his disappearance. Crowley's occult activities were always flavored with shenanigans of this sort, which has led some biographers to portray him as an unqualified charlatan, but it was probably this very playfulness that drew Pessoa to him. Here was a man who could be passionately devoted to the quest for spiritual truth and yet not take it completely seriously. Pessoa, whose skepticism prevented him from taking anything too seriously, seems to have been inspired by Crowley's example.

page 99
the good wishes it contains: For Pessoa's birthday, June 13th.

Mother's condition: Pessoa's mother, who in 1911 moved with her second husband and their children from Durban to Pretoria, had recently suffered a stroke.

page 100
Manuel Gualdino da Cunha: Pessoa's great-uncle.

The communications (. . .) anonymous: In fact, Pessoa was already receiving communications signed by Henry More, one of which [138/55] instructed him not to divulge their contents to his Aunt Anica.

I consulted a friend: Mariano Santana, a habitué of the Café Brasileira whose name is mentioned in several automatic communications.

page 101
Café Brasileira of Rossio: There were two Café Brasileiras—the one at Rossio, Lisbon's busiest downtown square, and the one at nearby Chiado, the neighborhood where Pessoa was born. The latter is still in business.

page 103
[30 Astral Communications]: Previously unpublished. The archival reference numbers are: (1) 138/37, (2) 138/36, (3) 138/49–51, (4) 133I/24, (5) 138/33, (6) 138/38, (7) 138/39, (8) 138/44, (9) 114¹/64, (10) 138/42, (11) 138/54v, (12) 138/48, (13) 133I/98, (14) 133L/94, (15) 144D²/112, (16) 133J/91, (17) 133I/34, (18) Sinais 5, (19) 133I/

63, (20) 144Y/22, (21) 144Y/31, (22) 144Y/35, (23) 144Y/42, (24) 138/52–3, (25) 133J/
3–5, (26) 133L/11, (27) 133A/38, (28) 133I/75, (29) 49A⁶/52, (30) 133F/86.

page 106
Orpheu: See SENSATIONISM AND OTHER ISMS.

page 107
The Key to the Tarot (*Papus*): The full book title is *Absolute Key to Occult Science: The Tarot of the Bohemians*, translated from the French and published in London in 1892. Papus was the pseudonym of Gérard Encausse (1865–1916), an active promoter of the occult sciences. He cofounded the Martinist Order, a para-Masonic association, in 1891.

page 110
Marnoco e Sousa: José Ferreira Marnoco e Sousa, a Portuguese professor and scholar of law, was born in 1869 and died in March of 1916, the same month that Pessoa began to write automatically. The Pessoa archives contain an isolated bibliographical reference [48B/39] to a history of Roman law by Marnoco e Sousa.

who married many: "who married much" in the original.

page 113
a man who made Joseph: Joseph Balsamo (the alias of Cagliostro — see the introduction to this section), who signed communication #18 and part of #19.

He is interrupting me: Interrupting his handwriting, which at this point in the manuscript becomes jagged and uncontrolled, as if produced with a struggle.

page 115
20: Written on or after January 13, 1917, the date of an unfinished English poem that precedes the communication.

page 116
transversal backward line: Beneath More's signature.

page 118
Love gives back to each man himself: "Love gives back himself to each man" in the original.

is for a need to exist: "is to exist a need" in the original.

page 120
your martial tendencies: Refers, perhaps, to the astrological influence of Mars.

Essay on Initiation: Pessoa left a number of typewritten pages, in English, for this projected essay that dates from the 1930s. They were first published in *Fernando Pessoa e a Filosofia Hermética*.

page 121
the path taken: "the path that is taken" in the original.

Treatise on Negation: Original Portuguese published in *Textos Filosóficos.*

page 131

before my family arrives: After the death of his stepfather in 1919, Pessoa's mother, half sister, and two half brothers returned from South Africa to Lisbon. Pessoa undertook to find and lease an apartment for the family, which arrived on March 30, and he himself lived there until his death in 1935.

Osório: An office boy who delivered letters between Fernando and Ophelia.

page 132

Rua do Arsenal: The two sometimes met in a bookstore on this street.

Mr. Crosse: As noted in the section THE MASTER AND HIS DISCIPLES, Pessoa competed in newspaper games under the name of A. A. Crosse, presumably the brother of Thomas Crosse and I. I. Crosse.

page 133

at home: The new apartment mentioned in the March 22 letter.

page 134

Nininho: One of Ophelia's pet names for Pessoa, probably derived from Fernandinho, the diminutive form of his first name. He sometimes called her Nininha.

C. D. & C.: C. Dupin & Cia. was the name of the firm where Ophelia had recently begun working, having transferred there from the office where she met Pessoa.

page 135

Rossio train station: Ophelia's older sister, with whom she often stayed, lived opposite this station, in downtown Lisbon.

Ibis: Another pet name, used by Pessoa to refer to himself as well as to Ophelia. Ibis was also the name of a printing press that Pessoa unsuccessfully tried to set up in Lisbon, in 1907.

page 137

May 11th decree: A government decree, issued on May 11, 1911, made it possible for mentally ill patients to commit themselves to a psychiatric hospital.

page 140

Petition in 30 lines: From a letter written by Ophelia the same day, we can deduce that Pessoa, in a phone conversation, had asked her for a kiss, had expressed jealousy because she showered kisses on her eight- and ten-month-old nephews, and had promised he would send her this "petition in 30 lines."

page 141

aren't really aunts: The two women, according to Ophelia's letter from the day before, were her brother-in-law's aunts.

Pombal: A small town north of Lisbon, but also the Portuguese word for dove-cote. Pessoa used doves as an amorous metaphor in several letters (see the first one dated October 9, 1929) and in some verses to Ophelia, as she recalled in her next letter to Fernando.

losing weight: In a letter written the previous day, Ophelia reported having lost weight since her relationship with Pessoa had been rekindled, two weeks before. She also wrote that she had no appetite, wasn't sleeping well, and thought incessantly of Fernando.

page 145
Mouth of Hell: A dramatic rock formation (*Boca do Inferno* in Portuguese) on the coast beyond Cascais. See the note on Aleister Crowley, p. 329.

page 147
The Return of the Gods: All the passages (of which only the first and third are actually marked *Return of the Gods*) were published in *Páginas Íntimas*, but my translation of the fourth passage is based on a different reading of the manuscript [21/43–4], especially toward the end. One of Pessoa's publication plans [71A/2] confirms (as alluded to in the introductory note) that he hesitated whether to attribute this work to António Mora or to Ricardo Reis.

page 149
Christism: Disparaging term for Christianity often used by Mora and by Ricardo Reis.

page 153
Preface to the Complete Poems of Alberto Caeiro: The four passages were published in *Páginas Íntimas*, but my translation of the first one is based on a somewhat different reading of the manuscript [21/73].

page 155
Julian was a Mithraist: Mithra was a Persian and Indian god of the sun, whose slaying of a sacred bull had created life on earth and would be the means to human redemption and immortality. Mithraism, as practiced in the Roman Empire, involved a seven-step initiation and embraced astrology.

page 158
PORTUGAL AND THE FIFTH EMPIRE: The texts included in this section, all written in Portuguese, can be found in *Sobre Portugal*. The first one was written for a projected manifesto titled "Atlantism"; the second one is taken from an interview published in *Revista Portuguesa*, Lisbon, 13 October 1923; the third one is from Pessoa's preface to *Quinto Império* (The Fifth Empire), a book of poems by Augusto Ferreira Gomes (Lisbon, 1934); the fourth one is from a series of questions and answers published in Augusto da Costa, *Portugal Vasto Império*, Lisbon, 1934; the fifth one is from a projected essay titled "Sebastian-

ism"; the last three, though not labeled, were no doubt meant for essays such as "Atlantism" and "Sebastianism."

page 160
a long poem titled "Anteros": In a letter to João Gaspar Simões dated November 18, 1930, Pessoa explained that his English poems "Antinöus" (1918) and "Epithalamium" (1921) corresponded to Greece and Rome in a five-poem "imperial cycle" about "the phenomenon of love in its various expressions"; the last poem in the cycle, "Anteros," corresponded to the Fifth Empire.

page 162
Teixeira de Pascoaes and Guerra Junqueiro: Two writers initially much admired by Pessoa, who became more critical of them as he got older. Pascoaes (1879–1952) was the leader of Portugal's *Saudosista* movement, which promoted nostalgia as a literary and spiritual value. Guerra Junqueiro (1850–1923), extremely influential in his day, began as a satirical, anticlerical poet, but as time went on his verses became increasingly informed by a pantheistic mysticism.

page 164
Book of Revelation: Chapter 6, verse 2: "And I saw, and behold a white horse: and he that sat on him had a bow; and a crown was given unto him: and he went forth conquering, and to conquer."

page 166
King João IV: The first king of the Bragança dynasty, who stepped onto the throne in 1640, marking the end of sixty years of Portuguese submission to Spanish rule.

page 167
THE ANARCHIST BANKER: It was in an undated letter sent to the editor of *Contemporânea*, the magazine where "The Anarchist Banker" had recently been published, that Pessoa referred to his story as a "dialectical satire."

page 197
PESSOA ON MILLIONAIRES: The three fragments [138/22–26, 138A/7–8, 138A/9] were previously unpublished.

page 198
Mr. Ford (. . .) reincarnation: Henry Ford (1863–1947) told his interviewers that he came to believe in reincarnation when he was twenty-six years old.

would have been done in: "would have been done too" in the original. Pessoa presumably left out the "in" after "done" because of the example of Portuguese, in which *feito*, meaning "done," can also mean "done in," with no added preposition.

page 199
a belief in reincarnation: A reference to Henry Ford. See the penultimate note.

page 200
ENVIRONMENT: Published in 1927. The penultimate sentence, *Estar é ser*, which is impossible to render adequately in English, affirms that what we take to be temporal, spatial being (*estar*) is in fact essential, true being (*ser*).

page 201
[SELF-DEFINITION]: The actual heading on the manuscript is *Preface (use for "Shakespeare"?)*.

page 202
EROSTRATUS: The selection corresponds to Texts 2, 59, 37, 23, 33, 17, 50, 51, 63, and 54, in that order, from the complete, annotated edition of the essay published in *Heróstrato e a Busca da Imortalidade*. All of them were written in English.

page 205
Woman Clothed with the Sun: "And there appeared a great wonder in heaven; a woman clothed with the sun, and the moon under her feet, and upon her head a crown of twelve stars" (Revelation 12:1). This description became the basis for representations of the Immaculate Conception in Renaissance painting.

page 206
properly speaking: "properly such" in the original.

page 211
legitimate right: "correct right" in the original.

page 212
Faguet said (. . .) posterity likes only concise writers: Émile Faguet (1847–1916), when commenting on George Sand's verbosity in his book *Dix-neuvième siècle: études littéraires*.

page 213
[The Task of Modern Poetry]: [139/28]. This and the following piece, "Shakespeare," are previously unpublished passages written (in English) for a preface-in-progress to the five-poem "imperial cycle" described on p. 332, in the note about "Anteros."

peoples as separate: "peoples separate as far" in the original.

page 214
the Aeolian cave: "the Aeolus' cave" in the original.

[which it behooves]: "that is the province of" in the original.

therefore: "then" in the original.

page 215
Shakespeare: [139/15]. Pessoa left many passages for a projected essay on Shake-

speare, but this passage, though it was titled "Shakespeare," belongs to his unfinished preface to *Five Poems*. See the note to the preceding selection.

page 216

Shakespeare's lack (. . .) *is ordinary:* The original sentence reads, "The lack of
sense of proportion, of sense of unity, of sense of development and interaction
shown by Shakespeare are so extraordinary, as the fact that they happen to a
Christian poet is an ordinary one."

[On Blank Verse and Paradise Lost]: Pessoa labeled the manuscript copy "*Erostratus*
(or the like)." It was published as Text 65 in *Heróstrato e a Busca da Imortalidade.*

"Tithonus," or "Ulysses" or "Oenone": All by Tennyson.

properly speaking: "properly such" in the original.

page 217

Charles Dickens—Pickwick Papers: The first four paragraphs, typed by Pessoa,
were published in *Páginas de Estética.* The continuation of the text, written by
hand on the reverse side of the typescript (19/97), was previously unpublished.

page 218

the two Wellers: Sam Weller (Mr. Pickwick's valet) and his father.

one-eyed bagman: A character who appears in Chapter 14 and again toward the
end of the novel. A bagman was a traveling salesman, so called because he carried his samples in a bag.

Concerning Oscar Wilde: None of Pessoa's writings on Wilde has previously
been published. The first of the four passages transcribed here [14E/69] carries
the title "Concerning Oscar Wilde," which appears on several lists of Pessoa's
planned and in-progress works. The other three passages [14E/73, 55I/89, 55I/
94] were labeled "Oscar Wilde." Pessoa's horoscope and biographical chronology for Wilde are in notebook 144Y.

page 220

he had begun (. . .) *have been able:* "he began with pictures, he will never be
able" in the original.

page 221

unconscious: "conscious" in the original, presumably by mistake.

lack of purpose: "dispurposedness" in the original.

page 222

[The Art of James Joyce]: Translated from an unpublished note [144/70]. Pessoa
owned the 1932 Hamburg edition of *Ulysses.*

[The Art of Translation]: First published in *Pessoa Inédito.*

involved in parodying: "involved in translating" on the original typescript, presumably by mistake.

the other case a certain: "the other one" in the original.

page 224

ESSAY ON POETRY: Envelope 100 of the Pessoa archives contains two typed copies of the long opening section (published in *Pessoa por Conhecer*). The transcription is of the second, cleaner but incomplete copy for as far as it goes, switching at that point to the earlier one. The other sections (beginning with "I now pass on") were previously unpublished and have been transcribed from autographs found in Envelope 13A. Written at different times and not collated by Pessoa, the essay's various pieces (most but not all of which are included here) have been ordered on the basis of internal evidence.

page 226

expounding: "exposing" in the original.

page 227

Spencer: Herbert Spencer (1820–1903), the English philosopher. Professor Jones is apparently not familiar with Edmund Spenser the poet.

page 228

but: "only that" in the original.

page 230

long and pointed ears: "a long and pointed ear" in the original.

page 231

FRANCE IN 1950: The first and last passages [138A/2, 138A/1] were published, in French, in *Pessoa por Conhecer*. The three middle passages [55E/87, 133F/38, 55E/86] have not previously been published. The essay, retitled "La France à l'an 2000," was scheduled to appear in the second issue of *Europa* [144D²/42]. The narrator of the piece was identified as Japanese not only in a "List of Publications" [48B/66] but also in a list of pamphlets to be published [144D²/6]. Another pamphlet on this latter list was titled "On the Necessity of Creating Male Whorehouses."

page 234

RANDOM NOTES AND EPIGRAMS: Archival references and published sources: (1) 133E/84, (2) 133E/83, (3) 75A/22, (4) 93/88v., (5) 26C/21, (6) 92D/3, (7) 21/119 (published in *Páginas Íntimas*), (8) 15B³/86 (Text 21 in *The Book of Disquiet*), (9) 22/95 (published in *Textos Filosóficos*, v. I, but the translation is based on a different reading of the original), (10) 133F/55, (11) 15⁴/2, (12) 75A/28, (13) 133E/91, (14) 144D²/32 (last sentence published in *Pessoa por Conhecer*), (15) 20/68 (published in *Páginas Íntimas*), (16) 75/23, (17) 14⁵/30, (18) 134A/46.

Item 2 was written on an envelope postmarked in Madrid in 1923, and item 8 was dated March 24, 1929.

page 239
TWO LETTERS TO JOÃO GASPAR SIMÕES: The first letter contains a P.S. not translated here.

"Hymn to Pan": A poem by Aleister Crowley. See the note for Crowley on p. 329.

page 240
your article about me: Originally published in *Presença* under the title "Fernando Pessoa and the Voices of Innocence."

page 242
Café Brasileira of Chiado: A Lisbon café popular among intellectuals, including Pessoa. See the note on p. 330.

page 245
"O church bell of my village . . .": One of the first two poems published by Pessoa as an adult, in 1914.

Directory of the Republic: The leadership of the Portuguese Republican Party, which controlled the provisional government of the young republic, established in 1910.

page 247
Figueira: Figueira da Foz, a fishing village and beach resort where residents of Coimbra often spend their holidays.

page 248
Portugal, *a small book of poems*: The book Pessoa published in 1934 as *Message*, with forty-four poems.

page 252
a Leader or Chief: Pessoa employed the Portuguese word *chefe*, whose pronunciation is virtually identical to the French *chef*.

rational Sebastianist: See the section PORTUGAL AND THE FIFTH EMPIRE.

prize offered by the National Office of Propaganda: Pessoa won second prize, apparently because his book did not meet the required length of one hundred pages.

page 256
"Slanting Rain": See note on p. 322.

"Triumphal Ode": See note on p. 322.

page 257
"Opiary": See note on p. 322.

page 258
> *Ferreira Gomes:* Augusto Ferreira Gomes (1892–1953), a long-standing friend of Pessoa, shared his interest in astrology and the occult sciences.

page 260
> *"Eros and Psyche":* "Eros e Psique," published in the May 1934 issue of *Presença.* The epigraph in question reads: ". . . And so you see, my Brother, that the truths you received at the Neophyte stage and those you received at the Adept stage are, even if contrary, the same Truth."

page 261
> *[Another Version of the Genesis of the Heteronyms]:* The original Portuguese text [20/74-7] contains an unfinished sentence, not translated here, that addresses a potential audience of readers. This suggests that the passage was intended for a general preface to Pessoa's works.

page 272
> *Vigny:* Alfred de Vigny (1797–1863), French author of poems, essays, plays, and a novel. Disillusioned in love, unsuccessful in politics, and unenthusiastically received by the French Academy, he withdrew from society and became increasingly pessimistic in his writings, which recommended stoical resignation as the only noble response to the suffering life condemns us to.

page 277
> *Vieira:* Father António Vieira (1608–97), who spent much of his life in Brazil, is one of the greatest prose stylists in Portuguese. His enormous output includes about two hundred sermons and over five hundred letters. (See the introduction to PORTUGAL AND THE FIFTH EMPIRE.)

page 290
> *Cascais:* A beach town southwest of Lisbon.

page 296
> *"Any road (. . .) the World":* In Thomas Carlyle's *Sartor Resartus: The Life and Opinions of Herr Teufelsdröckh.*

page 297
> *epopt:* An initiate in the highest order of the Eleusinian mysteries.

page 304
> *Greek philosopher:* Protagoras.

page 305
> *Buridan's donkey:* The fourteenth-century French scholastic Jean Buridan, concerned with the problem of free will, is supposed to have asked what a donkey would do if, suffering equally from thirst and hunger, it stood at a point equidistant from a bucket of water and a bucket of hay.

page 309

Disjecta membra, *said Carlyle:* In *On Heroes, Hero-Worship, and the Heroic in History.* Carlyle's exact words were: "*Disjecta membra* are all that we find of any Poet, or of any man."

page 314

LETTER FROM A HUNCHBACK GIRL TO A METALWORKER: In the second half of the letter, before the paragraph that begins "You go back and forth," Pessoa left blank space for inserting text that remained unwritten, except for the following phrase: "and so why am I writing you this letter if I'm not going to send it?"

BIBLIOGRAPHY

PUBLISHED SOURCES FOR THE PROSE SELECTIONS

The following list contains published sources for the Portuguese originals and previously published sources for the English originals, but many of the translations are based on new readings of the manuscripts, and all selections written by Pessoa in English are direct transcriptions. The Pessoa Archives are housed at the National Library of Lisbon.

Campos, Álvaro (Fernando Pessoa). *Notas para a Recordação do meu Mestre Caeiro*, ed. Teresa Rita Lopes. Lisbon: Editorial Estampa, 1997.

Centeno, Yvette K. *Fernando Pessoa e a Filosofia Hermética*. Lisbon: Presença, 1985.

Lopes, Teresa Rita. *Pessoa por Conhecer*, vol. 2. Lisbon: Editorial Estampa, 1990.

Pessoa, Fernando. *O Banqueiro Anarquista*, ed. Manuela Parreira da Silva. Lisbon: Assírio & Alvim, 1999.

——. *The Book of Disquiet*, tr. Richard Zenith. London: Penguin Books, 2001.

——. *Correspondência 1905–1922*, ed. Manuela Parreira da Silva. Lisbon: Assírio & Alvim, 1998.

——. *Correspondência 1923–1935*, ed. Manuela Parreira da Silva. Lisbon: Assírio & Alvim, 1999.

——. *Heróstrato e a Busca da Imortalidade*, ed. Richard Zenith. Lisbon: Assírio & Alvim, 2000.

——. *Obra Poética*, ed. Maria Aliete Galhoz. 7th ed. Rio de Janeiro: Editora Nova Aguilar, 1977. (1st ed. 1960.)

——. *Páginas de Doutrina Estética*, ed. Jorge de Sena. Lisbon: Editorial Inquérito, 1946.

——. *Páginas de Estética e de Teoria e Crítica Literárias*, eds. Georg Rudolf Lind and Jacinto do Prado Coelho. Lisbon: Edições Ática, 1966.

——. *Páginas Íntimas e de Auto-Interpretação*, eds. Georg Rudolf Lind and Jacinto do Prado Coelho. Lisbon: Edições Ática, 1966.

——. *Pessoa Inédito*, ed. Teresa Rita Lopes. Lisbon: Livros Horizontes, 1993.

——. *Sobre Portugal—Introdução ao Problema Nacional*, eds. Maria Isabel Rocheta, Maria Paula Morão, and Joel Serrão. Lisbon: Edições Ática, 1978.

——. *Textos Filosóficos*, ed. António de Pina Coelho, vol. 2. Lisbon: Edições Ática, 1968.

——. *Ultimatum e Páginas de Sociologia Política*, eds. Maria Isabel Rocheta, Maria Paula Morão, and Joel Serrão. Lisbon: Edições Ática, 1978.

Soares, Bernardo (Fernando Pessoa). *Livro do Desassossego*, ed. Richard Zenith. Lisbon: Assírio & Alvim, 1998.

Teive, Barão de (Fernando Pessoa). A *Educação do Estóico*, ed. Richard Zenith. Lisbon: Assírio & Alvim, 1999.

WORKS CONSULTED FOR THE ESSAY MATTER (BUT NOT CITED ABOVE)

Benjamin, Walter. *Reflections*, ed. Peter Demetz. New York: Schocken Books, 1986.

Bréchon, Robert. *Étrange étranger: une biographie de Fernando Pessoa*. Paris: Christian Bourgois, 1996.

Jennings, Hubert D. *Os Dois Exílios: Fernando Pessoa na África do Sul*. Oporto: Fundação Eng. António de Almeida, 1984.

Lopes, Teresa Rita. *Fernando Pessoa et le drame symboliste—Héritage et création*. Paris: Fondation Calouste Gulbenkian, 1977.

——. *Pessoa por Conhecer*, vol. 1. Lisbon: Editorial Estampa, 1990.

Pessoa, Fernando. *Fernando Pessoa & Co.—Selected Poems*, tr. Richard Zenith. New York: Grove Press, 1998.

——. *Poemas Ingleses*, vol. 2 (Alexander Search), ed. João Dionísio. Lisbon: Imprensa Nacional—Casa da Moeda, 1997.

Queiroz, Ofélia. *Cartas de Amor de Ofélia a Fernando Pessoa*, eds. Manuela Nogueira and Maria da Conceição Azevedo. Lisbon: Assírio & Alvim, 1996.

Simões, João Gaspar. *Retrato de Poetas que Conheci*. Oporto: Brasília Editora, 1974.

——. *Vida e Obra de Fernando Pessoa*. 6th ed. Lisbon: Publicações Dom Quixote, 1991. (1st ed. 1950.)

CPSIA information can be obtained
at www.ICGtesting.com
Printed in the USA
JSHW020525090922
30315JS00001B/6

9 780802 139146